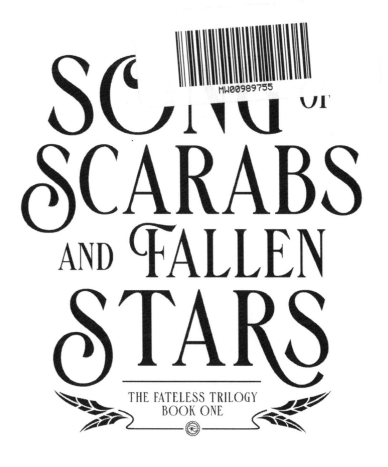

SONG of
SCARABS
AND FALLEN
STARS

THE FATELESS TRILOGY
BOOK ONE

LINDSEY SPARKS

RUBUS PRESS

SONG OF SCARABS AND FALLEN STARS

THE FATELESS TRILOGY
BOOK ONE

LINDSEY SPARKS

RUBUS PRESS

Editing by Fresh as a Daisy Editing

www.freshasadaisyediting.com

Cover by We Got You Covered

www.wegotyoucoveredbookdesign.com

9798429633350

ALSO BY
LINDSEY SPARKS

ECHO WORLD

ECHO TRILOGY
Echo in Time
Resonance
Time Anomaly
Dissonance
Ricochet Through Time

KAT DUBOIS CHRONICLES
Ink Witch
Outcast
Underground
Soul Eater
Judgement
Afterlife

FATELESS TRILOGY
Song of Scarabs and Fallen Stars
Darkness Between the Stars

LEGACIES OF OLYMPUS

ATLANTIS LEGACY
Sacrifice of the Sinners
Legacy of the Lost
Fate of the Fallen
Dreams of the Damned
Song of the Soulless
Blood of the Broken
Rise of the Revenants

ALLWORLD ONLINE
AO: Pride & Prejudice
AO: The Wonderful Wizard of Oz
Vertigo

THE ENDING WORLD
(writing as Lindsey Fairleigh)

THE ENDING SERIES
The Ending Beginnings: Omnibus Edition
After The Ending
Into The Fire
Out Of The Ashes
Before The Dawn
World Before

THE ENDING LEGACY
World After

For more information on Lindsey and her books:
www.authorlindseysparks.com

Join Lindsey's mailing list to stay up to date on releases AND
to access her free starter library:
https://www.authorlindseysparks.com/join-newsletter

AUTHOR'S NOTE

Dear reader,

What a wild ride this book has been to write! I cannot wait for you to join Tarset on her time travel adventures and to immerse yourself in the scorching sands and lush intrigue of ancient Egypt. But first, a warning.

Tarset's story is darker and steamier than the previous two series in the Echo World. This book includes depictions of torture, psychological manipulation, implied sexual assault, graphic violence, and death, as well as sexually explicit scenes and references to the historical death of a parent. Proceed with caution...

And, as always, happy reading!
Lindsey

THE PLAYLIST
(IN CHRONOLOGICAL ORDER)

Subscribe to my newsletter for a detailed list of the songs and the scenes they correlate with from the book:
https://www.authorlindseysparks.com/join-newsletter-

What Other People Say - Sam Fischer, Demi Lovato
Angels Like You - Miley Cyrus
Closer - Nine Inch Nails
Zombie - Damned Anthem
Stand By Me - Ki:Theory
Lion - Saint Mesa
Still Have Me - Demi Lovato
Jesus Christ - Brand New
Castle - Halsey
Darling - Halsey
Bells in Santa Fe - Halsey
Astronomical - SVRCINA
The Tradition - Halsey
Heaven In Hiding - Halsey
Feel - Fletcher
Sowing Season (Yeah) - Brand New
Gimme What I Want - Miley Cyrus
Nightmare - Halsey

Lifts - Lia Marie Johnson
Change (In the House of Flies) - Deftones
Anyone - Demi Lovato
Losing My Religion - BELLSAINT
Little Did I Know - Julia Michaels
Ghost - Adaline
1121 - Halsey
Issues - Julia Michaels
Shadow Preachers - Zella Day
Beautiful Crime - Tamer
Easier than Lying - Halsey
Wrong Direction - Hailee Steinfeld
Born Alone Die Alone - Madalen Duke
Mad World - Demi Lovato
Smoke & Mirrors - Demi Lovato
How Villains Are Made - Madalen Duke
Up Down - Boy Epic
Slip Away - UNSECRET, Ruelle
Love and War - Fleurie
Scars - Boy Epic
Killing Strangers - Marilyn Manson
War of Hearts - Ruelle
Can't Help Falling in Love - Tommee Profitt, brooke

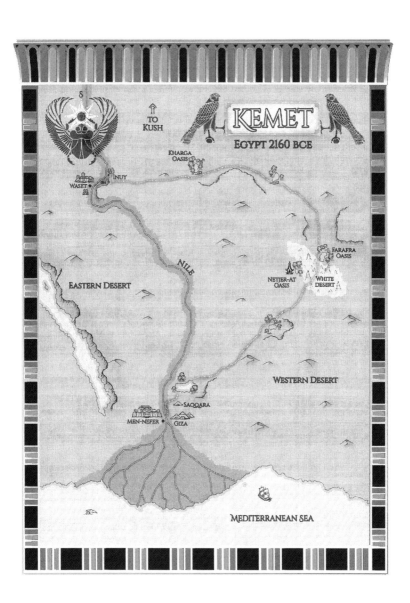

1

"**T**HESE ARE DARK TIMES," I said, resting my elbows on the table and leaning in closer to the microphone to add my personal commentary to the prescribed broadcast I had just read aloud. "Trust me, I know. There are *literal* gods attacking our world. But we're all in this together."

At sunrise and sunset every day for the past week, I emerged from my Saharan hidey-hole to broadcast a daily public service announcement updating both humans and immortals on the current state of the war. I delivered the message—*Don't give up, we're working on it, and things* will *get better*—because the world knew me. Trusted me. Loved me. I was Tarsi Tiff, the chart-topping singer-songwriter beloved by all. Well, not *all*. One only needed to check out my social media to see that.

"I know how hard this is, I really do," I told listeners. "I, um—" A faint, breathy laugh caressed the microphone. "Well, I've been working on something for you all." I crossed my ankles under my folding chair and sat a little straighter, a small smile curving my lips. "A new song, just for you."

An arid breeze fluttered the canvas flap covering the doorway of the broadcast tent. The tiny hairs on my arms and the back of my neck stood on end, and I shivered despite the sweltering desert heat. I glanced to one side, then peeked over my other shoulder, making sure I was still alone.

"I hope this will remind you to stay strong. To never give up. We *will* get through this—and we'll do it *together*." I cleared my throat and inhaled, filling my lungs in preparation to hum the first notes.

It had been ages since I last sang for an audience. Okay, maybe it had barely been a week, but I was used to regular doses of the sweetest sound in existence—the roar of a crowd of adoring fans. I missed it. Missed *them*.

I craved the swell of energy that poured onto the stage as a crowd's anticipation mounted and the hush that fell right before I sang. The last bastion of social media went down three days ago, so I couldn't even rely on virtual adoration. This war had cut me off from my fans, from their love, and I was jonesing for a fix.

My dad wanted me to make these broadcasts quick. *Deliver the message and get back to the oasis*, he would say. The longer I lingered out in the open, the more likely it was that one of my people's almighty ancestors, the Netjers, would detect me. They were like bloodhounds, hunting for the scent of a Nejeret's immortal soul.

But I just wanted to sing a song. Surely my dad couldn't begrudge me that. It was just a song. One little song. No harm ever came from singing a song.

I closed my eyes and released the first string of notes.

A brutal pain stabbed into my back, and my eyelids flew open. I cried out, the inhuman sound strangling the beginning of my song as the pain burrowed deeper, boring through my chest. My lungs seized, and the cry gurgled out.

Eyes opened wide and mouth gaping, I stared down at my chest and watched the tip of a gleaming iridescent sword blade sprout from my sternum. My diaphragm flexed and spasmed, straining to make my lungs work.

I felt pressure on the back of my shoulder, followed by a rush of searing agony as the blade disappeared, yanked free of my body. My vision momentarily whited out.

But then the worst of the pain receded, and I could breathe again. Sort of.

My lungs worked in fits and starts. The first shallow inhale carried with it the sensation of drowning.

"Wha—" The half-formed word came out with a gush of blood.

I coughed, sputtering crimson onto the textured white surface of the folding card table and down the front of my tank top. Drops of blood splattered the exposed skin of my thighs below the frayed hem of my cut-offs.

My vision grew fuzzy, slowly narrowing my view of the world to a dim tunnel. I slumped forward, banging my cheekbone against the microphone. It tumbled off the table, hitting the canvas floor with a dull *thunk*.

My arms hung limply on either side of my chair as blood dribbled from my mouth. It pooled on the table under my cheek, hot against my chilled skin.

The darkness continued to close in until it was all I could see. Until it was everything.

I felt a lingering sadness that the world would never hear my song. My last song. But soon enough, even that faded away.

I WOKE TO A pounding headache, ringing ears, and sand so far up my nose that if I started crying, it would probably come out in my tears. I flared my nostrils and inhaled through my mouth, intending to blow the breath back out through my nose to clear it. Massive backfire. Now I had sand up my nose *and* in my mouth.

Spitting sand, I rolled from my stomach to my side and cracked one eyelid open to blinding sunlight. The sun beat down from high in the sky, saturating my exposed back with its pervasive heat. I immediately squeezed my eyes shut again.

Gritting my teeth, I forced my eyelids open and raised my throbbing head, squinting against the bright sunlight. It took my eyes long seconds to adjust. It took my fuzzy brain even longer to process what I was seeing.

Sand. So much sand. An endless sea of the stuff stretching out in undulating dunes, surrounding squat peaks formed of craggy limestone like white-capped waves. I craned my neck, peering all around me. The expanse of desert continued in all directions, vast and endless.

"What the shit?" The words came out creaky, like my voice hadn't been used in days.

I laid my head back down and squeezed my eyes shut. Clearly, I was in the desert—specifically, Egypt's Western Desert. That made sense as the last thing I remembered was reading the morning broadcast in the radio tent outside the Netjer-At Oasis.

But where was the canvas tent? Where was the buggy? Where was the satellite and radio tower?

My mind registered the press of skin on skin where my torso touched my inner arm. I was positive I had been wearing a tank top when I left the oasis. I had been known to let the girls hang out in private, much to the joy of the paparazzi who made it their business to be all up in *my* business, but I wasn't in the habit of walking around topless *around my dad*. However, I sure as hell didn't seem to be wearing a shirt now.

I risked another raise of my eyelids to peer down at my body. Yep, I was naked as the day I was born.

"What the actual shit?" I mumbled, completely baffled.

Don't get me wrong, I had been living in LA for the better part of the last decade. I'd had some wild times, resulting in more than my fair share of WTF wake-ups, but this—waking up face-planted in the sand and buck-ass naked in *literal* Bumfuck, Egypt—was a new one for me.

I rolled onto my back and flung an arm over my eyes to shield them against the sunny daggers stabbing down from the sky. I took a deep breath and delved deeper into my tender mind, searching for any possible explanation for my current, totally bonkers situation.

Last thing I remembered, I was in the broadcast tent. I had finished reading out my dad's morning update, and I was about to sing my new song. I was excited. It's a pretty fucking fantastic song.

A flash of memory seared through my mind. A mere flicker, there and gone in a heartbeat.

> A *lightning bolt of pain struck my back, and a gleaming sword blade burst out of my chest.*

I gasped, sitting bolt upright. My eyes flew open, and I searched my bare chest with frantic hands for the bloody, gaping wound. But there was no sign of it.

Before I had recovered from the disorientation of the first, another flicker of memory flashed through my mind.

> *I floated through a streaming rainbow, being sucked toward a dark, looming void.*

I whimpered, curling up my legs and hugging my knees to my chest. My heart galloped, adrenaline flooding my veins. That looming darkness frightened me more than the memory of the killing blade.

I buried my face between my knees, hiding from the disturbing scenes. It did no good. The vivid flickers of memories continued to invade my mind, choppy and incomprehensible, there and gone in a flash.

I was in the rainbow stream again, only this time I wasn't floating. I was drowning. A violent, suffocating undertow dragged me away while I thrashed wildly.

Panic gripped me, and my breaths came faster. I focused on slowing my breathing, on drawing the hot, dry air deep into my lungs before releasing it in a measured exhale.

What were those flashes—genuine memories? Or leftovers from some horrific nightmare? I honestly couldn't tell.

I felt like I had blacked out. My recollection of everything from the broadcast tent onward was too slippery, those flashes too brief. I couldn't make sense of *any* of it, and the harder I tried, the more intensely my headache pounded.

Regardless of the how and why of it, my strange situation remained the same. I was naked and alone in the desert in the middle of the day. I needed to find shelter from the blistering sun, and soon, before my delicate skin really did burn to the point of blistering. I was Nejeret, descended from the all-powerful Netjers currently assaulting our world, which made me immortal—so long as nothing killed me—but not indestructible.

Once the panic receded some, I raised my head and squinted, waiting for my eyes to adjust to the bright glare of the midday sun. I curled my legs underneath me and sat on my knees, raising one hand to shield my eyes. In every direction, jutting limestone outcroppings and rolling dunes stretched to the horizon, where they met the cerulean sky. A few wispy clouds broke up the unrelenting expanse of blue overhead, but they were worthless for providing shade.

I craned my neck to examine my shoulder. The coppery flesh had yet to take on the telltale rosy hue of a sunburn. I pressed a finger into the skin to be sure. Nope, not burned. Yet. I couldn't have been out here for very long.

Frowning, I pulled on my shoulder to get a better look at my back. I hadn't noticed it at first, what with the sand coating my skin. My pristine, unmarked, un*inked* skin. My clothes weren't the only thing missing.

Last I checked, the phases of the moon were inked onto my back, running down the length of my spine. It was a beautiful piece, given to me by my aunt Kat on my eighteenth birthday. The black ink faded to gray once my Nejeret traits manifested and my body started to reject it. I twisted this way and that, brushing away the sand to make sure my eyes weren't playing tricks on me.

They weren't. The tattoo was gone. Not faded. *Gone.*

"What the hell is going on?" I said, my voice more than a little shrill as I grew increasingly distressed.

Hastily, I glanced down at my forearms, twisting my wrists to expose the undersides. The string of music notes on my left forearm and lyrics on my right were missing as well.

I wasn't just naked. My skin was *brand new.*

My brows bunched together, and I shook my head, attempting to dislodge the cobwebs tangling my most recent memories. I scanned my immediate surroundings, this time using a more critical eye. No broadcast tent. No satellite or radio tower. No buggy.

I chewed on the inside of my cheek. It was as though I had been plucked out of the tent—and out of my clothes—and dropped in some random part of the desert.

I adjusted my feet so the soles pressed into the warm, coarse sand and placed my palms on the ground, pushing myself up into a crouch. My joints creaked, my muscles protesting at the movement. I felt bruised all over, like I had tumbled down the side of a mountain, pinballing between trees and boulders. Groaning, I straightened until I was standing about as steadily as a rheumatic octogenarian.

I rubbed the center of my bare chest with my fingertips as I peered around, feeling a ghost of that blade skewering through flesh and organ and bone. But there was no actual pain, no tenderness, only the memory of searing agony. I inhaled, filling my lungs completely, relieved to find no sense of drowning.

My hand fell away from my chest when I spotted what I was looking for. There, near the horizon, I could make out a massive mound of craggy, sand-swept limestone boulders. The Netjer-At Oasis.

I smiled to myself and trudged through the sand toward the oasis. I didn't relish the idea of waltzing in there naked, but if I didn't get out of the sun soon, I really would start toasting.

Ten minutes into the trek, a terrifying possibility struck me: the Netjers.

If those frightful flashes weren't from a nightmare, but pieces of actual memories, then those bastards must have found me while I was broadcasting. It didn't explain how I had ended up naked and relocated—or *not* dead. I clearly recalled the sensation of a blade stabbing me through the chest, which should have been a killing injury, even for an immortal-ish Nejeret.

The hows and whys fled my mind as fear gripped my heart. I picked up the pace, stumbling forward through the bone-dry sand until I was running.

If the Netjers had found me, I feared they would find the other Nejerets hiding in the oasis soon enough. If they hadn't already. Everyone I loved was there—my dad and Lex, Aset, the twins, little Reni . . .

A sob clawed up my throat at the thought of the Netjers attacking my sweet baby sister, and I covered my mouth with one hand. I tripped in the sand, barely catching myself on my hands and knees.

I loved Reni like I had birthed the kid myself. If the Netjers found her, they would kill her. Their mission was to search and destroy. No Nejeret was safe, no matter how young or innocent. Especially not a special Nejeret like Reni, who carried a rare *sheut* within her tiny toddler body, affording her some yet-to-be-revealed magical power.

I took heaving breaths, wrestling the wild fear into submission, and pushed back up to my feet. I ran the rest of the way to the oasis as fast as I could. I needed to get there before the Netjers. I had to warn my people.

I was gasping for breath by the time I reached the veritable mountain of limestone shielding the oasis from the world. Gripping my side and gulping air, I stumbled around the perimeter of the massive mound, searching for the mouth of the tunnel that burrowed through the limestone barrier to the idyllic haven concealed within. When I reached the opening, I stopped in my tracks.

"No, no, no . . ." I lunged forward and slapped my hands against the solid barrier covering the entrance to the oasis.

The tunnel was blocked by a thick, opalescent sheet of *At*, the otherworldly substance created when the very fabric of space and time was pulled into the physical dimension and given solid form. The solidified *At* shimmered, iridescent in the unrelenting sunlight. Super pretty. Also, super impenetrable.

Only a few Nejerets could wield At, and two of them were supposed to be inside the oasis right now. Had they done this? Had they sealed themselves inside the oasis to protect the Nejerets hiding within from our far more powerful ancestors? It would only buy them time. Once the Netjers realized my people were in there, those monsters would tear through the dome of *At* shielding the oasis like it was cheap wrapping paper.

"Come on!" I wailed, pounding the sides of my fists against the unbreakable barrier of *At* blocking the only way into the oasis.

I dropped my arms to my sides and leaned my forehead against the indestructible barrier. The *At* was smooth and warm, but not hot to the touch like the limestone surrounding it.

"*What* is going on?" The words fell from my lips, little more than a whisper.

I turned around and, back pressed against the *At* barrier, slid down to the ground. Something dark and terrible slithered in my chest, constricting around my heart. Dread, sickening and insidious, settled in my belly. Those flickering still frames shifted around in my mind, expanding and gaining substance.

I knew. I knew what had happened to me—why the others had sealed themselves in the oasis—and the truth was too horrifying to face.

I hugged my knees to my chest, feeling wretched and exposed. My chin trembled, and tears welled in my eyes, quickly spilling down my cheeks. I squeezed my eyelids shut and pressed my cheek against my knee. My shoulders shook as silent sobs racked my body.

Images flooded into my mind, coalescing into scenes and fusing into a cohesive sequence. Into a full-fledged memory.

I was in the broadcasting tent, staring down at the tip of the shimmering blade protruding from my chest. The blade was yanked free of me, and I fell forward, drowning in my own blood and lamenting the song that would never be sung.

Suddenly, I was floating above my body, staring down at myself. The change in perspective was disorienting, but oddly enough, not disturbing. It was as though all my fears and worries died with my physical body. I slowly floated backward, my discarded body shrinking as distance separated me from it.

With a pop, I passed through a filmy barrier and floated into a gently swirling sea of vibrant colors. The soul-energy. I was in Duat, I realized, the blissful realm where mortal souls mingled after death. An overwhelming sense of peace and calm settled into me, and I basked in the serenity of it all.

The tranquility vanished as I passed through another barrier. This one was a dark and menacing void. It was the cold absence of life, of light. It clung to me, oily and clammy. Viscous. Hungry. The fear I thought I had left behind surged forth, and for an infinite moment, that nightmarish darkness held me captive.

There was a strange, suctioning sound, like pulling a boot free from the mud, and a cool, glittering mist replaced the dark void. It was silvery and so thick I could hardly see through it. I felt my chest, but I could find no wound. No stain of blood on my tank top. I turned around and around, peering into the mist. Into the utter stillness. The complete silence. This had to be Aaru. The inescapable land of the dead. The prison the Netjers built to hold

Nejerets' immortal souls.

A whisper of sound cut through the silence, and I moved toward it. A shadowy silhouette took form. I rushed forward, the slap of my sandals on hard-packed ground echoing through the mist. As I ran, more silhouettes became visible, other Nejerets.

Before I could get close enough to see anyone clearly, a blinding flash of light vaporized the mist, and I was surrounded by shouting. Screaming.

Silence fell, sudden and deafening.

I blinked, and Aaru—and all the other Nejerets—vanished. I was back in that rainbow sea of soul-energy, in Duat. Only this time, the current wasn't gentle and welcoming. It was violent and raging, throwing me about. Sweeping me away. Tearing me apart. I tumbled and rolled, unable to get my bearings.

Just when I thought I couldn't take any more, the mystical maelstrom stopped. Once again, I floated along in a lazy current, my soul bruised and battered. I sensed the barrier into Aaru before I saw it, the dark, looming wall. The sucking void. It drew me closer, a moth to a fatal flame.

But before Aaru could reclaim me, an invisible hook caught in my heart. I gasped as something tugged me backward, away from the looming abyss. My arms and legs trailed through the rainbow current, disturbing the flow of the soul-energy.

I heard a pop, and another blinding flash of light consumed the world.

My eyes snapped open, and I raised my head, searching the horizon but seeing another time. Another dimension. Another life.

It hadn't been a nightmare.

I died. And when my life ended, I was sucked into Aaru, just like every Nejeret who had died before me.

Narrowing my eyes, I studied my sandy surroundings. I was still in Aaru. I had to be. Aaru was a one-way trip. Not even an all-powerful Netjer could escape the dark, imprisoning shell surrounding the immortal underworld.

So, where was everyone else I had seen in that strange mist? I frowned and glanced down at my au naturel state. And where were my clothes? When I first arrived in Aaru, I had been wearing the same tank top and shorts I'd been wearing when I died. I returned my attention to the endless stretch of sand and limestone.

I knew a fair bit about the Nejeret land of the dead. Aaru was filled with an endless and varying array of landscapes, like some infinite and twisted theme park, ruled by strange, wish-like magic. The denizens of Aaru were able to think things into existence. In fact, the first Nejeret who ever entered Aaru was the one who thought the labyrinthine structure of the place into existence. So far as mythical underworlds went, it wasn't half bad.

I stood and peered down at myself, imagining a tank top and shorts covering my extreme nakedness.

Nothing happened.

My brow furrowed, and I tried again. I pictured myself wearing that stupid outfit until a sharp, stabbing pain joined the dull throbbing inside my skull.

But still, nothing happened. I remained as naked as ever.

With a sigh, I gave up. Clearly, there was some trick to the strange magic. Either that or I was no longer in Aaru. And *that* was impossible.

I STALKED AROUND THE rocky mound covering the Netjer-At Oasis. Being on my feet and moving helped my mind work, giving clarity to my muddled thoughts.

The longer I pondered my predicament, the more the impossible became probable: I couldn't get Aaru's strange magic to work because I wasn't *in* Aaru.

I died, that was a certainty. And like all Nejerets who had died before me, I had been immediately sucked into Aaru. But somehow, the impossible had happened. I had escaped—or rather; I had been spat back out—and then *reborn*. My brand-spanking-new body was a testament to my unexplained resurrection.

"It must've been Kat," I speculated aloud as I chewed on my thumbnail.

My aunt was the only being in this universe more powerful than a Netjer. She must have somehow cracked Aaru open, letting my immortal soul escape. It was the only plausible explanation, not that I could come up with anything more specific than the vague certainty that Kat had somehow resurrected me.

I glanced over my shoulder, then up at the sky for the umpteenth time. Having been stabbed through the back by a Netjer left me paranoid and jumpy. Were those bastards still around? Still hunting us? Or had Kat taken care of them as well? Not that there was anything I could've done about it if they *were* still lurking about. Well, other than not linger here and lead them right to the oasis and to all the Nejerets hiding within.

"Isfet, grant me the serenity to accept the things I cannot change," I murmured under my breath. "The courage to change the things I can, and the wisdom to know the difference." The serenity prayer had become something of a security blanket for me during my *troubled years*. I often fell back on its simple, no-nonsense guidance when life grew too heavy.

The Netjer situation—whatever its status—was out of my hands. But I *could* do something about my precarious naked-and-stranded-alone-in-the-desert predicament.

I reached the blocked entrance to the tunnel that led into the oasis and stopped, crossing my arms over my chest. I glared at the impenetrable *At* barrier barring my way. There was no way through, at least, not for me. Here was another of those things I couldn't change.

I needed to move on, to find shelter elsewhere. And water. If my gut was right and I had been miraculously resurrected, my shiny new body wouldn't remain alive for much longer without water, especially not at the rate I was melting in this heat.

I angled my face up toward the sun and squinted, studying its position in the sky. I estimated six or seven hours of full daylight remained in the day. Once the sun set, the air would cool, buying me some more time.

"What's that rule?" I muttered as I shifted my focus to the horizon, far beyond which I would find the Farafra Oasis. "Something about threes..." I pursed my lips. "You can survive three minutes without air, three days without water, and three weeks without food?"

I frowned. I couldn't imagine holding my breath for three whole minutes, and the idea of not eating for even a week made my stomach groan in protest. I wasn't sure how long it would take to walk to the Farafra Oasis from here. It was about an hour's drive. Did that equate to less than three days of walking?

I let out a breathy, semi-hysterical laugh. "Does it matter?"

It wasn't like I had any other options. I could either hoof it to the Farafra Oasis, or I could sit here and feel sorry for myself while I slowly died of dehydration. Or heat stroke. Or both.

Huffing out a breath, I turned my back to the blocked tunnel and marched into the desert. I was about a half-mile out when I paused and turned to peer back at the rocky mound covering my people's ancient home.

What about my family? My dad, Lex, Reni, and the others who were supposed to be in the oasis. Had they been among the silhouetted Nejerets I had seen in Aaru? What if they were fine and *were* still holed up in the oasis? Maybe if I just sat tight near the tunnel entrance, eventually someone would come and remove the *At* barrier to let me in.

"Accept the things you can't change," I reminded myself in a sing-song voice.

I *could* wait by the *At* barrier, and someone *might* find me there and let me into the sanctuary of the oasis. Or a Netjer could find me, then find the Nejerets hiding in the oasis and kill them all. *Or* I could sit there until my body shriveled up, waiting for someone to come who wasn't even in there. It was safest to assume that the oasis was empty and that I was on my own.

I let out a sigh, turned, and continued onward, delving deeper into the wilds of the Western Desert. As I walked, I cataloged my extremely limited knowledge of survival skills. A Jack-of-all-trades, I was not. I was the dreaded master of one. I knew a lot about one thing—music—and not much about anything else. Certainly not much about anything that might help me survive out in the desert on my own. Well, my dad *had* taught me to fight, but that wasn't the type of survival skill I needed right now.

I mentally berated myself for not taking up my ex, Wolf, on his offer to feature me as a guest on his survival show. *Wolf in the Wild* was an international sensation. Not as big as me but big enough to get between us. Of course, he would never have admitted that. He would probably fire back with something lame, like saying there was no room for his career to get between us with my ego taking up all the space.

"Ugh," I grunted.

But what *had* I learned from listening to Wolf drone on and on about survival craft? I must have soaked up something. Cognitive osmosis is a thing, right?

I knew not to drink untreated water from a natural source. Doing so risked exposure to all kinds of nasty bugs. But I didn't have any way to treat water—let alone know how to do such a thing. I thought maybe iodine was involved. Or was it bleach?

"That doesn't make any sense," I mumbled, shaking my head. Why would anyone voluntarily drink bleach? Surely doing so would kill anyone who tried it faster than any parasite.

I weighed the merits of dying of straight-up dehydration versus diarrhea-induced dehydration. If I found water and didn't drink it, I would most definitely die of dehydration. If I *did* drink it, there was a chance I would contract something like giardia and die in the least glamorous way possible. *But* there was also the chance that I would be fine. And, bonus—I would be alive.

"In a worst-case scenario, you can always drink your pee."

I gagged as Wolf's remembered words whispered through my mind. "Not going to happen, bucko." Way too gross. With some of the things that came out of his mouth, it was a miracle I ever even wanted to have sex with him.

And then there was the issue of food. The rule of three applied to humans, and while Nejerets were originally born of humans—Nuin, the Netjer who created this universe, boinked and impregnated a human woman many thousands of years ago—humans and Nejerets were different enough that I feared the three-weeks-without-food rule wouldn't apply to me.

Our relative immortality was born of the gift of hyper-regenerative cells. A Nejeret's body kicked healing and renewal up into overdrive when injured, but the regeneration process required a ton of energy—in other words, food—and coma-like rest. A Nejeret in the throes of healing was held captive by the gorge-rest cycles that dominated the process. Theoretically, we could live forever, so long as nothing injured us beyond our hyper-regenerative means.

I had no doubt that the damage caused to my body by dehydration or—shudder—a waterborne parasite would trigger my body's built-in regenerative process. Which meant that if I suffered from either, I would need food—right away and a lot of it.

What was edible in the Sahara? I might as well have been on Mars for all the plant life visible at the moment. It was all sand and rocks as far as the eye could see. Far ahead, I could just make out the first hints of lumpy white chalk formations poking out of the sand. I was entering the White Desert, which was a welcome sign because it meant I was heading in the right direction. It was less welcome for the extreme lack of anything alive in that portion of the Sahara.

I had never personally experienced a regeneration cycle. I was twenty-five years old, and as was standard with my kind, my Nejeret characteristics had only manifested a few years ago. I didn't actually know what my energy needs might be if I tripped on a stray chunk of chalk and sprained my ankle while trekking across this stupid, barren desert. I shifted my focus from the horizon to the sand right in front of me, suddenly more mindful of where I placed my feet.

My shoulders were feeling slightly roasted, and I glanced down at my forearm. The coppery skin was definitely darker and rosier than usual. No sunburn press test required.

Would a bad sunburn trigger a regenerative cycle? I wasn't sure.

I picked up the pace.

At least it wasn't crazy hot. I estimated the temperature to be around ninety degrees, which was a little cooler than the desert had been lately. It seemed like every time I emerged from the pseudo-cavern of the oasis, I was smacked in the face with a hundred-degree wall of hot, dry air. Not that I minded.

My friends joked that I had the aged, skin-damaged soul of an eighty-year-old snowbird, but I preferred to call myself a sun chaser. Misery was spending more than a day or two under overcast skies and dodging rain showers. Or worse, snow. When I wasn't touring, I was out basking in the sun, under the protection of a thick layer of SPF 100.

While my soul was well acclimated to spending long periods of time under the sun, since manifesting my Nejeret traits, my skin was another matter entirely. I couldn't tan. My skin cells constantly shed and renewed. It meant I would never wrinkle, never get freckles or moles or sunspots, but I also would never develop calluses, leaving the bottoms of my feet hypersensitive and the tips of my fingers prone to bleeding when I played the guitar. And if I ever dared to spend an extended period of time in the sun with unprotected skin, I *would* burn.

About an hour into my desert trek, I was well into the White Desert, and the skin on my shoulders was feeling decidedly crispy. All around me, white chalk formations jutted out of the golden sand like meringue peaks.

I should have reached the desert road by now. Even if sand completely covered the road itself, the darker limestone blocks periodically marking the route should have been easy enough to spot among the sea of stark white chalk. But I hadn't seen a single road marker.

Awkwardly, I climbed to the top of the nearest chalk formation, one that looked like a ten-foot cresting wave, and raised my hand to my forehead to use as a visor. I scanned the petrified sea of white chalk, my heart sinking deeper and deeper into my stomach with each slight rotation.

"Come on," I murmured. "Where's that stupid road?"

A pile of golden rocks, standing out in stark contrast to the white chalk, caught my attention, and I squinted to focus. It was in something of a valley between a string of taller, tree-like chalk formations. Rocks didn't just stack themselves up like that, especially not limestone rocks in a place where chalk dominated the landscape. Even from a good two hundred yards out, I could tell it was a man-made cairn.

I hustled down the side of my dune and hurried toward it. As I drew near, a large limestone block came into view another hundred yards or so beyond the stacked stones. Finally, road marker.

I grinned, wincing as my dry lips cracked and split.

"Ow…" I touched a fingertip to my bottom lip, and it came away crimson. I licked my lips to moisten them, despite knowing doing so would only dry them out further. I couldn't help it.

The cut had already healed, but I was prepared to be more cautious with my smiles.

"This is a no-fun zone," I chastised myself under my breath. Then I laughed—without smiling—the sound a little too shrill. As if I needed any reminder of that.

I passed the cairn but paused at the larger limestone block marking the route. The road itself was completely sand swept, and the marker was half-buried, as though nobody had traveled this way in decades. Hands on my hips, I pursed my lips and quirked them to one side, studying the block for a long moment before looking up the road one way, then down the other.

"This is weird," I told myself. "Really, *really* weird."

I had been on this road barely a week ago, and it had appeared well-traveled. There hadn't been any notable sandstorms since then, so how had the desert suddenly reclaimed the road?

I returned my attention to the limestone road marker. The block's edges were the sharpest of any ancient road marker I had ever seen. Most had been extremely eroded by wind and sand over the thousands of years that had passed while they stood sentry.

Groaning, I let my head fall back as my hands slipped from my hips. "I'm so thirsty," I whined and wallowed in self-pity for a solid thirty seconds.

I inhaled purposely and raised my head before blowing out the breath. Water wasn't going to deliver itself to me from the Farafra Oasis. I needed to get my crispy butt there myself. And so, after a deep breath, I started along the desert road.

Another couple of hours passed, and the soles of my feet were feeling decidedly raw. I was too much of a wuss to look, knowing that seeing the no-doubt ravaged state of my feet would make the pain ten times worse. Dehydration was setting in, fogging my brain. Three times now, I would have sworn I saw the shimmer of water in the distance, only to have it vanish in a blink. Stupid mirages.

I sang to myself to help pass the time and to distract my mind from my body's increasing aches and pains. I worked on half-finished songs, adding new verses and lyrics.

"Damn," I said when I—*finally*—sang the perfect final verse in a song I had been writing and rewriting for the better half of a decade. "That was epic. Baz'll make it a lead single for sure."

My manager was going to pee his ridiculous plaid pants when he heard the finished song. I could already see the glazed-over look in his eyes, the ghosts of dollar signs spinning in his soulless pupils.

I considered scratching myself deep enough to draw blood so I could jot down the lyrics on my skin. I really didn't want to forget them. But even as I considered doing so, the exact shape and form of the verse slithered away.

My eyes stung with a sudden welling of tears. I stopped in my tracks and bowed my head, my shoulders slumping as I fought the urge to cry. I couldn't believe I was on the verge of tears. Over song lyrics, of all things.

I didn't even know if Baz was still alive. The entire music industry might be dead, for all I knew. The Netjers had been smashing cities left and right for days. But this—forgotten song lyrics—was going to be the thing to break me down?

Not dying—or being inexplicably resurrected. Not wondering if my family was okay. Not finding myself stranded, naked and alone, in the middle of the godsforsaken Western Desert. And not walking for hours on raw feet, my skin singed and throat parched.

No, nothing sensible like that. I was falling apart over stupid fucking song lyrics.

Growling in frustration, I combed my fingers through my hair, pulling chunks of the long dark strands free from the loose knot I had tied at the base of my skull. "Get your shit together, chick. Come on." I gripped my hair tight at the roots and pulled. "Come *on*. Get it together."

I inhaled shakily and raised my head, setting my jaw. I. would. Not. Cry. Not right now. Not about this. I wasn't that self-centered. I couldn't be.

Except, I distinctly recalled that my last conscious thought before I died was of a song. Not worry for my family, who the Netjers were sure to find. Oh no. A song.

"You were right, Wolf." I took a step. Then another. And another. "I'm completely fucking obsessed with myself."

When this was over, I was going to do a serious reassessment of my priorities. I would be making some big changes in my life. I would learn how to be less of a selfish asshole.

When this was over.

"Left. Right. Left. Right. Left. Right . . ." The words were little more than grunts, but they kept me going.

I staggered onward, my skin scorched and my bloody feet caked with sand. I was going on hour six or seven of trudging along the desert road. The smooth white chalk formations jutting out of the sand had gradually given way to darker, craggier limestone.

I had long since lost the ability to gauge the passage of time, but the sun clued me in. It had slowly sunk toward the horizon off to the right of the road and now hovered there like it was purposely delaying setting. What a dick.

I considered dropping to my knees to crawl for a little while, giving my soles a chance to heal. But if I got down on the ground, I wasn't sure I would be able to get back up, and I had made a promise to myself not to stop until I reached the oasis. Until I reached water and salvation.

The distant sound of children's laughter reached my ears, carried by a gentle breeze. The sound lured my gaze up from the rock-strewn sand covering the patch of road immediately in front of me. I couldn't recall the last time I had looked up. It took energy away from walking, from convincing each brutalized foot to lift and touch back down on the coarse, burning sand.

When I did look up, I was a little surprised to find the road ahead of me sloping downward. I felt like I was trekking up a steep incline. I was even more surprised to see tall stone pillars silhouetted by the tangerine sky.

Squinting, I trudged onward. Not pillars. *People.*

My eyes opened wide, and I stumbled forward. I was too weak and clumsy to catch myself, and I ended up sprawled out on the road, face in the sand.

I spat out sand and lay there for a few seconds, my forehead resting on my forearm as I caught my breath, working up the nerve to raise my head. To look. To *see*.

If it was a mirage. If the people were suddenly gone, I wasn't sure I could make myself stand up again. To keep going.

This was so hard. Too hard. I couldn't do it.

A wretched sob rattled around in my chest, clawing its way up my throat. When I opened my mouth, I released a hoarse cry.

"Please be real. Please be real. Please be real." The words were a whispered wish, barely audible. After a few more ragged lungfuls of air, I slowly raised my head.

The people were still there, several dozen of them, robed in white from head to toe. They still looked like stone pillars to my sluggish mind, except stone didn't move. And there was some kind of animal. Camels? No, the shape was wrong. Horses? But that made no sense. Horses didn't do well this far out in the desert. But I didn't really care because there, beyond the cluster of white-robed figures, was water. Glorious, drool-inducing water.

The small, pristine pool of water glittered amber in the golden light of the setting sun, surrounded by a border of greenery.

I swallowed glue-like saliva, imagining it was cool, clear water, then licked my cracked, peeling lips with a tongue like a tacky eraser and pushed myself up to my hands and knees. After a deep, fortifying breath, I gingerly placed one foot on the ground. And whimpered. It was like stepping on hot coals.

I forced myself to transfer my weight to that foot and straighten my leg as I placed my other foot on the ground, earning a muted cry. I squeezed my eyelids shut, my eyes stinging with tears I couldn't shed. I was so close. So damn close. The water was right there.

I could *not* give up now.

After a deep inhale, I blew out the breath and opened my eyes. I lifted my right foot and took a step. Then I stepped forward with my left foot. Each step brought forth a starburst of pain and a muffled sob, but I did not stop.

As I drew nearer to the people, I saw that the animals were donkeys, their backs laden with woven baskets and hide waterskins. Something about that seemed off, but I didn't have the mental energy to figure it out.

I attempted to arrange my face into a warm, friendly expression. I was just a woman out for a nice, peaceful stroll through the desert. But deep down, I knew there was no way to disguise the desperation in my eyes.

And then I remembered I was naked and burned to a crisp, and I wondered why I was even trying to pretend that anything about this situation was casual or normal.

All stares were focused on me as I approached. I tried to see myself through their eyes. I probably looked half dead and fully nuts. The white-robed figures murmured among themselves, some tilting their heads to the sides as they watched me. A few of the smaller figures—children—giggled and ducked behind adults, peeking out around their robes.

A lone figure stepped forward from the group and cautiously approached me.

I stopped walking. It was all I could do to remain on my feet. To not drop to my knees and beg this stranger to take pity on me and fetch me a handful of water. Just one handful. It didn't even need to be clean water. At this point, I would gladly have slurped from a mud puddle.

"What has happened to you, child?" the figure asked, voice feminine but seasoned with the gravel of age. It took my shriveled mind eons to process the meaning of her words. She stopped a half-dozen paces away, and I focused on what I could see of her aged face under her linen cowl. As she studied me, concern deepened the lines in her brown, leathery skin.

"I'm Nejeret," I told her, betraying every survival instinct in my body. But she needed to know the Netjers would hunt me. Being near me meant danger to her and her people. If they were smart, they would run away from me and never look back.

Confusion clouded her dark, shrewd eyes. She studied me for a long moment, and then she stunned me speechless by dropping to *her* knees. She bowed her head, holding her hands out, palm up. Her knuckles were bulbous and gnarled, but her hands were steady.

At first, I thought she must have recognized me as Tarsi Tiff, international superstar. She wouldn't have been my first elderly fan, but she may have been my most unexpected. I supposed I should have been flattered, or maybe embarrassed. I didn't deserve such deference. But I didn't have energy for anything beyond lusting after the natural well a scant hundred yards away. I couldn't even manage a halfhearted effort at covering what I could of my nudity with my hands and arms.

The woman spoke without raising her head. "You honor us with your presence, divine one."

Again, it took me ages to comprehend her words, and even longer to discern the reason for the delay. It wasn't because extreme dehydration slowed my mind. Or, rather, not *only* because of the dehydration. I was having a hard time understanding her because she was speaking a language I hadn't heard since I was a young child: my native tongue, Old Egyptian.

Among humans, the language had been dead for thousands of years. And this old woman was decidedly human. Nejerets didn't age, at least not in the traditional, physical sense. So, how could she possibly be fluent in that ancient language?

Only then, once my brain code-switched to Old Egyptian, did I fully process what she had said. Specifically, what she had called me. Divine one. It was an honorific that humans used for my kind during ancient times. The title hadn't been used in hundreds, possibly thousands, of years—in *any* language.

This woman hadn't recognized me as Tarsi Tiff; she had recognized me as *Nejeret*.

Despite the lingering end-of-day heat and my extreme dehydration, an icy chill cascaded over my skin. I shivered as things that had seemed odd or out of place shifted, and I reoriented myself in the world.

I had wondered why my people would have replaced the *At* barrier blocking the tunnel to the Netjer-At Oasis. But now I could see that it hadn't been replaced at all. Rather, it had never been removed. And the limestone blocks marking the desert road were in such remarkable condition because they had yet to be eroded by eons of sandstorms.

When I was expelled from Aaru, I had tumbled through Duat for what felt like an eternity because I hadn't jumped straight from Aaru to the same time and place of my death. I had been dragged back to the distant past. To the time and place of my *birth*.

It was impossible. Miraculous. *Almost* unheard of.

I had, like my beloved stepmom before me, unintentionally traveled backward in time.

PRESENT DAY

⊆LETTER FR⊙M THE ⊆GUEST ℰDIT⊙R

ARCHAEOLOGY TODAY MAGAZINE

Dear reader,

Not long ago, I was in your metaphorical shoes. I was an average Jane graduate student. I knew the rules of the world and understood the limits of humankind. There was no place for immortals or soul mates or time travel in the real world—such things were relegated to works of fiction. Until I learned I was an immortal. Until I met Heru and bound my soul to his. Until I traveled through time.

So much has happened in the two decades since I learned the truth of the world—that I am Nejeret. I witnessed the death of a god—Nuin, the father of all Nejeretkind—and became his interim successor. My babies, Susie and Syris, have grown into near omnipotent beings. My little sister, Kat, has transformed into a veritable goddess powerful enough to protect not just the world, but the entire universe.

I learned that existence extends beyond the physical realm. I learned of At and anti-At, the elemental building blocks of this universe. I learned to enter and view the Echoes, the higher dimension where I can view all past, present, and potential future events like a streaming video. I learned about Duat, the higher dimension filled with a rainbow river of soul-energy, the source of all mortal souls. I learned that as a Nejeret, I have an additional part of my soul called a ba, which, in the event of my death, will be lured into and trapped within a separate, self-contained dimension beyond Duat, called Aaru.

And I learned that some Nejerets have yet another soul element called a sheut, which gives us incredible otherworldly abilities. I borrowed Nuin's sheut for a short while and wielded his terrifying power over time and space. Now, I have my own sheut that allows me to pull raw At into the physical realm and shape it to my will. My husband, Heru, can teleport from one location to another. Kat's drawings take on a life of their own, and her unique connection to the universe allows her to draw on not only At and anti-At, but also on the vast river of soul-energy.

It seems like magic; I know. Like the familiar world is no longer bound by the rules of physics. Like there is no place for science in this new reality. But as Arthur C. Clarke said, "Magic's just science that we don't understand yet." I know it's scary. I know these recent revelations require an enormous paradigm shift within each of us. But you will get through this. We all will—together.

Remember, Nejerets may descend from Nuin, a nearly omnipotent being from another universe, but we also descend from you—from humans. My mother was human. My grandmother was human. I was, until my Nejeret traits started to manifest when I was twenty-four years old, human. We are not the enemy. The other. We are of you. And we must all remember that in the difficult days to come.

I have worked closely with the editors and writers of Archaeology Today to bring you this special issue on the history, science, and archaeological record of my people. If you have any further questions or concerns after reading this issue, please reach out to the Nejeret Human Relations Agency.

Sincerely,
Alexandra Larson

ᴀND THE ꙅTARS ᴡILL ꟻALL ꟻROM ꜰEAVEN

AN OP-ED PIECE FROM
ARCHAEOLOGY TODAY MAGAZINE

Do the gods now walk among us? Are we entering the end of days? Who are these mysterious immortals who call themselves "Nejerets" and why are they here? It may feel as though the Nejerets have invaded our planet—that they are the ancient aliens so many conspiracy theorists have long hunted. These immortals couldn't possibly be as native to Earth as you or me, right? Evidence suggests a bit of both. Let's examine the archaeological record to understand a little more about the origins of the Nejeret species.

EVOLUTION OR DIVINE INTERVENTION?
According to Heru, one of the Nejeret leaders, his species is *homo sapiens nejeret,* an offshoot from our own *homo sapiens sapiens*, much like our cousin species, the more familiar *homo sapiens neanderthalensis*. However, unlike Neanderthals, with whom we share a common ancestor, the Nejerets are direct descendants of our species. During a candid press conference, Heru explained that Nuin, one of the near-omnipotent creators of our universe, implanted himself into the womb of a pregnant human woman many thousands of years ago. He lived as one of us, and his progeny, born of human mothers, became the beings we now know as Nejerets.

His kind have inherited many enviable perks from their "Great Father," including—but not necessarily limited to—heightened senses and enhanced cellular regeneration, the latter of which leads to their extreme longevity. Heru, though unwilling or unable to pinpoint his exact date of birth, insinuated that he has been alive for over five thousand years—and he is not even the oldest among his kind. While these traits may seem like something straight out of a fantasy novel, some of the world's top geneticists have been studying Nejeret blood and tissue samples since their public "coming out" last month. In the weeks since, these devoted researchers have detected several genetic markers that they believe cause the notable differences between our two species.

Egyptologists have been scouring the historical record for evidence of Nuin, as well as Heru (more commonly known as "Horus" to mythology buffs), Hat-hur (more commonly known as "Hathor," the supposed ancient alter-ego of Alexandra Larson), Aset (more commonly known as Isis), Nekure (Aset's son, known as "Nik" among devoted admirers), Tarset (Heru's daughter and beloved pop star better known as "Tarsi Tiff") and many more. Temples, tombs, and other preserved historical sites spread across Egypt support Heru's claims.

There is even mention of an ancient Nejeret homeland in a lost oasis, long buried under the sands of the Sahara. When asked about the events that led to the ancient diaspora of his people, Heru turned the microphone over to his wife, Alexandra, who claimed that the events surrounding Nuin's death destroyed the oasis—though this hasn't stopped archaeologists and treasure hunters from seeking it. Alexandra knows this because she was there, a modern woman supposedly transported across a vast chasm of time to the ancient past.

Time-traveling? Teleportation? Surely such abilities are impossible—

5

⁺LEX

I BLEW OUT AN annoyed breath and tossed the open magazine down on the coffee table in front of me. How had everything gone so wrong so fast? For two days after the special issue of *Archaeology Today* released—moving record copies, I might add—it looked like we were making genuine progress on the human-Nejeret relations front.

But then the Netjers invaded, smiting cities all over Earth in their effort to exterminate all Nejeret life. We did the only thing we could do—we fled to the safety of our hidden oasis. I may have exaggerated the level of destruction there, just a smidge. It *had* been lost for millennia, hidden under a mountain of limestone and thousands of years of sand, but beneath all of that lay the ancient Nejeret settlement, perfectly preserved and awaiting our return.

Of course, humanity had a completely understandable reaction to us fleeing. They blamed us—for everything. For abandoning them in their time of need. For drawing the Netjer's attention to this universe in the first place. For the destruction and devastation caused to this planet. In the eyes of most humans, we were responsible for every death that resulted from the immortal war. And I could hardly blame them for that.

A squeal drew my attention to the wrestling match taking place on the floor of the playroom. Syris struggled under the dual assault of his tiny attackers. My baby girl, Reni, giggled maniacally as she clung to my full-grown son's back like a barnacle, while her partner in crime, Bobby, rained tickles of fury upon Syris' feet.

The corners of my mouth tugged upward, but my worries weighed too heavily upon my mind to result in anything beyond the tiniest of smiles. We had been hiding in the oasis for well over a month now. The Netjer threat was gone, driven away by Kat during the epic battle that led to the destruction of Aaru and the resurrection of all our people. Now, it was the humans who had us cowering in fear. Or, at least, what remained of them.

Again, I could hardly blame them for their hatred. Their condemnation. Billions of people died—and remained dead—while every Nejeret who had fallen as a casualty of the immortal war had been granted a miraculous rebirth. It wasn't remotely fair, and it *was* our fault. But the continued aggression served no purpose other than to fuel humanity's hatred of Nejerets.

They wanted us gone. But we had nowhere else to go.

I looked to the doorway as Susie walked into the playroom. She eyed her twin brother wrestling with her younger siblings on the floor, smirked and shook her head, then turned her attention to me. She crossed the room to where I sat perched on the edge of an *At* bench, her brow furrowing when she spotted the open magazine on the coffee table in front of me.

"Mom," she said, a faint hint of exasperation in her tone, "why do you beat yourself up with that thing?" She flicked her hand toward the discarded magazine. "There's nothing you could have said differently in there that would have made this situation better." She stopped near the end of the table and crossed her arms over her chest, raising her eyebrows for emphasis. "It is what it is. We can only move forward from here."

I let out a single, dry laugh. "I think we both know that's not entirely true." Our family had a bad habit of hopping this way and that around in the timeline. Even if Kat had put a kibosh on any further time travel before her powers burned out, there was always a chance for temporal displacement. I knew that better than anyone.

Susie rolled her eyes. "I'm sure Dad's waiting for you," she said.

With a sigh, I stood and brushed a whole lot of nothing off the front of my linen pants. "Yes, I'm sure he is." I pointed to the low table tucked into one corner of the playroom with tiny chairs arranged around it. "The kids' snacks and waters are right there," I told her.

We had done what we could to make the space comfortable, but our resources were extremely limited out in the middle of the desert. It wasn't like there was an Ikea nearby to furnish all the palaces in the oasis. In the last month and a half, we had made do with fabricating what we could from solidified *At* and repurposing the few creature comforts we had hauled out here *before*.

Had it really only been a month and a half since everything went down? Since the war ended? Since we died and were reborn? Since Tarset vanished?

It felt like a lifetime ago.

A squeal followed by a peal of laughter shook me out of my daze, and a smile curved my lips as I watched Syris chase Reni and Bobby around the room, stomping after the smaller children and roaring like a deranged T-Rex.

It was probably time for me to stop thinking of Syris as a child. He was twenty years old now and nearly as large as his dad. But for the leaner build of youth, I could almost mistake him for Heru from behind. But Syris was *my* child, my baby boy, my first-born son. He would always be my baby, regardless of how big or strong he grew.

"We'll be fine, Mom," Susie said, linking her arm with mine and tugging me toward the doorway, away from her siblings. "Take a breath. Go to the meeting. And *don't* worry."

I cast one last, uncertain glance at Syris and his toddler charges before stepping out into the hallway. The trio was oblivious to me leaving. Somehow, that stung more than it reassured me.

I frowned as Susie pulled me further down the hallway. We were on the second floor of the oasis palace that had been my husband's home in ancient times. Most of the bedrooms and more private living spaces were located on this level and the one above. Heru had turned one such space into his office, where Susie currently led me. Half of my mind was on Heru—and the upcoming meeting with the rest of the heads of clans—but the other half lingered back in the playroom, on my grown boy, my baby girl, and my adopted son.

Susie and Syris may have been my first children, but ridiculously complex time-travel circumstances had prevented me from experiencing the joys and struggles of raising them. Rearing Reni and Bobby was my first true mothering experience, and my helicopter parenting tendencies disturbed me to no end. But they *had* died on my watch. In my arms.

I swallowed the sorrow, shoving the memory of those horrifying last moments into a locked vault in my mind. They were okay now, and the Netjers were gone. Nothing like that would ever—*ever*—happen to my children again.

I glanced over my shoulder as Susie led me further down the hallway. "If anything happens while we're at the meeting—"

"Nothing's going to happen, Mom," Susie cut in.

"But if something *does* happen and you need any help—," I persisted, anxiety twisting in my gut.

Some nights, I didn't sleep a wink. I just laid there in bed, thinking through all the worst-case scenarios, imagining every bad thing that could happen to my babies. Not even Heru could distract me from the horror show playing out in my mind, not while he battled his own demons.

"Get grandma," Susie said, finishing for me. She added an eye roll for good measure. "I know."

We slowed as we approached the open doorway to Heru's study. The faint hum of Tarset's voice told me my beloved was watching one of Tarset's many recorded interviews. Susie and I stopped in the doorway and peered in at Heru. He sat at his desk, hunched forward on his elbows, his back bent and shoulders slumped. Only the top of his buzzed head was visible over the upper edge of his laptop screen. It was so strange to see his powerful figure bowed and his dazzling charisma dulled by such heavy burdens. Not just his role as the leader of our people, but his heartbreak over losing Tarset.

I pressed my lips together, the corners dipping down into a frown as my heart broke for my husband, my bond-mate, the man whose soul resonated in perfect harmony with mine. Our unique connection meant I felt his pain on a visceral level. Not quite as if it were my own, but close.

He had been watching recordings of Tarset obsessively since the dust settled after Kat resurrected us and defeated the Netjers. It was when we first realized Tarset was missing. I wasn't sure what he thought he would find in those videos, but it certainly hadn't brought us any closer to finding her.

All it had done was reinforce Heru's belief that he had failed in his role as Tarset's father. He blamed himself for what happened to her, not that we had any clue of what that might actually be.

Susie loosened her hold on my arm and dragged hers free. I glanced at her face to find her features arranged in a mirror image of mine. She gave me a slight nod of understanding, her eyes filled with pity, and inched backward. When she was out of arm's reach, she turned and retreated at a quicker pace.

I watched her go, waiting until she disappeared around the corner, then turned my attention back to Heru. I inhaled deeply, grounding myself in my own emotions to resist the undertow of his turmoil, and stepped into the study.

Heru didn't look up as I crossed the room. I doubted he even realized I was there. I rounded his desk and planted myself behind his low-backed chair, slipping my arms around him and resting my chin on his shoulder. The soft fabric of his linen button-down shirt brushed against my forearms. He pressed the side of his head against mine in silent greeting.

On the screen, Tarset sat in an elegant upholstered armchair, one leg crossed over the other, her usual poised, bubbly self. She looked glamorous and gorgeous, as always, her copper eyes glittering with good humor, and her long, dark hair tied back in a sleek high ponytail that trailed over one shoulder.

"But, yeah," Tarset said, smiling like she was talking to her closest girlfriend in the universe, "we're still friends. Wolf and me—we were right for each other for a little while, but not for forever, you know?"

"Hmmm, yeah," the interviewer said, and the camera cut to her. "I think we can all relate to that." She was the curvy journalist from *Celeb News Now*—Miranda *something*—which meant this was *that* interview.

I held in a sigh.

"So, tell us," Miranda started. "What has it been like to grow up as an ancient Egyptian magically transported to modern times?"

Tarset laughed, the sound musical, like every other sound that came out of her mouth. Her expression remained warm and open as she answered. "Honestly, I couldn't tell you. I mean, how many people remember much from before they were, you know, four years old?" She shook her head, shrugging. "This world—" Tarset held out her hands, gesturing to the world beyond the set of the interview. "This is all I've ever really known."

The camera cut back to Miranda, capturing her thoughtful nod. "You've been notoriously tightlipped about the actual circumstances that led to your move from ancient times to our modern world. Can you tell us anything about what happened—about how you ended up here?"

Tarset laughed again. "You mean, can I tell people how to travel through time?" She grinned. "I hate to disappoint your viewers, Miranda, but it was kind of a onetime deal."

"Surely you must be able to share something," Miranda persisted. "Maybe not the *how* of it—but what about the *why*? You were born at the end of the Old Kingdom in Egypt, during the final years of the incredibly long reign of Pepi Neferkare, if I'm not mistaken."

The camera cut to Tarset's wilting smile, but it only lingered on her for a second before returning to Miranda.

Miranda leaned forward, her face locked in that dog-with-a-bone journalist's expression that I knew for a fact Tarset despised. "*Why* did you leave that time? Why jump forward four thousand years?"

The camera cut back to Tarset, capturing the last ghost of her smile as her gaze grew distant, her eyes unfocusing. The darkness from her childhood cast shadows on her usually sunny, effervescent personality. The shadows vanished almost as soon as they appeared, and Tarset's smile returned, but it looked forced.

I clenched my jaw, hating Miranda whatever-her-last-name-was for forcing Tarset to dredge up those haunting memories. What right did this woman have to push and push and *push*? Tarset was a *person*, but all this woman saw was a story.

More than once, I had heard Tarset confess she felt like she was public property, that it was part of the whole fame gig. She would say it with a single-shoulder shrug and a lopsided smile, like the masses thinking they owned her didn't bother her. But here, now, in this interview, it clearly did.

"I was sick," Tarset finally said, pausing to clear her throat.

The heartache in her voice shoved me back to those traumatic events, and in a blink, the memory replayed in my mind.

"Something's wrong," Heru said, stopping before the columned entrance to the palace. He looked up at the descending sun, still hours from the horizon. "They never go in this early. There's still much to do..."

Heru took the stairs leading up to the palace's arched doorway two at a time, me close on his heel. Vomit and sweat scented the air, and I suppressed a gag. "Sesha?" he called out to his wife.

There was no response.

"Sesha! Where are you?"

A groan came from one of the back rooms, accompanied by the faint sound of weeping.

Heru made his way through several sparsely furnished chambers and down a long hallway that led to the back of the palace, to the cozy room where the three youngest children slept.

Sesha kneeled on the floor beside one of three polished, wood-framed beds carved to display a bevy of animals native to Egypt, her head resting on her curled-up arm on the edge of the bed and her body shaking with each of her faint sobs. Tarset lay atop the bed, her skin pallid and coated in a sheen of sweat, her breaths quick and shallow. A brief glance at the other beds told me the children occupying them were also unwell, but not nearly as ill as Tarset.

"Sesha..." Heru strode into the room and dropped to his knees beside his wife. When Sesha didn't look up, didn't show any sign of having heard him, he shook her shoulder. "Sesha!"

She raised her head and turned red-rimmed eyes on him. With a wail, she threw herself into his arms and cried harder.

While Heru attempted to comfort her, I made my way around the room, checking on the other two children. They were both burning up, but neither seemed to be having as much trouble breathing as Tarset was having.

I stopped at the head of Tarset's narrow bed and stared down at her. Her eyes were closed, her mouth open, and each ragged, rattling breath was clearly a struggle. My stomach knotted, and fissures laced through my heart. Not her. Not the little girl I had grown to love so deeply.

"What happened?" I swallowed roughly. "How—"

Without warning, Sesha spun on her knees and wrapped her arms around my thighs, hugging my legs. "I beg of you, save her!" She stared up at me with hope-filled eyes. "Please!"

Slowly, I shook my head. "I don't know how to—"

"Please," she cried, desperation making her voice hoarse. "Please! You must be able to do something. Whatever you say, you have the powers of the gods... I know you do. Please, Alexandra! Use this great power you have. Save my little girl. Please!"

"Do not drink any water—it's been poisoned," Aset said as she rushed into the room, Nik close on her heels. She scanned the beds quickly. "Ah... but I see I am too late."

"Can you save them?" Heru asked his sister, his voice rough.

Aset approached the foot of Tarset's bed and shook her head. "I can do nothing for her, but the other two I may be able to save." She moved to the youngest boy's bed and bent over the child.

My throat constricted. Aset—a renowned doctor in the future—was a healer even now. But not even her skills could save the little girl who'd snuggled her way into my heart. Tarset was going to die. A sob lodged in my throat. Not her...

"Please..." Sesha's hands were clutching the backs of my leg so hard that it was painful. "Help her!"

"There was no way to save me using the medicine available *then*," Tarset said, her voice dragging me back to the here and now. "And well . . ." Her forced smile on the screen faded as the shadows of the past returned and her gaze grew glassy. This time, she didn't banish the darkness with a smile. "I was delirious. I don't really know how much is memory and how much is from a fever dream. My mom—"

Her voice broke, and she averted her gaze to her lap, where she fiddled with the thick gold band encircling her left thumb. It had been her mother's. She closed her eyes and took a deep breath.

"Lex, my stepmom—" Tarset opened her eyes, and a tiny smile touched her lips. "Well, you know who she is. The entire world does. She saved me the only way she could, by turning me into a type of otherworldly statue, preserving my body here on Earth while my soul waited in some other dimension outside of time and space—it's all super complicated," she said, interrupting her own explanation.

To call the events that had led to Tarset's shift from the distant past to the present *super complicated* was a gross understatement. I had been there, and it had been epic—in every possible meaning of the word.

"Long story short," Tarset said on the screen, "I remained frozen in time for four thousand years until medicine advanced far enough that I could be *un*frozen and saved." She shrugged, the shadows in her eyes clearing as her smile widened. "And then I was here."

The camera shot lingered on Tarset.

"Wow," Miranda said, slowly shaking her head. "I can't imagine what that must have been like." Her features shifted into an exaggerated expression of sympathy. "So, just like that, you left your family behind."

"Part of my family," Tarset corrected her. "I still have my dad and Lex and their kids, and I have more cousins and aunts and uncles than I know what to do with." She laughed, clearly trying to steer the conversation back onto lighter ground.

"But your mother," Miranda said, refusing to shift gears. "You must miss her."

I let out a derisive snort. What a stupid thing to say. Of course, Tarset missed her mom. Sesha was amazing. I missed the damn woman, and she still owned a sliver of my husband's heart.

A hint of irritation flashed across Tarset's face, so quick and subtle that if I hadn't known her—the real Tarset—I would have missed it.

Heru balled his hands into tight fists on the arms of his chair. Beneath me, I could feel the tension humming through his muscles, and I tightened my arms around his shoulders.

"Yeah, I miss her," Tarset said. "I suppose it's the same for any kid who loses a parent when they're young. I mean, it doesn't matter if they died four years ago, or four millennia ago. It will always hurt, always be fresh . . . always raw." A tear breached the brim of Tarset's eyelid and streaked down her cheek. "So, yeah, I miss my mom. I miss her every day." Tarset inhaled a shaky breath, her nostrils flaring, and turned her face away from the camera.

Tears filled my eyes and spilled over. I sniffed and wiped them away.

Tarset was our ambassador, the public face intended to help humanity accept Nejeret kind. I had watched her give countless interviews in this role since the big Nejeret coming out, and she almost never showed such vulnerability. She had always been so careful to conceal her inner scars, even around family. Such an open, raw display of pain was rare.

I had long assumed she held everything in because she didn't want to seem ungrateful. She bottled up all of her longing for the life—the mother—she left behind in ancient times and only projected what she believed others wanted to see in her. Calm, happy, friendly, cheerful, kind—those were the adjectives that fit Tarset. Or rather, that fit her public image as Tarsi Tiff.

When had her public face invaded her private life? It seemed like the polished, plastic version of Tarset was all we saw these days, even behind closed doors.

I reached past Heru and tapped the laptop screen to pause the video.

Heru expelled a breath like he had been holding it for minutes. "I should have seen it," he said, the silken baritone of his voice vibrating against my chest. "How much she was struggling." He exhaled a laugh, brief, muted, and bitter. "I didn't. I couldn't. I was so focused on our people, on the bigger picture and the war, that I failed to see what was going on with my daughter."

Closing my eyes, I turned my head toward Heru, pressing my face into the crook of his neck and inhaling his intoxicating spicy scent. Then I placed a soft kiss against his smooth, golden-brown skin, sighed, and opened my eyes, pulling away just enough to see his strong profile.

"Tarset is a performer," I reminded him. "She's an expert at putting on a show to make her audience see and feel whatever she wants them to see and feel. She didn't want you to see her pain, to feel it with her, so she didn't let you."

Heru sat motionless for a long time, but slowly, the tension eased from his muscles and he relaxed beneath me. He shifted his hands to my forearms crossing over the front of his chest. We remained that way for nearly a minute, not moving, not talking. Just being together. Sometimes that was enough.

Heru slid his left hand into mine and rotated it to place a gentle kiss on my palm. He exhaled a sigh, the sound slow, deep, and rough, and turned his chair away from the desk, angling his body toward me. Hands on my hips, he pulled me down to sit across his lap before raising his hands to cradle either side of my face. He kissed me softly, gently.

When he wrapped his arms around me and pulled me in close, it felt as though he was seeking refuge in my embrace. I melted into him, pressing my cheek against his shoulder and twining my arms around his neck, lending him what strength I could.

"It's been five weeks," he said, resting his cheek against the top of my head. "Where is she?"

I squeezed him more tightly in response but said nothing. He wasn't looking for an answer from me so much as he was putting the question out there, hoping Isfet, the soul of the universe, might take pity on him and answer.

Was Tarset dead? After the Great Resurrection, we honestly didn't know what happened to Nejerets when their new bodies died. Aaru had been destroyed. Where would our souls go now? Would they float for all eternity in the stream of soul-energy in Duat? We couldn't merge with the collective soul-energy there; our souls were eternal. Apart.

Was there a chance that some part of Aaru had survived the implosion and that Tarset was trapped there? Or had the Netjers stolen her away when Kat drove them out of our universe? Did something happen to her during that final battle that somehow destroyed her, body and soul?

I held in a sigh. Would we ever know for sure?

I twisted my wrist and peeked down at my watch, checking the time. "They'll start gathering soon," I said, loosening my hold on Heru. "We should prepare."

6

KAT

LIPS PURSED INTO A perma-frown, I flipped a fourth card from the deck of tarot cards, adding it to the three cards already laid faceup on the small patch I had cleared on the dining table in front of me. Half-finished sketches lay scattered around the tarot cards, the fruits of a brief but productive manic drawing session.

Scowling at the partial tarot spread, I took a gulp of whiskey—breakfast of champions—then set my empty glass down with a *thunk*. I flipped another card, the motion jerkier.

"Mother fucker," I muttered.

I flipped another card and slapped it down.

"Mother fucking mother fucker."

When I flipped the next card, I didn't even bother laying it in the spread on the table with the others. I held it pinched between my fingers and glared at the image displayed on its face. The tarot card quivered.

The Star card displayed Tarset, nude, kneeling at the edge of a pool of water surrounded by palm trees and sand, arms extended over the pool and water dripping from her cupped hands. Seven stars hung above her in the twilight sky, looking like silver asterisks. Near the horizon, in the place of an eighth star, a black scarab hovered, its wings flared up and around a golden disk. Upright, this card represented hope and creativity, which seemed fitting for Tarset. But upside down, as the card kept appearing, The Star suggested loneliness and defeat.

The spread of cards was the same as before. The same as always.

The silence filling the cabin grated on my nerves. The endless falling snow outside muffled all the noise of the surrounding world. A world that had become far too quiet. We may have vanquished the enemy, but they had left brutal scars on the earth.

Growling, I unleashed my frustration on the useless tarot cards, shoving them off the table with a violent sweep of my arm. Several sheets of paper fluttered to the hardwood floor, covering some of the cards.

With a harsh scream, I shoved my chair back and stood partway. Another, angrier arm sweep sent more sketches flying, along with my empty whiskey glass and a few discarded pens. The glass smacked against a cabinet door, then rolled on its side down the length of the aisle between the kitchen island and the row of cabinets. A couple of sheets of paper made it all the way to the rug in the living room beyond the far end of the table.

Breathing hard, I leaned forward, my palms planted on the table's smooth oak surface. I had been raw and on edge since that final showdown with the Netjers, like the colossal force I had channeled had overloaded my synapses and singed my nerve endings. The smallest things set me off these days, and the most minute use of my powers exhausted me.

Nik had brought me here, to this cabin in the remote Alaskan wilderness, to give me a chance to recuperate in peace. I had no idea what was going on *out there*, in the rest of the world. Though I supposed I would find out today, when we met with the Nejeret clan leaders at the oasis. It would be my first time revisiting the scene of the battle.

I straightened and reached out to my right to snatch the half-full whiskey bottle off the end of the counter. I yanked the stopper free, took a long pull of the burning amber liquid, then stuffed the stopper back into the neck of the bottle.

Rage bubbled up, boiling over. With a hoarse howl, I chucked the bottle across the cabin. It hurtled toward the picture window in the living room. I hadn't actually intended to throw the bottle at it, but that's where it was headed, and part of me gleefully anticipated the impending explosion of glass.

The bottle froze feet from smashing into—and likely through—the window. It hovered in front of the glass, the idyllic winter wonderland displayed beyond remaining undisturbed by my tantrum. A delicate vine of iridescent *At* coiled around the neck of the bottle, the other end of the vine rooted in the floor.

In the entryway beyond the living room, the cabin's front door stood open. Nik stepped inside holding an armful of firewood, his tall, imposing figure framed by a serene, snowy backdrop. The early morning light tinted the snow behind him rose gold. He had been out since I woke up some forty minutes ago. Now I knew where he'd been—chopping wood. Sometimes, he needed physical activity to expel his frustration. I wasn't oblivious enough to think *I* wasn't the root source of most of that frustration.

Nik stomped his boots on the entry rug and scanned the chaos on the floor around the table before fixing his attention on the hovering bottle. A grim expression hardened his stunning angular features. At his direction, the *At* vine lowered the whiskey bottle, gently setting it on an end table beside the couch. The thin vine unwound from around the neck of the bottle and withdrew, fizzling away in a glittering mist.

Nik took another step into the cabin and kicked the front door shut. "I thought we talked about this, Kitty Kat." He speared me with his pale blue stare, one eyebrow elevated. "It would seem you and I have different definitions of the word *rest*."

I raised my right hand, thrust it out in front of me, and flipped him the bird.

The corner of Nik's sinful mouth tensed, and he narrowed his eyes to irritated slits. In the same heartbeat, a new vine of *At* snuck up from the floorboards at my feet and snaked around my outstretched wrist.

Nik tutted and shook his head. "Such crude manners. Somebody should really teach you a lesson."

My stomach did a little flip-flop at the dark promise in his words. I tugged my arm, attempting to pull free from the vine's hold, but it was useless, like being cuffed in an iron manacle. Before that final, no-holds-barred battle with the Netjers, I easily would have been able to shatter the *At* vine with focused thought. But at the moment, the task was utterly impossible.

Nik crossed the living room to the oversized hearth in the far wall, taking his time. Letting me struggle. He crouched and set down the firewood, stacking it in a neat little pyramid in the recessed cubby beside the fireplace. By the time he stood and faced me, I had stopped struggling.

I couldn't break free, not in my current state. I assumed that was the whole point of this little display of his power. And of my lack thereof. Nik wanted me to face my weakened state. To acknowledge the lingering effects of the battle. The war was over, but the trauma from the fight lingered in my body. In my soul.

Nik crossed his arms over his chest and stood in front of the hearth, simply staring at me. His eyes trailed lazily down the length of my body, taking in the baggy sweats and T-shirt I had taken from his dresser when I crawled out of bed. When his gaze finally returned to mine, his pale eyes glinted dangerously.

"Since you seem to be incapable of resting on your own," he said, slowly stalking toward me. He unzipped his checked wool coat and shrugged out of it, shedding his lumberjack disguise and tossing the coat aside like it contained the last shreds of his civility. "It falls to me to *make* you rest."

I gulped, a zing of anticipation shooting down my spine, striking my core. I licked my lips, my chest rising and falling faster than before.

Another vine of *At* shot out of the floor and captured my other wrist. Those twin vines holding me captive pulled my hands down and dragged me backward, toward my abandoned chair. When the back of my right calf hit the wooden chair leg, two more *At* vines burst up from the floor and coiled around my ankles, climbing up my calves and around my knees. They forced my knees to bend, and I resisted for only a few seconds before dropping into the chair.

As soon as I sat, the vines holding my limbs latched onto the arms and legs of the chair, restraining me. I instinctively struggled against my bindings, but by the time Nik reached me, I had fallen still.

His heated, hyper-focused gaze roved up and down my body. He was hunger. Need. Desire. And he was just a little bit scary.

I watched him, motionless save for the rapid rise and fall of my chest. I had a rough idea of where this was headed, but Nik could be extremely creative. I could only imagine what he had planned for me. The only thing I knew for sure was that I would love every damn second of it.

Nik leaned in, looming over me. He set his hands on the arms of my chair, directly behind my elbows, and bent his arms, sinking deeper into my personal space. A low, rough noise rumbled in his chest as he nuzzled the hollow of my neck, his nose barely skimming that sensitive flesh.

The *At* vines twining around my legs crept higher, inching up the insides of my thighs. They forced my knees further apart until the outsides of my legs were flush against the chair's armrests.

Nik pulled back enough that I could see his achingly beautiful face. His gaze skimmed over my features, dark lust burning in his pale irises. His face was naked of his signature piercings, but his neck displayed the goddess Isis tattooed in black ink, her wings outstretched to embrace him.

I had done that. Marked him. *My* ink stained patches of his skin, all over his glorious body. A small, possessive smile curved my lips.

"You want me to punish you, don't you?" Nik said, his voice a low purr. His attention lingered on my lips before returning to my eyes. "Do you want pain or pleasure?" He licked his lips as they curved into a slow, wicked grin. "Or both?"

"I—" My voice caught in my throat, my heart hammering and my whole body flushing. Don't get me wrong—my sexual tastes were far from vanilla. But Nik was every other fucking flavor in the ice cream shop, and he made me feel like an inexperienced young virgin at least once a day. "I want—"

But Nik's focus abruptly strayed away from me, and my words faltered. He fell still, absolutely and completely. Even his *At* vines ceased their slow, incessant creep up my body. I watched as the desire bled from his eyes. As his eyelids opened wider. As something that looked a hell of a lot like fear took root in his shocked stare.

"What?" I craned my neck to see what had captured his attention.

Something on the floor. But all that was down there were my scattered tarot cards and the dozens of half-finished, hastily sketched drawings.

Straining the muscles and tendons in my neck, I glanced from Nik to the drawing I thought had captured his attention and back. "What is it?"

The *At* vines restraining me vanished, leaving me startlingly free to move. I twisted my wrists, increasing the blood flow to my fingers.

Nik stepped away from my chair and crouched to pick up the sketch. He stood and extended his arm, holding the sketch out in front of me. "What is this?"

I scanned the drawing. It was one of the first I had done this morning. Like all the others, it featured a winged scarab holding a circle over its head in its buggy pincers, much like the scarab on The Star card. Aesthetically, this particular rendition of the winged scarab was very much in the style of the ancient Egyptians.

"It's a drawing," I said dryly. Duh.

Nik didn't react to the sarcasm dripping from those three words. It wasn't like him to ignore my pokes and prods. He liked it when I gave him shit, and he enjoyed dishing it back out even more. Unease settled in my belly, replacing the need Nik had stoked just moments ago.

Nik locked eyes with me. "Why did you draw this, Kat?" The paper shivered as he shook the drawing for emphasis.

He called me Kat. Not Kitty Kat–just *Kat*. This was bad.

My brow furrowed and my lips parted. Again, I looked from Nik to the drawing and back. I searched his eyes, trying to understand why this sketch had shaken him so badly. I didn't get it.

"I was trying to find Tarset," I admitted. He was going to *love* that, especially after I had promised not to even try to use my powers when I was alone. Lately, I had a bad habit of ending up unconscious when I pushed myself too hard, magically speaking.

A bitter laugh bubbled up from my chest, and I flung a hand, gesturing to the rest of the unfinished sketches littering the floor. Each displayed some variation of the same scarab symbol in different artistic styles.

"Clearly, I'm broken," I added, my shoulders slumping as I lowered my arm. "I give up. You win. No more powers. I'll rest."

Nik ignored my admission of defeat, which was unlike him. His eyes remained locked on the drawing in his hand. "Do you know what this represents?" His gaze flickered up, meeting mine for a fleeting moment before returning to the sketch. "This symbol?"

I shook my head, frowning as I studied the drawing more closely. "I mean, other than the sun. Right? That's what the scarab is holding—the sun?" At Nik's minute nod, I continued, "So maybe it represents Re or Amun or another of the divine manifestations of the sun?"

Nik finally tore his stare away from the drawing. His eyes locked with mine once more. "Atum," he said, naming one of those solar gods. "It represents Atum."

I shook my head slowly, unwilling or unable to make the necessary mental leap quickly as fear iced through my veins. Atum was a Nejeret myth. A legend. He was our version of the bogeyman, said to hunt naughty Nejerets and kill them in their sleep. And I had drawn *his* symbol—over and over—while trying to find Tarset.

I swallowed roughly. "But—" I cleared my throat and held Nik's haunted stare. "But Atum is a myth. He's not real."

"Yeah, sure," Nik said. But despite his quick agreement, his voice lacked conviction. "Whatever you say, Kitty Kat."

NIK

I HUNG BACK AS Kat strode toward the magical gateway drawn on a sheet and pinned up on the living room wall. Heading outside dressed in only jeans and a T-shirt felt wrong when the cabin's windows provided a view of knee-deep snow. But then, we weren't heading outside *here*. Kat's hand-drawn gateway would transport us to the other side of the world, to the oasis, where a Who's Who of the Nejeret world was probably already gathering.

I leaned back against the edge of the kitchen island and crossed my arms over my chest. "I don't think we should go."

We had made a deal. If she could create the gateway without overexerting herself and passing out, then we would go to the meeting. I wasn't too proud to go back on my word. Not if it meant keeping her safe.

Kat halted mid step, two paces from the gateway. She stood with her back to me for a solid ten seconds before slowly turning to look at me, her eyebrows raised. She looked ready to go to battle in her black leather coat and combat boots, and with her sword, Mercy, strapped to her back. But despite her appearance—and trademark fuck-off attitude—I knew her nerves were eating her alive.

The corners of my mouth tensed as I anticipated an outburst. Being with Kat was like riding a roller coaster built on emotional extremes every second of every day. It was fucking exhausting. And exciting as hell. She wasn't just volatile. She was a fucking volcano. And nobody—not even me, the person who shared a soul bond with her—could predict when she was going to blow.

"They don't need us," I said, not backing down. "Let's sit this one out."

Her scowl deepened with each word.

"We'll hit up the next gathering," I went on. "Give you a little more time to—"

Her expression hardened, her eyes flashing with rainbow luminescence as she subconsciously drew on her unique connection to the soul-energy. It had been happening more and more often, and neither of us knew why or what it meant. The battle had damaged her soul so badly that she couldn't even feel it when she channeled soul-energy. Most of the time, she didn't even know it was happening unless I told her.

The vibrant, burning colors filling her eyes faded almost as soon as they appeared, giving way to the dark brown irises I drowned in every night . . . and morning . . . and afternoon . . .

Fuck. I wanted her. Right now. Always.

I pushed off the counter and stalked toward her. If I could just get my hands on her body, I knew I could convince her to stay.

Kat widened her stance and reached over her shoulder, drawing her sword in one smooth motion. The cabin filled with the ringing of the *At* blade. "Back off, Nik."

This time, I was the one to stop mid step. I raised my hands, quietly surrendering. Slowly, deliberately, I slipped my hands into the front pockets of my jeans to let her know I wouldn't try anything more. She wasn't beyond fighting me to get what she wanted. Even if we both knew she wouldn't beat me, she would still try.

"We're going," she said, staring at me for a moment longer before trusting my show of defeat and sheathing her sword. "Deal with it."

Before I could even think about arguing further, she spun on her heel and stomped through the gateway.

I blew out a breath and followed her. Looked like it was an eruption kind of day.

The gateway transported us to the portico outside the arched front entrance of Heru's palace. Kat stood on the edge of the porch and stared out at the oasis. I stepped forward to stand beside her. There were hints of green, growing things everywhere I looked. The land was coming back to life, now that the Netjers had ripped away the mountain of limestone that had shielded the oasis from the rest of the world.

I angled my face upward, taking in the deep purples, oranges, and reds staining the sky while secretly keeping a close watch on Kat. If she felt like I was hovering—or if I dared to inquire about her wellbeing—she might just deck me. It wouldn't have been the first time.

The corner of my mouth tensed as I suppressed a grin. Not that I minded.

Without warning, Kat trotted down the porch steps and started along the paved pathway that would lead toward the gathering area at the heart of the oasis. I begrudgingly followed her, a glowering shadow.

By the time we reached the small, sunken amphitheater our people had used as a gathering space for thousands of years, the curved bench seats were already packed with immortal bodies, leaving little room for us. I spotted my mom on the far side, seated in the row behind Heru and Lex. Heru was on his feet, addressing the gathered Nejerets.

Kat stopped near the entrance to the South stairway, her hands balled into tight fists at her sides. She was losing her nerve. But if she walked away now, she would see it as backing down from a challenge, something she was practically allergic to. She would hate herself for the perceived show of weakness, and she didn't need that on top of all the other shit she was dealing with.

I placed my hand flat against her lower back and guided her around the outside edge of the amphitheater, heading for the East stairway. We quietly descended the stairs and slipped between the rows, squeezing in beside my mom.

"Good to see you, dear," my mom murmured, curving her arm around Kat's shoulders and giving her a side hug.

"You too, Aset," Kat said, her rigid expression warming momentarily as she leaned into the embrace.

My mom released Kat and reached across her back to grip my shoulder. Her eyes locked with mine, her stare overflowing with questions—about Kat, about me, about how we were doing and what we had been up to. There was a silent admonition in there, too, for being so out of touch.

"Later," I mouthed.

She nodded and returned her attention to the debate happening in front of us. Heru was still on his feet, but a woman across the amphitheater had joined him in defiance of whatever he had been saying. Her name was Saskia, and she was the leader of one of the Baltic clans. I hadn't been paying attention to their debate, but her body language told me it wasn't a friendly discussion. I tuned in now.

"... is not our place to force them to cohabitate with us," Heru countered vehemently. "If they want to form human-only settlements, we must allow them to do so."

"Human-only—" Saskia sneered and shook her head. "Open your eyes, Heru. They're not human-only. They're anti-Nejeret. And these so-called 'safe havens' are little more than breeding grounds for anti-Nejeret terrorists." She sniffed in disgust. "We need to snuff this problem out before it grows. How many more of our people need to be captured and tortured to convince you of that? How many more of our people need to *die*?"

Saskia flung her hand out, pointing a single, slim finger straight at Kat. "Behold, our great savior." Sarcasm dripped from her words.

All eyes turned to Kat, who tensed beside me. Lex glanced over her shoulder, surprise at seeing us there melting into an apologetic smile for Kat being drawn into the argument.

Tension vibrated in my muscles, making my body go rigid. This was exactly the kind of thing I had been hoping to avoid.

Saskia lowered her hand. "Weak, power depleted." Her gaze swept across the assembly. "Who's to say if the great Katarina Dubois will ever return to full power? We can't rely on her to once again resurrect those of us who are slain. We are bleeding people. How many Nejerets have been killed by these *human* purists? The situation is spiraling out of control, and we must act swiftly and with a firm hand before we lose our foothold in this new world order."

Anger radiated off Heru. The surrounding air seemed to thicken. Those nearest him could sense the change, even if only subconsciously. I didn't think they realized they were doing it, but all around Heru, Nejerets leaned away or even scooted on their benches.

I watched Kat out of the corner of my eye. She seemed to shrink in on herself, and I reached for her hand, gripping it tightly. Her slender fingers felt frail, so unlike her.

Coming here was a mistake. We had barely been sitting here for two minutes and Kat had already been attacked for her current, depleted state. A state she was only in because she had saved these ungrateful pricks.

"More violence will only reinforce the position of these wayward groups," Heru countered, his voice low and carefully controlled. "We would be feeding fuel to their fire. If you want to see a situation that is out of control, by all means, Saskia, launch an attack."

Saskia scoffed. Apparently, she was shit at reading people because she continued her verbal onslaught on Heru. "Oh, and I suppose you want us to turn a blind eye to all these attacks? To roll over and let them push us back into the shadows?" She flung her arms out to either side. "This is our world, too, Heru. We deserve to stand in the light as much as humans do."

"But it is also *their* world," Heru said, his voice getting very quiet. It was his don't-fuck-with-me tone, which meant shit was about to hit the fan. "And *our* war has nearly destroyed it. We made a mess, and now we must clean it up."

"By going back into hiding?" Saskia bit out. "By pretending we don't exist?"

"That's not what I—"

Another Nejeret stood, joining the argument. I didn't even see who as I shifted all of my attention to Kat. Her body trembled beside me, and a faint tingle thrummed between us everywhere we touched, from hips to shoulders to hands.

My focus snapped up to her face. Her eyes were squeezed shut, her expression a pained grimace. The rising energy in the group awakened her connection with the soul-energy, and if that connection continued for much longer, she would pass out right here, in front of everyone, only strengthening Saskia's anti-human arguments.

"Shit," I hissed.

Thankfully, the attention of the assembly remained locked on the verbal sparring match. Nobody was paying Kat any attention.

Quietly and unobtrusively, I stood and pulled Kat up to her feet and out to the aisle. Wrapping an arm around her shoulders, I guided her up the stairs and away from the charged amphitheater. I tried to hurry her along, but it was like dragging someone who was half-asleep.

"It's going to be okay, Kitty Kat," I assured her, stopping and turning to face her.

I rested my hands on her shoulders, skimming my thumbs up and down her neck as I studied her face. No change, at least, not for the better. I clenched my jaw and scooped her into my arms, cradling her body close to mine as I jogged toward a secluded spring hidden by a semicircular rock outcropping nearby.

Once we were concealed by the barrier of limestone, I eased Kat down onto the barren ground. I needed to get her in the water, to mute the influx of sensory input. That was the closest thing to an off switch we had found for her haywire connection. Well, that and sex, but that only worked in the earlier stages. When it was bad, like this, the sensory deprivation seemed to be the only thing that could help her regain her inner balance, and through that, her control over her connection to the soul-energy.

She was shivering, unable to assist me as I removed her sword harness and guided her arms out from her coat sleeves. I pulled her tank top off over her head, then got to work untying her bootlaces.

She hugged herself, her eyes squeezed shut. "I—I'm sorry," she said through chattering teeth. "You w-were right. We sh-sh-shouldn't have c-come."

Damn fucking straight I was right, but I wasn't about to throw an *I told you so* in her face right now. Not while tears streamed down her cheeks and soul-energy flooded her every cell. The charged tingle surrounding her grew increasingly uncomfortable, and I gritted my teeth as I pulled her boots off her feet. I yanked her socks off next, then moved higher to unbutton her jeans.

I pulled my hand away when my bare skin contacted hers. It was like touching a live electrical socket. I shook out my hand, then carefully unbuttoned and unzipped her jeans. There was no way I was going to get them off her lower body with her sitting like that. I could just leave them on, but bare skin worked best.

"Lay down, Kitty Kat," I told her. "Just for a second."

She seemed locked in that position, and it took her a painfully long time to relax onto her back.

I finally pulled her jeans off and tossed them away. Kneeling at her feet, I surveyed her nearly naked body. For once, the sight didn't induce even a hint of lust. There was no room for desire right now, not when the need to protect her consumed everything within me.

Now, for the hard part. I stood, moved to her side, and crouched. I inhaled deeply, holding my breath. This was going to hurt.

Jaw clenched, I sucked in a breath and slid one arm under her knees, the other under her shoulders, then lifted her off the ground. The shock of energy was so intense, it momentarily locked up my muscles. I pushed through the pain, forcing our way forward. By the time we reached the edge of the pool, I was gasping for air and covered in sweat.

An image of tossing a live toaster into a bathtub flashed through my mind, and I paused at the water's edge. This was the worst she had ever been, but even so, the water never reacted to the soul-energy flowing through her like it would to actual electricity. I knew I would be fine entering the water with her—I had been every time before—and I silently told my survival instincts to *fuck off*.

With no further hesitation, I stepped into the pool, pushing forward toward the deeper section. I formed a snorkel out of *At* before submerging Kat under the water, sinking down myself until I was immersed up to my neck. The tepid water soothed the sting of touching her. And—hey—I hadn't been electrocuted, so things were looking up.

Ever so slowly, Kat's trembling subsided, and her body relaxed in my arms. I waited until she went completely limp, and then I eased her out of the water, holding her close as I waded toward the edge of the pool. She was unconscious, wiped out by the battle for control within her body. Her scarred soul. It would be hours until she woke.

This was why I didn't want her using her powers, not when she could no longer do so without tapping into her connection to the soul-energy. She shouldn't have to go through this. Not after everything else she had already been through to save us. She *deserved* to rest, to take it easy for once in her damn life.

So why wouldn't she fucking do it?

I closed my eyes and drew in a deep breath, then released it, slow and controlled.

She wouldn't—couldn't—take it easy, because she was Kat. Because she was either on, or she was off. There was no room for a dimmer switch in her life. I knew that when I bound my life—my soul—to hers. But it didn't mean she couldn't still drive me batshit crazy sometimes.

I formed a thin, pillowy bed of At on the ground near the edge of the pool and gently set her down on the shimmering surface. Kneeling, I straightened her arms and legs until she looked comfortable and brushed her hair out of her face with a sweep of my shaking hand, then covered her in a soft blanket of At.

Leaning forward, I pressed a kiss to her brow and rested my forehead against hers. She always woke disoriented and frightened after one of these episodes. I wouldn't let her wake to face that confusion—that darkness—alone.

Upon hearing the crunch of footsteps in dry, cracked earth, I straightened and looked around. I was in the mood for a fight, and if anyone—*anyone*—even looked at Kat wrong, I would rip their fucking eyes out.

"It's just me," Lex said, picking her way down the rocky path to join us by the edge of the pool. Her face displayed unguarded concern as she peered past me at Kat. "How is she?"

"She has good days and bad days," I said, standing. I walked around Kat's makeshift bed to meet Lex on the other side.

Lex's eyes trailed over me as I approached, her gaze assessing. "You're soaking wet."

I shrugged one shoulder. "It happens." I sank to the ground to sit and watch over Kat while I waited for her to wake. I propped my forearms on my upturned knees and nodded toward Kat's slumbering form. "We're going to be here for a while," I told Lex, then looked at the ground beside me, silently inviting her to join me.

Lex chewed on the inside of her cheek, her brow furrowing. She stepped forward and lowered herself to sit beside me, hugging her knees to her chest and resting her chin on one knee. "Does this happen often?" She tore her stare away from Kat to look at me.

I nodded, more of a rocking of my body than a bobbing of my head. "More often than I'd like, that's for damn sure."

Lex was quiet for a long moment. "Is she getting worse?"

I shifted my attention from Lex to Kat. She was so still, her only movement the slight expansion and contraction of her ribcage with each breath.

"It's hard to say," I admitted. "If she'd stop pushing herself every time I turned my back, she might actually make some progress and heal. But I don't know if she'll ever recover fully." I picked at a hangnail. "If she'll ever be the Kat *they* want her to be."

Lex let out a brief, harsh laugh. "*They* don't know what *they* want." She shook her head, clearly annoyed by the argument in the amphitheater. "Saskia and her cohort think Kat's the answer to everything, like she should be able to wiggle her nose and fix all our problems." Lex scoffed. "Like Nejeret society didn't function just fine without her for thousands of years."

Sighing, Lex reached for me, placing a hand on my arm. "It's barely been a month. Give her time. She's been through more than any of us can comprehend." Lex laughed again, the sound softer than before. "She deserves decades to recover, and if that's what she needs, then that's what we'll give her. The clan leaders be damned."

I covered Lex's hand with mine and bowed my head in thanks. Her words were kind but pointless. "You know she'll never go for that," I murmured, removing my hand.

Lex pulled hers back as well. Again, she sighed. "I know."

"It was a mistake for us to come here," I said, my focus returning to Kat. "Too much, too soon. Don't expect us back for a while."

Lex nodded. "Whatever you guys need. I'm here for you."

A surge of otherworldly energy warned me we would soon have company. Lex must have sensed it as well because she glanced over her shoulder at the same time as I did.

Heru appeared in a burst of rainbow mist, my mom at his side, her fingers curled around his upper arm. Fuck, I wished I could teleport. What a sweet ability. But no matter how many times I tried or how hard I focused, I couldn't expand my *sheut*—the part of my soul that housed my magic—to enable that power.

Heru was a thundercloud beside my mom's calm serenity. The ancient gods Horus and Isis, in the flesh. They had been yin and yang as twins in the womb, and their counterbalancing relationship continued to this day.

Lex stood and hurried toward them. She traded places with my mom, placing her palm on Heru's chest over his heart and murmuring softly. Some of the tension eased from Heru, his shoulders relaxing and his stony expression softening. They were one of the few other Nejeret couples who shared a soul bond, like Kat and me. It was so strange to see it at work from the outside, now that I had experienced the intensity of the bond first hand.

My mom headed my way, and I stood, glancing down at Kat to assure myself she would be all right without my full attention for a few minutes. I strode toward Kat's discarded leather coat and dug through her pockets until I found the folded-up drawing. I pulled it free and turned to meet my mom.

"There's something you need to see," I said before she could dive into an interrogation about Kat's recovery—or lack thereof. Ever the healer, my mom.

I lured her back over toward Heru and Lex with the mystery of the folded paper.

She shot an endless string of furtive glances over her shoulder as we walked, her instinct to help Kat wrestling with her curiosity over what was on the paper.

"She'll be fine," I told her as we drew near Heru and Lex. "You can examine Kat as soon as we're done here." I unfolded the paper and handed it to her. "I promise."

My mom pressed her lips together, accepting my terms, and turned her full attention to the sketch of the scarab. She stumbled, missing a step, and I caught her elbow to keep her upright.

"Where did you get this?" she asked, looking from the scarab to me. The color had drained from her face, leaving her looking like she might be sick.

"Aset?" Heru asked, closing the distance between us. "What is it?"

My mom handed him the paper.

Heru studied the sketch for all of two seconds and scowled. "Is this some kind of joke?"

"What?" Lex asked, craning her neck to peer down at the sketch. "That's a solar scarab," she said. "A representation of Khepri-Atum, the rising and setting suns." She looked up from the drawing, her brows bunching together. "Unless it means something else to Nejerets?"

Lex was so ingrained into our society now, it was easy to forget that she hadn't grown up among our kind. She was often unaware of the finer nuances of Nejeret lore. Like this one.

"She drew this?" Heru asked, glancing past me at Kat. His hawkish gaze refocused on me.

I nodded. "This morning," I explained. "She drew dozens of them." I paused before adding, "While she was searching for Tarset."

Heru hissed an ancient curse I hadn't heard for centuries.

"I don't understand," Lex said, looking from Heru to my mom to me. "Why would Kat draw this"—she glanced down at the sketch—"while searching for Tarset?"

Tension clouded the air all around us, fueled by our extended silence.

"The legend of Atum is," my mom started, then paused as she searched for the right word. All eyes focused on her, but her attention was on the drawing. "Complicated," she finally said. "He is far more than the mythological deity you know from your studies of ancient Kemet." She looked at Lex. "Our lore claims Atum lurks in the shadows, waiting to emerge from Rostau to punish Nejerets who stray too far from the light."

"Rostau?" Lex said. "Like, Osiris's fiery realm from the Book of Two Ways?"

"Rostau is surrounded by fire," Aset said. "Not in flames, itself."

"It's not an actual place," Heru added. "Just as Atum isn't a real person. He's a myth. Nobody has ever actually met him." *And lived,* hung unsaid between our little group.

"Nobody?" I stared pointedly at the side of my mom's face.

My mom stood a little taller, which wasn't saying much with her petite stature, and turned her back to us. She took several steps away, gazing out at the setting sun. "Atum is not a myth," she said quietly. "A legend, yes, but not a myth." Her shoulders rose and fell with a deep breath, and then she turned to face us. "He's real." Her eyes locked with her brother's. "I've met him."

"When?" Heru demanded.

"A very, *very* long time ago." She tugged on a delicate gold chain hidden under the collar of her linen shirt and fished the pendant free—a medallion of iridescent solidified *At* about the size of a quarter, displaying the scarab symbol from Kat's drawing—and held it out for us to see.

"I healed him," she explained. "I saved his life, and he gave me this token. He said it would provide me safe passage through the flames surrounding Rostau if ever I found myself in need of sanctuary." She looked at me, a quizzical smile curving her lips. "You knew all along, didn't you?"

I glanced at the medallion. It was made of *At*, after all, and I had sensed it for millennia as well as the symbol displayed on its face. "I suspected," I said, locking eyes with her. "When did you heal him, exactly?" I shook my head. "I can't remember when you first started wearing that."

My mom tucked the pendant back into the collar of her shirt. "It was a few decades after Lex visited us in ancient times," she said and arched one eyebrow higher. "I don't recall the exact year. You were off somewhere." She looked away like she was annoyed with me.

For not telling her I knew? That was laughable. If anyone should have been annoyed right now, it was me. *She* was the one who had hid this *huge fucking thing* from me.

"A couple of decades after Lex visited," Heru thought aloud. "That would have been around 2160." He frowned, his eyes narrowing on the drawing. "What does this mean?" He shook the paper, dragging our collective focus back to the sketch. "Does Atum *have* Tarset?" He looked from me to my mom and back. "Or is he hunting her?" Heru's throat bobbed as he swallowed roughly. "Did he already—" What I assumed was the word *kill* caught in his throat, and he crumpled the paper in his fist.

His focus shifted past me, to Kat, unconscious on the bed of *At*. "She has to try again," he said, his voice ringing with command. "Perhaps if she searches for Atum instead of Tarset . . ." He trailed off, his thoughts leaping around to all the options. "We can make him talk."

Heru shouldered past me and marched toward Kat.

I snagged his arm at the elbow, holding him back. "Leave her. The fuck. Alone."

Heru turned partway, glancing down at my hand on his arm, then slowly raised his gaze to meet mine. A dangerous challenge glinted in his golden eyes.

I took a step closer. Leaned in. "You don't scare me." That same dangerous challenge dripped from my words. I held his stare for a long moment before I released his arm.

Heru took a step back, putting some distance between us.

"Every time Kat draws on her connection to the universe, she backslides," I told him, figuring an explanation would ease the sting of the refusal. "She gets weaker. If you want her to have a chance in hell at finding Tarset, you need to give her the space and time she needs to heal. She'll help when she's ready."

ANCIENT TIMES

TARSET

A SHADOW BLOCKED THE moonlight, and I blinked up at Ineni. She was the matriarch of this clan of gentle souls who had saved my life. Ineni's daughter, Tiy, had generously gifted me a white linen shift and a gauzy, multi-layered robe, which protected my still healing skin from suffering another bout of second-degree burns. Not that the moon posed much of a threat in that arena, but it wouldn't be night forever.

I had blistered and scabbed all over. The healing process was unbearably itchy and left me feeling ravenous, but at least I hadn't dropped into a healing coma. I had slurped down enough water to rehydrate an elephant and had eaten whatever Ineni offered me, and now I rested on a woven mat Tiy had laid out for me a few yards from the pool. By morning, I figured I would be good as new.

Aside from the whole lost-in-time situation.

"We are leaving, divine one," Ineni said, groaning as she eased her arthritic body down to sit on the ground beside me. Her pale gray hair shimmered like strands of moonstone in the silvery light.

Panic flitted to life in my chest, and I pushed myself up to my elbows. "You're leaving?" My Old Egyptian was rusty, my accent horrendous. But Ineni seemed able to understand me well enough. My brows bunched together, and I shook my head as I sat up the rest of the way. "Now? Where are you going?"

Ineni rested a gentle hand on my shoulder. "Be calm, divine one," she said, her low volume softening the gravel in her voice. "We head to Waset. This was only a stop along our journey." She sighed and stared out at the crystalline pool. "The land is changing. The oases do not provide as they once did. My eldest daughter settled with her husband near Waset, so we will head there to join her. Perhaps Iteru will provide better than the oases can."

Iteru was the ancient name for the great river that provided this land its lifeblood, so I figured Waset must have been a city along the Nile. I silently berated myself for my spotty knowledge of the ancient landscape. I had no clue where along the Nile Waset was located or which future city had been—would be—built atop the ancient structures. I supposed it didn't matter. At this point, I was essentially a stray puppy; I would have followed Ineni anywhere.

I held in the urge to whine, "But what about me?" Instead, I shifted my attention from Ineni to the glimmering surface of the natural well. What would I do here, all alone? Wander closer to the Farafra Oasis? I wasn't even sure how far out this well was from the main lake. And then what—was I going to sit tight and hope someone in the distant future figured out a way to rescue me from *whenever* I was? And that was assuming anyone who cared enough to miss me had even survived the war to notice I was gone.

"You are welcome to travel with us," Ineni said, addressing my unvoiced fears.

I looked at her, my eyebrows raised. "Really?" The panic receded as hope swelled within me.

Her smile was gentle, like everything else about her. She bowed her head, lowering her gaze to the ground. "It would be our greatest honor to travel with a god of time among us." She straightened her neck, her smile deepening the wrinkles fanning from the outer corners of her eyes.

I sniffled, blinking back a sudden welling of tears, and covered Ineni's hand with my own. "Thank you, Ineni," I said, bowing my head to her in turn and gently squeezing her gnarled fingers. "You are the one who honors me. I would be grateful to travel with your clan."

Once again, I walked along the desert road, only this time, I wasn't alone. It was the early hours of the morning, well before dawn, and a full moon hung heavy in the sky in the place of the golden sun. The robe's thin layers of linen shielded me from the faint chill carried by the early morning breeze, and soft, sturdy leather slippers protected my tender feet. I wore a borrowed waterskin on a woven strap across my body, filled near to bursting with cool water from the natural well.

The clothing, the shoes, the waterskin—Ineni and Tiy professed they were gifts, but I silently vowed to repay them.

Squat palm trees sprang up among the desert brush the closer we drew to the spring-fed lake. I walked at the tail end of the caravan as we headed into the oasis proper, alone with my racing thoughts. Now that my life was no longer in immediate danger from the threat of dehydration, my mind had free rein to spin and churn. To process the very precarious nature of my little time slip. Walking in solitude helped my brain work through the insanely complex situation.

I was stranded in the ancient past. Thousands of years stretched out between the current moment and the future I was desperate to return to. Even the slightest change to this past could alter that future, potentially destroying the people I loved. I was the proverbial bull in a china shop, and I needed to tread very, *very* carefully.

No pressure. Right.

I resolved to make as minimal of an impact as possible on the lives of the members of Ineni's clan, not to mention any other ancient people I came across. Until I figured out a way to return to the present—or, rather, the *future*—I would remain anonymous. Unknown. And I *had* to find a way to get home to my family. If I could travel backward in time, there had to be a way for me to travel forward again.

"There's always a way."

Kat's voice whispered through my mind, and I smiled to myself. That had been one of her go-to sayings when I was growing up, and not once had it failed me. There *was* always a way.

My out-of-time situation was a puzzle. I only needed to view the various pieces from the exact right angle to make them fit together and show me the solution. The way home was simple: time travel.

Problem was, *I* couldn't time travel. At least, not on my own. So far as I could tell, it had taken the combined effort of the collective soul-energy flowing through Duat to transport me back to—well, I wasn't exactly sure *when* I was.

Ineni didn't know the name of the current ruler. She and her people spent almost all their lives hopping from oasis to oasis, and it often took years for news from the Nile valley to reach them. The last ruler she could recall had been Neferkare, and she believed it had been a couple of decades since his death. She claimed he was the only ruler she had ever known, meaning he must have ruled for a long time. Finding out the name of who currently ruled Egypt was on the top of my to-do list for when we reached Waset. I didn't have the names and dates of all the ancient rulers memorized, but there was always a chance I might recognize the current one.

Regardless of the current year, I figured the best way for me to return to the future was to find someone with the ability to travel through time at will. So far as I knew, only a few people had such an ability, and I knew of one such Nejeret who had been born in ancient Egypt. Her name was Aramei, and she had spent the first part of her life as a priestess in the Hathor temple in Men-nefer, the ancient name for the city that would one day become Cairo and, for millennia, had been the ancient Nejeret seat of power.

I didn't know the exact date of Aramei's birth, but I was fairly certain it was some time in the Middle Kingdom. Once I figured out *when* I was, I would have a better idea of what to do next. If finding Aramei was my plan, then I only had one option: go to the Hathor temple. Once there, I would either find her and beg her to let me hitch a ride with her back to modern times, or I would wait for her to be born and come into her full power, and *then* I would beg her to carry me back to my home in the future.

Once we reached Waset, getting to Men-nefer wouldn't be too complicated. Every city in ancient Egypt bordered the Nile, so Waset's exact location didn't matter. I would take a boat to Men-nefer. Easy-peasy.

With my plan settled, my thoughts wandered to my family in the future. Were they okay? Had they realized I was gone? Was anyone even still alive to notice, or had they been among the crowd of Nejerets in Aaru? If so, had they been thrown out of the land of the dead, as well? Had they, too, been resurrected? Were they together, or had they been scattered throughout time?

"I'll find you guys," I vowed, the words a quiet murmur.

"What language is that?"

I blinked and glanced to my right. A child walked along beside me. I looked up and around. Where the hell had this kid come from? "What?" I asked, consciously switching back to Old Egyptian.

"Mother says I'm not supposed to talk to you," the kid said.

The cowl of the kid's robe was up, covering their hair, and they were young enough that I couldn't tell whether they were a boy or a girl, especially not with the long linen robe covering their clothing. I guessed the kid was somewhere between five and ten years old. Older than Reni and Bobby, but I didn't know enough kids well enough to estimate age better than that.

"Grandmother, too," the kid added.

I laughed under my breath. "And yet, here you are."

The kid shrugged. "They're busy," the kid said and pointed up past the string of donkeys and small clusters of people toward the front of the caravan. "So, what's it like to be a god of time?"

"I'm not a god," I responded automatically. It was one of my speaking points as Nejeret ambassador to the human world, and the issue came up so often that refuting my people's nature as divine had become second nature. "But you healed so fast," the kid said. "Grandmother wasn't sure you really were a god of time until you started to heal. But then she knew." I sighed, my shoulders slumping. "Fine, yes. I am one." I didn't want to be a total jerk to this kid, but I also wanted to be left alone.

There was no way to know how even the tiniest interaction might impact the greater timeline. Maybe it was a mistake to stay with these people, but whatever Wolf said about my high opinion of myself, I knew my limits. I wouldn't survive out here in the desert on my own, and I certainly wouldn't make it all the way to Men-nefer.

"What kinds of things can you do?" the kid asked.

I shot the kid some serious side-eye. "What do you mean?"

"Can you make things float in the air?"

My brow furrowed. "No."

"Can you fly?"

"No."

"Can you run really fast?"

"I don't know," I said with a shrug. "I don't think so."

"Can you make yourself invisible?"

"No."

"Can you burn things with your touch?"

"No."

The kid let out an exasperated sigh like I was the greatest disappointment imaginable. "Well, what *can* you do?"

I frowned, feeling altogether lame. "I can sing," I said, my tone mildly defensive.

The kid scoffed. "So can I."

I smirked. "Not like me." And I drew in a lungful of air to prove my point.

I started the song by humming a string of notes I only ever heard in my dreams. The melody belonged to an ancient song my mom used to sing to me when I was a little girl. I didn't remember the exact words, but it was a folk song, which meant the lyrics were fluid, changing with the regions and times. As I sang, I thought about how strange it was that I could recall this song, which I only ever heard sung by my mom, but the memory of her actually singing it was long gone.

My voice faltered at the start of the third verse. Movement up ahead drew my eye as our caravan slowly angled toward the side of the road. I pressed my lips together, suddenly on high alert.

"Why'd you stop?"

I glanced at the kid, then pointed up the road. Another caravan was heading toward us in the opposite direction.

The kid squinted. "What is it?"

"People," I said, figuring it was too dark and the approaching caravan was still too far away for the kid to see it.

A tingle floated in the air, making the hairs on my arms and the back of my neck stand on end. My spine instinctively straightened. There was no mistaking the feeling of that otherworldly energy. There were other Nejerets among the people in the approaching caravan. Several, judging by the strength of the sensation.

"Shit," I hissed.

I was committed to making a minimal impact on the lives of Ineni and her people. That was merely a precaution. They were short-lived humans. But it was imperative that I had zero impact on the lives of *any* Nejerets. A Nejeret's life could span millennia, increasing the risk to the timeline exponentially.

"Go find your mother," I told the kid. When the kid looked ready to argue, I snapped, "Now!"

The kid's eyes widened, and they scampered off.

I pulled up my cowl and slunk to the outside of our caravan. I crouched as I walked alongside one of the pack donkeys, hoping to go undetected by the other Nejerets.

Our caravan stopped when the head of the approaching caravan reached ours. I bit back a string of curses for fear of the whispered words reaching sensitive Nejeret ears and mimicked the members of Ineni's clan as they dropped to their knees in veneration, arms extended in front of them, palms upraised.

I could feel the other Nejerets as they passed, and I begged Isfet to conceal the telltale thrum of otherworldly energy wafting off my soul. I held my breath, too afraid to lift my face enough to sneak a peek to see if I recognized any of them. I was too afraid to move at all, for fear of drawing their attention to me.

But then they were past me, apparently too engrossed in their conversation to sense my presence. I didn't let myself relax until the Nejerets' caravan was clear of ours.

I ignored the curious looks thrown my way from the members of Ineni's clan. They wondered why I hadn't greeted my brethren. They were probably recalling the state they had found me in—naked, alone, and near death—and suspected they harbored some sort of rogue Nejeret. A fugitive. Someone dangerous.

Would they ask for an explanation? Would they demand answers?

They could try, but they would get none. And if push came to shove, I would leave and find my own way to the Nile, and eventually, to Men-nefer. Or, at least, I would try.

I SAT ON THE lip of a narrow canal near our day camp, my bare feet dangling in the warm water as I scratched letters in the patch of sand by my right hip with the tip of my index finger. *Tarset was here.* My robe lay folded on a rock nearby, along with my waterskin, and I savored the gentle breeze coming in off the Nile as it caressed my bare shoulders and neck. Alone time was rare for me these days, and I had no doubt Bek would join me soon. Ineni's granddaughter was my shadow, always at my side, always chattering about something.

We traveled at night during our journey, hopping from one water source to another, be it a well, a spring, or a full-blown oasis. I was surprised by how much water could be found in this desert if one knew where to look. And lucky for me, Ineni's clan always knew exactly where to look.

But even so, chunks of days would pass by without a fresh drop of water. Then, our waterskins were as good as gold. Not even the children dared to spill a single drop.

It took thirty-seven exhausting days to reach the Nile. Every night but one an endless slog through the desert. We rested for a single day at the lush Kharga Oasis before tackling the longest, driest stretch of the journey yet. I could happily go a few decades without seeing another lazy dune or craggy limestone formation. I was so tired of having sand in my mouth or digging stray grains from my eyes. It was everywhere. Literally *everywhere.*

My sun-worshipping days were over. I was officially in recovery. I now craved the feeling of raindrops on my skin. Or even—gasp—the kiss of snowflakes on my face. Not that I was likely to find either in the Nile valley, but a girl could dream.

We spent the past two daytime rest periods camped under the shade of acacia trees and enjoying the steady supply of fresh water carried by agricultural canals. Last night, we walked along the west bank of the Nile for miles and even passed through a small farming village that went by the name Iuny.

I almost cried at the sight of even such a rudimentary example of civilization. No offense to Ineni and her clan, but I needed more people. More variety of conversation. More stimulation. *More.*

A gust of wind whipped my hair around my face, and I raised my hands to rebraid my long hair, then awkwardly tied a leather cord around the end. I would have killed for an elastic hair tie. I missed my messy buns desperately.

By the time a fresh braid trailed over my shoulder and I returned my attention to nature's sketchpad, the words I had written in the sand were all but erased. It felt like I, too, was being erased. Every day I spent in this ancient time, anonymous and unknown, a little more of myself slipped away. I hadn't realized so much of my identity was tied up in what other people thought of me—the real me, not this ghost I was pretending to be. That people knew my name. That they thought of me at all.

Tonight, we would cross the Nile and finally reach Waset. From the way young Bek described Waset, it was a thriving metropolis. Of course, everything she knew about the town was hearsay, as she had spent all nine years of her life in the desert oases and this was her first time visiting the Nile valley.

Based on the landscape here, with the abrupt, snaking curve in the Nile and the steep limestone cliffs so near the west bank of the river, I was fairly certain that Waset was the city I knew of as Luxor in modern times. One day, it would be called Thebes, but some whisper of memory made me think *that* name came from the Greeks. If I had been a better student of history, I could have used this information to narrow down the window of time to determine *when* I was. *Before the Greeks* was as specific as I could get. So, that placed the current era at a really, really, *really* long time ago, as opposed to just really, really long ago.

As the sun sank deeper behind the cliffs to the west, I shivered. It was almost time to don my desert robe. Rectangular holes pocked the stepped face of the cliffs more to the north in what seemed a random pattern, but I knew them to be marking the locations of tombs. Stone facades with carved columns surrounded some of the dark spots, while others were simple openings cut into the face of the cliff. I stared out at the collection of tombs, imagining what wonders were sealed within each one.

Movement in one such dark rectangle caught my eye, and I sat up straighter. I leaned forward, resting my elbows on my knees, and focused on the tomb's entrance. Apparently, this one *wasn't* sealed.

A figure emerged, followed by two more people, so tiny and distant that they looked like creeping ants as they climbed a path zigzagging up the side of the cliff, lumpy bundles strapped to their backs.

I raised a hand to shield my eyes from the setting sun and squinted as I watched them. Were they workers packing out their tools after toiling to prepare some wealthy Egyptian's tomb for the day he or she would need it to assist in the transition into the afterlife?

But then I noticed the glint of gold on one of their backs, and the bundles took on new meaning. These people weren't packing out tools. They were packing out *treasure*.

Horrified, I scrambled to my feet.

Another figure emerged from the tomb, dragging what appeared to be a life-size statue of a person, likely the deceased owner of the tomb. I doubted one person alone would have been able to move a stone statue of that size, and I figured it was carved from wood. My heart dropped into my stomach as I watched the tomb robber shove the statue over the edge of the landing. It bounced along the steep slope until it fell out of sight.

I covered my mouth with one hand, holding in a gasp. These monsters weren't just stealing from the dead, they were defiling their tombs. Destroying their eternal legacy. My blood heated and my body trembled with an unexpected rush of outrage. I balled my other hand into a fist, my nails digging into my palm. It was despicable.

I may have grown up in the modern world, but I was still a child of Egypt, where the need to prepare for the transition to the afterlife was as necessary as access to clean water, food, and air. For without a tomb or the offerings within to provide the deceased with all they would need in the land of the dead, their afterlife would be bleak—if it would happen at all.

"Hunger makes beasts of all men," Ineni said from beside me.

I jumped, startled, and pulled my hand away from my mouth as I looked at the small elderly woman standing beside me. I hadn't heard her approach, too engrossed in watching the atrocity on the cliffside.

I studied the lines of Ineni's face, noting the weariness camouflaged by her deep wrinkles and leathery skin. The exhausting trip sapped much of her strength. Every day that passed, she seemed a little older and slightly more frail.

Ineni's clan had left the string of oases, hoping the food and resources weren't so scarce along the fertile black land bordering the Nile. Now, disappointment rang loud and clear on her face. The drought that was drying up the oases was evidently impacting the lush river valley, as well.

I returned my attention to the grave robber scrambling up the cliffside trail to join his companions, his pilfered goods wrapped in a bundle strapped to his back, and then I glanced over my shoulder. The rest of the members of Ineni's clan were packing up, storing their meager belongings in woven baskets and securing them to the donkeys' backs. Bek hurried from animal to animal, offering each donkey a last drink of water from a bucket while the adults secured the beasts' burdens.

How much had these people been hurting for food during the trip, and I had been oblivious to their struggle? I thought back to each of the meals we had shared, one at sunset and one at sunrise every day, for over a month. They wasted nothing. Every crumb of bread, every strand of jerky, was eaten. I had politely declined the fire-roasted locusts every time they had been offered, preferring to go without protein for those meals. I just couldn't bring myself to bite into their plump insect bodies. I recalled the baffled expression on Ineni's face the first time I refused to eat the insects, like she hadn't been able to believe anyone would turn down something edible.

I had been looking forward to reaching Waset for many reasons, chief among them the chance to fill my belly with a more substantial meal. My focus had been entirely on what was lacking from the food I had been so graciously given, not on gratitude for being given anything at all. Ineni's clan had shared their increasingly sparse resources with me, and I had barely noticed their struggle. Their fear that what little they had would soon dry up, leaving them to starve.

"I didn't realize it was this bad," I said quietly, shame burning my neck and cheeks as a sick feeling took root in my belly. I returned to watching the cliffs. The grave robbers were gone, leaving the necropolis serene once more.

Ineni rested a hand on my forearm, the gesture gently patronizing. "It is not so bad for your kind, I'm sure," she said, her gravelly voice carrying only a hint of bitterness. "Merely for the rest of us."

I jutted my jaw forward, my eyes suddenly stinging with tears.

"I pity them," Ineni said, pointing toward the cliffs with her chin.

I looked at her, my brows drawing together. "The thieves?"

Ineni sighed and shook her head. "No, divine one." Her lined, weathered features arranged into a mask of deep sadness. "The dead," she clarified. "They must have spent their entire lives preparing for their deaths, making their mark on eternity. They never actually lived."

She closed her eyes and bowed her head toward the tombs pocking the cliff face as though she was honoring all the lost souls, giving them what recognition she could without ever having known them. "And now they will be forgotten," she said. "A life never lived and no longer remembered. What a waste."

I looked from Ineni to the tomb entrances darkening the face of the cliff.

A life never lived and no longer remembered. What a waste.

I couldn't help but feel like Ineni wasn't just talking about the dishonored dead. I felt like she was also talking about *me*.

How long until I was forgotten in the distant future? How long until the more pressing, urgent struggles of people's daily lives pushed any memory of me—of my music—to the backs of their minds? Fan love was fickle, requiring constant feeding and regular attention. It was so different from the love of my family members, my dad and Reni, Kat and Lex and little Bobby.

Now that those relationships were out of reach, I regretted how much I had neglected them. I had traded in the few deeper connections in my life for the superficial love of the masses.

During one of our final, epic showdowns, Wolf had accused me of being addicted to love. To the rush of being adored. To the flood of affirmations on social media and the roar of a crowd chanting my name. I had spat a string of defensive comebacks, though I could no longer recall what I had said.

Now, I was forced to face the truth in his barbed words.

In my absence, my fans would move on. The only people who would still love me were the ones I had all but forsaken. Their memories of me would be my last tether to the world I had left behind.

A life never lived and no longer remembered. What a waste.

That was me. I had never really lived, and soon, I would be forgotten. I had wasted my life, all for the sake of my legacy. But my misguided strategy had backfired. My legacy was worthless because my life had meant nothing.

When I returned home—and I *would* make it home—I vowed to reassess my priorities. No longer would I take advantage of those few relationships that truly mattered. I would nurture and feed them as much as I did my adoring fans.

I would no longer only live for my legacy. I would live to *live*.

"**Y**OU COULD STAY WITH us," Bek said, a slight whine in her voice. Bek was always nearby, but knowing our paths were about to diverge had amped her clinginess to baby-monkey status.

We walked the last stretch of the journey to Waset together at the tail end of the caravan, the limestone cliffs rising up from the desert beyond the barley field on our left, moonlight gleaming off the surface of the Nile on our right. Bek and I were responsible for ensuring the trailing trio of donkeys didn't fall too far behind the caravan or stray from the road.

Tiy walked a short way ahead. Her frequent glances back at us told me she was ready to step in and pry her daughter from my side if I needed a break.

"I can't stay, Bek," I reminded the girl for about the hundredth time as I absently brushed a stray lock of hair from my face. "I have to get back to my people. They're waiting for me."

I heard a strange, whizzing sound and cocked my head to the side, searching the field stretching out along the left edge of the road. What was that? Some enormous bug? Maybe a beetle zipping through the air? The crescent moon gave off just enough light to create barely-there shadows in the swaying barley that played tricks on my eyes.

"I know," Bek whined, "but—"

An arrow thunked into the stretch of tilled soil bordering the barley field, mere feet from the road. I grabbed Bek's arm, jerking her to a stop, and froze mid step.

A second arrow joined the first, this one embedding itself into the hard-packed dirt at the very edge of the road. One of the donkeys in our charge screamed and reared back, an arrow protruding from its flank.

The wounded animal hovered precariously on its hind legs for a second or two. My heart skipped a beat as time seemed to stand still.

The donkey collapsed sideways, crushing the baskets strapped to its back. My heart recovered, beating triple-time.

"Get down!" I shouted as I wrapped my arms around Bek and picked her up, tossing her over my shoulder. I was no weightlifter, but the kid was a toothpick, barely weighing anything at all. I hauled her toward a squat boulder bordering the barley field, snagging Tiy's arm as we passed her and dragging Bek's mother along behind me.

The three of us huddled together behind our rocky cover. Tiy held her daughter close, Bek's head tucked under her mom's chin. I was breathing hard, my thoughts racing. Spinning. Stumbling.

We were under attack, obviously. What was I supposed to do? Flee? Let the timeline run its natural course? Was this always supposed to happen? Were these kind, generous people supposed to die at the hands of road bandits?

Or had I delayed the caravan's progress? They might have reached Waset a day earlier if they hadn't had to pause outside the Farafra Oasis to nurse my crispy self back to health. If that was the case, was it better to stay and fight? To defend them? To do what I could to preserve their lives—and the timeline?

"Shitshitshitshitshit . . ." I breathed, paralyzed by indecision. I had absolutely no clue what to do.

They were dead—Bek, Tiy, Ineni, and every other person in the caravan. In the future, they had all been dead for thousands of years. When I finally made it home, Ineni's clan would be dust and bone, long since forgotten by everyone but me. Would it even matter how they had died?

Probably not.

I should run. Look out for myself. It was the smartest thing to do. The safest. Both for my life and for the timeline.

But what if a member of Ineni's clan was supposed to do something important? What if one of Bek's descendants would one day be pharaoh or invent the printing press or discover antibiotics?

A quiet hiss alerted me to another volley of arrows. A couple landed to the right of our hiding spot. Close enough to tell me our attackers knew we were huddled behind the boulder.

A cry sounded further down the road, clearly human. Someone had been hit. Screams filled the night as the scene on the road devolved into pure chaos. Donkeys bolted, knocking over a few older members of Ineni's clan. Some people ran for cover, while others stood frozen in the road.

I looked at the girl quietly sobbing against her mother's chest. What if Bek died here, tonight, because I ran?

Her life would be over, and I would go on. But *my* life would be the one wasted. The life without value. The life unlived. I had spent the last decade building myself a tomb in music and lyrics, in fan mail and *likes* and followers. In things that didn't really matter. But Bek and the rest of her clan—they made the most of their brief time on Earth. Their lives held purpose and meaning *to each other*, not to strangers. The value of their lives far outweighed mine.

My eyes stung with a sudden welling of tears. I set my jaw, my blood turning to fire. Bek wasn't dying tonight.

I. Would. Not. Run.

Which left one option. I had to fight.

I narrowed my eyes, centering myself. I was a child of Heru. My father had ingrained in me the need to defend others, and like all of his children, he had been training me to be that defender almost since I took my first steps as a toddler. I had trained with the best trio of teachers in existence: my dad, his badass protégé, Dominic L'Arange, and the legendary Katarina Dubois. I could do this.

I could *do* this.

Peeking around the edge of the boulder, I was just able to make out several shadowy, dark-robed figures creeping through the tall barley, making their way closer to the road. One headed straight for our hiding spot.

I turned to Tiy and gripped her shoulder. "Stay here," I said, locking eyes with her. Her cheeks were wet with tears, but she otherwise appeared composed. "Stay hidden."

Tiy nodded emphatically.

I faced forward and took a deep breath. My heart hammered in my chest, and my blood roared in my ears. Another deep breath. As I inhaled a third time, I lunged out from behind the boulder, diving for the two arrows that stuck out of the ground nearby.

The sound of quick, heavy footsteps crunching on dry earth alerted me to the bandit bearing down on me.

My hands closed around the errant arrows, and I rolled to the side. I popped up and spun on my knees, fisting one of the arrows, the sharp wooden point sticking out a few inches from my curled fingers like a stubby dagger. I punched out my arm as the bandit tackled me, throwing me backward.

Gritting my teeth, I plunged the tip of the arrow into my attacker's sinewy neck. He stiffened, landing crossways on top of me.

I grunted and jerked the arrow free. Blood spurted out of the gaping wound in his neck, coating my hand and forearm. I partitioned the horror of that sensation into some other part of my mind to deal with later. With this much blood, I must have hit an artery. It was more dumb luck than skill, but I would take it.

The man was dead weight on top of me, and it took me a solid ten seconds to wriggle out from under him. The glint of metal on the ground nearby caught my eye as I struggled to get free. I crawled around my motionless attacker and found a dagger on the ground a few feet from his outstretched hand. He must have dropped the weapon as we tumbled to the ground. He had probably been planning to use it on me, but I had stabbed him first.

I curled my fingers around the wooden hilt of the dagger. It felt sticky in my bloodied hand.

Pounding footsteps behind me alerted me to another incoming bandit.

I gathered my feet under me and, still crouching, spun around. There, a half-dozen paces away, heading for Tiy and Bek's hiding place. He was a towering shadow robed in darkness, and he carried a long knife with a slightly curved blade.

I cocked my arm back, then flung it forward, letting the dagger fly. The knife shot out of my hand and struck the bandit in his gut. He stumbled to the ground, crawling toward the cowering mother and child, almost like he was begging them for help.

I stalked toward the wounded bandit, more animal than thinking, coherent person at this point. When I reached him, I dropped to one knee, the second of my scavenged arrows gripped tight in my fist. He grasped my forearm with calloused hands as I shoved him onto his back. Blood stained his lips.

I didn't hesitate as I plunged the arrow into his eye. There was a sickening *pop*, and then the pointed wooden tip of the arrow scraped bone. His body seized, and his scream chilled me to the bone. Vitriolic fluid spurted out from around the arrow shaft, and I angled my face away to avoid the spray even as I increased the pressure on the arrow. The tip broke through the thin membrane of bone at the back of his orbital cavity and sank deeper into his skull, piercing his brain.

He fell still, like I had hit an off switch on his life.

My stomach turned, bile rising in my throat. The battle rage receded, and I was suddenly shockingly aware of my vicious actions. Of the lives I had just ended. My awareness tunneled until blood and vitriolic fluid were all I could see. All I could smell and taste and feel.

I bowed my head and retreated within myself, hiding from this savage creature I had become.

A hair-raising scream broke through the momentary fugue, and I snapped my head up, brutal reality crashing home around me. Back on the road, a half-dozen bandits still assaulted the scattered members of the caravan.

I gripped the hilt of the dagger protruding from the dead man's gut, then pried the long-bladed knife from his death grip. I spun on my knees toward Tiy and Bek, tossing the smaller dagger toward the mother.

Another scream drew my attention back to the brutal scene on the road.

"Go," Tiy said, her voice hard, steady. When I turned back to her, she gripped the dagger in one hand, her expression fierce. "We'll be fine." She nodded toward the road behind me. "Help the others. *Please.*"

I stared at her for a long moment. And then I stood, turning to face the road.

The situation spreading out along the hard-packed stretch of dirt was pure chaos. A few donkeys lay unmoving on the ground, but the rest of the caravan's herd bucked and fled, braying as they trampled anything—or any*one*—unfortunate enough to get in their way. A handful of white-robed lumps lay sprawled on the road, motionless. Likely dead. If Ineni was among them, I couldn't tell.

I picked out five more bandits among the scattered members of the caravan, their dark robes marking them as the enemy. Three faced off against white-robed opponents who were holding their own. I dismissed them. It was the other two bandits who earned my full attention. They seemed to be targeting the weaker members of the caravan—the young and the elderly.

I locked on the one attacking an older man, Ramus, who cowered protectively over a small, weeping child clinging to a motionless body—likely that of Sila, Ramus' wife. I bolted straight for them, a resurgence of the battle rage burning through my blood.

A few paces before I reached them, Ramus cried out and crumpled forward against his attacker. I streaked past the stumbling pair, a single stroke of my long, curved blade slicing into the backs of the bandit's knees.

He shrieked and dropped Ramus's limp body.

I circled back with a roundhouse kick that sent the hamstrung bandit sprawling on his back on the road. I lunged for him and planted one knee on his chest. With no hesitation, I sliced my stolen blade across his throat.

His scream came out as a gurgle. The blade caught in his trachea, and I grunted as I yanked it free.

A body slammed into my side, hard.

I was thrown onto my back beside my latest victim, and my knife went flying. This guy was the largest bandit I had faced yet, and without the element of surprise or any kind of weapon, he easily overpowered me.

I attempted to scramble away, but he grappled me to the ground and straddled my body.

The bandit wrapped his massive hands around my neck and squeezed, choking off my air supply. I slapped and clawed at his arms and face. I bucked my hips and frantically kicked my feet, but my struggles did no good. He was too big. Too strong.

It wasn't long until my face felt bloated and swollen and dark spots danced around the edges of my vision. I stared into my attacker's dark eyes, seeing nothing but hatred and rage. He was killing me, and I was utterly helpless against him.

But even as I lay dying, I didn't regret my decision to fight. Because, for once, I had done something that mattered.

Tiy's feral face coalesced beside the bandit's. In the next moment, she swept the dagger I had left with her across my attacker's throat, and a crimson waterfall gushed from the gaping wound. Hot blood sprayed onto my face, pooling in my mouth. I choked and sputtered.

The bandit's hands loosened, then fell away from my neck as he slumped forward.

I twisted my head to the side, gagging and spitting out blood while simultaneously attempting to draw in a lungful of air. It was nearly impossible with the full weight of the dying man crushing me.

"He's too heavy," Tiy said to someone out of sight. "We have to roll him off her."

A moment later, the suffocating body was hauled away. I curled up on my side, coughing and choking. The linen fabric of my robe and shift clung to me, saturated with blood. I couldn't escape from the metallic scent, and it made my stomach heave.

"Are you all right, divine one?" Tiy asked, gripping my arm and shoulder to drag me upright.

I nodded as I coughed some more. Tiy knelt beside me and patted my back.

The worst of the nauseousness slowly abated, and I dazedly scanned my surroundings. The attack was over, and the remains of the caravan's supplies lay scattered about on the road. There wasn't a live donkey in sight, but from the looks of it, most of the people had survived. That was something, at least.

A figure coalesced from the shadows off to the left of the road, emerging from the swaying barley. Ineni. And Bek was with her. Both appeared rattled, but uninjured.

Some of the tension within me eased. Bek and Ineni survived. That knowledge far outweighed the horror I felt at recalling my own savage brutality. I had taken human lives. They had deserved to die, but now I had to live with the memory of ending them.

A laugh bubbled up from my chest, obscene and inappropriate, but I couldn't do a damn thing to stop it. It erupted from my mouth, musical and tinged with a hint of hysteria. I slapped my bloody hands over my mouth, embarrassed by my depraved laughter. By the sudden, absurd swell of pure joy.

I had spent so long living for yesterday and tomorrow that I had been living half a life. But for a few moments there, in the heat of battle, every cell of my being had been engaged in the here and now. I had been truly present.

For the first time in my life, I felt blissfully, terrifyingly alive.

MY HEART WAS HEAVY as I walked away from Ineni's clan. Bek stood in the middle of the road, her expression crestfallen. She had been in a state of mute shock since the bandit attack, but as soon as the sun rose and those of us who had fought had changed out of our bloody clothes and washed ourselves clean in a nearby canal, some of the light had returned to her eyes, though she remained uncharacteristically quiet.

I hated leaving her right now, after what she had just been through. But I had interfered in these people's lives enough. With each minute I lingered among them, I felt like I was goading fate to make *this* the moment that mattered. The one that changed too much. That shredded the timeline.

Which meant it was time for me to leave them. Past time.

I walked away from the people who had become a second family to me knowing I would never see them again. I wore sandals that had belonged to one of the dead and another of Tiy's white linen shifts. It was a little worn and more of an off-white at this point, but it was a vast improvement over the torn and blood-stained dress I had left behind.

"You saved my life," Tiy had said as she pressed the new garment into my hands. "And my daughter's life, as well. I would gladly give you the clothes off my body and walk into Waset naked, and still, it would not be enough to repay my debt."

"There is no debt," I told her before pulling her into a tight embrace. "You saved my life, too." When I released her, I turned to Bek, who was hovering near her mother. "Come here," I said, holding my hand out for the girl to take. "I want to tell you something. A secret."

Bek moved closer, curiosity lighting her haunted eyes as she slipped her small hand into mine.

I crouched in front of her and leaned in close. "You have to promise to never, *ever* tell anyone."

Bek was quiet for a long moment. "Never tell anyone what?" she said, her voice barely above a whisper. I thought it may have been her first words since the attack.

I smiled then, a small, secret smile. "My name."

I refused to look back as I walked away. I wiped a tear from my cheek and inhaled a shaky breath. The fresh goodbyes lingered in the forefront of my mind, along with the gratitude I felt for the gifts Ineni and her people had given me. I had arrived in this ancient time with nothing. Now, I felt wealthy in comparison.

To my name now, I had one leather waterskin, sturdy leather-soled sandals, a dagger and longer knife—both bronze from blade to hilt—and matching leather sheaths, which I wore on a leather weapons belt poached off the first man I had slain. I wore the belt fastened as tight as it would go, but it still hung low on my hips, far from fashionable for the era. Who knew, maybe I would start a new trend. The few unbroken—un*bloodied*—arrows I had scrounged up were tucked into the belt, as well. I figured they must be worth *something*, which was a hell of a lot better than *nothing* when heading into a situation involving bartering.

But most importantly, I walked away from Ineni's clan with a newfound and very unexpected sense of self-worth that had nothing to do with what others thought of me and everything to do with what I thought of myself. It felt strange, like my entire center of self was shifting. Strange, but I liked it.

The river road led me to a wide, shallow cove on the west bank of the Nile. A long quay built of limestone blocks stretched out from far into the riverbank toward the Nile proper, the surface of the man-made walkway about five feet above the water level, emphasizing just how severely the decades-long drought had impacted the land.

The water in the cove rippled in the cool breeze, reflecting the early morning sunlight like bands of liquid gold. Several slender boats floated on either side of the quay, moored by woven lines to bulbous stone cleats sticking up from the edge of the limestone walkway. The bows and sterns of each boat narrowed as they swooped up toward the sky.

The occupants of two such boats appeared to be asleep, stretched out on the decks of their small crafts. I headed for the third boat and the man kneeling within who rubbed oil onto the paddle of a wooden oar with a dark-stained rag.

Gulls launched into the air as I crossed the quay, disturbing the serene scene. At their squawking, the boatman looked up. He carefully folded the rag he had been using to oil the oar and tucked it into a pouch affixed to the inside of the hull. He stood slowly, his slender craft barely wobbling from the movement, and rested his elbows on the edge of the quay. He watched my approach, his gaze assessing.

"Good morning," I said, stopping well out of arm's reach.

The boatman peered up at me with a pleasant, youthful face. He wore a white linen schenti, the kilt knotted around his waist and the lower hem reaching his knees. His torso was bare, displaying lean muscle honed from his daily work on the river. His head was clean shaven, as was his tanned face. Overall, his whole appearance reminded me so much of how I remembered my dad looking in ancient times that I was tempted to believe I hadn't landed too far off from my original, abandoned native era. I had been born around the year 2185 BCE, and I had been frozen in At four years later. I tentatively set 2180 as the current date, give or take a few centuries.

That temporal anchor, however speculative, spurred a new, irresistible train of thought. What if my mom was still alive?

My heart beat faster, and tears welled in my eyes. Suddenly, my mom was all I could think about. What if I could see her again? What if—

"Divine one?" the boatman said, his tone suggesting those two words hadn't been his first. I had missed whatever else he had said, distracted by the tantalizing prospect of seeing my mom again.

Blinking, I refocused on the boatman. "I'm sorry. What did you say?"

His tentative smile bared white teeth that were only slightly crooked. "Are you looking to cross the river?" His accent differed from that of Ineni's clan, with longer vowels and a slight lilt at the end of each word.

"Yes," I said, returning his smile. "Yes, I am." I pulled the three arrows from my belt and held them out. "Would you accept these in payment?"

The boatman tilted his head to the side, examining my offering. After a long moment, his eyes returned to mine, and he nodded.

He crouched in his boat, retrieving a rolled ladder made from braided ropes and narrow wooden rungs. He hooked a pair of loops at the end of the ropes around two small stone pegs jutting up from the edge of the quay and let the ladder unfurl the five or so feet down to the water. Stepping backward while keeping one hand on the quay to steady the boat, he reached up for me with the other.

I was far from graceful as I climbed down the ladder, and once I was in the slender boat, trying my hardest not to shift my weight, I was that much more impressed by his ability to move about without disturbing the craft. I caused it to wobble precariously from side to side by simply breathing.

When I was safely settled on a low bench built into the boat's midpoint, facing the western riverbank, the boatman retrieved and rolled his ladder, stashing it near what I took to be the stern, in front of me. He untied the two lines mooring us to the quay, coiled them neatly and stashed them alongside the ladder, then sat on a second built-in bench at that end of the boat. He pushed off from the side of the quay with the paddle of one oar.

Up close, I could see the miniature hippo heads topping the slim wooden spires extending upward from the bow and stern.

"Did you travel far, divine one?" the boatman asked, steering the boat with the careful guidance of his oars.

As it turned out, his end was the bow, not the stern, and he rowed with his back toward our destination on the eastern bank. I couldn't make out anything that looked like buildings on the far side of the river yet, and I assumed Waset must sit tucked behind an embankment to protect the town from flooding during the annual inundation. Either that, or it was much less substantial a town than I had been imagining.

"Yes," I said, shifting my focus from the eastern riverbank to the boatman. "I have traveled *very* far."

The boatman's gaze skimmed over my belt with the two pilfered weapons. His bemused expression confirmed my assumption that my styling was far from fashionable. "And did you have trouble on the road?" He asked, his eyes returning to my face.

"Some. Bandits." I averted my gaze and forced a tight smile, donning a placid mask as images of killing those men flashed through my mind. I bottled up a resurgence of revulsion and met the boatman's curious stare. "They won't bother anyone again."

Much to my surprise, the boatman laughed, low and rumbling. "I am pleased to hear the roads will be safer." He paused, not missing a beat in his rowing, then added, "For a little while, at least. Until a new batch of desperate men takes their places."

I nodded, my attention drifting back to the far bank of the river, still so distant. I wished the boatman's words provided me some comfort, but they only compounded the unease twisting in my gut.

The ripples of killing those bandits spread so much farther than I had previously considered. New bandits would rise, people who may have found some other way to make ends meet had this illicit void not been created by someone who never should have been present in this time period to begin with. The potential impacts of my actions fanned out before me in an intricate, infinite pattern.

I swallowed my rising nausea. I couldn't help but feel I had made a mistake. I never should have killed those bandits. I never should have interfered at all, regardless of my noble motivations. It was a mistake I vowed to never make again.

My thoughts drifted back to my mom. If she truly was alive right now, would I be able to resist going to her? Speaking with her. *Knowing* her?

Would I be able to resist revealing my true identity to her? Maybe it was better if I never found out whether she still lived.

As our boat gradually closed in on the eastern bank, I weighed my options. I would head downriver to Men-nefer as soon as I could charter a larger riverboat to carry me. If my mom *was* still alive, she would be there, where she and the rest of my family had lived out the remainder of their lives after leaving the Netjer-At Oasis.   •

When I reached Men-nefer, I could either head straight to the Hathor temple to inquire about Aramei, my time-traveling ride home, *or* I could scope out my family's estate–after figuring out where it was in the first place—to see if my mom was there. I would just look in on my family from afar, making sure they were doing okay, and *then* I would head to the Hathor temple.

Oh, who was I kidding? Like there was even a choice. There was no way I *wasn't* going to check on my family. But I was fully committed to not interacting with them. I could not interfere in their fates. I *could not*. I had meddled far too much already.

I just wanted to see my mom one more time. I wanted to imprint an image of her face into the nearly infallible vault my mind had become when my Nejeret traits manifested. When I thought of her, I wanted to see *her*, not the fuzzy, diluted image I carried with me now, formed from a combination of my imperfect child's memory and the idealized likenesses displayed in her tomb.

Just once, I wanted to hear her voice. Her laughter. Her singing. I wanted to watch her smile. I wanted to gather up all these little pieces of her like priceless treasures and stash them away in a chest that was mine alone. Then, my mom would live on in my heart, always.

I had been given a gift. An opportunity. I couldn't pass up this chance to make my heart whole. I *would* see them—see my mom—just one more time.

W HEN I REACHED THE small harbor on the east side of the river, I headed straight for the larger ships at the opposite end of the T-shaped quay. I wanted to secure my ride downriver to Men-nefer as soon as possible. I had no clue how much it would cost, and my bartering supplies were limited to the stolen blades and the leather weapons belt slung around my hips.

The eyes of sailors and dock workers followed me as I made my way along the quay. Either they weren't used to seeing women in the harbor—so far as I could see, I was the only one present—or they recognized me as Nejeret.

The nearest ship was docked on the riverbank side of the quay, just past an intersection with a limestone walkway that connected back to dry land. The ship bore a similar form to the smaller craft that had ferried me across the river—long and narrow, with arching protrusions that swept upward at the bow and stern—but its larger scale was such that the deck was nearly flush with the surface of the walkway, some five feet above the water.

The ship's hull was painted turquoise, with deep crimson and sunny yellow accents. A single, thick mast stood tall in the center of the ship, the crimson sail collapsed and tied to the lower of the two long wooden spars crossing it. The paddles of eight oars stuck out from the visible side of the hull, and a squat, square cabin stood on the stern side of the mast. A trio of men wearing only white linen schentis, their torsos bared to the morning sun, moved about on the deck, while another man stood nearby on the quay, directing the sailors' work with sharp gestures and barked commands.

I approached the bossy man standing on the dock, taking him to be the captain of the ship. He was short and sturdily built, with skin the leathery brown that came from decades of exposure to the sun. He eyed me, his gaze trailing first down the length of my body, then back up, part assessment, part leer.

"Good morning," I said, angling closer to the edge of the quay as I drew near. I stopped and plastered a friendly smile on my face. "Are you the captain of this ship?" I glanced at the boat in question.

"Aye," the captain said, finally dragging his eyes the rest of the way up to meet mine.

I forced my smile to hold despite the slimy residue left behind by his gaze. "I'm seeking transport to Men-nefer."

He glanced to the side, watching the sailors working on his ship. "It just so happens my ship is headed that way in three days."

My smile turned genuine.

"We could carry another body." His eyes met mine once more, and he raised his eyebrows. "For the right price."

"Oh, yes, of course." I pulled the dagger from the sheath on my left hip. It was the finer of the two weapons, but I didn't want to offer both straight away. Starting low was the key to winning at bartering. At least, that's what my gut told me. I didn't actually have any experience trading goods, though I had done my fair share of negotiating contracts.

I held the bronze hilt of the dagger out toward the captain, offering him the weapon to inspect. "Would this be enough?" I asked, looking from his face down to the dagger, then back up.

The captain barked a laugh, the boisterous sound more dismissive than if he had actually said *no*.

I straightened my spine and raised my chin. If this was his reaction to the dagger, I wasn't holding out hope that adding the longer, cruder knife would help matters. However, even if I didn't have enough valuables to trade for passage aboard his ship, there was another card I could play.

"Do you know what I am?" I said, my words ringing with authority. My dad had taught me more than how to fight. He had also taught me how to command a room. Or, in this case, a harbor.

Nejerets were respected in this time, often revered, as had been the case among Ineni's clan. Perhaps this captain was unaware that I wasn't just some poor human woman. If he realized a so-called god of time—a *Netjer-At* in Old Egyptian—required his assistance, there was a chance he might even transport me to Men-nefer free of charge.

The captain chuckled. "Aye, *divine one*," he said, confirming he was aware I was a Nejeret. He managed to make the honorific sound cheap and somehow dirty. Or maybe that was the leer that accompanied the two words. "I can see full well what you are." Again, he chuckled, and when his eyes returned to mine, they were shadowed with impudence.

Clearly, reverence for Nejerets wasn't universal in this time.

The captain returned his attention to his sailors, watching them work on the deck of his ship. "Ain't no mistaking that," he said. "But I wouldn't carry Osiris himself aboard my boat without full payment—up-front. These are difficult times, after all, and I've been cheated out of due payment a few times too many."

I pressed my lips together, biting my tongue, and re-sheathed the dagger.

The captain looked at me directly, his stare unwavering. "There is *another* way you could pay your fare." His insinuation rang out loud and clear—I could pay my way to Men-nefer with my body.

My lip curled, my eyes narrowed, and heat scorched up my neck and cheeks. Acting on impulse, I stepped closer and reached for the captain's shoulders, the movement too quick and unexpected for him to evade. I gripped his shoulders and jerked my knee upward, ramming it into his groin as hard as I could.

Grunting, the captain bent double. The sailors on his boat *oohed* and winced, and I heard laughter coming from farther down the quay.

I took three stiff steps backward, then spat on his feet. "Pig," I hissed before turning on my heel and stalking away.

I marched straight back the way I had come, to the other end of the quay, where the boatman who had ferried me across the river once again knelt in his small vessel, oiling an oar. He watched me approach, his eyes glittering with mirth, making me wonder if he had been the source of the laughter I had heard.

I stopped near the edge of the limestone walkway and addressed him. "I would greatly appreciate it if you would ferry me back across the river." I drew the longer knife, flipped it so I was holding the blade, and reached down, offering him the bronze hilt. "Will you accept this as payment?"

The boatman stood in that slow, steady way that seemed second nature to him. He reached up for the knife, but instead of curling his fingers around the hilt, he pushed it back toward me.

My heart sank at the rejection, and I straightened, my arm drooping.

"I'll carry you free of charge," he said, his eyes dancing. "I'd ask for a kiss as payment, but I think we both know where that would get me." He glanced farther up the quay. "Though seeing Usur taken down like that is more than payment enough."

I peeked over my shoulder, pleased to see the insulting captain was still doubled over. I snickered.

The friendly boatman refocused on me. "Besides, I need to cross back to pick up more refugees. Not much paying traffic heads back that way these days," he said, nodding toward the west bank as he held his hand out to help me climb down the ladder to his boat.

As he pushed off with an oar, my momentary good humor faded, and I felt mildly sick to my stomach. I was preemptively disgusted with myself for what I was about to do.

If I was going to afford the trip to Men-nefer, I would need something more valuable than bronze knives to trade. I didn't have any useful or marketable skills, at least, not during this time. There was no way for me to earn enough to pay my fare downriver. Well, short of selling my body, and while I wasn't afraid of a little quid pro quo action, I would only enter such an arrangement on *my* terms. And I would never—*never*—enter such an arrangement with someone like Usur.

So far as I saw it, I had two options: either steal from the living, or steal from the dead. The choice seemed obvious to me as I stared out at the tombs pocking the face of the western cliffs. Tonight, I would rob the dead.

13

I CROUCHED IN THE shadows of a rocky outcropping high on the cliffs bordering the fields running along the west bank of the Nile and gazed down on the necropolis as I waited for the sun to set. The city of the dead was built into a natural bowl on the cliffside. Small rectangular mastabas looking like pyramids with their tops chopped off stood alongside tomb entrances marked by columned porticos built out from openings cut into the cliff wall. Even more tombs appeared to be literal holes in the wall.

As dusk darkened to night and the crickets tuned up their song, a couple of figures snuck along a cliffside path at the far end of the necropolis, a few hundred yards from my position, heading toward the cluster of larger tombs there. They wore dark robes, much like the bandits who had attacked the caravan, turning them into living shadows moving along the path.

My lip curled at the sight of them—grave robbers.

And then my stomach turned. I was no better than them.

I waited until at least an hour into full night to make my move, wanting to make sure no other enterprising grave robbers joined the fun without me knowing they were there. Looked like it was just me and the pair at the other end of the necropolis. So long as I kept an ear out for them as I hunted for treasure of my own, I figured I should be fine.

Careful of each foot placement, I crept down a narrow trail that snaked along the side of the cliff, leading me into the necropolis. One wrong step would send a waterfall of loose rocks tumbling down the steep drop off to my right, announcing my presence.

I stopped at the first tomb on my path, a small mastaba barely taller than me. I eased down to my knees and crawled into the structure just past my shoulders. The mastaba was all there was to this tomb; nothing larger had been dug into the cliff behind it. Whatever offerings had been left within had already either been plundered or smashed, and all that remained were the conical, stone-like remains of petrified loaves of bread, shards of broken pottery, and the faint odor of stale beer.

The burial shaft at the center of the small tomb had been uncovered. I crawled in another foot, up to my waist, and peered over the lip of the shaft. The crescent moon provided just enough light for me to see that the coffin's lid lay askew at the bottom of the six-foot hole, exposing a desecrated mummy to the elements.

I didn't even bother checking the coffin for hidden treasures. Whatever valuables had been stashed within would be long gone by now. Disappointing, but at least I had no reason to violate the deceased further than I already had.

Sighing, I backed out of the mastaba.

The second tomb was much the same. By the time I finished a brief search of a third compact mastaba, I understood why my unsavory companions were targeting a different part of the necropolis. This section had already been cleaned out.

I crouched beside the small mastaba and waited for any sounds that would mark the location of the other grave robbers. After about fifteen minutes, I heard them talking excitedly as they emerged from a tomb, still on the far side of the necropolis. Apparently, they were having better luck over there.

I chewed on the inside of my cheek, considering what to do. I could wait until the other thieves were gone and then explore the larger tombs in the area where they were focusing all of their efforts. But there was no guarantee they would finish up and take off early enough for me to explore that part of the necropolis before sunrise, which meant I would have to come back tomorrow night to continue this oh-so-fun experience. *Or* I could creep closer *now* and risk searching some of the larger tombs on the outskirts of their section while they still worked.

After a slow, deep inhale and exhale, I stood and snuck along a winding pathway that led toward the other side of the necropolis. I ducked into the nearest tomb when the scuffle of leather soles on dry, rocky earth announced the grave robbers' reemergence into the open night air.

This tomb had a porch-like portico with a series of four stone columns. I slipped between the first two and crept toward the tomb's entrance. It was unsealed, which didn't bode well for me making any lucrative discoveries while I hid within. I had to crouch slightly as I passed through the squat rectangular entrance. The dim moonlight was enough for me to make out ghosts of the images and colors decorating the walls of the tomb's cramped antechamber.

I moved deeper into the tomb, heading for the doorway carved into the back wall. A shard of pottery crunched under the sole of my sandal.

I winced, freezing for a moment and holding my breath as I listened. No sounds indicated that my thieving companions had heard me, so I continued deeper into the tomb, moving even slower and being even more careful about where I stepped.

In the next chamber, I found an enormous sarcophagus carved from some kind of granite. It was impossible to tell whether it was black or gray or red in the dim moonlight, even with my enhanced Nejeret vision. But what I could make out of the sarcophagus made my heart leap. It was sealed shut, the slab lid resting flush against the massive base. Which meant the valuables that had been hidden with the dearly departed within the sarcophagus were likely still in there.

I made a slow circuit around the sarcophagus, examining it from every angle. I ran my fingertips over the surface as I walked, making a mental image of the intricate designs carved into the smooth stone. Not hieroglyphs, and not images of daily life or spells from the coffin texts. They felt more geometric, almost like an art déco pattern.

Based on the size of the sarcophagus and the quality of the engravings, I was betting there were some high-value items sealed within, likely jewelry and amulets, and maybe some trinkets, all stored on and around the mummy. All I needed to do was get the lid open.

And soil my soul by defiling the dead.

The memory of looting this poor corpse was likely to haunt me until my dying day. But even such a debase act could easily be justified if it helped me make my way home before doing irrevocable damage to the timeline. Assuming I hadn't already.

I wasn't sure how the whole time-space continuum worked, but I was hoping my continued presence in this time period meant I *hadn't* changed things enough that the events that led to me being here had been altered. That paradoxical logic *mostly* made sense in my head.

Standing at one corner of the sarcophagus, I gave the lid a test push. It didn't budge.

I pushed harder. Still nothing.

I pressed my lips together, starting to suspect why this sarcophagus remained undisturbed while the tomb itself had clearly been plundered.

I stepped back, angling my body toward the sarcophagus for better leverage, sucked in a breath, and shoved the edge of the lid as hard as I could.

My muscles strained until my entire body shook with the effort. Despite that, the lid didn't shift.

I expelled my held breath and straightened. My arms trembled as I relaxed them at my sides. There was absolutely no way I was going to open this thing. At least, not on my own. It was too heavy.

I narrowed my eyes, studying the sarcophagus. *Unless there was some trick to it.*

I made another, slower circuit around the sarcophagus, following the seam between the lid and base with a fingertip, searching for a notch or gap or hidden latch. I circled it again and again, poking and prodding the sarcophagus, running my hands up and down its carved sides, searching for any irregularity that might clue me in on how to open this damn thing.

Until finally—reluctantly—I accepted the truth. There was no trick to opening it, no secret button or hidden latch. The sarcophagus had been constructed to prevent anyone from opening it. Ever. Period. I wouldn't find an easy way in. I wouldn't find *any* way in at all.

Defeated, I turned away from the sarcophagus and leaned back against the cool, carved granite to slide down to the floor. As I sat there, working up the motivation to continue my hunt for treasure, I absently traced the narrow cracks between the stone floor tiles.

The tile immediately to my right shifted minutely, giving off the faintest groan of stone grinding on stone.

I stopped tracing the crease between the tiles and cocked my head to the side. Curious, I retraced the same crease. The sound came again. One of the floor tiles was loose.

Eyes narrowed, I peered down at the tile in question. It looked the same as all the others—rectangular, unpolished limestone, about one foot wide by two feet long. I shoved my finger deeper into the crease until the end of my nail reached the underside of the tile, wincing as the edge of the neighboring tile scraped my cuticle.

The loose tile was maybe an inch thick. It would be heavy, but not too heavy for me to move it on my own. I glanced at the sarcophagus. It was more than I could say for that stupid slab of granite.

I scrambled onto my knees, facing the loose tile, and hastily gouged out the sand and dirt that had settled in the surrounding creases. I wedged my fingertips into the seam on the far side and pulled the tile closer to me, widening the gap on that side. Once the edge of the tile was flush against the one beneath my knees, I crawled around to the other side and dug my fingers deeper into the crease. Rough stone scraped against my skin, but I hardly noticed the pain.

My heart leapt when my fingers were far enough under the tile to make me fairly sure that a hollow space lay beneath. Giddy, I hoisted the limestone floor tile up a few inches and ducked my head to peek beneath the slab of stone. And grinned.

A narrow, deep hole had been carved out of the bedrock beneath the tomb's floor. It was a perfect hiding place for something valuable. I just hoped that whatever had been hidden here hadn't already been discovered.

I slid the tile off to the side and eased it down, taking a moment to shake out my hands. I sat up straighter, stretched my neck first one way, then the other, and wove my fingers together to crack my knuckles, working up the nerve to reach into that dark abyss. Not even my excellent vision could pierce the blackness, and any number of creepy crawlies could have made the recess their home.

I took a deep breath, then blew out the air and bent forward, reaching into the hole. "Please don't be scorpions," I murmured, imagining the stinging insects lying in wait at the bottom of the dark recess. "Please don't be scorpions. Please don't be scorpions . . ."

My arm was in the hole up to my shoulder when my fingertips finally skimmed something solid. Thankfully, it was hard and flat-ish, and my hand's presence didn't cause anything to skitter about.

Emboldened by the lack of bugs, I felt around the edges of the roughly square-shaped recess, then swept my hand across the center of the hole.

There! Something similar in size and shape to a narrow shoebox.

I pulled my arm out. Squinting, I braced a hand on either side of the opening in the floor and stuck my head into the hole, attempting to see what was down there, but it was too dark.

I sat up and stretched my back, then reached in with my right arm once more. I wedged my fingertips under the bottom edge of the small box and lifted it. Aged, rotted wood crumbled in my grasp, disintegrating like dry sand.

"Damn it!" I hissed, breathing hard.

But I wasn't about to give up. Something must have been *in* the box.

I combed my fingers through the crumbling splinters, my heart skipping a beat when I found what felt like small, irregularly shaped pebbles scattered among the debris. I scooped up a couple and sat back, moving my hand into the weak, silver moonlight seeping in through the doorway to the antechamber. I uncurled my fingers to reveal two small tokens a little larger than my thumbnail, one shaped like a thread spool, the other like a cone. Both glinted gold in the moonlight.

My lips parted, and my heart rate sped up. Breathlessly, I raised the cone-shaped piece to my mouth and bit down. When my teeth sank into soft metal, I knew the tokens weren't just gold-plated. They were solid gold. And even better—I recognized the shapes. These were game pieces for senet, which meant there would be more of them down in that hole. *Many* more.

I suppressed a squeal and reached back into the hole to sift through the crumbling remains of what must have been the game board. The pieces would have been stored in a drawer tucked under the playing surface.

I found sixteen more game pieces, all made of solid gold. Once I was sure I had mined the recess for all it had to offer, I stashed my treasure near the bottom edge of the sarcophagus and sat back to cut a six-inch strip from the bottom of my shift. I bundled the linen scrap around the gold tokens, then re-wrapped the bundle a few more times for good measure.

Clutching my prize tightly, I snuck out of the tomb. When I made it back to my hiding spot from earlier in the evening sheltered in a crevice high on the cliffs, I hugged the bundle to my chest like it was the most precious thing to me in the world—because, at the moment, it was.

I couldn't believe my good fortune. My chest quaked with silent laughter that slowly morphed into muffled sobs. I had more than enough to pay my way to Men-nefer.

Nothing could stop me now.

I WAS STARTLED AWAKE, roused by the sensation of something skittering over the top of my foot. A scorpion. Pale yellow with a dark brown stinger at the tip of its fat, curling tail. At least as big as my thumb.

I shrieked and kicked out my leg, sending the potentially deadly bug flying before it could sting me, then jumped to my feet. I shimmied and shook my whole body to make sure nothing else had snuggled up with me while I slept.

I paused in the middle of sweeping my hands down my left leg and looked around. Where was I?

I stood in a narrow spot of shade created by a crevice in a rocky mound jutting up from the ground, but I was surrounded by bright sunlight. I squinted and turned around, raising a hand to protect my eyes from the golden sun hanging low over the eastern horizon. Just a few steps away, the ground dropped off at the edge of a cliff. I must have fallen asleep while I waited for the sun to rise after searching the necropolis.

The necropolis. The tomb. The hole in the floor.

My treasure.

Heart suddenly racing, tripping over itself, I turned in a frantic circle as I scanned the surrounding ground, searching for the valuable linen-wrapped bundle. I patted down my body. Where was it?

For a panicked second, I feared I had kicked my prize—my lifeline—over the edge of the cliff. But then I spotted the small bundle wedged into the very back of the crevice where I had dozed off.

I hurried forward and crouched to scoop it up, hugging the linen-wrapped bundle to my chest and shooting furtive glances around to make sure nobody was spying on me.

Out in the middle of nowhere.

Paranoia may have been making me just a smidge irrational.

Letting out a shaky laugh, I made my way to the edge of the cliff. I brushed flyaway strands of hair from my face as I took in the breathtaking view of the necropolis below, the life-giving Nile cutting through the verdant land beyond, the *meryt* filled with vendor stalls near the quayside on the east bank of the river, and the compact walled town of Waset tucked behind an embankment built up beyond the marketplace.

Once again shielding my eyes with a raised hand, I peered out at the sun hovering over the eastern horizon. It was still morning, maybe an hour or two after sunrise. I glanced back at my shelter and shook my head. I couldn't believe I had fallen asleep. At least my luck of the previous night had held out, and nobody robbed me while I slumbered.

I hurried back down to the riverbank, where I found my favorite boatman sitting on the edge of the quay, feet dangling over his boat as he repaired a braided line with new plant fibers—maybe reed or papyrus. He glanced my way as I approached.

When I reached him, I stopped and held out my hand, uncurling my fingers to reveal a single gold cone-shaped game piece. The rest of the game pieces remained wrapped in the linen bundle, which I had tied to my belt, right next to the dagger's sheath.

The boatman raised his eyebrows, then looked up at me. "Well done, divine one."

I nodded, flashing him a relieved smile and moving my hand closer to him. "For your kindness yesterday." My smile widened, my eyebrows raising. "And for a ride back to Waset, if you're not too busy."

He shook his head, eyeing the gold piece. "It is too much."

"Take it," I said, crouching down beside him. "Please."

The boatman studied the token for a moment longer, and then his lips spread into a broad grin. He plucked the gold game piece from my palm. "How could I refuse such a generous offer?" He tucked the treasure into a fold in his kilt, then turned and fluidly slipped over the edge of the quay to climb down the rope ladder, the motion reminding me of a seal sliding into the water.

I settled on the passenger bench at the midpoint of the slender boat, feeling truly hopeful for the first time since arriving in this era. The weight of the pouch on my hip countered the heaviness in my heart, and I felt lighter than I had since before the war broke out in the far distant future.

When we docked in the harbor on the east side of the river, I lingered near the familiar boat and peered down the quay where the larger ships were moored, hesitant to part ways with my boatman. We hadn't even exchanged names, but I considered him a friend. Possibly my only one in this place, now that Ineni and her clan had moved on.

"Do they head down river often?" I asked the boatman as he climbed the rope ladder.

"That depends." He glanced toward the larger ships, then knelt to tighten his lines around the bulbous stone cleats protruding up from the edge of the quay. "How far are you looking to go?"

"I need to get to Men-nefer."

The boatman whistled and gazed up at me. "A ship heads down that way every couple of months. It's a long voyage." He flashed me an apologetic smile. "Unfortunately, Usur makes that trip the most frequently."

I sneered, earning a chuckle. "Out of the question."

"I figured as much." The boatman stood and planted his hands on his hips, studying the selection of moored ships. "I would check with Misha. He captains the *Wedjat*," he said, pointing to a ship much like Usur's docked at the very end of the quay.

The hull was painted emerald green, with lapis-blue and golden-yellow accents. The sail was unfurled while a sailor repaired it, displaying a black eye of Horus—a Wedjat—painted on a white background. I grinned. My father's symbol. It was perfect. Almost like the universe was sending me a sign.

"He usually makes the trip to Men-nefer once per season," the boatman continued.

So, three times a year, since the ancient Egyptians only recognized three seasons—Akhet, Peret, and the current, dry season, Shemu. I was a little impressed with myself for remembering that much from my childhood.

"He hasn't gone in a few months." The boatman said. "Which makes me think he is likely planning a trip that way soon."

"Is he fair?" I asked, returning my focus to my boatman. "And honorable?" In other words—would I be safe with him?

"Misha?" the boatman frowned, then nodded and looked at me sidelong. "He's a crotchety old sailor, but he'll offer you a fair price for the trip—assuming he has the room to spare—and he'll make sure you have plenty to eat and that no harm comes to you while you're on his ship." After a moment, he added, "For the right price, of course."

My brows lowered, and I scowled at the boatman.

He raised his hands defensively, suppressed laughter making his broad shoulders jump. "Not *that*, trust me." Still chuckling, he shook his head. "We've all learned our lesson there."

I tensed the corners of my mouth, my lips pressed together. "What would be the right price?"

The boatman squinted down at the linen-wrapped bundle tied to my belt. "How many of those gold pieces did you find?"

I snorted a laugh. "I'm not telling you that." He may have been my only friend, but I *had* only known him for a day, and contrary to what my haters may shout across social media, I wasn't an idiot. My recent nap near the necropolis notwithstanding.

The boatman grinned, his warm brown eyes dancing. "Any reasonable captain would transport you down to Men-nefer for five gold pieces like the one you gave me." He squinted his eyes thoughtfully. "Maybe six. Not more than that."

I nodded to myself, staring downriver, to the place where the Nile met the horizon. I had seventeen gold game pieces left after grossly overpaying for my last two river crossings. Even if the journey downriver cost an exorbitant seven gold pieces, the remaining ten had to be more than enough to trade in the market for the things I needed to survive—clothing, hygiene supplies, better weapons—as well as for food and board here in Waset for however long I needed to sit tight while I awaited departure.

I refocused on the boatman. "Thank you," I said. "For everything."

His responding smile was broad and kind, and he bowed his head deeply. "I wish you well, divine one."

I turned away from the boatman before I could get too choked up and took a single step, then sucked in a breath and faced him once more. "I don't suppose you could recommend an inn as well? And perhaps tell me how to find my way there?"

He did so without hesitation.

"Thank you," I told him again. "Truly." I stepped closer and leaned in, pressing a kiss to his smooth cheek.

When I pulled back, shock widened his eyes.

"Goodbye," I said. Without another word, I turned away and headed up the dock.

15

SIX GOLD PIECES SECURED me a spot on the *Wedjat*, including a bedroll, food, water, and beer during the journey—had to love a culture that considered beer a staple part of their diet—as well as the guarantee that no man on Misha's crew would touch me. He would be taking the *Wedjat* upriver to the first cataract to trade in Swenett, then return to Waset to swap out goods and make any necessary repairs before heading downriver to Men-nefer, likely in four weeks' time. Just one more month.

It wasn't until I had agreed to the terms and was walking up the quay toward the riverbank that I realized the ancient Egyptian week had ten days rather than the modern seven. I didn't just have to wait *a month*; I would be sitting tight for closer to a month *and a half*.

At least I had a comfortable place to wait. Three of the gold game pieces bought me a full service, all-you-can-eat stay at the *Wandering Gull*, to be paid in increments during my time there.

I found the inn exactly where the boatman had said it would be, along the short stretch of road from the harbor to Waset, tucked behind the embankment bordering the edge of the town walls. The long mudbrick villa stretched far beyond the road, with a wide, open-air courtyard at the front of the building that functioned as a common room and dining area. A single hallway extended out from the back of the courtyard, lined on either side by rudimentary wooden doors to the inn's rentable rooms.

My room was the fourth door on the left, about halfway down the hallway. The narrow space was sparsely furnished, with a low table surrounded by a half-dozen floor cushions, the once vibrant colors no doubt muted by the many washings they had received, a ceramic chamber pot tucked behind a plain screen of woven plant fibers, and a niche with a long, low platform built into the back wall topped by a thin pad—what passed for a mattress nowabouts. I wasn't all that excited about sleeping on the used pad, but it helped to know ancient Egyptians were notoriously committed to the prevention and eradication of all insects that liked to dwell on or with people—fleas, lice, and bed bugs were not tolerated. People bathed daily, washed clothes and other home fabrics often, and were big fans of hair removal.

I would need to take care of my own hair situation soon. Not only was my long hair increasingly annoying in a time before the invention of the elastic hair tie, but it was inconveniently unfashionable. I was trying to blend in. To make minimal waves. But with a braid that nearly reached my waist, I stood out like a sore thumb.

Plus, when I was resurrected, my body had been brought back au natural. As in, fully haired. Pits, legs, lady bits—my whole body was in need of a long, intensive grooming session. I wanted to feel the sting of wax. Lots and lots of wax. As soon as I acquired the things I needed from the market, I would indulge in some extensive hair removal.

I only had a few minutes to examine my room before someone knocked on the door. I unlatched the interior lock and pulled the door open, letting in two servants, both young women dressed in simple white linen shifts nearly identical to mine save for the added aprons tied around their waists. The first carried a reddish-brown ceramic basin and matching jug for washing, the second a broad tray laden with the considerable feast I had ordered when I checked in.

The tray held a thick wedge of hard white cheese, a shallow basket holding an assortment of fresh fruits—figs, grapes, and a berry I didn't recognize—a second smaller basket holding dried dates, a steaming bowl of lentil stew, and a pair of round, squat bread loaves with a golden-brown crust. A ceramic pitcher—beer, from the smell of it—finished off the spread.

My mouth started watering as soon as the aroma of the food hit my nostrils, and it was all I could do not to dive into the food until after the servants had left me alone in the room. I hastily latched the door lock—a simple wooden bolt that slid into a notch gouged in the stone doorframe—then rushed back to the table and dropped to my knees on one of the cushions. I gorged myself until I was painfully full, then leaned my back against the wall to nurse the beer while I digested enough to cram more food into my stomach.

I had lost weight during my time with Ineni's clan. Even without the help of a full-length mirror, I could tell I was Calvin-Klein-model thin—a far cry from the natural curves I had started with.

By the time I set the empty tray on the hallway floor outside my door and collapsed on the bed platform, the amber light streaming in through the trio of small, square windows cut into the wall near the ceiling over the bed niche suggested it was late afternoon. The thin pad was lumpy and did little to soften the hard mudbrick surface beneath.

It didn't matter. I was asleep in a matter of seconds.

I woke ravenous, as though my stomach knew a ready supply of food was nearby and wanted to make up for all the lost calories during the journey through the desert. The small window cutouts high in the wall above the bed let in cheerful sunlight, telling me I had slept through the night and well into the following day.

Stiffly, I sat up and scooted to the edge of the bed, my jaw cracking with a yawn. I stood and stretched, reaching my arms high over my head and arching my back. I rolled my neck, attempting to relieve the sharp crick hindering my range of motion. My body did not appreciate the hard bed. Even the ground during the desert journey had been more forgiving.

After taking care of my most pressing need—my full-to-bursting bladder—I poured tepid water from the ceramic pitcher into the matching basin to wash up. I set the chamber pot on the floor outside my door on my way out of the room and padded down the hallway to the sunny courtyard, the strap of my waterskin slung over my shoulder and the weapons belt snug around my hips.

I had been too focused on food and rest the previous day to notice the barren planters and flower pots and the scraggly, wilted date palms in the courtyard, or that the rectangular recess for a pool at the center of the space stood dry. More evidence that the drought was impacting the river land as well as the string of oases.

Inn patrons sat on floor cushions around a few of the low tables scattered about the courtyard, eating and chatting with their table companions. I followed the enticing scent of baking bread through the columns lining the left side of the courtyard, heading for a doorway in the side wall. I stopped in the doorway and gaped at the bounty.

Two wheels of cheese, a half-dozen loaves of bread, and a basket of fresh fruit had been laid out on the long, narrow table lining the far side of the larder. Through another doorway at one end, tall red-brown ceramic jugs filled another, smaller storeroom, stacked three-high. At the other end of the room, bright sunlight streamed in through another doorway in the outer wall.

A servant bustled in through the outer doorway holding a tray laden with fresh-baked loaves of bread. I recognized her as one of the young women who had served me in my room the previous day.

"Are you hungry, divine one?" she asked as she set the tray on the table and unloaded the fresh loaves beside those already lined up.

The honorific barely registered as I nodded, greedily eyeing the bread.

The serving girl turned to me and leaned back against the edge of the long table, wiping her hands on the stained linen apron tied around her waist. "Go ahead and sit," she told me, her focus shifting past me to the courtyard at my back. "I'll bring a tray out for you."

"Thank you." I unslung the strap of my waterskin. "And would you fill this as well?" I asked, holding out the leather jug. "With water, please," I added, just in case it wasn't obvious. I did not want to forever taint the taste of any water it held with the essence of stale beer.

"Of course," she said and stepped forward to take the waterskin.

I nodded my thanks and retreated into the courtyard. After eating my fill—or slightly more than—I headed out, following the limestone causeway back toward the *meryt* at the quayside, where vendors had set up stalls within a walled enclosure to peddle their wares to the gathering sailors and townsfolk alike.

Despite being an ancient Egyptian by birth, I knew very little about my people's ways. In my mind, I had imagined Waset to be laid out like an Italian village, with a central square surrounded by mudbrick buildings situated close together, a warren of narrow streets winding through them.

In reality, there wasn't any reason for me to enter the town proper, not when everything I needed *should be* back by the river's edge. I followed a young mother and her two small children to the *meryt* but soon lost them as they passed through the break in the walls surrounding the market and blended into the gathered crowd milling about from stall to stall.

I stepped through the break in the wall and stopped a few feet into the market, my mouth falling open. I couldn't believe the variety of goods and wares available under the shade of the thick stretches of white linen overhead that blocked out the worst of the relentless midday sun. There was everything from fresh fish, fruits, and vegetables to prepared foods like bread and stews to luxury items like sandals and jewelry. There were even a couple of stalls that offered a hodgepodge of items, like the ancient equivalent of a general store. And that was just what I could see down the main aisle. It would be easy enough to find everything I needed here.

I grinned to myself. I loved shopping. This wouldn't just be easy; it would be fun.

Turned out, I had a knack for bartering. I supposed all that experience haggling with managers and record labels for more favorable contract terms paid off. Who would have thought?

I moved from stall to stall through the open-air market, trading creatively to acquire the things I needed. After a couple of hours, I had in my possession a large woven basket much like an oversized tote bag, filled with a half-dozen white linen shifts of the finest weave available, a compact toiletry chest that I stocked with kohl and a few applicator brushes, a bundle of tooth sticks, and a trio of small ceramic jars filled with natron paste for teeth cleaning and BO prevention, honey ointment for minor wounds, and a thick, aloe-based moisturizing balm. I also found basic mending and fish hook kits, a second water skin, a whetstone, some leather-soled sandals, and upgraded knives and their accompanying sheaths. And last but far from least, I stocked up on the sugar-based wax mixture I needed to thoroughly de-hair my body.

I was browsing a jeweler's stall when I felt the sudden suspicion that I was being watched. I set down the wide gold cuff bracelet I had been considering splurging on and peeked over my shoulder, scanning the booths and stalls lining the far side of the market.

I found the watcher at the very end of the market, a human man leaning back against the mudbrick wall surrounding the market enclosure, his arms crossed over his broad chest. My belly gave an appreciative flip-flop. Holy hell, he was a prime specimen of man. I would have noticed him even if his stare wasn't practically burning a hole through me. I would have noticed him in the middle of the crowd at a packed concert. He was the kind of man I would have noticed *anywhere*.

Tall and muscular, he towered over the people milling and bustling around the market. The dark umber skin of his bared shoulders, torso, and arms displayed an intricate pattern of small scars, symmetrical and harshly beautiful. A fine white linen schenti wrapped around his lower body with enough elaborate folds and knots to suggest his elevated, wealthy status. The silver- and gold-banded hilt of the sickle-shaped sword at his hip confirmed it.

This striking stranger was someone important. And his attention was locked on me. He watched me closely, his dark gaze filled with intrigue.

Heat crept up my neck and flushed my cheeks. My lips curved into a coy smile.

The stunning stranger lowered his chin, his eyes lighting with interest.

Feeling slightly overheated, I turned back to the jewelry stall and picked up a delicate gold bracelet inset with a carved lapis lazuli Wedjat. My father's symbol. Even if I couldn't make my identity known, it would still be nice to carry a piece of my heritage with me.

"Please, no!" a girl cried out further down the market.

My head snapped to the left, and I searched the crowd for the source of the disturbance, absently clutching the bracelet.

A girl who couldn't have been a day older than sixteen had been cornered behind a fishmonger's stall on the far side of the market by a pair of armed brutes. The larger of the two wrapped his arms around the girl, her back to him, and lifted her feet off the ground, while the other speared the nearest vendors and market patrons with a death glare.

"Help! Please!" the girl sobbed, kicking frantically as they carried her back toward the break in the walls. "Please, no! Please!" Her cries grew fainter as she was dragged out of the market and out of sight.

I searched the faces of the people around me, expecting to see someone going after the girl. Someone stopping the men who were obviously abducting her. But all I found were bowed spines, hunched shoulders, and averted gazes. Not a single person even glanced down the alleyway after the girl.

Were they afraid of drawing her abductors' attention their way? Were they really willing to sacrifice a teenage girl just to remain unnoticed? Had they *no* honor?

I clenched my jaw, glaring at anyone who dared to make eye contact with me, including my stunning admirer, who seemed completely unruffled by the trouble at the other end of the market. He was a coward. These people were all cowards. Each and every one of them.

"I'll be right back," I told the jeweler, setting the bracelet down on his table before dropping my basket of goods. "Watch this for me? There will be gold in it for you." When he nodded, I hurried after the trio.

They had a fair head start and were already past the inn by the time I reached the exit. I ran after them, but they had vanished into the warren of narrow streets and alleyways winding through Waset by the time I reached the town walls. I paused on the main road, just inside the walls, and turned my head to the side, letting my ears lead me. With the girls' cries and the brutes' cruel laughter, they were easy enough to track down an alley between squat mudbrick structures.

The alley widened as the buildings on either side grew larger and more spread apart. Warehouses and workspaces, based on the few doorways I poked my head through to listen.

I tracked the trio to a warehouse filled with oversized linen sheets hanging to dry on long stretches of line crisscrossing the cavernous space, the fabric dyed cerulean blue, sun yellow, and blood orange. The girl's cries had died down to muted whimpers, and I hoped I wasn't too late.

I fought the urge to draw my dagger. I had vowed not to kill anyone else, and if I closed my fingers around the hilt of either of my blades, I didn't trust myself not to slit a rapist's—or attempted rapist's—throat.

Moving silently between yards of linen dyed crimson and orange, I crept toward the back corner of the warehouse. I lifted a wooden paddle a little longer than my arm from the rim of a large stone vat filled with steaming sapphire liquid.

Peeking through the crack between two red sheets, I clenched my jaw to hold in my disgust. They were playing with her, like a couple of cats with a terrified mouse. They shoved her back and forth between them, groping her each time they caught her. One man's back was to me, while the other faced me, too distracted by his prey to notice me spying on them.

I raised the paddle, holding it like a baseball bat, and slipped through the crack between the sheets. I stalked forward, each step slow, each foot placement deliberate, and drew in a deep breath, holding it as I swung.

The eyes of the man facing me widened a fraction of a second before I smacked his buddy. The end of the paddle struck into the side of the other guy's head, the impact reverberating up my arm. He dropped like a stone.

I rushed forward, grabbing the girl's arm and jerking her backward. "Get out of here," I urged.

The girl stared at me, her eyes wide and wild.

"Go!" I shouted.

I barely had the chance to shove her out of the way before the second brute lunged at me. As I scrambled backward, I watched the girl stumble between a pair of crimson sheets and out of sight.

I turned my full attention to the irate man barreling toward me. I needed to finish him off before his buddy roused, or I wouldn't have a chance in hell at escaping this alive, at least not while attempting to handle this humanely. Then, it truly would be kill or be killed. And I *would not kill*.

Eyes, ears, nose, throat, temples, solar plexus, groin, feet.

I could almost hear my dad's voice in my head, reciting the weak points in a human body. Points that were easy to injure, even when facing a larger, stronger opponent. I just needed to disable this guy long enough to flee without him following.

I sidestepped my opponent's attempted tackle at the last possible second. He reacted faster than I had expected, snagging my arm in a bruising grip and yanking me off balance. I lashed out with my free arm, swinging it in a wide arc and smashing the heel of my palm against his ear.

He grunted and released my arm, shaking his head, momentarily dazed. Taking advantage of the brief reprieve, I went on the offensive, gripping his shoulders and jerking my knee up into his groin. The air whooshed out of his lungs, and he doubled over. A knee to the groin worked every time.

I skittered back a few steps, grinning like an idiot as adrenaline-spiked blood roared through my veins. Breathing hard, I drew back my foot and soccer kicked this asshat in the face. His head tilted up, his body arched backward, and he collapsed crossways over his unconscious companion.

I stared at the men's collapsed forms for a moment, making sure they were really down, and then I spun around and fled through the maze of colorful fabric. I hurried out into the alleyway. I would have headed straight back to the inn, but I needed my basket and all the things I had purchased, which I had left with the jeweler in the market.

When I reached the market, I slowed to a fast walk, blending into the crowd on the main thoroughfare. Someone grabbed my arm, and I whirled, fists clenching and arms flying up to attack.

It was the jeweler, my bulging basket slung over his shoulder. He released my arm and backed up a step, hands raised in the universal gesture of surrender.

I lowered my arms, still breathing hard, and hastily scanned the surrounding crowd. No sign of the two asshats yet.

The jeweler handed me my basket, then extended one hand toward me, the delicate gold bracelet adorned with a lapis lazuli Wedjat emblem resting on his palm. "Please, take it," he said.

I looked from the bracelet to his face, my brows drawing together. I shook my head, pretty sure *I* was the one who owed *him* gold. "I don't have time to barter," I said, glancing past him to scan the crowd for the two brutes. "I have to go." I started to turn, hiking the handles of my basket further up on my shoulder.

"Please," the jeweler said, stepping closer. He caught my wrist and pressed the bracelet into my hand, then released me. "Take it."

I glanced down at the bracelet in my hand before raising my eyes to meet the jeweler's stare.

"A gift," he said, bowing his head. "A *thank you*. For your bravery." His eyes were glassy, almost like he was holding back tears.

I nodded, my fingers curling around the bracelet. And then I turned and hurried away from the market, back to the safety of the inn.

I LOUNGED ON MY sleeping platform in one of my new dresses, letting my scrapes and bruises from the scuffle in the warehouse, as well as the swollen skin from my overzealous hair-removal session, heal. The shift I had worn to the market hung on a wall peg, drying, the faintest ghost of bloodstains marring the white fabric. I hadn't noticed the blood spattered on the white linen until I retreated into the safety of my room and stripped down to scrub my skin clean of the grimy residue from the men's hands. But no amount of scrubbing, waxing, or grooming had been able to wipe away my self-loathing.

I angled my face away from the peekaboo view of the burnt sunset visible through the small window cutouts high in the wall and draped my arm over my eyes. I never should have gone after them. But as I had watched the girl being hauled away, all thoughts of protecting the timeline had fled from my mind.

Going after them had been stupid and reckless. I made a fist, my fingernails digging into my palms. I had to stop interfering. *Now* was the past. Done. Over with. The future was what mattered.

My stomach groaned, reminding me I hadn't eaten a midday meal. My body wasn't exactly in the best shape to go without food at the moment, so I hauled myself up and trudged toward the door, my bare feet dragging on the cool mudbrick floor.

A commotion ahead made me pause halfway down the hallway to survey what I could see of the torchlit courtyard. Nothing seemed out of sorts, so I crept forward, hanging back in the mouth of the hallway.

Armed men moved about the space, simple banded leather cuirasses protecting their upper bodies and sickle-shaped swords like I had seen on my admirer in the market hanging from their hips, over their white linen schentis. There was at least a half-dozen of them, by my quick count. Were they soldiers? Or maybe some sort of town guard?

Whoever they were, they moved through shadows and pools of torchlight, stooping beside each table to study the faces of the people seated on the floor. One stood in the doorway to the larder, visible through a pair of columns, dressed and armed the same as the rest but more petite and notably curvier.

I turned my head to the side, narrowing my eyes as I focused on the input reaching my ears from that direction. The timbre of her voice confirmed my suspicion that she was a female warrior, an extreme rarity in this time.

"Have you seen her?" the armed woman asked whoever was within the larder, likely one of the serving girls. There was a long moment of silence. Of waiting. "No harm will come to her," she added, as though the servant needed convincing. "You have my word."

The armed woman backed out of the doorway, letting the hidden servant pass through and into the shadowy space between the columns and the wall. The girl scanned the courtyard, then looked toward the mouth of the hallway. Her eyes locked with mine, apology written all over her face.

I stiffened, my heart stumbling to a gallop. Her expression told me all I needed to know. The *her* they were looking for was *me*.

Instinct took over. I spun on my heel and sprinted down the hallway, heading for the back door. I exploded into the cool evening air, leaping down the three mudbrick stairs.

And straight into the arms of the stunning, scarred man from the market, who crowded the path between the back door and the vegetable garden behind the inn. He caught me before I fully crashed into him, gripping my upper arms to steady me. His midnight eyes were opened wide, his full lips parted. He was as startled by my sudden appearance as I was by running into him back here.

I stepped back, gathering my wits about me, and tugged against his hold. His grip on my arms remained firm, his expression stony.

"Release me," I demanded, shooting a panicked glance at the door hanging open behind me.

With a twist and a jerk, I yanked one arm free, earning a friction burn from his fingers, but the man's grip held fast on my other arm.

"What are you *doing*?" I continued to tug and pull. "Let me go!"

Those dark, striking features softened, curiosity lighting his gaze.

"Please," I begged, easing my struggles. I peered up at him, falling still and filling my eyes with a plea. "I have to go. Please, let me *go*."

The corners of his mouth tensed, and his eyes narrowed, just a little. And then he released me.

I stumbled backward a few steps before turning and racing down the path that followed the back of the inn, no clue where I was headed but knowing I had to get away, as far and as fast as possible. Back to the quay maybe? If I found the friendly boatman, perhaps I could convince him to carry me down the river at least part of the way to Men-nefer.

I heard thundering footsteps before some of my pursuers rounded the corner of the inn. It was two of the armed men from the courtyard. They slowed when they spotted me.

I skidded to a stop, wincing as chunks of gravel in the hard-packed dirt gouged the sensitive soles of my bare feet. My heart jackhammered in my chest, my stomach sinking, a leaden knot.

Hands partially raised, I slowly backed away even as the armed men advanced on me.

Until the slap of leather on stone behind me announced the arrival of even more company. A glance over my shoulder revealed it to be the armed woman and two more of her companions emerging from the back door. Another pair from the group appeared around the far corner of the inn.

I frantically scanned my surroundings, a wild, cornered creature. I considered fleeing into the garden, but then what? There was nothing but fields of waist-high grain everywhere I looked, leaving me nowhere to hide if I did run. On top of that dire reality, I was hungry and exhausted from the events of the day. And these people looked fresh and spry. They would be on me in a heartbeat.

"Didn't want to get your hands dirty?" the woman said as she trotted down the inn's back steps.

The scarred man gave her a flat look as she passed him.

I turned my attention back to the armed men nearest me. If I could get my hands on one of their curved swords, there was a chance I would be able to cut them both down and flee around the corner of the inn. Then, if I made it to Waset proper before they caught me, I might be able to disappear.

I stopped backing away and settled into a defensive stance. But even as I considered fighting my way out of this, a process that would invariably end up getting someone killed—either them, or me—my conviction to fight wavered and died.

I had already killed people. I had already removed lives that were supposed to go on. And I had vowed to never—*never*—do it again.

Shoulders slumping, I lowered my hands and hung my head. "Please," I said to nobody in particular. "You don't have to do this. Just let me go. Let me walk away."

Fingers curled around my arm. "We have our orders, divine one," the woman said from my side. "We have to bring you in."

One of the men in front of me stepped forward, taking hold of my other arm. Together, they pulled me into motion. I dragged my feet for all of three steps, then begrudgingly walked alongside them toward the back corner of the inn.

"Wait," one man behind me said, his voice a deep rumble that seemed to resonate within me. It was him—the scarred man. Though I had not yet heard him speak, I knew with every fiber of my being that the voice belonged to him.

We stopped, and all three of us looked back at him.

He stared pointedly at my feet.

The woman gripping my arm sighed, then made eye contact with another of the men further back and nodded toward the door to the inn. "Ask the serving girl to let you into her room and fetch her shoes."

The woman's lackey hustled back into the inn.

While we waited, I studied the scarred man indirectly, gratitude for his consideration of my comfort battling with hatred for him delaying my escape. His focus on me was far more direct, and needing a distraction, I turned my attention to the woman at my side. So far as I could tell, she was in charge.

"Where are you taking me?" I asked, studying her profile as she stared after her man. She had the black hair and bronze skin common to this region. Soft features contrasted the steely glint in her dark eyes.

"To see Inyotef," she told me.

"Who's Inyotef?"

She eyed me sidelong, like she wasn't sure what to make of me. "The overlord." She looked ahead. "Inyotef runs Waset and the surrounding territories."

My lip curled. "Well, he's not doing a very good job."

At a muffled snort of masculine laughter, we both glanced toward the small group of warriors, but it was impossible to say which of the men had hidden the laugh. Was it him—the scarred man? I pushed my shoulders back and stood a little taller as I returned to looking at the woman. At least *someone* agreed with me that this *overlord* was doing a shit job at running Waset.

"What does Inyotef want with me?" I asked.

The woman shrugged. "He doesn't explain himself to me." She frowned and shook her head. "He wanted me to bring you to the palace, so I'm bringing you to the palace."

I huffed out a breath, frustrated with the useless answers. "Well, am I to be a prisoner?"

"Don't know," she said. "Don't care."

I ground my teeth together, biting back a retort as I considered the extreme lack of information she was giving me. The way I saw it, either the overlord—this *Inyotef*—wanted to see me because of the incident in the market today or because I was Nejeret. Either way, I needed to keep my head down and my mouth shut.

If Inyotef wanted to talk, I would listen. If he wanted to punish me, I would take it. This was all temporary. I was a reed in the wind of his will; I would bend, but I would not break.

And I would not kill. Not again. Never again.

ONCE MY SANDALS WERE on my feet, I was escorted through the quiet town to a main road that led north of Waset. Here, it was all sprawling orchards and grain fields as far as the eye could see. To the right of the road, the Eastern Desert rose from the horizon in shadowed mounds that blotted out the stars. Fanning date palms and bushy acacia trees blocked whatever view the scant moonlight may have afforded of the Nile or the limestone cliffs beyond the far bank of the river.

The woman apparently in charge of my escort walked at my side the entire two-hour jaunt through Waset and the outlying northern territory, though she released my arm as soon as we left the town proper. The scarred man brought up the rear of our group, while the rest of the men spread out ahead of and behind us.

Every once in a while, I snuck a peek back at the scarred man. He intrigued me to no end, and not only because of his striking appearance, though that certainly didn't dampen my interest in him.

He wasn't Egyptian, at least, not in the cultural sense. Place of birth was irrelevant here so long as one adopted the local culture. Which meant the ancients of this land came in every possible shade of skin, from lily white to the deepest ebony, so it wasn't his dark skin that set him apart or even his towering stature and bulky build compared to his companions. But scarification absolutely was *not* a part of ancient Egyptian culture. The intricate designs cut into his skin all over the front of his torso, shoulders, and arms marked him as *other*.

So who was he? And why was he so fixated on *me*?

About half a mile outside of Waset, our group veered off the main road and headed up a narrower pathway that followed a canal cut between two grain fields. At the end of the path, the fields opened to a palatial structure. Starlight gleamed off the ten-foot wall guarding its front, suggesting the wall was constructed of limestone rather than the cheaper and more readily available mudbrick favored in Waset. The wall's height dropped a couple of feet at the center, over a rectangular wooden gate.

The scarred man picked up the pace, passing us as we approached the closed gate. He raised his fist and knocked on the wood door, the rhythmic pattern too long and precise not to be a code, or maybe a password.

A moment later, there was a deep, creaking sound on the other side of the gate, and then the door swung inward. The scarred man had to duck to pass through the gateway without scraping the top of his shaved head against the underside of the stone head jamb, the threshold of which couldn't have been higher than six feet. Plenty high for the rest of us, but not even close to high enough for him. As soon as he was through, he turned to the left and disappeared from view.

The woman stuck close to my side as I passed through the gate, but the rest of the escort slipped away. Straight ahead, polished limestone stairs led from the open-air entryway to a shadowed reception hall filled with vibrantly painted columns. As soon as we were inside the palace walls, the woman led me to the left, following in the scarred man's wake.

We caught up to him in a courtyard surrounded by tall date palms and other shorter, fruiting trees. A long, rectangular pool filled the center of the courtyard. The scarred man stood under an arbor near the side wall, talking with a man who barely reached his chin. The smaller man was lean, the bronze skin of his torso bared to reveal a toned physique.

He turned toward us as we approached, revealing a face that was boy-band pretty, with light eyes that contrasted with the black kohl drawn along his lash lines. His gaze scanned me from head to toe before slowly trailing back up.

My escort grabbed my arm and pulled me to a stop a few paces shy of reaching the pair. I glanced at her, then returned my attention to the smaller of the two men, who watched me closely. Was this Inyotef, the overlord of Waset, the leader of these lands? If so, he was far younger than I had expected.

"If that is all you require of me?" the scarred man said, his voice a low rumble.

It was only the second time I had heard him speak, but once again, I was struck by the rightness of his voice. He sounded exactly how he should, not that I had any clue how or why I would think that.

"Yes," the smaller man said, not taking his eyes off me. "Thank you, Temu."

The scarred man—Temu, apparently—bowed his head, turned, and passed through a doorway in the wall at the back of the courtyard, retreating further into the palace. In his absence, the silence stretched out, filling the night.

I rubbed my thumbs against my fingers, fidgeting under the hushed scrutiny. "You must be Inyotef," I said when I couldn't take the quiet any longer.

The man's lips spread into a sly grin, and his eyes glittered with intelligence. "Indeed, I am—Inyotef, Great Overlord of Waset, at your service." He bowed his head in greeting. "But I'm afraid you have me at something of a disadvantage. You know who I am, but nobody in Waset seems to have any idea who *you* are." He scanned my body again as he raised his head until his keen-eyed stare focused on my face. "What is your name, divine one?"

The corners of my mouth tensed. "*Divine one* will do for now." I noted the faintest twitch around Inyotef's eyes, despite his smile holding steady. He wasn't used to being disobeyed. Good to know.

"A woman of mystery," Inyotef murmured. "How intriguing."

His smile faded, and he gestured toward a stone bench set off to the side of the courtyard, bordered by a pair of tall date palms. A tray rested on the center of the bench, holding a pair of faience chalices and a matching pitcher with a single, curved handle.

"Sit with me, won't you, divine one?" Inyotef started toward the bench. "Let us share a cup of wine and get to know one another."

I glanced at my escort, raising my eyebrows. What the hell was this? Chatting over wine? I had been steeling myself to be tossed into a dungeon.

My escort shrugged unhelpfully.

Reluctantly, I followed Inyotef. He lowered himself onto one end of the bench, and I hesitated only for a moment before easing down on the other end. Inyotef angled his knees toward me. I sat straight-backed and stiff, one leg crossed over the other, my dangling foot pointing away from him.

I watched my escort retreat to the edge of the courtyard, where she stood out of the way but continued to keep watch.

Inyotef lifted the pitcher and filled the cups two-thirds of the way full with wine that was the deep red of garnets, then held one chalice out for me to take. Flickering torchlight gleamed off the thick gold cuffs on his wrists, illuminating the winged scarabs made up of semi-precious stones.

I reached past the proffered cup of wine for the other, still on the tray. Just in case. I watched Inyotef's face carefully, but his friendly mask remained this time. Not even an eye twitched to betray him if he was annoyed by my mistrust.

This close, I upped his status from boy-band pretty to movie-star handsome, with disarming hazel eyes—an unusually pale eye color for someone with his bronze complexion—and confidence and charisma rolling off him in waves. Had he been born four thousand years later, he would have fit right in with all the A-listers whose elbows I so frequently rubbed.

We stared at one another, his gaze tracing pathways all over my face. I held my chalice with the base resting on my knee, waiting for Inyotef to take the first sip.

Inyotef inhaled deeply through his nose and angled his head to the side. "Tell me, divine one, what has brought you to my humble land during these dangerous times?" He raised his wine cup to his lips, tilted it back, and swallowed.

I averted my eyes to my own chalice. The faience cup was formed out of long petals reminiscent of a lotus blossom. I traced one such petal with the pad of my thumb, considering how to respond.

"I'm just passing through," I finally said and raised my cup to take a small sip. The wine was light and fruity, with just a hint of tannins and earthy undertones, reminding me of a pinot noir. It really was quite nice.

"On your way to Men-nefer," Inyotef amended for me.

I forced myself to swallow, to *not* choke on the wine, and did my best to hide my surprise behind my cup.

He must have been asking around about me down at the harbor. Who had he spoken to? The friendly boatman? Misha, the captain of the *Wedjat*? Usur, the captain of the scumbags?

I suppressed a snort at the thought of what Usur might have said about me.

"Did you travel far?" Inyotef asked, not missing a beat. "I heard you arrived with little more than the clothes on your back, though it seems you have acquired more since then."

I lowered my chalice to once again rest the base on my knee and stared down at the glistening ruby surface of the wine. "I traveled light, and over some distance," I said, choosing my words carefully. "Thankfully, I was able to replenish my resources quickly upon reaching Waset." I raised my eyes, meeting Inyotef's, and curved my lips into the polite, practiced smile I usually reserved for annoying members of the press.

Inyotef's expression mirrored mine, calculating smile for calculating smile. He sipped his wine. I did the same.

"Did you have any trouble on the roads?" he asked, his eyebrows climbing higher and drawing together, as though he was extremely concerned for the safety of my past self.

I returned to studying my wine, focusing on pushing away the disturbing flashes of memory lured to the surface of my mind by his words. "Nothing I couldn't handle," I said quietly.

"Yes, well," Inyotef started, "the road to Waset can be quite dangerous, but Waset itself is often worse."

I gritted my teeth together, biting back a retort. This was his territory. *His* town. If things were so bad—and he knew just how bad they were—then why wasn't he doing something about it?

Inyotef drank from his chalice, then set it in a shallow recess cut into the wall behind us at chest height. I hadn't noticed it was there until he made use of it.

Elbow resting on the lip of the recess, Inyotef leaned in toward me, his expression serious, his stare steady. "I heard about the incident in the market," he said, his voice pitched low. "Whispers on the street speak of retaliation, though they hesitate because of what you are." He gave me a meaningful look. "That hesitation will not last indefinitely."

I set my cup on the bench and crossed my arms over my chest, pressing my lips together. It was growing harder and harder to hold my tongue.

"I had Kiya bring you here for your protection," Inyotef explained, either oblivious to or unperturbed by my increasing annoyance. "You are no longer safe at the inn, and I would be remiss if I allowed a Netjer-At to be harmed in my territory." A sly smile touched his lips. "Especially one so lovely as yourself."

I narrowed my eyes ever so slightly, not buying his altruistic facade for one second.

"My palace has high walls and is guarded day and night," Inyotef said. "I wish you to stay here, divine one, where you will be safe."

I blinked, surprised. I had not expected to be invited to stay here *as a guest*. "I have a choice?" I clarified. "I can leave whenever I want?"

Inyotef laughed, the sound soft and silken. "You are not a prisoner, divine one." He shook his head, sobering quickly. "While you are here, you are my *most honored* guest." His eyes locked with mine, heat igniting in his gaze.

I reclaimed my chalice and lifted it to my lips. "I've booked passage on a ship heading downriver in four weeks' time."

"The *Wedjat*," Inyotef said. "Yes, I heard."

I flashed him a brief, tightlipped smile. "When that ship leaves, I *will* be on it."

"If that is your desire," he said, leaning back against the wall. He reached for his wine cup. "*Or* you could join me on *my* ship. I am heading to

Men-nefer myself in two weeks. I would be happy to carry you downriver, as my most honored guest."

My eyes widened, then narrowed. Why? *Why* was he so persistent about helping me? Nothing in life was free. Inyotef wanted something from me beyond his apparent carnal interest—something he had been interested in attaining before he ever laid eyes on me. But *what* did he want? My Netjer-At connections? If that was the case, I definitely wouldn't be sharing with him that I was, for all intents and purposes, estranged from my people.

"You leave in two weeks?" I asked. "Truly?"

Inyotef nodded.

Taking him up on his offer would cut my waiting time in half, plus I could save the six gold tokens I had set aside to pay my fare, as well as the two I owed the innkeeper for my room and board for the remainder of my stay. *And*, if Inyotef spoke the truth about the thugs I had beaten up in the warehouse, and they really were after me, I couldn't stay at the inn anyway.

"Besides," Inyotef expounded, "I daresay the accommodations here in the palace and on my ship will be a great deal more comfortable than those you had arranged."

I watched Inyotef closely as he spoke, studying his eyes, searching for signs of deceit. His hands remained steady on his cup. His gaze never faltered. His voice didn't crack, and his tone didn't waver. He didn't stutter or stumble over his words. He was calm, confident, and comfortable.

I sipped my wine, considering Inyotef's offer. No matter what angle I examined the situation from, I snagged on the same question.

"Why extend such generosity toward me?" I asked, voicing my primary concern.

Of course, there was always the timeline to think of, especially if I was going to be hanging around the ancient Egyptian equivalent of a governor. But if I kept my head down and my mouth shut—and parted ways with Inyotef as soon as we reached Men-nefer—I figured the potential harm to the timeline would be far less than if I bumbled through the land on my own.

Inyotef returned my assessing stare. "One never knows when one might need to call in a favor owed for a favor given."

I nodded to myself, put at ease by his open admission that he wasn't helping me out of the goodness of his heart. He would expect something from me in return. Not right now, but one day.

Well, he didn't know that one day, I wouldn't be here. One day, I would be thousands of years away, where he couldn't reach me to call in his favor.

"Very well," I said, bowing my head to hide any duplicity Inyotef might have read on my face. "I accept your offer."

I WOKE TO THE muted orange light of dawn streaming in through the window-like openings cut out of the wall near the ceiling, giving me my first good look at my room in Inyotef's palace. It was very similar to my room at the inn—long, narrow, and sparsely furnished—if perhaps marginally more spacious. It came with the added upgrade of a minimalist wood bed frame rather than a mudbrick sleeping platform, covered by a slightly more robust pad. All in all, the bed was a noticeable improvement. I still woke with a crick in my neck, just not one quite so severe. However, the door–or lack thereof–was a major downgrade.

I tossed and turned all night. Every time I drifted off, I startled awake, imagining I had heard someone pushing aside the heavy linen curtain that blocked the doorway. But once I was awake, heart pounding and eyes straining in the darkness, I heard nothing but silence within the room.

Eyes gritty and swollen from the poor night's sleep, I sat up and reached my arms over my head, arching my back until my whole body shook with the stretch. I had always been more of a night owl than an early bird, enjoying a nice, long morning linger.

I dropped my arms and stared down at the thin wannabe mattress. I wondered if the ancients purposely made their beds so uncomfortable to prevent such morning laziness, because I seemed to have transformed into a morning person since I started sleeping on them.

I climbed out of bed and padded over to the chamber pot tucked behind a screen to take care of my morning business. Once finished, I retrieved the thick ceramic basin and water pitcher from where I had placed them just inside the doorway the previous night—my poor man's alarm system—and moved them to the low table tucked into the corner of the room, pushing the empty food tray from my evening meal out of the way.

I removed my shift and gave myself a thorough sponge bath, then pulled the thin linen dress back over my head. I made a mental note to ask Inyotef to retrieve my things from the inn. I was *so* over wearing the same clothes for days on end. Besides, I wanted my weapons.

At least the room came with a toiletry chest. Kneeling on a floor cushion, I cleaned my teeth with a frayed tooth stick and some natron paste, carefully applied kohl around my eyes, and combed out my hair before weaving it into a long, thick braid that hung down my spine. As soon as I had my blades from the inn, I was chopping off most of my hair's inconvenient length.

I headed toward the curtained doorway, debating between searching for the kitchen to snag an early breakfast or exploring the palace and grounds before the sun rose fully and the whole place awakened. I wasn't all that hungry yet, and by the time I pushed the azure curtain aside, I had settled on exploring.

I yelped and slapped a hand over my mouth when I spotted someone leaning against the wall to the right of my doorway. I took a few, skittering sidesteps and clutched my chest, like doing so might somehow calm my racing heart.

It was the woman who had led my escort party the previous evening, wearing the same masculine uniform as before—banded leather cuirass, white linen kilt, and sword belt with one of those strange, scythe-like blades.

She eyed me sidelong, her arms crossed over her chest, her shoulders bobbing with a lazy chuckle. *Gotcha* glittered in her dark eyes.

I allowed myself a full three seconds to glare before lowering my hands and willing my tensed muscles to relax. "What are you doing sneaking around outside my room?"

Mock innocence widened her eyes. "I'm not sneaking," she said. "I'm standing." She flashed me a sly grin. "Well, technically, I'm *leaning*."

I studied her through narrowed eyes. "Are you spying on me?"

"Spying? No." She pushed off the wall, widening her stance and casually glancing up and down the hallway. "Inyotef assigned me as your primary guard. Figured you would be more comfortable with me than any of the men. Plus, they're all idiots." She flashed me a tightlipped smile. "And I'm not."

I frowned, surprised by Inyotef's consideration. "All right, well . . . I was going to go for a walk." I started down the hallway. "So I'll just be on my way."

I was three steps past her when I heard quiet footsteps behind me. I stopped and slowly turned around, my lips pursed and my eyes narrowed. "What are you doing?"

She blinked guilelessly. "Following you."

"Perhaps I was unclear," I said. "I would like to go for a walk *alone*."

"Noted."

I nodded once, confident we had reached an understanding, and turned away to continue down the hallway. Again, I heard footsteps behind me as she followed.

I whirled around, my eyebrows raised and hands planted on my hips. "I said I wanted to walk alone." My tone was razor edged.

She remained uncowed. "You did. And I said 'noted' to let you know I heard you." She flashed me a quick smile, there and gone in a blink, but it didn't touch her bold stare. "But *I* want to avoid being whipped for disobeying orders." She wrinkled her nose. "Where you go, I go. Sorry." She was clearly not sorry.

Would Inyotef really have her whipped for not following his orders? The more I thought about it, the less shocking it seemed.

I inhaled deeply through my nose, then released the breath through my mouth. "I guess I don't have much of a say in the matter, do I?"

The guard shook her head. "No, you don't."

My hands slipped off my hips to hang at my sides. "All right," I sighed. "Well, I guess we're going to be spending some time together. You're name is Kiya?"

She bowed her head. "It's an honor to serve you, *divine one*."

I snorted a laugh at her impudent tone.

"And what should I call you?" Kiya asked as she straightened. "Or shall I cycle through the terms of address used for your kind?" She followed her question with another of those too-innocent blinks and vacant smiles.

I grinned, suppressing another laugh. I kind of liked this chick. Her friendly irreverence was refreshing.

I considered continuing to go nameless—it had worked well enough among Ineni's clan—but I wasn't sure I could handle many more cheeky honorifics from Kiya. Surely it couldn't hurt anything to pick a name to go by, especially if that name wasn't actually *mine*. I thought of young Bek, the only person in this time who knew my true name, and smiled to myself.

"Bek," I said, putting one degree of separation between me and my true identity. "You can call me Bek."

"Well then," Kiya said with a deeper bow of her head. "It is an honor to serve you, Bek." This time, the words didn't drip with quite so much sarcasm.

As Kiya straightened, I gestured to the hallway with a sweep of my arm. "You might as well walk with me rather than trailing behind." I resumed walking down the hall, and Kiya fell in step beside me. "Would you mind showing me around? I'd love to see the grounds."

"If that's what you would like," Kiya drawled.

After a right turn and a left, the hallway led to a larger reception hall, lined by columns painted with vibrant greens, yellows, blues, and whites to resemble bunches of white lotus flowers. Kiya guided me toward a large rectangular doorway at one end of the hall, which dumped us into a smaller chamber with narrow doorways cut into the walls on either side and the closed and barred wooden gate straight ahead. A pair of armed men guarded the exit.

"Open the gate," Kiya commanded, stopping in front of the gate.

The guards exchanged a look. "But the sun has not yet risen," the one on the left said.

"Open the gate," Kiya repeated, no change to her tone.

The chattier guard inhaled, as though planning to protest further, but Kiya silenced him with a look. The mute guard moved to stand in front of the gate, his back to us. His buddy begrudgingly joined him, and together, they lifted the thick wooden beam holding the gate closed. Once they—and the beam—were out of the way, Kiya stepped forward to haul the heavy door open.

"Lock the gate behind us," she tossed over her shoulder as we strode outside.

The palace complex was essentially a huge, self-sustaining farm with all anyone would need to survive. On her tour, Kiya showed me through a stunning walled vegetable garden and an orchard, around pens and pastures holding cattle, donkeys, sheep, and geese, and into an enormous granary holding row after row of huge storage containers shaped like brick beehives. There were actual beehives, too, back by the orchard and garden.

We strolled between rows of grapevines in the vineyard that extended behind the villa's back wall, the sun peeking over the mountainous dunes at the edge of the Eastern Desert beyond the vineyard. I stopped when I spotted movement at the crest of one of the nearest, shortest dunes. I squinted, focusing, and a distant figure took on a more distinct, distinguishable shape. A man.

And not just any man. The scarred man, who I found so incredibly fascinating. Temu, I recalled Inyotef calling him the previous night.

Kiya continued ahead of me, but stopped and turned to face me when she realized I was no longer trailing behind her. She peered over her shoulder, following my line of sight toward the horizon. "Ah, yes, the prince," she said, turning back to me.

She retraced her steps, coming to stand nearby. "Nobody knows exactly what he does out there, all by himself. He goes to the edge of the desert every morning at sunrise and spends an hour doing *something*." She gazed out at him, his figure no doubt indistinct to her human eyes. "I think he's praying," she added.

Her first words finally registered, and I glanced at her, only taking my eyes off Temu for the briefest moment. "Did you say, *prince*?"

Kiya nodded distractedly. "From Kush," she explained.

I wasn't positive, but I wanted to say Kush was an ancient name for Nubia.

"Beyond the first cataract?" I clarified, and when she nodded, I had my confirmation. "If he's a prince, why is he here—and why is he taking orders from Inyotef?"

Kiya frowned. "You know, I never really thought about it. He just showed up one day." She shrugged. "I figured he was here as leverage—a way for us to ensure the Kushite king behaves."

"How fascinating," I murmured, watching Temu's intriguing ritual with renewed interest.

Kiya and the other humans living in Inyotef's palace may have had to speculate about what Temu did each morning out on that dune, but my eyesight was good enough that I could see exactly what he was up to. In one hand, he held a small dagger with a gleaming black blade. Roughly every ten seconds, he carefully flicked the tip of the blade over his skin, drawing a bright bead of blood. So far as I could tell, he seemed to be retracing the pattern of his scars with the blade.

I couldn't look away. Was Kiya right and this was some form of prayer?

After minutes of watching the strange ritual, I felt too much like a voyeur. I turned away from the eastern horizon—and from the enigmatic prince—and retraced our steps, fighting the urge to look back.

19

THE WALK AROUND THE palace grounds roused my appetite, and by the time Kiya and I reached the front gate, I was more than ready to find the kitchen.

"In a moment, Bek," Kiya said when I voiced my desire for food as we entered the villa. "Inyotef will want to see you first."

I pressed my lips together but didn't argue. Doing so wouldn't get me anywhere, not with her.

Kiya led me back into the courtyard from the previous evening, through the doorway on the left side of the entry chamber to the palace. In the cheerful morning sunlight, the courtyard was a lush, verdant space. The surface of the water in the long, rectangular pool rippled like molten gold around lily pads and blue lotus flowers, and tiny birds flitted from tree to tree, singing their good mornings.

Inyotef occupied the same stone bench as before. Only now, the chalices and pitcher were perched on the recessed alcove in the wall behind him, and in their place, the tray beside him on the bench overflowed with fresh fruit, disks of flatbread, and a bowl of something that looked like mush, but might have been a soft cheese. I didn't care. My mouth watered at the feast, regardless.

Inyotef stared blankly up at another man, who stood before him in only a linen schenti—no weapons or armor—recounting an extremely abbreviated series of violent and troubling incidents in what I took to be Inyotef's morning briefing. When Inyotef spotted us approaching, he held up one hand, and the man standing before him fell silent.

"We'll finish this later," Inyotef said in dismissal.

The other man bowed before turning and heading for a doorway at the far end of the courtyard.

Inyotef's expression brightened as his eyes locked on me. "Divine one," he said, standing.

We stopped a few paces away, standing near the edge of the pool.

Inyotef was even more dashing in the daylight, like the warm tones of his skin and eyes soaked up the sunlight and reflected it. And without Temu around to dwarf him, he didn't seem small at all.

"I looked for you in your room first thing this morning," Inyotef said, "but you were not there, and I grew worried." His bunched brows emphasized his words.

"I wanted to explore," I said, purposely not apologizing or confirming to make sure my exploring was all right with him. I would not ask him for forgiveness or permission—for *anything*. Doing so would imply that he had any say at all over my actions, and I was determined to keep a tight leash on my own agency during my stay here.

Inyotef had claimed I wasn't a prisoner, but I couldn't rid myself of the fear that all his talk about my status as a guest was mostly lip service. I was tempted to pretend to leave if only to see how he would react.

"Perfectly fine, of course," Inyotef said, giving his approval anyway. "Sit, won't you?" He gestured to the vacant end of the bench. "Break your fast with me. I know the Netjer-At are known for having large appetites, and I would hate for you to feel mistreated in my home."

"Very well," I said, moving closer.

Inyotef's focus shifted past me as I neared the bench, locking onto Kiya. "Next time, notify me if you plan to leave the palace walls with our guest." A command, not a request.

My hands balled into tight fists at the remark, and I forced my fingers to unflex. So many things bothered me about that simple order. Inyotef wanted to keep tabs on me, but he hadn't *asked me* to keep him informed of *my own* whereabouts. He had commanded Kiya to keep him in the loop. Like I was a child who needed close tending, not a responsible adult who could take care of herself.

"Leave us," he ordered, his tone sharp, and lowered himself back down to the bench.

I clenched my jaw and held my tongue as I sat, wishing I could go with Kiya. I wasn't all that excited about navigating the dangerous waters surrounding a private tête-à-tête with the overlord of *this entire region*. Keep it light. Small talk. Chit chat. Talk about the weather. Were there any sports in this time period? I could ask him about the plants in the courtyard, and if there were any fish in the pool.

When Inyotef's attention returned to me, I offered him a pleasant smile, my mind continuing to flip through an imaginary Rolodex in search of mundane topics of conversation. The smile touched my eyes. I knew because I had practiced this same smile thousands of times in front of a mirror.

"Did you enjoy your walk?" Inyotef asked, reaching behind the bench for the pitcher tucked away in the recessed alcove. He poured rose-colored wine into both chalices and handed one to me.

"I did, thank you," I said, taking a sip of wine when what I really wanted was coffee. But I knew all too well that none was to be had.

I set my cup beside me on the bench and picked up a flatbread from the tray. It was soft and squishy, and still slightly warm from the oven.

"You have a beautiful estate," I told Inyotef before tearing off a piece of bread and putting it in my mouth. A little bit nutty. A little bit sweet. A little bit salty. Yum.

Inyotef sipped his wine, smiling to himself.

"Temu is a prince," I said, unable to stop myself from blurting out one of the less mundane topics at the forefront of my mind.

I watched Inyotef's face closely, curious if he had purposely withheld that information from me. He certainly hadn't offered it up last night. He hadn't even introduced us to one another—the Nejeret and the prince staying in his home. Did he not think me worthy of introduction? Or was it Temu who fell short in his estimation?

Inyotef's eyes widened, then narrowed, his focus locking on Kiya's retreating form as irritation flickered across his features. So he *had* been trying to hide it. Why?

"Indeed he is," Inyotef said after a moment, his friendly expression returning when he refocused on me.

"I saw him on the hill at sunrise," I said, wondering what more Inyotef might inadvertently tell me if I pursued the subject.

Powerful men loved explaining things to others, especially women they wanted to impress. I mean, *mansplaining* is a thing, after all.

I tilted my head to the side, my brow furrowing. "Was he praying?"

Inyotef shrugged one shoulder and leaned back against the wall behind the bench. "Perhaps," he said, staring across the courtyard, his gaze unfocused. "I asked Temu about it once, and he told me he was honoring the dead. He wouldn't tell me more, no matter how much I pried." Inyotef's eyebrows crept upward. "Or how much wine I poured into his cup."

I considered that bit of insight as I chewed my next bite.

If Temu was honoring the dead out there at the edge of the desert, did that mean each scar represented a life—or, rather, a life *ended*? Whose lives? His people in Kush? His ancestors? There had to be hundreds, maybe thousands, of scars on his torso, shoulders, and arms. None on his back, which made sense if they were self-inflicted. His cuts must have been very shallow, mere nicks. And did he cycle through which scars he reopened each morning? I hadn't noticed any scabs on him the previous evening, and I had spent plenty of time sneaking glances his way.

I plucked a fig from the tray, turning it around and around in my fingers. "He truly goes out there every morning?" I raised the fig to my mouth and bit into its soft flesh.

"Every day since he arrived here," Inyotef said, a sharp edge to his tone.

I felt his eyes on the side of my face, but I didn't look at him. He wanted my attention focused on him. It ruffled his feathers when I asked about Temu, which was perfect because I preferred to keep Inyotef off balance when he was around me. The universe knew I'd had plenty of practice with dealing with powerful men like Inyotef. *Cough, cough*—my dad.

"Why such an interest in the prince, divine one?" That sharp edge was more pronounced now.

I suppressed a smirk. Jealousy was such a beautifully predictable emotion.

Inyotef was interested in me as a woman, as he had made clear enough the previous night. His interest would only grow if he believed *me* to be interested in *someone else*. So long as I didn't give him any reason to believe I had acted on that other interest, he would put more and more effort into winning me over. I wondered if I might even be able to get him to set sail for Men-nefer early. Perhaps to separate me from Temu?

"Just curious," I said and glanced at Inyotef sidelong, a coy smile twisting my lips.

Physically, he and Temu were night and day from one another, but Inyotef was just as easy on the eyes. I couldn't say much yet about their personalities, comparatively, but Temu had given off some serious strong-silent-type vibes in the short time I had known him, a stark contrast to Inyotef's commanding, charismatic presence.

It wouldn't be so difficult to string Inyotef along. I thought I might even enjoy the game.

"Curious about Temu?" Inyotef clarified.

"Mmhmm," I murmured dreamily, raising my cup to take a sip of wine. I sighed and lowered my chalice, resting it on my palm and curling my fingers around the base. I played the infatuated woman for another few seconds, then cleared my throat and sat up a little straighter. "What I mean is—" I finally looked at Inyotef. "I haven't had the chance to interact with many people from Kush, and I enjoy learning about unfamiliar cultures."

"I see," Inyotef said cooly. "And what of *your* culture, divine one? Your accent is unique. I have heard nothing quite like it. From what region do you hail?"

I picked up another flatbread from the tray, carefully thinking through my response. These were some of the dark, dangerous waters I had been trying to avoid. "My homeland is very far away from here," I said, considering what more I could safely share. "It is a place called *America*."

Surely revealing that couldn't hurt—Inyotef would be thousands of years dead by the time the name of America was ever used to refer to the great continent across the Atlantic Ocean.

"America," Inyotef said, testing the word out. "I have never heard of such a place."

I nodded. "It's beyond the Western Desert," I explained. "Far, far beyond the desert and across a vast sea."

"I shall have to take your word for it," Inyotef said. "What is this *America* like? Filled with handsome suitors vying for your attention? Perhaps a husband?"

I chuckled, the reaction genuine. "You must not be too familiar with my kind's customs. We rarely settle," I explained. "We prefer to keep our options open."

It was the truth. Pairings like my dad and Lex, or Kat and Nik, were rare, driven by their soul bonds. Most Nejerets rarely entered monogamous relationships. Likely a product of our crazy long lives. Usually, it was only the young—like me—who still clung to such human traditions. And after the messy ending to my relationship with Wolf, I was ready to be done with monogamy as well.

Inyotef's eyes glittered disarmingly as he studied my face. Flecks of leaf-green, slate-gray, and honey-gold warred for dominance in his irises. "But you didn't say you lack suitors in your land."

I didn't bother to conceal the sly smile that curved my lips. "No, I didn't."

"Merely that your options are open."

"Always." Demurely, I lowered my gaze to the bowl of fruit on the tray and picked at a bunch of tiny purple grapes with skin so dark it was almost black.

At the sound of someone approaching, Inyotef tore his attention away from me.

I looked up as well, a grape pinched between my thumb and the tip of my forefinger, forgotten halfway to my mouth.

Temu approached from the front of the courtyard, his stride quick and sure.

My focus instantly locked on his chest, where I had distinctly seen him draw blood with the tip of that black-bladed dagger. There were no open cuts. There was no hint of redness. No scabbing. No sign beyond the existing scars that his skin had ever been broken.

Eyes narrowing, I scanned all the visible skin on his body. All the *unbroken* skin. I had seen blood. I knew I had. No human could have healed that fast.

I pressed my lips together and raised my gaze to Temu's face, scrutinizing his strong features as I searched for any sense of that otherworldly tingle that charged the air around Nejerets. But there was nothing. He looked—and felt—human.

But he wasn't. He couldn't be. Humans didn't heal that quickly.

Which meant Temu was Nejeret.

His attention shifted from Inyotef to me as he drew closer. When his dark eyes met mine, they held a challenge. He knew. He knew *I* knew his secret. And for whatever reason, he didn't want Inyotef to know, too. His stare dared me to reveal the truth he had so carefully concealed.

I smirked, enjoying this little bit of power I now held over Temu. I nodded infinitesimally, letting him know I would hold my tongue.

For now.

"I 'LL RETURN AT FIRST light," Kiya said, standing just inside the doorway to my room, the azure curtain providing a striking backdrop behind her. It would have been a great selfie background—had cameras existed. "You'll never even notice I'm gone."

Feet rooted to the floor in the middle of my room, I bit back a snide remark. I would notice her absence because I would *know*. I would know it wasn't Kiya posted outside my room all night but some guy Kiya introduced as Taki. I thought he may have been one of the guards who had been a part of my escort to the palace, but I couldn't be sure.

Kiya arched one eyebrow higher, and the corner of her mouth twitched, like she could sense my bottled-up retort. "You'll be asleep, and by the time you wake, I'll be here." Her lips curved into a closed-mouth smile.

"I'm sure I'll be fine without you," I said, projecting the easy calm I wanted to feel. Fake it till you make it. And in my profession, faking it was an art form.

I was ashamed to admit that Kiya had become something of a security blanket to me over the *single day* we had spent together. I hadn't realized just how much I was relying on her presence to make me feel safe in Inyotef's palace until she informed me she was off duty for the night.

I fought the urge to beg her not to go. To offer my floor—hell, she could take my bed and *I* would sleep on the floor—if only she would stay.

"Goodnight, Bek," Kiya said, bowing her head.

I consciously kept my hands relaxed at my sides, my features placid. "Goodnight, Kiya," I said, the embodiment of serenity. On the outside.

And then Kiya turned, pushed the curtain aside, and was gone.

Unease twisted my stomach into knots, and I chewed on my thumbnail as I paced back and forth across the room. Every time I turned to retrace my steps, I glanced at the curtained-off doorway. My new guard, Taki, was on the other side of that heavy blue curtain. He would continue to be there until Kiya returned in the morning, and unless I planned to pace the room all night, I figured I should just go to bed already.

I huffed out a heavy breath and made my way to the small pile of my things arranged against one of the longer side walls. They had been waiting for me here when I returned to my room after the morning meal with Inyotef. Him having ordered my things retrieved from the inn without my even having to ask both surprised me and calmed my nerves about staying here. But I still wasn't cool with the lack of a door.

As quietly as possible, I moved all of my possessions over to the doorway, recreating my booby trap from the previous night with the added items from the inn. Once everything was arranged just so, I stepped back to assess my work. A basket full of clothing, a small wooden case, a toiletry chest, a washbasin, and a pitcher—hardly enough to stop anyone determined to enter the room, but at least any intruders were likely to trip over the clutter and make enough noise to wake me.

Nodding to myself, I retreated to the bed at the far end of the narrow room. I stretched out on the thin pad, noting that it was just as uncomfortable as I remembered. But I was exhausted from walking around the palace grounds and exploring within the villa, and I fell asleep quickly.

It was staying asleep that was the issue. Every hint of a whisper or scuffle from outside roused me, and by the time pale dawn light poured through the window cutouts high in the wall beside my bed, I was wide awake, waiting to rise and shine.

I dragged myself out of bed, limbs heavy and mind fuzzy from the restless night, and cleared away the tripping hazard in front of the doorway. Once everything was back in its rightful place, I washed up, donned a new shift, applied fresh kohl around my eyes, strapped on my weapons belt and sandals, and headed for the doorway. I was on a mission this morning. I needed to confirm what I had seen on that dune. I had to make absolutely sure Temu was Nejeret before I confronted him.

I pushed the curtain aside and stepped out into the hallway, bracing myself to encounter a stranger.

"You're up early," Kiya said, lounging against the wall opposite my doorway, her hand resting on the pommel of her sword, cool chick vibes rolling off her in waves. "Again."

I brightened instantly, my lips spreading into a broad grin. "Kiya!" I toned down my giddiness a few notches and cleared my throat. "I didn't think you'd be back this early."

She raised one eyebrow and cocked her head to the side. "Did I not say I would return at first light?"

"Well, yeah," I admitted, laughing under my breath.

"Then you didn't believe me?" Both eyebrows were up now.

"Not exactly." I glanced away.

Kiya pushed off the wall. "Bek," she said, coming to stand in front of me and looking into my eyes point blank. "You have trust issues."

She had no idea. I had *fill-in-the-blank* issues. Trust issues. Mommy issues. Daddy issues. Timeline issues. Resurrection issues. My life had turned into a Mad Libs of suckage.

A hysteria-tinged laugh burbled up from my chest and burst out of my mouth before I could stop it. I clapped a hand over my mouth, not wanting to wake the rest of the palace, especially not Inyotef. I had a mission to complete before he tracked me down and commandeered my day.

"Come on," I said, linking my arm through Kiya's and pulling her down the hallway alongside me. "I don't want to be late."

"Late?" Kiya threw me some serious side-eye. "For what?"

I glanced at her sidelong, suppressing a giggle. "You'll see."

"All right," Kiya drawled. "At least tell me if this surprise appointment of yours is going to take place outside of the palace because I'll need to let Inyotef know."

My steps slowed and my face fell. I had forgotten about Inyotef's command regarding my comings and goings around here. "Do we have to go see him *now*?"

Kiya laughed dryly. "No. He told me to notify him if you were planning on leaving the palace walls." She flashed me a sneaky smile. "He'll be notified, just not by us." She leaned in close, pitching her voice low like she was sharing a secret. "I'll send one of the gate guards to his room. To wake him. And notify him. As requested." With each added phrase, her smile widened. "He's not known for being an early riser."

I couldn't help but grin in return. Inyotef should have been more careful about the precise verbiage of his command. The devil was in the details, after all. An early morning wake-up call served him right for trying to boss me around.

When we reached the front gate, Kiya sent one of the gate guards scurrying off to notify Inyotef that we were leaving—after he helped his buddy unlock the gate, of course. As he hurried away, we strolled out of the palace with not a care in the world.

I led the way back to the vineyard we had visited the previous morning and walked between two rows of vines toward the easternmost edge. The first sliver of the sun had just peeked over the eastern horizon when we reached the edge of the vineyard.

"What are we doing out here?" Kiya asked, looking around.

I pointed out toward the dunes and the tiny figure of a man trekking up the side of the nearest one. "Watching," I murmured, narrowing my eyes to focus more clearly on Temu.

Kiya moved closer to me, squinting as she strained to see him clearly. Or at all. "Can you really see him all the way out there?"

I nodded.

"Clearly?"

"Uh-huh," I confirmed, distracted.

When Temu reached the peak of the dune, he unfurled a woven mat and laid it out on the ground. He knelt and drew his black-bladed dagger, angling the tip of the blade toward his abdomen.

"What's he doing?" Kiya asked, her voice a low whisper.

I glanced at her, just for a moment. "Some sort of ritual with a knife."

I couldn't tell her he was cutting himself, because then *she* would wonder about his lack of wounds and, in time, come to the same conclusion I had. Secrets were powerful. If his secret came out, I would lose what little power I had over him.

I watched Temu's strange ritual until he cleaned his dagger and re-sheathed it on his belt. By my count, he had cut himself at least six hundred times. Every few minutes, he set down his knife to scoop up a handful of sand and rub it on the freshest wounds. I winced every time he did it. What a strange thing to do. And painful.

My eyes widened and my lips parted as I finally realized the purpose for the sand—the scars. That must have been how he made himself scar. I hadn't been able to figure that part out, since Nejerets healed so perfectly. But Temu's scars were like tattoos—the sand slowed the healing process and left behind raised marks, for a while at least. Just like with tattoos, if he didn't constantly reopen and re-sand the wounds, they would heal until they vanished. Thus, the daily ritual.

The sun had fully risen by the time Temu stood and picked up his mat, shaking it out before rolling it back up and once again tucking it under his arm. He made his way down the side of the dune.

Whatever doubts I may have harbored about Temu's true nature had been obliterated by what I just saw. He was Nejeret.

I turned to Kiya, reaching for her elbow.

She looked a little startled by my sudden movement.

"Do you know what route Temu takes to return to the palace?" I asked.

I wanted to head him off so I could speak with him outside of Inyotef's earshot. Temu was hiding his true nature from Inyotef and everyone else here, and I was determined to find out why.

Reading my urgency loud and clear, Kiya nodded. "Come on," she said, turning and diving back into the vineyard. "It's this way."

KIYA AND I FOLLOWED a well-worn path out toward the desert, bordered on both sides by lush barley fields. The stalks swished and swayed in the light breeze coming up from the Nile. We had ventured well beyond the palace grounds, but if straying so far bothered Kiya, she kept her mouth shut about it. Either it wasn't an issue, or she knew this battle wasn't one she would win.

I was just beginning to wonder if Kiya had mistaken the trail when Temu appeared over a rise ahead. The corners of his full mouth tensed when he spotted me, but he didn't slow. Gods, he was magnificent.

"Can you give us some time alone?" I muttered to Kiya without taking my eyes off the approaching Nejeret. I supposed it didn't matter if his sensitive ears picked up my words, but speaking softly when other Nejerets were around was second nature to me.

"How much time?" Kiya asked, her tone dry.

I glanced at her. The wry twist of her lips and lascivious glint in her eyes told me exactly what she thought I was up to with Temu. I couldn't blame her for the gutter-minded leap. He was a stunning specimen of a man, like a Friesian stallion among Shetland ponies. Nothing against the adorable little horses, but damn. That man was a big, beautiful stallion.

"Stop it," I said, smacking Kiya's arm with the back of my hand even as my neck and cheeks flushed from thoughts of doing all kinds of naughty things with Temu. "It's nothing like *that*." My focus returned to Temu, and I pushed away all thoughts of getting down and dirty with him. Or, at least, *most* thoughts. "I just want to talk to him," I said, my tone carrying a sharp note of defiance.

Kiya snorted.

"I mean it!" I insisted and leveled a beseeching look on her. "Do you mind walking ahead—just for a little while?"

Kiya pursed her lips, uncertainty bunching her brow.

I faced her fully and raised my right hand, three fingers extended in the scout's honor salute. "I promise not to stray from sight," I said and lowered my hand, all seriousness now. "I swear, I just want to talk to him."

After a deep inhale and exhale through her nose, Kiya nodded. "But I'll walk behind the two of you, so I can keep an eye on you."

Without another word, Kiya marched down the trail toward Temu, while I hung back, fidgeting with my fingers. My hands were suddenly clammy, and I wiped them on the skirt of my shift.

When Kiya reached Temu on the trail, she snagged his forearm, and the two paused for a brief stare down. He dwarfed her, not that their size difference seemed to have any impact on her bravado. "I'm watching," she said, her words low and cold when they reached my ears. Had I been human, I definitely wouldn't have heard her warning.

Temu didn't respond, at least not with his voice. Instead, he sent a pointed look down at the place where Kiya's hand gripped his arm.

Kiya made a show of letting go and bowing, sweeping one arm up the trail toward me, inviting him to continue on his merry way. Her mastery of nonverbal sarcasm was incredibly impressive. I thought Kat would have liked her.

My focus locked on Temu as he left Kiya behind—and headed straight for me.

When he reached me, he stopped a few paces back and bowed his head. "Divine one." The gentle rumble of his voice was like a caress, sending a tingle down my spine, and once again, my thoughts took a naughty turn. Would anyone really mind if we rolled around in a barley field for a little while?

Inyotef.

I mentally slapped myself with an image of my admiring host. My ticket downriver. Inyotef would most certainly mind. And what was worse—much worse—was that his wounded ego might force him to turn me out on my ass, no shelter from those who hunted me in Waset, and no ride to Men-nefer.

I cleared my throat and smirked at Temu, thinking a little snark should silence my roaring libido. "Just to be clear," I said dryly, "when you say *divine one*, are you referring to yourself, or to me?"

Temu straightened and studied my face, his bold features locked in a cautious but considering expression.

"Because, the way *I* see it," I went on, taking a small step closer and scanning the intricate pattern of tiny scars decorating his chest and shoulders, "we both have a bit of the divine flowing through our veins." I took another step and raised my hand to ever-so-lightly trail my fingertips over the raised scars fanning along his biceps. Probably not the best idea, but I couldn't resist touching him, just once. I raised my eyes, meeting his. "Helping us heal." I tilted my face up and involuntarily licked my lips.

The black of Temu's pupils expanded, swallowing his warm brown irises. Was that *desire* suddenly burning in his gaze? Because it sure as hell looked like desire. And holy shit, did I want it to be desire.

My breath hitched, a tsunami of lust slamming into me, washing away all cautionary thoughts of Inyotef. My heart raced, and my breaths came too quickly.

Embarrassment over my extreme reaction to Temu snapped me out of the carnal haze, and I withdrew my hand. I blamed the unusual dry spell. It had been years since I had gone longer than a week without getting naked with someone. Until now.

Averting my eyes, I took a hasty step backward and, again, cleared my throat. A full-body flush made me wish that wimpy breeze would ramp up to a hurricane-force gale.

I dragged my stare back to Temu's face, taking in his clenched jaw and the inferno burning in his eyes. At least it wasn't just me who felt this attraction.

"Inyotef doesn't know, does he?" I said, attempting to course correct. I ignored the slight quaver in my voice and shook my head, still studying Temu's face. Even now, all of my senses told me he was human, not Nejeret. "I wouldn't have figured it out if I hadn't seen you cutting yourself out there." I pointed toward the dunes rising behind him with my chin, not taking my eyes off his.

Temu glanced over his shoulder, peering out at the sandy hills, then returned his focus to me. His eyes narrowed. "You watched me."

Now that he knew I had seen his ritual, I felt even more like a voyeur. "I had to be sure," I said defensively. "If someone else saw you—what you really do out there—they would figure it out, too," I added, attempting to redirect the focus of the conversation away from me and back to him. "Why risk it?"

"Because I must." The corner of Temu's mouth tensed, inching upward, and his stare burned into me. "Did you enjoy watching me?"

Renewed heat crept up my neck, but I refused to look away. "I was simply returning the favor." I tilted my head to the side, studying this Nejeret who could somehow pass as human. "Why do you conceal your true nature?" My brows bunched together, and I laughed under my breath, shaking my head wryly. "Everyone I meet knows what I am as soon as they see me."

And I meant *everyone*. I genuinely missed the self-involved obliviousness of the humans from my future time.

Temu's lips curved into a curious smile. "You blaze with otherness like a fallen star," he said, the timbre of his voice resonating deep within me. How did he *do* that? "Even a blind man could see you are not entirely of this world." His stare bored into me, heated and intense, like he was trying to unlock all of my secrets with his eyes alone.

"But not you," I murmured, searching the dark depths of his eyes. "There is nothing at all *other* about you." Again, I shook my head. "How do you do it?"

Temu's expression softened, the intensity in his gaze abating. "I have always been able to keep a low profile."

I scrutinized his features, considering whether to push for more of an explanation. He was being purposely vague, which meant he was hiding something. Many things, most likely.

"Will you keep my secret?" Temu asked, a guarded mask sliding over his momentarily open features. I hated seeing the warmth and friendliness disappear.

I nodded. "I will."

He didn't smile, but some of the warmth returned to his dark eyes. "We should head back to the palace." Temu looked past me to the trail stretching out beyond. "Inyotef will wonder where you are."

I rolled my eyes, instantly annoyed. I didn't want to return to the palace or to Inyotef. I wanted to stay out here with Temu, to unlock more of his secrets. Even so, I fell in step beside him as he started down the path, heading back the way I had come.

"Will you give me your name?" Temu asked as we strolled. "Or must I continue to call you *divine one*?" The hint of a smile touched his lips.

I eyed him sidelong, studying the curve of his sensual mouth. Raising one hand, I fanned myself. It really was an exceptionally warm morning.

"I have one of your secrets," I said, returning my focus to the way ahead. "It only seems fair to give you one of mine. My name is—" I hesitated, vacillating between telling him my true name or the false one I had given Kiya. I wanted Temu to know me, but not nearly as much as I wanted to protect my family in the future. "Bek," I said, erring on the side of caution.

Temu was quiet for a long moment. "An exchange of secrets is only fair if both parties share honestly."

I pressed my lips together, my stomach knotting. My hesitation must have given me away. Or maybe it was my racing heart.

"I'm sorry," I blurted. "I—I can't tell you who I am. It is dangerous information."

"No matter," he said. "Tell me something else about yourself, and all will be forgiven."

I looked at him, my eyebrows raised. I liked this side of him. "What do you want to know?"

Temu took his time considering what to ask me. "You are unusually skilled at combat for a woman," he finally said.

"What—" My eyes opened wider, and my lips parted. How could he possibly know anything about my fighting skills? Unless . . .

I stopped walking, grabbing his elbow to hold him back.

Temu stopped and turned partway to peer down at me.

"The market," I said, releasing him. "You followed me into Waset—into the warehouse." My eyes narrowed to slits. "You followed me, but you did nothing. You didn't help." I laughed bitterly and speared Temu with a haughty gaze. "Now who likes to watch?"

"You had everything under control," Temu said, unruffled. "Had I interfered, I would have been in the way." He tilted his head to the side, studying me like I was the most interesting person in the entire world. "You didn't know that girl. Why did you help her?"

"Because I'm not a monster." I ground my teeth together, inhaling and exhaling a slow, deep breath. "Why *didn't* you help her?"

"Who taught you to fight?" he asked, steamrolling my question.

"My dad," I snapped, bristling at Temu's avoidance. I sniffed and looked away. "He makes a point of ensuring all his children can protect themselves."

"And others, it would seem," Temu mused. "Tell me, *Bek*, do you make a habit of interceding on another's behalf?"

I crossed my arms over my chest and turned a glare on him. "Why didn't you step in? Before they took her away—when they were dragging her from the market. Why didn't you at least *try*?"

Temu studied me for a long moment, the intensity returning to his stare. I must have struck a nerve. His nostrils flared with his next inhale, and he leaned in, invading my personal space. "Because freedom is an illusion, and free will is a luxury," he said, his voice carefully restrained. He was so close that I could feel his breath on my skin. "And I have neither."

He brushed past me and stalked up the trail.

I turned to stare after him, struck dumb by his response. What the hell did all of *that* mean?

"So," Kiya said, drawing out the word as she approached behind me. "How did it go with the prince?"

I watched Temu's back as he walked away. "Not at all the way I expected."

22

"I'M SORRY."

Temu stared at me from three paces away, his head tilted to the side, his steady gaze assessing, like he was searching my soul for the worth of my apology. I was very aware of Kiya standing further down the path, watching us closely.

"What I said the last time we spoke—" I paused, sucking in a deep breath. "It was unfair of me, and I am sorry." I bowed my head, holding the position as I waited for Temu's response.

It had taken me two whole days to work up the courage to face Temu again and speak those two words. Two days to wrangle the snarls of guilt writhing within me—not only about lashing out unfairly at Temu but about my impulsive vigilantism and extremely reckless behavior. I had put the life of a single, ancient young woman before those of my family and friends—of literally *everyone*—in the future, and my anger with myself had been quietly festering within me.

By the time I reached the palace gate after the unexpectedly explosive ending to my initial chat with Temu, I realized I had been projecting my self-loathing onto Temu. I didn't know the first thing about his situation. Why was he here? Why serve Inyotef? Was he even a Kushite prince, or was that just a cover for his true Nejeret mission?

Temu took his time in responding. The slow crunch of footsteps on the path heralded him drawing nearer. He stopped closer to me than was comfortable and reached out one large hand toward me.

I held my breath, anticipating his touch.

He raised my head with gentle fingertips under my chin. Our eyes locked, and my heart stumbled over the next few beats.

"I will forgive you," he said, his voice a low thrum that rolled through me. "If you tell me your true name."

My held breath whooshed out of me, and I closed my eyes, needing a reprieve from the intensity of his stare. I couldn't think with his burning brown eyes searing my soul.

What was the harm in telling him? In letting one person know me? I wouldn't tell him I was from the future or anything about what was to come. My name was common enough in ancient Egypt. There was no reason to suspect he would link me to Heru's daughter who supposedly died as a little girl back in the Netjer-At Oasis.

My will to hold out wavered, then crumbled. I was surprised to discover just how badly I wanted to tell Temu my name. To these ancient people—the ancient people of my birth—a person's name was one of the many parts of their soul. And I felt it, the lack of my name, like part of me—of my soul—was missing.

"Tarset," I breathed and opened my eyes, staring at Temu, drowning in his dark gaze. Joy swelled within me as the two syllables left my lips, and a tear snuck over the brim of my eyelid. I inhaled a shaky breath. "My name is Tarset."

Temu watched the tear glide down my cheek, catching it with the pad of his thumb when it reached my jawline. "Why are you here, Tarset?" My name on his tongue was like a caress of its own, giving rise to a cascade of goose bumps.

I sniffled, curving my lips into a quivering smile. "I'm trying to get home."

Temu withdrew his hand. "To Men-nefer?"

I shook my head and wiped under my eyes to prevent any more tears from falling. "It's just a stop along the way."

Temu's focus slid past me, like he was watching something farther up the path, but when I peeked over my shoulder, all I saw was Kiya. "Thank you for your honesty," he finally said, refocusing on me.

I nodded once. "I would appreciate it if you didn't tell anyone else my name. As I said, it's dangerous knowledge."

"Dangerous to whom?"

"To everyone," I whispered.

Temu was quiet for a long moment. "Names are powerful," he finally said. The corners of his mouth tensed, like he was suppressing a frown, or maybe a smile. "I will keep your secret so long as you keep mine."

It was only fair. "Of course," I said, with another, briefer bow of my head.

Temu extended one arm up the trail. "Walk with me? I would be glad of the company."

My eyebrows rose. "Truly?" I said even as I fell in step beside him. "You wouldn't prefer to be alone?"

A dry laugh rattled around in Temu's chest. "Believe me when I say I have had more than enough solitude in my long life."

"Oh?" I looked at him, studying his strong profile.

Nejeret faces were ageless, our skin cells locked in a permanent cycle of rejuvenation. Temu could have been the thirty or so years old he appeared to be, or he could have been three thousand.

"And how long is that?" I asked, blinking innocently as I returned my attention to the path stretching out before us. Asking a Nejeret's age was a bit of a faux pas, but I felt we were past such formalities.

Temu chuckled. "Long enough for me to grow bored with my own company." Without missing a beat, he asked, "Are you enjoying your stay in the palace? I assume Inyotef is playing the attentive host."

I snorted a laugh. "Oh yes, he is *very* attentive." I rolled my eyes.

Every time I left my room, Inyotef found me, offering me wine or gifts or probing questions. Yesterday afternoon, he showed up while I was stripped down and soaking in the communal baths at the back end of the villa. I doubted it was a coincidence, us bathing at the same time. At least, he was perfectly respectful, not leering or trying to cop a feel. I had retreated to my room after that, not venturing out again until this morning.

"Be careful of Inyotef," Temu said, casually scanning the outlying barley fields at the far edge of the palace grounds. "He can be a very dangerous man."

I nodded to myself. My gut had been telling me the same thing since I first met Inyotef.

Kiya stepped off into the tall barley beside the trail, letting us pass.

I smiled and nodded my thanks to her. I waited until we were well past her to speak again, only doing so after I peeked over my shoulder to ensure she was out of earshot. "So, tell me, *Prince* Temu, why are you here?" I watched Temu out of the corner of my eye, studying his immediate reaction to the question.

The corner of his mouth tensed in an almost smile. His mannerisms may have been subdued, making him seem cold and stony, but I was learning to read him. There was a lot going on under that calm surface.

"I have my reasons," Temu said, making me think he enjoyed preserving his air of mystery.

"You're not really a prince from Kush, are you?"

"No," he said. "I am not really a prince *from Kush.*"

I frowned, curiosity piqued by the emphasis he placed on the words, *from Kush.* "But you *are* a prince—" I looked at him fully. "From elsewhere."

"A prince is merely the son of a king," he said, drawing out the mystery.

I laughed under my breath. Was he saying his father was greater than a king? "So, you're what—the son of an *emperor?*"

My smile wilted, and another laugh lodged in my throat. Realization washed over me, chilling me to the bone. "Or the son of a god?" I asked, my stare glued to the side of his face.

Temu's sidelong glance told me everything I needed to know. He was the son of the father of our species, the Netjer who created this entire universe.

"Nuin is your father," I said breathlessly.

Holy shit. Holy fucking shit. In the future, none of the first generation Nejerets still lived. Well, unless all the dead Nejerets who had been trapped in Aaru had been released and resurrected when I was. Then, I supposed, they would all be alive again. But I had never actually met one. Well, maybe I had met my grandfather, Osiris, when I was young—before the whole time displacement situation that saved my life, but I hardly remembered him beyond a vaguely imposing figure in my memory. And Temu was his brother. One of Nuin's children. Wow.

Temu wasn't a prince, at least, not *merely* a prince. He was so, *so* much more.

"So, why *are* you here?" I asked, unable not to repeat the question after he dropped that bomb on me. "And why are you letting Inyotef order you around?"

"As I said," Temu began. "I have my reasons."

I STARED INTO THE marshy bank from my nest of cushions under the canopy at the center of Inyotef's flat-bottomed fishing barge, covering a yawn. Yet another flock of waterfowl burst forth through the bushy tops of the papyrus plants in a nearby patch in a quacking, squawking cloud of webbed feet and feathered wings. One bird barely made it free of the foliage before an arrow struck its small body. It flapped its wings wildly as it tumbled back down to the water.

Inyotef hooted from his perch at the bow of the barge. I assumed it was his arrow that had struck the unlucky bird. He lowered his bow and turned, beaming at me across the deck.

My lips curved into a bored smile, and I raised my cup, saluting him with my chalice before taking a sip of wine. If that lackluster congratulation wasn't enough to cue him in to how disinterested I was in hour three of observing his personal vendetta against the local waterfowl, the glazed-over look in my eyes had to be a dead giveaway. The amount of effort I put into feigning interest in our little duck hunting excursion was inversely proportional to how long we had been out here. I was over it. Had been for a while now.

Maybe I would have been enjoying myself more if Kiya or Temu were around—Kiya to make subtle, sarcastic comments under her breath, and Temu to exchange weighty glances while Inyotef's back was turned—but neither had joined us. Instead, Inyotef and I had set out after breakfast with a retinue of a half-dozen guards who had, so far as I could tell, been selected based on their prowess with a bow. Or rather, their lack thereof.

Their collective inability to land a shot on even a single bird made Inyotef's mediocre skill with a bow seem on par with a sharpshooter.

Inyotef handed his bow to the guard at his side. "That should be enough," he said, slapping the other man on the shoulder. "Let us retrieve the birds and be on our way." With that, Inyotef started across the barge's deck toward my shaded perch in the middle of the craft.

"Enough for what?" I asked as Inyotef lowered himself onto the cushions spread out beside me.

Inyotef sprawled lazily on his side, his head propped on his hand, his lips curved into a pleased smile.

"Enough to noticeably thin out the local bird population?" I added dryly.

Inyotef's smile widened to a grin, and his healthy ego glittered in his eyes.

I suppressed an eye roll. His type was so predictable—an ego with a bottomless appetite. So long as I continued to feed his ego, he would keep coming back for more. Just thirteen more days of this—or less, if I played my cards right.

"We're having a dinner party tomorrow evening," Inyotef said, his attention shifting to the trio of men bent over the bow of the barge, fishing his kills out of the water. "I'm surprised Temu didn't tell you during one of your morning walks."

My eyelids tensed, attempting to narrow, but I refused to react in such a predictable way.

"We're expecting a very special guest to visit," Inyotef explained, watching me out of the corner of his eye.

"Oh?" I said, affecting a look of wide-eyed curiosity.

"Queen Nitocris, herself," Inyotef revealed. "We will have the pleasure of hosting her tomorrow night, while she rests during her return trip from visiting the upper Nomes."

I turned my full attention to Inyotef. There were about a million things to unpack from what he just shared—Egypt currently had a *queen*—but one shoved its way to the forefront of my mind.

Return trip.

Was the queen returning to Men-nefer? It had been the royal seat for much of Egypt's ancient history. If she was only staying at Inyotef's palace for one night, did that mean she would be back on her ship—and on her way to Men-nefer—the next morning? The chance to be on my way even earlier than planned, and without Inyotef breathing down my neck, was too tempting to pass up. What could I do to make sure *I* was on the queen's boat, too?

"The queen is coming here?" I said, glancing away to conceal the full extent of my interest in her. I sipped my wine.

"Indeed." Inyotef's keen gaze trailed over the side of my face. "And I am sure she will be very excited to meet you, what with the gods of time in Men-nefer having practically disappeared in the last two decades."

Because Nuin died. That had to be what he meant. After the catastrophic events at the Netjer-At Oasis that led to his death when Lex was visiting the past, my people had withdrawn from the public sphere, pulling back from influencing human politics for a long time.

Here was yet another hint at *when* I was—approximately twenty years after Nuin died. Twenty years *after* my four-year-old self was first frozen in *At*. My mom would be in her early fifties if she was still alive.

I gripped the corner of the pillow beneath me, twisting it until the coarse linen burned against my fingertips with the need to be released. If she *was* still alive, I had to see her. Just once.

Inyotef twisted to reach for the wine pitcher behind us. He filled a cup for himself, then refilled mine.

I flashed him a brief smile of thanks.

"I have arranged for a seamstress and a jeweler to bring a selection of their wares to the palace this afternoon," Inyotef said, setting the pitcher back down behind us. "I know you're purposely traveling light, but I thought you might wish to pick out some special items to wear for the queen's visit." When he faced forward once more, his keen attention trailed over my body. "Not that you need any additional adornment. You sparkle finer than any gemstone."

I glanced at him, my cheeks heating with an unexpected blush. "You flatter me."

"I only speak the truth," Inyotef countered, his gaze intense.

Absently, he fiddled with the hem of my shift, rolling a fold of the fine white linen back and forth between the pads of his thumb and index finger. His focus dropped to my lips, where it lingered for long enough that I thought he might lean in to kiss me. I would let him if he did. It would be a minor sacrifice to get me what I needed. Besides, there was always the chance that I would enjoy it. A slight chance, but a chance, nonetheless.

Inyotef looked away, staring upriver. "I must apologize for being so absent during your stay."

I hardly would have called him *absent*. He always seemed to track me down when I least expected it. But now that he brought it up, I realized I hadn't seen him much at all over the past few days, since learning of Temu's true identity—not as a prince of men, but as a prince of gods.

"I wish we could spend more time together," Inyotef went on, "but the world is filled with minor rebellions, and if left unchecked, even the faintest spark will blaze into an inferno." He continued to stare into the distance, his mind clearly preoccupied with the heavy responsibilities of his office.

Head tilted to the side, I studied Inyotef's angular profile, wondering how he had come to be the leader of this region. This unguarded display of vulnerability intrigued me. He rarely removed his overlord mask, and I thought this might have been my first true glimpse of the man he really was, not the face he showed the world. It made him surprisingly relatable.

"Well," I said, resting my fingertips on his forearm, just for a moment. "You're here with me now."

Inyotef looked at me, a slow smile banishing the ghosts from his stare. "Indeed, I am." Once again, his focus lingered on my lips before drifting back up to my eyes. "I hear you have been spending quite a bit of time with Temu." The seemingly innocent statement was cocooned in razor wire.

It was my turn to stare out at the horizon, though all of my senses were still homed in on Inyotef and his dangerous jealousy.

Perhaps it had been unwise of me, but I had fallen into a morning routine of my own these past few days since Temu and I forged our truce in shared secrets. I rose before the sun, walked with Kiya to the edge of the vineyard to watch Temu complete his ritual, and then I met Temu on his way back to the villa and walked with him. Our conversations were filled with gently probing questions as each of us attempted—unsuccessfully—to uncover more of the other's secrets. We had quickly become each other's favorite curiosities.

"He tells me about his homeland," I said, purposely not saying Temu's name. Names had power beyond the part they played in one's identity. They implied interest. Focus. Attention. "Such a fascinating place, Kush." I glanced at Inyotef sidelong. "Do you not agree, Inyotef?" I asked, purposely using *his* name.

"I suppose so, in a primitive way," Inyotef said, his tone cool. He released my hem and withdrew his hand.

I reached out and rested my fingertips on his forearm once more, peering at him through my lashes as I traced the edge of one of his jeweled scarab cuffs. "Perhaps tomorrow morning, *you* will walk with me," I said, curving my lips into a coy smile. "I would very much enjoy your more civilized company." Even as I voiced the words, my gut twisted at the thought of missing out on my alone time with Temu.

Inyotef's eyes locked with mine. He took hold of my fingers and raised my hand to his mouth, gently brushing his lips over the backs of my knuckles. "That would be my greatest pleasure."

I LAID ON MY back on the bed, staring up at the square cutouts of gray light at the top of the wall. For the first time in what felt like forever, I wanted to roll onto my side and spend a lazy morning dozing in and out of sleep. *Even* on this uncomfortable bed. The prospect of walking with Inyotef was having the opposite effect on my desire to get out of bed from my usual morning rendezvous with Temu.

But, I supposed—reluctantly—it had to be done.

Sighing, I dragged myself out of bed to prepare for a morning spent in Inyotef's company. Once I was cleaned up and ready to dazzle, I settled in to wait. I paced back and forth across the length of the room for a solid half hour before growing impatient with waiting.

I yanked aside the curtain barring the doorway, revealing Kiya in her usual spot, back leaned against the opposite wall of the hallway, arms crossed over her chest. A quick scan up and down the hall revealed we were alone. Yesterday, Inyotef had been all hot and heavy about walking with me this morning, so where the hell was he?

To be fair, we hadn't set an actual time. When he said he would come to my room to retrieve me for *our* walk, I had assumed he meant he would come to me at my usual time. I headed out to walk the grounds before sunrise every morning. Not like it was some great secret.

Apparently, I had assumed wrong.

"You look ready to tackle the day," Kiya commented, absently glancing down the hallway. In my present mood, I had no doubt that she meant *tackle* in the literal sense.

"Has Inyotef come by yet?" I asked, making a conscious effort to *not* snarl at Kiya. This was Inyotef's fault, not hers.

Kiya shook her head, her focus returning to me, a tiny frown turning down the corners of her mouth. "I'll let you know when he's here," she offered along with a conciliatory smile.

"Thanks," I murmured and retreated into my room.

I blew out a breath as I looked around the sparse space. My new acquisitions from the in-house shopping spree yesterday were displayed on the low table in the corner. I considered trying out different combinations of accessories and jewelry, but I had no idea how long I would be waiting, and Inyotef showing up to whisk me away when I was in the middle of doing something would only annoy me further. I needed him—for now—which meant I needed to keep him happy. *Which meant* I needed to not be a pissy prima donna.

I settled on pacing the length of the room, alternating between picking at imaginary hangnails and chewing on my thumbnail. He would be here soon. He *had* to be here soon.

When the gray light of dawn warmed to the golden light of sunrise and my thoughts turned to Temu, who would be in the middle of his daily morning ritual on the dune, I gave in and turned my attention to items on the table. I needed something to distract me from the simmering anger rising within me. I could have gone out earlier, walked the grounds with Kiya, and met up with Temu, like normal. Had I known Inyotef would be this late, I would have.

I narrowed my eyes as I studied the spread of glittering gold and gemstones on the table. Was that what this was about, making a point? Was Inyotef proving he could control me, even when I fought his invisible leash? Or was this a test? Did he want proof that he was my priority over Temu?

Or, was he really this oblivious and inconsiderate? I didn't think so. Inyotef struck me as the careful, calculating, chess-master type. He moved through life a dozen moves ahead of those around him.

I let out an irritated sound that was a cross between a groan and a growl. This was why I hated politics. Why I had resisted getting involved in the *family business* for so long. My father, Heru, was the uncrowned king of our people, and I had no interest in any of that. I'd had more than enough of tiptoeing around egos or making alliances in the record industry. Being the Nejeret ambassador to the human world had been easy enough because I was merely a mouthpiece. A figurehead. I didn't actually make decisions or affect change. Politicking hadn't been a part of the job.

But now, it had become my life. And I wasn't cut out for this.

I knelt on one of the floor cushions. As I stared at the assortment of semi-precious jewels set in collared necklaces, bracelets, rings, and earrings spread out before me, I vowed to find a way to convince Queen Nitocris to take me with her. When she sailed away from Waset tomorrow morning, I would be on that ship.

My stomach was groaning with hunger by the time Kiya's sharp whistle announced Inyotef's arrival. I glanced at the window cutouts. It was midmorning, based on the light. I had just enough time to stand and sidestep away from the table, where I was arranging jewelry combinations while trying—and failing—not to imagine Temu's reaction upon finding me absent on the trail.

Inyotef pushed the curtain aside and strode into my room, Kiya following close on his heels.

Inyotef carried a large woven basket, the straps hiked high onto his shoulder and the yeasty scent of fresh-baked bread wafting toward my nose. My mouth started watering immediately, and my stomach took over control of my body. In that moment, I would have followed Inyotef—and his basket of goodies—anywhere. Not that he needed to know that.

I pushed my shoulders back and held my head imperiously high, letting my irritation shine. "I expected you earlier," I said, the words dripping with reproach. I inched my chin higher.

"I know," Inyotef responded, his slight frown the only apology I would get. "I was unfortunately delayed."

I sniffed and crossed my arms over my chest, angling my face away from him. Of course, he was the type who couldn't take personal responsibility for the way his actions impacted others. Typical narcissist.

Inyotef moved closer to the table. I watched him in my peripheral vision. A small smirk twisted his lips. When he turned back to me, he flashed me a smile that was probably supposed to charm me. "I thought we could have a picnic."

I eyed his basket, my stomach rumbling its approval even if I wasn't ready to give in.

Inyotef must have heard it because his smile widened to a full-on Cheshire grin. "I can show you my favorite part of the grounds." He moved closer, angling his head this way and that in an attempt to capture my eyes. "I even have a wineskin filled with the red you like . . ." His eyebrows danced.

I worried the inside of my cheek and stared a hole into the basket. Damn him. I was a sucker for a dry, chewy red. It was my kryptonite, and this wine was fingertip-kissing perfection with all those scrape-your-tongue tannins and that mouth tingling acidity.

My irritation thawed, and I nodded once, my lips curving into the tiniest of smiles.

Inyotef beamed as if I had offered him my heart when really all I was giving him was my stomach. He held his arm out to me, which I took after a calculated hesitation. I was still annoyed, and I wanted him to know it, but I didn't want to ice him out. At least, not until we were docking in Men-nefer—assuming I didn't sail away with the queen in the morning. Then, I was planning on ghosting him, big time.

Inyotef respected my mood by remaining silent as we left the palace and strolled along a path that cut between a barley field and an orchard. Figs, from the looks of it, though I was no botanist.

The trail led to a slight hill, topped by a single, many-trunked tree weeping fluffy strands of tiny, blush-pink flowers. When we crested the gentle rise, we were awarded a breathtaking view of sprawling fields stretching toward Waset to the south and all the way to the Nile straight ahead, which snaked toward the northern horizon.

Inyotef stopped and released my arm, then slid the enormous basket from his shoulder. He set his burden on the dry earth and dug out a wool blanket woven with a pattern of alternating bands of mustard-yellow, carnelian, and crimson. He unfurled the blanket and laid it out on the ground in the shade of the tree, then gestured for me to sit.

I did so, curling my legs beneath me and leaning back on one hand, still admiring the view.

Inyotef withdrew the wineskin and a pair of ceramic chalices next, filling one cup with wine and handing it to me before doing anything else. Smart man.

"Am I forgiven now, or are you still cross with me?" he asked as he filled his own cup.

I sipped my wine and sighed, my eyelids drifting shut, just for a moment. It was impossible to feel anything but bliss with this liquid heaven rolling over my tongue.

Inyotef chuckled and resumed his rummaging through the basket. He pulled out more food than the laws of physics dictated should have been able to fit in the container. I gazed adoringly at a feast of crusty bread, butter, honey, and cheese, as well as some sort of spicy jerky, roasted almonds, and a delicious looking fig flatbread that would have fit right in on the menu at any fancy farm-to-table restaurant. I set my wine aside and dug in, spreading some goat cheese on the fig flatbread and drizzling it with honey.

"Oh wow," I said, shielding my mouth as I chewed. "It's *so* good."

Inyotef watched me, his eyes dancing with amusement.

I tore off a piece of my doctored flatbread and handed it to him. "Try it. You'll thank me," I said, and tore off another piece to stuff into my mouth. So, *so* good.

Inyotef nodded as he ate, not nearly as wowed by my concoction as I was. "Not bad," he said after he swallowed. "Not bad at all." He sipped his wine, studying me over the rim of his cup.

I admired the view, pretending I didn't notice his attention.

"Tell me more about your homeland," Inyotef said. "The exotic foreign land of *America*."

I snorted delicately as I chewed, thinking it sounded absurd for this man to call my part of America *exotic*. I split my time between LA and Seattle—or, at least, I had before the war—and both places were boringly normal. This place, this time period, these people—it didn't get much more exotic than this. Although, I supposed that was all a matter of perspective.

I glanced at Inyotef, then returned my attention to the food. "What would you like to know?" I asked as I broke off a chunk from a wedge of hard, aged cheese.

"Your family is there?" Inyotef said. He plucked a plain flatbread from the spread of food and turned it around and around between his pinched fingers.

I nodded as I chewed. Again, I covered my mouth with my hand to speak around the bite. "Some of my family, yes." I twisted the bracelet on my wrist, running my fingertip over the lapis lazuli Wedjat as I thought of my dad, thousands of years away. He was alive in this time, too, but he was hardly the same man as he would be in four millennia, and I knew that crossing paths with him would be catastrophic for the timeline.

Inyotef raised his eyebrows. "And the rest?"

I shrugged one shoulder. "Here and there." I reclaimed my chalice and raised it to take a sip of wine.

"In Men-nefer?"

I coughed, choking on the wine. I set down my cup and turned away from Inyotef to clear my airway. I loved big reds, but damn, they sure burned when they went down the wrong pipe.

"Divine one?" Inyotef patted my back unhelpfully. "Are you all right?"

I raised a hand, waving him away. "I'm fine," I said, my voice high and tight. I cleared my throat, my eyes watering, and turned back to Inyotef. "What else would you like to know about America?" I asked, hoping to redirect him away from the dangerous subject of my family in Men-nefer. I offered him a coy smile to hide my alarm at potentially having revealed too much.

Inyotef studied me for a long moment. "Everything," he said, his stare boring into me. "I want to know everything." Not about the vague, distant land of *America*. He wanted to know everything *about me*. Of that, I was certain.

I cleared my throat again and carefully sipped my wine. "What about you?" I asked, selecting a hunk of jerky. I tore off a strip. "Is your family here in Waset?" I glanced over my shoulder, looking back at the walled palace.

"Do they live here?" If any of Inyotef's relatives lived in the palace, I had yet to meet them.

When I turned back to Inyotef, his face was shadowed by some heavy emotion. He ran his fingertip around the rim of his cup as he stared into the dark red wine. "Alas, I am the last of my family."

His grief was raw and palpable, and it touched me more deeply than I would have expected. "I'm so sorry," I breathed.

Inyotef raised his eyes, meeting mine, and smiled gently. "Yes, well . . ." He sighed. "Now, I have the responsibility of building a new family."

Wait—was he implying that his new family might include *me*?

I was suddenly overcome with that strange awareness of my physical self that came with being intensely uncomfortable. I didn't know what to do with my face or where to look—at him, or away. What was I supposed to say? Or was silence a better approach?

Say something. Definitely say something. Redirect the conversation. We were in serious need of a subject change. Again.

"Was your father also the leader of Waset?" I blurted.

"No," Inyotef said, tearing his stare from me. He gazed out at the river. "My father was a scribe. He taught me his trade, and I served the previous three overlords." He glanced at me. "None of them lasted for long. When the position opened yet again after an unfortunate hunting accident, I had garnered enough respect from the people of this region to take the position." He let out a bitter laugh. "That was three years ago, and I've been cleaning up my predecessors' messes ever since."

He paused, but I didn't think he was done.

"Careful alliances have given me control over three other regions," he said. "And if all goes well tonight with the queen, perhaps we will finally have a united land again."

I eyed him curiously. Was he speaking of merging kingdoms with the queen—through a union of households? Through *marriage*? As soon as the thought crossed my mind, I knew it was correct.

"You're courting her," I murmured, surprise widening my eyes.

Inyotef looked at me but quickly averted his gaze to his wine cup. "I'm courting peace for my people."

I laughed through my nose, amused by his evasion, and returned to studying the view.

"Does that upset you?" he asked.

My eyebrows climbed even higher, and I swallowed a guffaw. "Does the idea of you courting the queen upset me?" He would probably like it if it did, so I donned a mask of forced disappointment. "I am surprised, that is all. I thought . . ." I laughed under my breath and shook my head. "Well, it doesn't matter now."

Inyotef inhaled deeply and held the breath in his lungs for a few seconds. With a heavy exhalation, he set his cup down on the ground beyond the edge of the blanket, then turned back to me.

"It doesn't have to change anything between us," he said, reaching for me across the picnic feast. His eyes met mine as he traced his fingertips along the hem of my dress, just above my knee.

I shivered, unused to being touched so intimately by Inyotef. By anyone.

It had been so long since anyone touched me in a way that wasn't purposeful or proper. I was used to being adored by legions of fans, to having potential lovers throw themselves at me day and night. Going for nearly two months without sharing my bed with anyone had left me achy and needy in a way I hadn't experienced before. My morning flirtations with Temu only made matters worse.

I stared at the fingers dancing delicately over my skin, both wishing Inyotef would stop and wanting more. I took a shaky breath as Inyotef's fingertips inched higher up my leg, his hand bunching the gauzy fabric of my skirt as it glided up my thigh.

Honestly, I had long since lost count of my *number* years ago. Physical pleasure wasn't something I was ashamed of. I liked my men adventurous and varied, and I wasn't one for settling down. Even my relationship with Wolf had been loosely monogamous. We had brought other people into our bed—together. And, okay, maybe I'd had a few dalliances on my own, too, but that was when I was on the road, and we had a *what happens on the road, stays on the road* agreement.

When it came to romance, I was more of a buffet girl. I liked to keep my options open, and I would have been lying to myself if I claimed to have no attraction to Inyotef, no matter how much he infuriated me with his power games. He was charismatic, intelligent, and easy on the eyes. And dangerous, but that only made things more exciting.

Inyotef's breaths came faster as he hungrily scanned the length of my body.

He withdrew his hand and crawled around the food to kneel in front of me. He extended his arm, curving his hand around the back of my head as he leaned forward to kiss me. The brush of his lips against mine was tentative at first.

Again, I was torn between wanting this to continue and wishing it would stop. But I was wary of angering Inyotef—I still needed him—so I parted my lips, opening up to him. The action earned me a soft growl from Inyotef. He deepened the kiss, and his hand was once again on my thigh and moving higher.

As his fevered kiss traveled down from my lips to my jawline to my neck, he kneaded the inside of my thigh. I squeezed my eyes shut, desire wrestling with unease in my gut.

At the crunch of dry earth beneath shoe soles, I opened my eyes and peered through the curtain of flower strands hanging down from the tree's branches to scan the trail that led up to the hilltop. I found the source of the noise, at the edge of the barley field, stalking up the gentle slope.

Temu.

He moved too quietly for Inyotef's ears, but not for mine. His stare was intense and challenging. I stiffened, flushing as I was flooded by unwarranted guilt mixed with disgust.

Inyotef seemed unaware of my mood change. His lips trailed kisses down the column of my neck to the valley between my breasts, his fingers inching ever higher.

Temu crested the hill and leaned his shoulder against one of the thicker trunks of the tree and cleared his throat loudly.

Inyotef froze, his entire body going rigid.

Oh, thank the gods. Or thank Temu. I was over this. Inyotef was a poor stand-in for the man I really craved.

"Pardon the interruption," Temu said, the deep timbre of his voice rekindling my smothered desire. "We just received word," Temu said, moving away from the tree to the far edge of the hilltop to stare out at the Nile valley. His skin gleamed with hints of brushed bronze in the late morning sunlight. He clasped his hands behind his back and angled his face toward us without actually looking our way. "The queen is headed to the palace now."

Inyotef cursed and drew away, pushing up to his knees. His lust-filled stare combed over me as he straightened and rearranged the folds of his schenti. My own linen skirt remained bunched up high on my thighs. His unguarded expression displayed the pain of unfulfilled desire. Even now, he wasn't committed to walking away. He needed a little encouragement.

"It's fine," I told him, once again propping myself up on my elbows. "Go. Greet your queen."

Inyotef growled and climbed jerkily to his feet. "This isn't over," he promised, towering above me. He looked at Temu, gesturing toward the food with a sharp jerk of his hand. "Clean this up and escort the divine one back to the palace."

Temu bowed his head.

Inyotef strode over to Temu, stopping close enough that he had to tilt his head back to look into the taller man's eyes. "And if you touch her," Inyotef said, his voice pitched low enough that were I human, I wouldn't have been able to hear what he said. "I will have you castrated." Inyotef turned away from Temu, raked his gaze over me one last time, then stalked away down the hillside.

Temu's eyes locked with mine, my stare issuing a new challenge. How badly did he want me? Enough to risk castration?

I stretched out on my back, resting one hand on my bared inner thigh. I traced my fingertips up and down the sensitive flesh. I was game if he was.

"Tarset..." My name was a plea on his lips. A warning. Oh, Temu wanted me, all right. Just as badly as I wanted him.

My intention was only to tease, but when Temu said my name like that, all rational thought fled from my mind.

"He said he would castrate you if *you* touched me," I said, my voice husky. I slid my hand higher and skimmed my fingertips over my slick core, sucking in a trembling breath. "He said nothing about *me* touching myself."

Temu took three halting steps toward me, then stopped, his hands balled into tight fists and his jaw clenched. Sexual energy arced between us, forging an electric connection.

"Tell me to stop, and I will." The words came out as a whisper on my exhale as I continued to caress my outer lips.

Temu was a statue, silent and still. And he absolutely didn't say *stop*.

The instant my fingertip pushed through my slit and grazed that tender, swollen bundle of nerves, I was lost to the exquisite, forbidden pleasure. To the thrill of letting Temu see what he did to me. How his mere presence undid me.

What would it be like to have his hand in place of mine? To have his fingers slipping into me. Stroking me. Coaxing me closer to release. Ever closer. So close.

I gasped, the sudden explosion of pleasure white-hot and blinding. I closed my eyes and writhed on the blanket as my core pulsed with the release.

I coasted on that glorious current of bliss, my every nerve ending hyperaware. The climax lasted almost as long as it had taken me to reach it.

The air shifted beside me, and I opened my eyes. Temu knelt at my side, his breaths quick and shallow. The rapid thrum of his heart beat an erotic rhythm to my sensitive ears that fanned my waning arousal even hotter and higher than before.

He reached out with one of those big, powerful hands like he might caress the side of my face but stopped shy of actually touching me. Palm hovering a hair's breadth from my skin, he traced the contours of my body, from my jaw down my neck and along my collarbone. He traced around my shoulder and over my breast and peaked nipple, then down to the dip of my waist and the swell of my hips. His gaze followed the course of his hand, and though he never touched me, I would have sworn I could feel him.

He flexed his hand, balling it into a fist, then stretching out his fingers before he caught the hem of my skirt between his thumb and forefinger and gently drew it down, covering me once more. The brush of linen over my skin gave rise to goose bumps, and I shivered, insanely aroused despite my recent release.

But still, Temu never touched me.

I pushed up onto my elbows, then sat up, and Temu withdrew his hand. I gathered my legs under me and knelt, facing him, my hands resting palm down on my thighs. I studied his strong jawline, his sharp cheekbones, his full lips, the noble slope of his nose, and the swell of his brow. I dove into the bottomless burnished bronze pools of his eyes, searching for some explanation for this connection we shared. This unexpected lure between us.

Was it possible—could it be the Nejeret soul bond? Or, rather, the *potential* to bond? Like my dad and Lex? Like Kat and Nik? The perfect compatibility of pheromones unique to our kind. The sublime harmony of Nejeret souls.

That was a terrifying prospect. Once a Nejeret bond was established, it could never be broken. The couple became literally addicted to one another, to the degree that separation for too long would lead to death.

"Would he really castrate you if you touched me?" I finally asked.

Temu was quiet for a long moment, his stare equally searching. "He would try." That Inyotef would fail in that attempt was implied.

I looked down at my hands, curling my fingers into fists to keep myself from reaching for Temu. "And what do you think he would do to me?" I asked, my voice small.

"I don't know," Temu admitted, his hushed tone sending a chill down my spine. "And we will *never* find out."

A FTER A GOOD SOAK and scrub in the baths that afternoon, I prepared for the party, taking Grammys-level care with my appearance. I chopped off a good foot and a half of my hair. I lined my eyes with kohl to double wing-tipped perfection. I painted my lips and dabbed my cheeks with a red ocher stain. A delicate diadem made up of an inch-thick strip of tiny amber and gold stars linked by thin strands of gold wire held my proper Egyptian middle part in place. I brushed gold dust on my cheeks, eyelids, and lips—just enough to add a shimmer, but not enough to look gaudy.

During the seamstress's visit the previous day, I had selected a simple sleeveless linen sheath dress with a deep V in the front and back that dipped nearly to my belly button. But I didn't want the dress in traditional white. Instead, I asked the seamstress to dye it black. Her expression at hearing my request told me just how odd it was, but when I returned from the baths, the dress was lying on my bed waiting for me, jet black, just as I had requested.

After catching Kiya making the same bewildered expression as the seamstress when she first saw the black dress, I banished her to the hallway. Once she saw the finished look, she would understand. I wasn't aiming to blend in tonight. Oh no. Tonight, I needed to be the flame to the queen's moth. I needed to be the most irresistible prize she never realized she wanted but that she suddenly, absolutely needed.

I added a thick belt of interwoven gold chains that cinched my waist and clasped at the front around a lapis lazuli scarab. Two feet of delicate gold chains dangled from the clasp down the centerline of my body, making a luxurious *whooshing* sound every time I moved my hips. A broad collar of tiny amber and lapis lazuli beads covered the top half of my chest and draped over my shoulders, clasping at the back.

A smattering of gold rings and bangles finished the look, joining the Wedjat bracelet I had been gifted for intervening in the market. No earrings. My ears had yet to be re-pierced since my resurrection. Besides, any more adornment would clash with the diadem and collar.

I had only my hand mirror held at arm's length from above to assess my completed look. Was the gold dust too much? It was hard to say in the smattering of late afternoon light. I could always brush some off.

"Kiya," I called to the curtained doorway, turning my head this way and that to examine my face from every angle.

In my peripheral vision, I saw Kiya push past the curtain. She stopped a few steps into the room and stared, her mouth opened into a tiny "o."

I turned to face her, holding my arms out to either side in a silent *ta-da* and flashing her a hopeful smile. "Well, what do you think?"

Kiya opened her mouth, then shut it. After a trio of blinks, she sucked in a breath. "Wow." She scanned me from head to toe, then back up again. "You look . . . well, divine."

I lowered my chin and grinned. "Perfect."

I was aiming to impress. I wanted Queen Nitocris to see me as every characteristic a Nejeret embodied in the minds of humans—powerful, valuable, and most importantly, *divine*. I needed her to be so enthralled with me—with what I might be able to offer her—that she wouldn't ever think of refusing me passage on board her ship.

Maybe it wasn't all that wise to spend too much time with the queen, but even I knew that during the era immediately following Nuin's death, Egypt had been ruled by a merry-go-round of failed monarchs. Even if Queen Nitocris was currently the most powerful person in Egypt, her rule wouldn't last long. This was an unstable period of Egypt's history, and there would be no ruler strong enough to unite the lands for at least another century. What harm was there in spending a few weeks with the current queen, doomed as she was?

I moved closer to the doorway and pulled the curtain back, angling my ear toward the hallway to listen. The murmur of voices, both male and female, drifted up the hallway from the front of the palace, telling me the party had already started. But was the queen out there? She was the only guest I cared about. I hated to waste my grand entrance on a room filled with useless nobles.

I let the curtain fall back in place and glanced at Kiya. "Do you think she's out there?"

Kiya frowned and shrugged.

"All right." I nodded to myself. "Let's go."

Kiya left first, making me wait until she scanned up and down the hallway before letting me emerge from my room. It was our usual routine—she had taken to rounding every corner and passing through every doorway ahead of me, just to be safe.

Tonight's gathering was happening in the colonnaded reception hall and the joined side courtyard, where I had been taken to meet Inyotef my first night here. When we reached the reception hall, Kiya paused at the wide doorway, for once allowing me to enter a room first.

I stood in the shadows of the doorway, taking in the crowded space. Torches flamed in sconces on the walls and columns, filling the hall with golden light and long, flickering shadows. Narrow tables holding a variety of finger foods and beverage options had been set up between alternating pairs of columns, turning the space into something of a labyrinth.

I scanned the faces of dozens of strangers, not recognizing a single person. Inyotef was nowhere to be seen. Temu was notably absent, as well. That most likely meant Queen Nitocris wasn't among this crowd either. I had little doubt that Inyotef, at least, would stay close to the queen. He was courting her, after all.

I backed through the doorway into the deeper shadows of the hallway. "Let's try the courtyard," I told Kiya.

Though I could find my way through the warren of hallways well enough by now, I let her lead as we took the long way around. With all these strangers in the palace, she would never let me walk at her side.

When we reached the doorway to the courtyard, I slipped through, once again hanging back in the shadows behind the colonnade as I scanned the twilit garden. Fewer sconces lit the outdoor space. There weren't as many people in the courtyard, either. Probably because all the snacks and booze were inside.

I counted at least two dozen heads out here. Definitely no Inyotef among them. I did, however, spot Temu lurking in the shadows between a pair of date palms along the outer wall of the courtyard. In addition to his usual white linen schenti, he wore a tailored cheetah skin draped over one shoulder like a toga and belted at the waist. His silver- and gold-hilted khepesh—as I had learned the vicious looking sickle-shaped sword was called—hung from his hip.

My heart beat faster at the sight of him, and a flush warmed my skin. For a moment, I was back on that hilltop with him, and a warm ache throbbed in my groin. Gods, I wanted him.

I moved forward, passing between two columns as I stepped into the flame-gilded twilight. The wave of heads turning my way pleased me, as did the murmur that spread throughout the courtyard, drawing the eyes of nearly all in attendance toward me. I moved sedately, serenely, my shoulders pushed back and my head held high, basking in the attention. Gods, I missed this.

I was Nejeret. A god of time. The most desirable, valuable, fascinating person here.

And tonight, I would make damn sure the queen knew it.

.

I GLIDED AROUND THE long, rectangular pool at the center of the courtyard, making eye contact with guests as I passed and nodding mute greetings, but not directly engaging with anyone. Temu slipped away while I wasn't looking, which sent my heart plummeting into my stomach.

Until I turned the corner at the end of the pool and found him approaching, a ceramic chalice in each hand. His eyes seared a trail over my body, slowly moving down to my bare feet, then back up. He stopped in front of me and offered one of the chalices. Dark red wine gleamed within.

"You are in your element," Temu murmured, his voice a caress, his gaze a brand.

"Thank you," I said, accepting the cup. I raised it to my lips and sipped, practically purring when the wine hit my tongue, the sharpness making my salivary glands tingle.

Desire flared in Temu's shadowed eyes, accentuated by the red and gold gleam from the flickering torchlight. His stare lingered on the lapis scarab on my belt, and then on the Wedjat displayed on my upraised wrist. I wondered what he made of the symbols. The scarab meant nothing to me, but the Wedjat was significant. Could he tell?

When his eyes returned to mine, they gave nothing away.

In the back of my mind, I wondered if he had already figured out that I was of clan Heru. I supposed it didn't matter. If everything went well tonight, I would be gone in the morning. We would be ships in the night, our fleeting time together over. The thought was a dagger twisting in my heart, even though the rational part of my mind knew it would be for the best. If—and that was a humongous *if*—we were potential bond-mates, then I needed to put some distance between us ASAP. Unless I wanted to end up trapped in the past with him, doomed to take the slow route home—the one that would take over four thousand years.

I cleared my throat and scanned the courtyard, taking in all the people pretending they weren't watching us, the exotic Kushite prince and the magnificent goddess of time. Temu's focus remained steadily on me, as though it discomfited him to have all those eyes on him.

"This is quite striking." I brushed my hand down the soft fur of the cheetah skin draped over the right half of his chest. "Is this the traditional garb of the Kushites?" I goaded, arching one brow as I looked up at him.

He stared down at my hand, his jaw clenched. When his eyes met mine, they were filled with warning. No touching. Right.

I cleared my throat and pulled my hand away, sipping my wine as I once again scanned the growing crowd. Temu seemed more uncomfortable with each additional pair of eyes directed our way.

"You do not seem to be in *your* element," I murmured, the corners of my mouth tensing in a teasing smile.

Temu grunted, and the low, throaty sound sent a tingly zing straight to my center. "I don't enjoy large gatherings," he said.

I studied his face. Clearly, being the center of attention at such gatherings was even more onerous. And yet, he had stepped out from the shadows and into the spotlight *for me*. Warmth spread through my chest at the gesture.

"Come," I said as I switched wine hands and linked my arm with Temu's. He tensed, but if Inyotef had any issues with such a benign touch, he could shove them up his possessive ass. "Walk with me. You can tell me who all these people are."

Nobles, merchants, and politicians, I learned, as we made a slow circuit around the courtyard before venturing into the reception hall for more wine. Some guests had come with Queen Nitocris, and some had traveled from the regions immediately upriver and downriver from Waset.

Temu and I settled in the shadows between two columns in the hall, facing one another with our backs leaned against opposite columns, his feet bordering mine. The rest of the guests could have disappeared, for all I noticed them.

At one point, I realized I had been gazing at Temu like a love-struck teen for far too long and made a cursory scan of the hall. "The queen has yet to make an appearance," I noted. "Inyotef, also."

Temu chuckled, sending another tingly zing to my lady bits. "Yes, well, they still had much to *discuss* when I left him in her room."

I looked at Temu sharply.

His eyes glittered with mirth and something darker. "Jealous?"

I snorted a laugh, not even justifying the question with an answer. "Did she seem open to his advances?"

The corners of Temu's mouth tensed with what looked like the start of a frown. "She was willing to listen."

I pressed my lips together, my eyes narrowing as I considered the implications of Inyotef forging his alliance with the queen *tonight*. I hadn't thought it would happen so quickly. She might not want to cross him by whisking me away if they had already agreed to terms that would unite their two territories.

"Whatever you're planning," Temu said, pushing off his column and leaning in toward me, "tread carefully." His fingers brushed against mine as they curled around my chalice, making me shiver. He stood there, his fingers touching mine, for a single heartbeat. And then he took my wine cup and walked away.

A murmur filled the reception hall, and heads turned toward the broad doorway. I sidestepped into the shadows between the colonnade and the wall as I watched Inyotef enter the hall with a petite woman on his arm, more gold adorning her body than was worn by everyone else gathered here combined. This had to be the elusive Queen Nitocris.

She had a curious appearance, with a boyish figure and sharp, androgynous features. Her eyes glittered with keen intelligence, and fine lines fanned across her temples, marking her age on an otherwise youthful face. I placed her in her mid to late thirties. Definitely still of a childbearing age, which was essential if Inyotef was planning to forge a unified hereditary monarchy with her.

Even from across the room, I could pick up the scent of sex wafting off them. I laughed through my nose. Perhaps ensuring her fertility was part of sealing their alliance.

Concealing a smirk, I glanced sidelong at Temu as he joined me in the shadows behind the colonnade, handing me my refilled chalice. He didn't even try to hide his smug grin. He had definitely picked up on their telltale scent, as well.

Inyotef spotted us in the shadows, his expression hardening as his stare momentarily lingered on Temu before shifting to me. He murmured something to Nitocris and slipped his arm from hers, striding toward us. He accepted a cup of wine from a servant on the way, but never took his eyes off us. Off me.

"I'll leave you in our host's capable hands," Temu said, bowing his head as he backed up a step. He turned away, making a beeline for the doorway to the courtyard.

As Inyotef drew near, his eyes lingered on Temu's retreating back. "Apologies for leaving you alone in this crowd, divine one," Inyotef said, refocusing on me. He reached for my hand, raising it to press a kiss against the heel of my palm. He peered at me through his long, dark lashes. "I was unavoidably detained."

The twelve-year-old part of my brain snickered, but I held my outward composure. "Think nothing of it." I looked past him, to the queen, who was chatting with a few of the other guests near the center of the hall, and lazily sipped my wine. "I wasn't alone."

Out of the corner of my eye, I watched irritation flash across Inyotef's face, there and gone in a blink. I probably shouldn't have mentioned Temu, however indirectly. Now that Inyotef was splitting his attention between Nitocris and me, there was a chance he would feel the need to overcompensate with his manly posturing toward me, and Temu might seem an even greater threat to my attention.

I crossed the first two fingers of my left hand, tucked close to my thigh. If all went well tonight, I would never have to consider Inyotef's delicate male ego again. I would be free of him and his attempts to get whatever it was he wanted from me. He would become irrelevant.

But he wasn't, yet. Not until I was on that boat. As things currently stood, I was still relying on him to help me reach Men-nefer.

I purposely molded my lips into a friendly smile and turned all of my attention onto Inyotef. I was a big fan of diversification. I hadn't become the highest-selling musical artist in history by carrying all my eggs around in a single basket. I knew the value of setting out many lines in the water. One hook may come up empty, but another might snag the prize catch.

"I'm glad you're finally here, though," I told Inyotef, curving my hand around the crook of his elbow. "Now, don't you want to show me off?"

Dark desire smoldered in Inyotef's shadowed eyes. "That isn't even close to what I want to do with you." His lips curved into a subtly wicked grin. "But it will do. For now."

I SPENT AN HOUR or two at Inyotef's side while the queen was busy with others, meeting countless important people whose names vanished from my brain almost as soon as they were out of sight. Eventually, Inyotef was pulled away by a pair of his guards, murmuring in hushed voices about some incident in town, leaving me to retreat alone to the dim courtyard. The shadows cast by the flickering torches were deeper and darker now, with only the half-moon and the stars sparkling above to dilute them.

I sat at one end of the pool, tapping my toes against the water's cool surface, mesmerized by the ripples as they spread and eventually died out. I watched Temu without staring directly, standing alone at the opposite end of the courtyard. He leaned one shoulder against a column, his arms crossed over his chest, the flames of a nearby torch highlighting the intricate pattern of his scars and the dark promise gleaming in his eyes.

But he wasn't looking at me. He was staring at Queen Nitocris, who burst into raucous laughter every minute or two. Either her companions were hilarious, or she was drunk. Maybe a bit of both.

It was probably about time for me to make my move, but I couldn't stop watching Temu watch *her*. Jealousy roused within me, heating my blood and making me feel reckless. Or maybe that was all the wine.

"He is quite striking, is he not?"

I tore my stare away from Temu, surprised to find Queen Nitocris gazing down at me across the corner of the pool. When had she abandoned her companions? And how had I not noticed her approach? To my sensitive Nejeret nose, she still reeked of Inyotef and their earlier indiscretion. She glanced at Temu, a coy smile curving her lips. Oh, right, I hadn't noticed her approach because I had been staring at him.

"He is, indeed," I said, glancing at Temu for the briefest moment, just long enough to know he was watching us. And listening. He was always listening.

Nitocris bowed her head, the gold beads dangling on six-inch strands from her diadem clacking with the motion. "It is a pleasure to meet you, divine one."

I bent my neck in return. "And you as well." I stretched out my hand, gesturing to the edge of the pool at her feet. "Won't you join me?"

"I would love nothing more," she said and sighed, easing down to sit on the ledge. She slipped her sandals off and tossed them aside, plunking her feet into the water. "You were smart to go barefoot." She sent a death glare at her pretty, gilded shoes. "I don't know why I bother wearing them. I always end up with blisters."

"I know exactly what you mean," I said, thinking of the state my feet would often be in after a show. I missed many things about home, but I absolutely did not miss high heels.

I leaned back on my hands and gazed up at the stars, the Milky Way stretching across the darkness like a river of glittering diamonds. The night sky didn't look like that anymore back home. There was too much light pollution, and probably regular old pollution, to provide such a pristine view of the heavens.

Silence settled over us, comfortable and companionable. I listened to the murmur of voices within the reception hall and the hushed whispers and low moans from the shadows out here, where a few amorous couples had snuck away for a modicum of privacy.

"Inyotef speaks highly of you," Nitocris finally said. "How long have you two been together?"

I looked at her, my eyebrows raised as high as they could go. "Oh, we're not together," I said, possibly too quickly and with too much vehemence. "I'm merely staying here in the palace while I await our journey downriver." I averted my gaze to the pool's surface. "There was some trouble in town when I first arrived. Inyotef assures me this is the safest place for me while I'm in the area."

"Ah, yes," Nitocris said, nodding slowly. "These are troubling times." She sighed. "It is difficult for one to know who to trust . . . who to ally with." She looked toward Temu, but her stare grew distant, like she wasn't really seeing him. "Some alliances breed fear among the masses, while others breed love."

"Which do you hope to achieve with an alliance with Inyotef?" I wondered aloud.

"I wish I knew." Nitocris raised a hand to rub the place where her neck met her shoulder. "It's such a fine line to walk—fear and love. But what value is there in the love of the masses when such love is conditional? When it's so fickle?"

Inyotef coalesced out of the shadows and joined Temu. The queen's focus latched onto her suitor.

"But fear . . ." She laughed under her breath dryly. "Fear is much easier to maintain. *But* once it is established, love is all but impossible." She sighed, gazing into the crystalline water.

"I don't envy you," I told her candidly. "I wouldn't wish to be in your position. The responsibility must be terrible."

Nitocris let out another laugh, this one distinctly bitter. "I don't wish to be in my position, either, but what choice do I have? No king has lasted more than a year in nearly two decades. Every man who attempts to lead this land is killed by those who claim to follow him." She looked at me, fear lurking in the shadows of her eyes, and nodded toward the warm glow pouring out through the doorway to the crowded reception hall. "How long until one of them comes for me? No matter what I do, it's never enough." She sighed, her focus drifting back to Inyotef.

The overlord was locked in an intense whispered exchange with Temu, neither paying us any attention.

"I will do what I must to preserve what I can of my people and our land," Nitocris vowed.

My heart ached for her. What a terrible position to be in—captaining a sinking ship. "I'm sure you will do the right thing," I told her.

Nitocris let out another of those bitter laughs. "The right thing . . ." She sighed. "Once, one of your people would have advised the ruler of this land on what to do. On figuring out the *right thing*. It is most unfortunate that your people have withdrawn from the public sphere." She looked at me, her expression beseeching. "I could really use your help right now."

I blinked, caught off guard. She was talking about the Echoes. The visions of the past, present, and future that were the crux of my people's power. Or, at least, they had been. By the time my Nejeret powers manifested last year, the way into the Echoes had long since been shut down—to protect the timeline from any meddling after certain integral events had happened. *Universe*-saving events. No time travel for those few with the ability, and no Echoes for the rest of us. We were relegated to experiencing the passage of time like humans.

I, personally, never even had the chance to view the Echoes. I hadn't considered that the way into the Echoes would be open now, in this time. I wouldn't even know where to begin to try to reach the higher dimension that would allow me to view the Echoes in the first place.

But I didn't tell Nitocris that. She had just unknowingly handed me my ticket onto her ship.

I offered her a small smile of apology and shook my head. It was time to play hard to get. "I fear my people's interference in the natural passage of time is part of what led us into this mess," I explained, offering her a version of the truth. She seemed like the kind of woman who valued honesty. "We have withdrawn with purpose and will meddle no more."

A single, brief laugh shook the queen's chest. "Spoken like Osiris when I petitioned *him* for help." She blew out a breath, her shoulders slumping. "It was worth a try."

I inhaled deeply but held my breath before speaking.

Nitocris raised her eyebrows.

"I will make a bargain with you," I started. "I will view a single Echo for you." It was a hollow offer. I would do no such thing. I paused, staring down at my empty wine cup.

"And what would you want in exchange?" she asked.

I twisted my chalice around and around in my hands. "You are leaving for Men-nefer in the morning, yes?"

I saw the queen nod at the edge of my periphery. "We leave in the morning. The trip will take a couple of weeks, but I am eager to return home."

"I don't suppose you could fit one more person on board?" I lifted my gaze, meeting the queen's hawkish stare.

Nitocris raised her eyebrows even higher. "You wish to join us?"

"I'm planning to join Inyotef on his journey to Men-nefer in thirteen days, but time is of the essence," I told her. "It would mean a great deal to me if I could travel with you and reach the great city even a few days earlier. I would be *much* obliged."

The corners of the queen's mouth tensed, and her intense eyes glittered with cunning. "Three Echoes," she countered.

I pressed my lips together, and after a long moment of false consideration, I nodded. "Very well, three Echoes."

I would have to slip away as soon as we arrived and find someplace to hide until Aramei came into power at the Hathor temple. But I had been planning the same thing when Inyotef was my ride, so it was no extra challenge.

Nitocris kicked a splash of water at my dangling feet, and one side of her mouth twisted upward into a wry grin. "You will be most welcome on my ship, divine one," she said with a slight bow of her head. "I think I will enjoy your company very much." She eyed the doorway to the reception hall behind her and the milling notables within. "At least I won't have to worry about *you* stabbing me in the back in a bid for power."

We shared a look of such perfect understanding that I knew I could trust this woman, even if she couldn't trust me. My lips curved into a grateful smile. "I can't tell you how much this means to me." I glanced at the empty shadows between the columns where Inyotef and Temu had been only a moment ago and lowered my voice. "And if I could ask you for one more favor . . ."

Nitocris pursed her lips, tilting her head to the side.

"Would you please not mention our arrangement to Inyotef?" I allowed my desperation to shine through in my eyes. "I don't think he would appreciate my early departure."

Nitocris nodded slowly, her eyes narrowed, considering the request. "Yes," she said after a drawn-out moment. "He is a man accustomed to getting what he wants." She bowed her head in assent. "You have my silence where he is concerned."

I grinned, my heart soaring. "Thank you."

THE SUN HAD SET hours ago, and I had drunk too much wine too quickly for my speedy Nejeret metabolism to burn through. Not enough for me to make a fool of myself, but just enough to make me throw caution to the wind and bypass the doorway to my room in favor of hunting down Temu's room. Every reason we shouldn't explore our electric attraction vanished from my mind until all that remained was the desire. The need.

"Bek," Kiya said, grabbing my wrist and holding me back as I blew past the curtained doorway to my room. She kept her voice pitched low, hushed. "Where are you going?"

"There's something I need to do," I said, tugging against her hold.

She stared at me for a long moment, her eyes narrowing. Finally, she released my wrist.

I turned away from her to continue up the hallway, then turned back, biting my lower lip. "Do you know which room is Temu's?"

I could probably have figured it out on my own by following my nose—the man smelled divine, like mulled wine sweetened with honey—but I preferred to save myself the indignity of sniffing the curtains to every guest room.

Kiya pursed her lips and crossed her arms over her chest. Now that she knew who—and likely *what*—I was after, she was less interested in helping me.

"Temu would never hurt me," I swore, stepping closer to her.

She frowned. "He's not the one I'm worried will hurt you."

Inyotef. She was worried about Inyotef—about what he would do to me if Temu and I hooked up. Temu had expressed concerns about the same thing.

My brow furrowed. Inyotef was possessive, yeah, but I couldn't imagine him actually hurting me. Besides, I would be gone in the morning, sailing away with Nitocris, far beyond his reach.

I waved away Kiya's concern with a brush of my hand. "Don't worry about Inyotef," I told her. "I'm taking care of it."

Kiya narrowed her eyes, looking far from convinced.

"Please," I said, gripping Kiya's upper arms and giving her a gentle shake. My brows bunched together and climbed higher as I implored her to help me.

This was my last chance to be with Temu. My only chance. Come morning, I would be gone, and I would never see him again.

"Which room is Temu's?" Desperation laced through my words.

Kiya sighed, her crossed arms loosened to hang at her sides, and she glanced up at the ceiling and shook her head like she couldn't believe she was about to do whatever she was about to do.

"Fine," Kiya said and brushed past me, heading up the hallway. "It's this way."

I squealed silently, then jogged to catch up with her.

Kiya led me all the way to the end of the hallway and around a corner, toward the barracks at the back of the palace. After rounding two more corners, we entered another long hallway bordered by curtained doorways. I had never been to this part of the palace, but it appeared to be another wing of guest rooms. Muffled, amorous noises drifted down the hallway to my ears, and I assumed some of the canoodlers from the courtyard had taken the fun back to their guest room.

Until Kiya stopped in front of the curtained doorway to the room that seemed to be the source of those noises. Dreadful anticipation twisted in my gut and my hand shook as I reached for the edge of the curtain.

I pulled the thick linen barrier aside a few inches, more than enough to get a good view of the room—as well as of the carnal scene within.

Temu lay sprawled on his back on a woven wool rug in the center of the room, his right shoulder to me, every inch of his scarred, bronze skin and hard-muscled body bared to the night. Nitocris sat astride him, her back arched and head thrown back as she rocked her hips. Her small breasts jiggled with each undulation of her lower body. Temu's long fingers dug into her hips, grinding her pelvis against his. Forcing himself more deeply into her.

I covered my mouth with one shaking hand, holding in a gasp. But I couldn't look away.

At that moment, I hated Nitocris more than I had ever hated another living being. More than I hated the bandits who attacked the caravan. More than I hated the attempted rapists in the market. More than I hated the Netjer who had killed me.

It should have been me in there, giving my body to Temu. He was supposed to be mine. He was *mine*.

And, suddenly, he was looking at me.

Temu's eyes burned into me like molten lava, and the hatred raging through my veins morphed into arousal so sharp and hot that I almost spontaneously orgasmed right then and there.

With a growl, Temu pulled the queen closer, until her chest was flush against his, and he flipped her onto her back. The way he moved, so beautifully powerful, like a panther taking down a kill, made me want him even more. Even as I watched him take another woman.

His eyes remained locked with mine, his expression savage. He covered her mouth with one large hand, muffling her cries as he rammed into her. She thrashed her head from side to side under his hand, and the throbbing sensation between my legs was so intense, it was almost like I could feel what she felt. Like Temu was pounding into me instead of her.

My breaths came faster, and my heart jackhammered in my chest. I had never been more pissed off—or turned on—in my entire life.

Temu's thrusting reached a crescendo, and every inch of hard, gleaming muscle on him went rigid, locked in the pleasure of his moment of climax. And even then, his eyes never left mine.

I stumbled backward, letting the curtain fall back into place. I barely registered bumping into Kiya before I spun away from her and fled.

Somehow, I found my way back to my room, Kiya close on my heels.

"Holy fuck," I murmured in English as I burst through the curtain and into the shelter of my dark room. Old Egyptian may have been my first language, but English was still my go-to for profanity. My whole body trembled as I paced frantically. "Holy fucking fuck."

I felt hot and cold all over, my blood burning with lust unlike anything I had ever experienced, even as ice coated my heart in a chilling rage. I rubbed my hands up and down my arms, over my neck and face, my lips. My skin was hypersensitive, my groin swollen and pulsing.

I *needed*. To be touched. Tasted. Filled. Fucked. Hard, fast, and deep, the way Temu would give it to me. The way I had seen him give it to Nitocris.

"Fuck!" I hissed.

"I hoped you would still be up," said a voice far deeper than Kiya's.

I froze, breathing hard, and slowly turned to face the man who had entered my room.

Inyotef stood shadowed in the darkness just inside the doorway, the curtain at his back. Kiya watched him with gigantic eyes, pressing herself back into the wall to his right so hard it looked like she was trying to disappear into the mudbrick.

My stare flicked to her, and I nodded that it was okay for her to leave.

She slipped silently behind Inyotef and out of the room, the curtain flapping from her abrupt exit.

My attention returned to Inyotef.

He wasn't the man I wanted, but he was still a beautiful man, and his eyes shone with the appropriate shade of desire. For me. And after watching Temu with the queen, I didn't give a fuck *how* my needs were met, or by *whom*, so long as they were met right fucking now. My libido had never been picky.

Inyotef stalked toward me, and I backed up, keeping pace with him until my shoulder blades touched the wall behind me. His gaze wandered up and down my body, lingering on my heaving breasts, on the expanse of cleavage exposed by the deep "V" of my dress.

I arched my back as he approached, anticipating his touch. Inviting it.

Inyotef stopped in front of me, leaving a few scant inches separating us. He slid his hands up my arms, gliding over my shoulders and stroking the column of my neck before hooking his thumbs through the straps of bunched black linen holding up the top half of my dress. He guided the straps over my shoulders and let them fall, baring my breasts to him.

A low, rough noise rumbled in his throat, stoking my desire higher. He moved closer, pressing his pelvis against mine as he palmed my breasts, kneading their fullness and flicking the pads of his thumbs over my nipples. The hot, hard length of his erection nudged against my swollen sex, and I ground against him, capitalizing on the added friction of the layers of fabric separating us.

Inyotef hissed, his jaw rigid, and dropped his hands to my thighs, greedily bunching up my skirt. I did the same with his schenti, grasping his bare shaft in a firm grip. The fingers of one of his hands slid between my legs, delving deep into my molten center, even as the other gripped my thigh and hitched my leg up, opening me to him further. I hooked my heel behind his thigh and guided him toward my entrance.

Inyotef thrust forward, hard, filling me in that single jerk of his hips. I squeezed my eyes shut as his body slammed into mine, again and again. The ache within me grew. The pressure built. The need for more became all-consuming.

More. But not from him.

In my mind, another man's hands gripped my hips. Another man's scent wrapped around me. Another man thrust into me, over and over and over.

But it wasn't enough. My release remained just out of reach.

Inyotef stiffened, reaching his own climax without me. He groaned, burying his face in the crook of my neck, his hands cinching the sides of my waist.

Panting and disappointed, I lowered my shaking leg to the floor.

Inyotef brushed a soft kiss against my neck and withdrew from my body, leaving me feeling more hollow than ever. He raised his head, and I thought he was going to kiss me, but he pulled back, gazing into my eyes in the most searching, unsettling way.

Could he tell I had been imagining he was someone else? Did he know? Did he care?

He leaned in close, but still, he didn't kiss me. "You are *mine*," he whispered, his stare intense.

Without another word, he released me and stepped back. Then he turned away and strode through the curtain.

"What the fuck?" I mouthed to the empty room.

For minutes, I stood with my back against the wall, breathing hard and choking on regret. I shouldn't have done that. I should *not* have done that. My gut told me giving my body to Inyotef had been a huge mistake.

I finally pushed away from the wall and, feet dragging, stumbled to bed. I sprawled on the hard, thin mattress and squeezed my eyes shut. A tear snuck free, streaking across my temple. I wanted to sleep, only so I could wake and discover this had all been a bad dream.

Temu and Nitocris.

Inyotef and me.

Please, let it all have been a terrible, twisted dream.

29

I NEVER DID MANAGE to fall asleep. There was no clock for me to watch the painfully slow passage of time, so instead, I stared up at the window cutouts high in the wall, watching the night slowly lighten to dawn. Once there was enough pale light for me to pack by, I rose and gathered my things together, stuffing everything I owned into a pair of woven baskets.

Everything except for the jewelry and clothing Inyotef had given me, because *fuck that guy*. I didn't belong to him, I didn't need his charity, and I certainly wasn't his whore.

I scrubbed my body as well as I could, but a sponge bath would never cleanse me completely of Inyotef's scent. Of the grimy residue of his *claiming*.

Images of our coupling flashed in my mind's eye, leaving me sick to my stomach. Only a good, long soaking would do the trick. A good, long soaking, and a lot of time.

I set my full baskets by the door and turned to survey the room. This would be the last time I stood here. As soon as I pushed through the curtain, I intended to track down Nitocris and latch onto her like a barnacle until we were on her ship and sailing away.

Despite my intensely negative feelings toward her while I peeped in on her dalliance with Temu, I didn't hate the queen. I could hardly blame her for leaping at the chance to jump Temu's bones, especially not when I had been desperate to do the exact same thing.

Rather, it was Temu who earned my ire. I felt like he had betrayed me.

An image of the way his gaze had burned into me while he had been buried deep inside Nitocris flashed through my mind, and I closed my eyes. He had wanted *me*, even then. Even when he was with her. So, why had he done it? Why had he taken *her* to his room?

Bile climbed up my throat, and my stomach lurched. I gripped my neck with one shaking hand, swallowing repeatedly. I refused to be sick over a man jilting me. I was better than that.

I inhaled deeply, blowing out the breath through my pursed lips. Another deep breath, and the nausea eased. Another, and *most* of the trembling abated.

Straightening my shoulders, I turned around and reached out to push the curtain aside. And blinked in surprise. Inyotef leaned his back against the opposite wall of the hallway in Kiya's usual place, his expression serious and his stare leveled on me.

"Divine one," Inyotef said in greeting. He pushed off the wall and stalked toward me.

I backed up a step, letting the curtain fall back in place.

Inyotef pushed through the curtain and entered my room.

"What are you doing here?" I asked as I hastily sidestepped, not interested in letting him back me against the wall again. I did *not* want a repeat of what happened last night. Just thinking about him touching me again made my stomach turn and sent imaginary bugs skittering all over my skin, and it was an effort not to shimmy and shake with revulsion.

Inyotef stopped three steps into the room and glanced at my packed baskets. "There is something we must discuss," he said, his stare returning to me.

Shitshitshitshit *shit*. He knew. That had to be what this was about. He knew I was planning on leaving with the queen. I gripped the sides of my white linen skirt with clammy hands. Was he going to try to stop me?

Oh, who was I kidding? There would be no *trying* about it. Stopping me would be easy enough. He was the one with a small army at his command, after all. I was comparatively powerless. Especially now that I had made the mistake of screwing him.

"Where's Nitocris?" I asked, hating the slight quaver in my voice. "I wish to bid her farewell." I would leave all of my things behind, so long as she took me with her.

A slow, cruel grin curved Inyotef's lips. "Alas, she is already gone. Her ship cast off at first light. But you'll see my betrothed again soon enough. We will be staying at her palace in Men-nefer, after all."

My heart sank into my lurching stomach, my expression falling with it. I turned away from Inyotef and pressed my palm into my belly, swallowing down a resurgence of bile. There would be no escape from this place. No escape from Inyotef. He was my only way downriver now. I needed him, and my focus shifted to considering ways to evade him in the meantime.

I was so thrown by the revelation that the queen had left—without me—that it took me a small eternity to process Inyotef's other words.

His *betrothed*. Did that mean she had agreed to marry him? To merge their two kingdoms? To unite all of Egypt? Was that why she had left me? Was leaving me behind part of the deal?

But—if she was marrying Inyotef, then what had been that thing with Temu last night? Was it just for fun? One last fling? Did Inyotef know? Maybe he didn't care who his intended fucked? Maybe he wasn't obsessed with possessing her the way he seemed to be with me?

"Oh." I forced a serene mask into place and turned to face Inyotef. "Well, I look forward to seeing her again." I glanced at the window cutouts, gauging the early morning light.

The sun would rise soon. If I could get rid of Inyotef quickly, I might be able to catch Temu on his way back to the palace from the dunes. I needed to know what was going on with him and Nitocris because my gut told me last night hadn't just been about attraction. At least, not on his end. There was a whole lot more going on, and I couldn't help but think it had something to do with why Temu was here in the first place.

"Come, sit," Inyotef said, strolling toward the low table. "Tell me about your family in Men-nefer."

My stare snapped back to Inyotef, my mind reeling with mental whiplash, and I watched him ease down to sit on a floor cushion. "My—my family?"

I twisted my bracelet around on my wrist, my thoughts automatically turning to the symbol of my clan, the lapis lazuli Wedjat emblem set into the gold. In my mind's eye, my siblings were still the children they had been when I left this time two decades ago, even though I knew they would be grown now, likely with young children of their own.

But I wasn't about to tell Inyotef any of that. My gut warned me to *never* tell him *anything* about them.

I glanced at the doorway as a servant pushed the curtain aside and carried in a tray of wine, cut fruit, cheese, and a loaf of bread still steaming from the oven. My stomach curdled at the thought of putting anything in it. The servant set the tray on the table and hurried from the room. I glimpsed Kiya pacing out in the hallway before the servant yanked the curtain closed.

"And which of Heru's wives is your mother—Meryet or Seshseshet?" Inyotef asked, dumping a bucket of ice-cold dread over me.

I stared at him wide-eyed, shock melting away my serene mask.

Inyotef smiled and nodded to himself, reaching for the pitcher to fill a chalice with rose-colored wine. "Nitocris has spent some time with your father," Inyotef explained. "She recognized him in your face . . . especially in your eyes. Once she mentioned it, well . . ." He glanced at my bracelet. "It made sense."

I swallowed roughly and released the bracelet, lowering my hands. I never should have worn the stupid thing in front of him.

"I wish nothing more than to reunite you with your family, divine one," Inyotef said, extending an arm to the floor cushions beyond the other side of the table. He smiled up at me, but his eyes remained cold.

Numbly, I approached the table and dropped to my knees on a cushion.

"In fact," Inyotef said, "I've moved up our travel plans. We will cast off in three days."

My brows rose, my lips parting. "Really?"

Inyotef nodded once, his eyes locking with mine. There was something dark and ominous about the way he looked at me that clashed with his friendly words. "But first," he said, "would you do something for me—to ensure we have a safe voyage?"

I swallowed roughly, completely off balance. "What would you like me to do?"

"Oh, nothing too difficult." Inyotef sipped his wine, looking away with overt nonchalance. "Just take a peek into the future and make sure it is safe for us to travel at this time." He glanced at me sidelong, his brow furrowed. "It seems reckless not to use every tool at our disposal. After all, these are such dangerous times."

I stared at him, stunned. Not blinking. Not breathing. I didn't know what I had expected, but it certainly wasn't this. Not the one thing I couldn't do.

This differed from the bargain I had made with Nitocris because Inyotef wanted me to view the Echoes *before* our trip. There was no way for me to shirk my end of the deal when I had to pay up front.

Ever so slowly, I shook my head. "I can't." I swallowed roughly. "I can't do what you ask."

Inyotef raised one shoulder and looked away. "If I can't guarantee your safety during our voyage, then I'm not sure I feel comfortable embarking on this trip at all."

I shook my head with more vehemence. Even if I was willing to do what Inyotef asked me to do—to view the Echoes—I couldn't have done it. I literally didn't know how.

And even if I knew how to view the Echoes, I would never view them for Inyotef, just as I wouldn't have followed through on my bargain with Nitocris. I wouldn't view the Echoes for *anyone* in this ancient time.

I splayed my hands palm down on the table. "I can't do what you ask," I repeated, enunciating each word carefully.

"You can't do it?" Inyotef asked, his voice dripping with malice. "Or you *won't*? Because Nitocris seemed to be under the impression you would view the Echoes for her . . ."

"I *can't*," I repeated. I looked at him beseechingly, tears welling in my eyes. "I just—I can't do it."

Inyotef's face turned stony as he dropped all pretense of friendliness. He believed me. He knew no words would convince me to help him in this. "Then our trip to Men-nefer is postponed indefinitely," he snapped. "If you won't guarantee our safety, then we won't be going anywhere."

"But—but—" I gripped the edge of the table, my nail beds blanching of color. "But you were planning on taking this trip before you even met me."

Inyotef laughed under his breath, the sound cruel. "Perhaps I shall go without you, as I had planned to do before I met you." He sneered, the expression so cruel, it was like I was staring at an entirely different person.

This was my first clear view of the man Kiya and Temu had warned me about. The man I had thought I could jerk around with my feminine wiles. Why, oh *why*, hadn't I listened to them?

Inyotef set down his wine and climbed to his feet. "Kiya," he called toward the hallway. "Come."

Kiya pushed through the curtain, followed by a pair of male guards. She avoided looking at me, causing icy dread to pool in my belly.

"You could have made this easy," Inyotef spat, looming over me imperiously. He glanced at Kiya and the guards flanking her. "Lock her up," he ordered before turning away and striding from the room.

Kiya's eyes flicked to me, just for a moment. She looked like she was about to vomit. Funny, because I *felt* like I was about to vomit. She turned on her heel, nodded to the guard at her left, then followed Inyotef out of the room, abandoning me to my fate.

I stared after Kiya, paralyzed by shock. I didn't even fight the guards when they closed in on me. When they gripped my arms and dragged me up to my feet and hauled me from the room. When they locked me away in a cell hidden in a cellar dug into the bedrock beneath the palace.

Because now I knew the truth. I knew why Inyotef had tracked me down in that inn. I knew why he had brought me here to his palace. I knew what he wanted from me.

He wanted a pet Nejeret. Someone to view the Echoes for him. To guide him in making decisions that would increase his power to near absolute status. He wanted me to abuse the timeline so grossly that the future I was trying to get back to would never come to pass.

Which meant this was it for me. The end.

Because *that* was something I would never—ever—do.

PRESENT DAY

KAT

G ASPING IN A BREATH, I sat bolt upright in bed. A sheen of cold sweat coated my skin, making the sheets tangled around my bare legs cling like plastic wrap. I kicked the stubborn covers away, appreciating the lick of cool air on my clammy skin, and dangled one leg over the edge of the mattress. Nik slept soundly on his back beside me, not yet disturbed by my abrupt wake up.

I saw her—Tarset—while I slept, and it definitely hadn't been a dream. Every once in a while, the universe liked to feed me Echoes while I slept. I was the only person who still seemed able to view them. Or, at least, I used to be. It hadn't happened for a couple of months, since before the showdown with the Netjers in the oasis. Since my connection to the universe went haywire.

But this, I felt certain, had been an Echo. A nightmarish Echo, but an Echo, nonetheless.

In it, Tarset stood in a cramped, dark room, surrounded by walls, a ceiling, and a floor of rough-hewn rock. The faintest trickle of light drifted into the small room through the crack under the door, leaving Tarset in near darkness. Her wrists were bound with tightly knotted rope and pulled taut over her head. The length of the rope looped through a ring secured into the top of the wall at her back, then tied to a knob near the door, well out of the reach of even her feet. Her fingers were curled tightly around the rope, likely to alleviate the stress on her shoulders. I could relate. I had experienced that pain firsthand.

As horrifying as the scene in the Echo-dream had been, it revived a spark of hope. Tarset was alive. Since first noticing she was gone, we hadn't known whether we should search for her—or for her body. But now I was certain. Tarset was still alive. A little worse for wear, but alive.

All I had to do now was find her. And if my connection to the universe really was repairing itself, then there was a good chance I would eventually be able to track her down.

I scrubbed my hands over my face, then combed my fingers through my hair. My fingers crackled with static electricity as they reached the tangled ends of my locks. I felt it then. The faint tingle, so subtle, humming in every cell of my body. If I looked into a mirror right now, my eyes would likely be glowing with vibrant swirls of soul-energy.

My connection to the universe hadn't gone dormant when I woke. It was still active.

With one trembling hand, I reached for the deck of tarot cards sitting on the nightstand beside the bed. I hadn't touched them in weeks, too afraid of the frustration and disappointment that came every time I tried—and failed—to find Tarset.

But this time would be different. I could feel it in my bones. In my soul.

I twisted the switch on the lamp to turn on the low-wattage bulb, tucked in my legs to sit tailor style, and hastily shuffled the tarot cards on one knee.

Beside me in the bed, Nik groaned and draped an arm over his eyes to block the light from the lamp. "What are you doing, Kitty Kat?" he asked, his voice rough with sleep. "You're making the air sizzle."

"Sorry," I whispered, wincing as I glanced at him. "I didn't mean to wake you. Go back to sleep."

Nik raised his arm just enough to peek out at me. "Are *you* going back to sleep?"

I shook my head, my lips pressed together into a frown as I shuffled the cards one more time. The shuffling wasn't strictly necessary. It was more of a delaying tactic than anything. After that Echo-dream, I had a feeling I would not like what the universe wanted to tell me.

"Then, neither am I," Nik said with a sigh. He sat up, his abdominal muscles bunching in the most deliciously distracting way.

His skin was more bare than inked, at the moment, which was unusual for him, but every day we made a little more progress on that front. In another week or two, the ratio of bare to inked skin would flip in favor of the ink. Nik said he felt naked without it. *And*, since Nik was one of those rare souls who inextricably linked pain with pleasure, I didn't mind indulging his urgent need for new ink one bit. It always—*always* worked out in my favor in the end.

And if I ogled him any longer while thinking about all the things we did together after I tattooed him, I was going to wuss out on this assuredly uncomfortable tarot reading in favor of something guaranteed to be *much* more comfortable. I tapped the tip of my index finger against the top tarot card in the stack, feeling the zing of otherworldly energy charging the deck. Sucking in a breath and holding it, I flipped the top card over and set it down in front of me on the bed.

The Star, reversed. Loneliness and loss of courage. Defeat. The card was much the same as before, displaying Tarset scooping water from that oasis pool, a winged scarab in the place of the eighth star near the horizon. The only notable difference in the design was that the scarab was gold instead of black.

I frowned, unsure what the change suggested.

Nik slid his arm around my lower back, his hand coming to rest on my hip, and propped his chin on my shoulder. "You saw her?"

I glanced at him, just for a moment. "Yeah," I said, then flipped the next card and set it down beside the first. A shiver traveled down my spine at the image displayed on the card.

Tarset appeared much as I had seen her in the Echo-dream. She was tied up against a stone wall, hanging by the rope knotted around her wrists, her white nightgown or dress in tatters. She was surrounded by darkness, her face obscured by shadows. The only bright element in the design was the golden scarab lurking in the very corner of the card.

The Hanged Man. Sacrifice. Delay. Waiting for some sort of transformation. This card wasn't usually as bad of an omen as the name suggested, but this time it had a decidedly sinister feel.

Nik inhaled deeply through his nose, held it for a few seconds, then let the breath out slowly. Only he could make a single breath sound so disapproving. "Are you sure this is wise?"

I snorted a laugh. No, I wasn't sure. But then, I wasn't sure of anything these days. Well, except for Nik. He was my rock. My anchor. And every once in a while, my ball and chain.

I drew the next card but hesitated before flipping it over. In my gut, I suspected which card it would be.

"She's a prisoner," I told Nik. "That's what I saw when I was sleeping."

His grip on my hip tightened, and tension coiled in his muscles, turning him to stone behind me.

I flipped the card and set it down.

The Nine of Swords, reversed. Powerlessness. Suffering. Despair. Again, the design showed Tarset in that cell, only this time, she sat on the floor, nude, her knees curled up to her chest and her face turned away. Her back was mostly visible, displaying the bloody image of a winged scarab carved into her flesh.

I touched the next card atop the deck, but it felt flat and lifeless. No hum of otherworldly energy charged the remaining cards in the deck. Everything the universe wanted to tell me was contained in the three cards lying faceup on the bed.

"Can you take a picture of this spread?" I asked Nik, not willing to take my eyes off the cards. I was barely even letting myself blink, afraid that if I looked away, even for a second, the designs would change.

The things I drew had a tendency to do that—to take on a life of their own and rearrange themselves. And considering I could still feel the electric zing of the soul-energy charging my every cell, the ink on the cards could very well shift at any moment.

Nik's arm slipped away from my back as he reached for his phone on his nightstand. He snapped a couple of photos, then set the phone down on the comforter in front of him.

I scooped up the cards, shuffled a few times, and drew the top three, laying them down in quick succession. The three-card spread was exactly the same as before. Same cards. Same order. Same orientation. Same designs. I gathered the cards and went through the process three more times. The results were the same each time.

"What does it mean?" Nik asked when I didn't immediately scoop up the cards after laying out the same three-card spread for the fifth time in a row.

"I'm not sure," I murmured, my eyes narrowed as I continued to study the trio of cards.

The universe had more to tell me. I could feel it. But clearly, the cards weren't going to do the trick. I gathered them again and straightened the stack before twisting to return the tarot deck to the nightstand. I opened the top drawer and pulled out a sketch pad, then fished around blindly for a pen. Once I was armed with ink and paper, I set the sketch pad on my lap and relaxed, letting the otherworldly energy take over.

I slipped into a trancelike state, my hand moving seemingly of its own accord, furiously covering the paper with black ink.

Until, without warning, the energy charging my soul fizzled out. My hand stilled, my connection to the universe going dormant.

I blinked, focusing on the sketch. It was a maze.

I squinted and pursed my lips. No, not a maze—a map. Of a city. But *what* city?

I lifted my hand, pulling the tip of the pen away from the last thing I had drawn—a small, distinct "X" like what so often appeared on a treasure map.

I shook my head and angled the sketch pad toward Nik. "Do you know where this is?" He was millennia old, and he had been *everywhere*. Even if I didn't recognize the layout of the streets, there was a good chance he would.

Nik narrowed his eyes, studying the map. "Maybe," he said, drawing out the word. He touched his fingertip to the tiny black "X" mark. "What's here?"

"Tarset," I said, her name little more than a whisper. "She's there."

I looked into Nik's eyes, my conviction and desperation overflowing in the form of a tear. I swallowed roughly, my chin trembling. "She's there, and she's hurting, Nik. I can feel her." My connection to the soul-energy suddenly flared back to life, fed by the swell of emotion within me. "She needs us, so please—*please*—tell me you know where this is."

Nik leaned in, catching that lone tear with the faintest brush of his lips. His pale blue eyes reflected the rainbow glow of the soul-energy saturating my gaze.

"I think it's Thebes," he said. "Or, I suppose it would be Luxor. My mom'll know for sure. We'll figure this out, Kitty Kat." Leaning in closer, he pressed a gentle, almost chaste kiss to my lips. "Just—" He rested his forehead against mine. "No more for tonight, all right?"

"All right," I breathed, letting my eyelids flutter shut as I focused on taking slow, even breaths in my attempt to reel the soul-energy back in.

Nik kissed me again, slow and lingering and definitely *not* chaste. "And if you were crossing your fingers," he said when he broke the kiss and pulled away, the sharp edge of warning in his voice mirrored in his eyes. "I'm going to take it out on your ass."

I shivered, equally thrilled and terrified at the prospect. I hadn't been crossing my fingers, but I sure as hell was now.

I held up my hand, ensuring Nik was fully aware of my need for his unique brand of punishment. I was pleased to see the multicolored glow had dimmed as my arousal flared. It usually did, and I absolutely did not mind that sex was Nik's go-to method for driving away the soul-energy to prevent me from losing consciousness due to what we had concluded were mystical overdoses.

Nik's eyes narrowed to slits as he focused on my crossed fingers, and a low growl rumbled in his chest. He clenched his jaw, making the angular lines of his face even more chiseled and defined than before.

He reclaimed his phone to snap a photo of the map, his thumbs racing over the keyboard on the bottom half of the screen as he sent the map to Aset for confirmation. When he finished typing out his message, he tossed the phone aside on the bed and turned the full, carnal force of his stare on me.

I gulped and scooted toward the edge of the bed. Away from Nik. My heart was suddenly hammering in my chest as some primitive instinct told me to run. Because the man sharing my bed was every inch a predator.

Nik grabbed my ankle, squeezing just shy of too hard, and jerked me closer to him. I yelped when he gripped my other knee and flipped me onto my stomach before I even had a chance to *think* about struggling. He yanked on one side of my panties, tearing the thin fabric to bare my backside. Apparently, he had meant *ass* in the literal sense.

A moment later, there was a loud smack and a sharp sting on my left cheek. Nik immediately massaged the sore flesh, the tips of his fingers dipping between my legs to just barely skim along my outer lips in the most enticing way.

Blood rushed to my groin, and I grinned into my pillow. "Come on, Nik," I taunted over my shoulder and raised my booty, wiggling it at him. "You can do better than that."

His lips curved into the loveliest, wickedest grin.

The sting of the next slap brought tears to my eyes, the sharp pain making the tantalizing sweeps of his fingertips between my legs that much sweeter. He grabbed a fistful of my hair, wrapping it around his hand to hold my head in place while he covered my body with his. His fingers delved deeper between my thighs, parting my outer lips and pinching my aching bud at the same moment as his soul brushed against the outer edge of mine.

I gasped, overwhelmed by the exquisite sensations. The combination of physical and spiritual bliss was almost too much.

Nik tightened his hold on my hair, making me arch my back, grinding my ass against him. "Naughty or nice, Kitty Kat?" he asked, his breath hot against my ear.

He slipped two fingers inside me and, again, skimmed his soul along the edge of mine. I squeezed my eyes shut, basking in the blinding pleasure, and arched my back further. I rolled my hips as I ground against his fingers in front and the hard length of him behind me.

I couldn't sense the soul-energy at all any more. There was only Nik.

Nik chuckled, low and rough. "Naughty, it is."

31

LEX

"T HIS IS IMPORTANT," HERU said, his voice low and controlled. He stood at the window in the second-floor study, his hands clasped behind his back, surveying the oasis spread out before him. The defined muscles in his forearms, bared by his rolled shirtsleeves, flexed and relaxed as he periodically clenched his fists.

"They should be here," he added. "*She* should be here. We might need her to commune with the soul-energy again—for more specifics about Tarsi's location."

I pushed off from the edge of the desk, where I had been leaning, arms crossed over my chest, staring at Heru's back. "Nik will never allow it."

Nik's text message to Aset was very clear. He and Kat would check in come morning—Alaska time—but until then, we were on our own. *Don't call us, we'll call you.* Those were Nik's parting words.

"If you show up on their doorstep unannounced . . ." I gripped Heru's wrist and raised his arm, ducking my head as I draped his arm around my shoulders.

So far as I knew, Heru had never gone head to head in a real fight with Nik, and while I had the utmost respect and admiration for my husband's considerable skills in hand-to-hand combat, I wasn't confident he could best Nik. And we did not need Heru limping around with a wounded ego, especially not with the heavy emotional burdens he already carried. *That*, superficial as it was, just might break him. Our people needed him right now, the uncrowned king leading us through the fallout of the greatest crisis this world had ever faced.

Heru pulled me in close to his side, pressing a kiss to the top of my head. "I just want to find my little girl."

I wrapped my arms around his middle. Tension thrummed through him, turning his muscles to electrified steel. "And we *will* find her," I assured him. I tilted my head back, gazing up at him. "Just give Aset a chance to lock in the location on Kat's map."

The map was of Thebes, or *Waset* as it had been known to the ancient Egyptians, circa the First Intermediate Period around 2160 to 2060 BCE. Little remained of that ancient city—almost nothing to use as a reference point in laying the sketch over a modern map of Luxor. *But* apparently, Aset had lived in Waset during that era, and she had recognized a few landmarks on the map and was puzzling out the modern location of the "X" right now.

Heru clenched his jaw, his nostrils flaring with his barely contained need to argue.

I gave him a squeeze. "Festina lente," I murmured. It was the original Latin behind one of his favorite maxims, which roughly translated to *slow is fast*. It was time for Heru to practice what he preached. It wouldn't do Tarset any good to have us running through Luxor like chickens with our heads cut off, raiding every building we came across.

Heru's cheek twitched in response.

"She's alive," I reminded him, resting my temple on his shoulder. "Thanks to Kat, we know that now, which is more than we knew an hour ago."

Heru made a rough, wordless grunt of agreement.

At the sound of multiple pairs of footsteps behind us, I raised my head and peered toward the doorway leading in from the hall. A deadly duo entered the study: Dom and Mari. Our very capable backup on the impending mission to Luxor, who looked like they had just walked off a catwalk in Milan.

Petite, polished, and pretty, Mari was, undercover, lethal, with a penchant for toying with her victims before she dispatched them to the hereafter. She, like Heru and me, was one of the rare, lucky Nejerets with an additional facet of her immortal soul—a *sheut*—giving her otherworldly abilities. Her *sheut* enabled her to pull the single deadliest element in the universe—anti-*At*, which was essentially solidified chaos—into the physical dimension and shape the obsidian substance to her will.

Onyx-like anti-*At* daggers were her go-to weapon. The blades were scalpel sharp and packed the added punch of being able to erase—as in completely eradicate—an immortal soul from existence. One touch of anti-*At*, and a Nejeret would be *unmade*, totally erasing them from the timeline and reshaping the universe around their absence.

Like I said, solidified chaos.

Dom, my tall, dark, and lethal half brother, on the other hand, practiced careful restraint in his execution of the deadlier arts. Make no mistake, he was a master of all things dark and deadly. Heru had found Dom when he was still a young Nejeret—sent out on a mission to assassinate Heru, no less—and had taken him under his wing, teaching Dom everything he knew about pain and killing, and how to use both to extract whatever information he hunted. Dom didn't have a *sheut* to give him additional otherworldly abilities beyond the usual Nejeret longevity and heightened senses, but it was probably for the best. I wasn't sure the world could survive Dom being even *more* deadly.

I flashed them both a smile, silently thanking them for agreeing to come on such short notice. We didn't know what we would be walking into—or, rather, teleporting into—and we wanted to be prepared.

I tensed at the sound of quick footsteps moving up the hallway. A moment later, Aset appeared in the doorway.

She hurried into the study, brandishing her phone in front of her like a battering ram, and shouldered between Dom and Mari with a muttered, "Excuse me." The bright excitement in her eyes told me she had a lock on the location marked on Kat's map.

"It's a Hilton," she proclaimed, marching straight for our post at the window.

Heru's arm slipped from my shoulders as he turned around to face his sister.

"As in—a hotel?" I clarified, my brows bunching together. Nik's text had included a troubling few lines about Kat *seeing* Tarset tied up in a dungeon.

Aset nodded and set her phone down on Heru's desk, the screen displaying a bird's-eye-view satellite image of what I assumed to be the aforementioned Hilton. Heru and I moved closer to the desk, leaning in to study the image on the phone's screen.

It showed a pretty fancy-looking resort, with a multi-pool outdoor lounge area, broad patches of pristine green lawn, and a whole slew of palm trees. It was all surrounded by several rectangular buildings, each of which was topped with another, more private pool and lounge area.

"The hotel has a dungeon?" I asked, certain I was missing something.

"Not exactly," Aset said, her eyes meeting mine for the briefest moment. "It's been a Hilton for almost a century," she explained. "But the site where they built the hotel has been many things over the years. Millennia ago, this was the location of the royal palace in Waset, and that palace likely would have had a dungeon dug into the bedrock."

"It did," Heru murmured. At my questioning look, he added, "I resided in that palace during Haty's reign." He glanced at me, but quickly returned his focus to the phone's screen.

I blinked, momentarily stunned by this reminder of exactly who I had married. The same man who had once been consort to the legendary Queen Hatchepsut.

Dom and Mari crossed the room, one standing on either end of the desk to get a look at the phone's screen.

"Yes, well," Aset said. "Parts of the palace's perimeter wall still stand—they incorporated the ancient front gate into the entrance to the resort's main restaurant, here." She tapped the tip of her fingernail against the screen, directly over a walled courtyard attached to one building. "It will give us a reference point."

Silence settled over our group as we studied the satellite image.

Heru glanced at his sister. "Do you truly think the ancient dungeon could still be intact—and *in use*?"

Aset shrugged one shoulder, her lips pressed together into a flat line. "It's the only explanation I have for what Kat saw." The apology in her eyes suggested she didn't think it was all that plausible. "Can you sense Tarsi there?" she asked Heru.

Heru closed his eyes, concentrating. Part of his *sheut*-given abilities enabled him to get a lock on an individual's essence and teleport to their exact location—most of the time. Certain types of electromagnetic fields could block his internal radar and prevent access via teleportation, as could a solid barrier of *At*.

After several heartbeats, Heru exhaled heavily, opened his eyes, and shook his head. "Still nothing." He clenched his jaw so tightly, I was surprised we couldn't hear his teeth grinding together.

I reached out, rubbing Heru's upper arm. "It doesn't mean anything." I studied his rigid profile. "Kat has found people you couldn't sense before," I reminded him, glancing at Dom.

She had found Dom when nobody else could, even if it had been in a roundabout way and had unintentionally resulted in his eventual death. I forced a hopeful smile and refocused on Heru, hoping his thoughts hadn't veered off in the same morose direction as mine. With the way his expression slowly hardened, I was betting they had taken that same unfortunate turn.

My eyes narrowed as I stared at him. Heru's copper skin seemed to shimmer gold, and his black-rimmed gold irises took on a distinctly luminous quality. My husband struck a stunning figure any day of the week, but now he looked positively divine. It was subtle, whatever was happening to him. Or it was all in my head. I really wasn't sure.

Heru studied the satellite image on the phone's screen for another ten seconds, then looked up, first at Aset, then at me. If he noticed my scrutiny, he didn't mention it. "Let's go," he said, extending his arm over the desk, his open hand palm up.

Aset placed her hand in Heru's, and his fingers curled around hers. "Brother," she said, drawing out the word as she stared down at his hand.

Mari and Dom each reached out to grip Heru's forearm. I moved closer to his side, and he curved his arm around my back as I wrapped mine around his middle. Before Aset could say more, a breath-stealing flash of colors surrounded us, and the world fell away.

For an eternal moment, we hovered in the space between life and death. Between existence and nothingness. I was everywhere, every*when*. I was one with all things.

We exploded back into the physical world in a shimmering cloud. The vibrant, wispy strands of otherworldly energy evaporated in a matter of seconds, revealing a broad stretch of mostly brown, overgrown grass bordered by a once-luxurious pool deck. The deck was covered in a chaotic jumble of teak lounge chairs, many of which lay on their sides or were completely overturned. More lounge chairs and a few umbrellas sat at the bottom of the murky pool.

Of the four of us hitching a ride with Heru, only Mari seemed unaffected by the spatial jump. Dom dropped to one knee, his head bowed as he caught his breath. Aset bent almost double, her hands gripping her knees for support, gasping for air. I hugged my middle and stared at the dead grass swallowing my feet, repeating a silent mantra in my head.

Don't throw up . . . don't throw up . . . don't throw up . . .

Heru hugged me close to his side and pressed a kiss against my hair. "Are you all right, Little Ivanov?"

"I'm fine," I assured him, closing my eyes and taking one more, deep, even breath before forcing a smile and looking at him.

But was *he* all right? Or had I just been imagining things? His skin and eyes appeared perfectly normal now—no ethereal glow—though it was hard to tell definitively when he was standing in full sunlight.

Heru released me and turned in a slow circle, scanning our surroundings.

The abandoned resort was a ghost town, and my chest tightened at seeing this evidence of just how much the world had changed in the last two months. We rarely left the oasis, where it was easy to forget that much of the world had suffered catastrophically in the wake of our war with the Netjers.

Heru started toward an ancient-looking stone wall on the far side of the lawn, Dom flanking him and Mari stalking along a few paces away. The heavy wood door set into the middle of the wall hung open partway. That must have been the ancient palace wall Aset had mentioned.

I followed Heru, Aset falling in beside me.

"Is it just me, or was my dear brother *glowing* before we jumped?" Aset asked, pitching her voice low, her words for my ears alone.

I glanced at her sharply. "You noticed it, too?" I whispered. Looked like it hadn't been my imagination, after all.

"Has anything like that happened before?" Aset asked.

I shook my head, frowning.

Aset's eyes narrowed as she studied her brother's back. "It was different from when Kat glows," she murmured, musing aloud. "With her, it is like she is too saturated with soul-energy and it has nowhere to go but out through her eyes and skin. But this—" Aset shook her head, considering. "It didn't feel electric or *other*, like with Kat. It was more like an inner glow."

"Like an aura," I said.

"Yes," she agreed, nodding. "That's exactly what it was like—an aura."

Heru and Dom slipped through the doorway and out of sight. Aset and I had fallen behind while we talked, but now we picked up the pace to catch up. We hurried through the doorway, entering the walled courtyard Aset had pointed out on the satellite image, and stopped to scan the space. The courtyard was filled with teak tables surrounded by matching chairs, and aside from a few of the chairs lying on their sides, the outdoor dining area seemed ready for a lunch crowd that would never come.

Heru stood in the center of the courtyard, his eyes closed and his expression locked in intense concentration. I figured he was imagining this place the way it had been when he had lived in Hatchepsut's palace thousands of years ago.

Heru's eyelids snapped open, and he turned to his right, marching straight for a wall of windows.

"Heru, wait!" I called after him, taking a step to follow.

Too late. He vanished in a cloud of multicolored smoke a heartbeat before walking into the glass. I spotted him reappear on the other side of the windows, a mere shadow through the tinted glass.

"Merde," Dom hissed, running toward the half-open double doors to the hotel at the far end of the courtyard.

Mari marched straight for the wall of glass. She slowly raised her hands in front of her as she walked, coaxing vines gleaming like obsidian from the earth and sending them climbing up one of the glass panels. There was an eerie creaking sound, like breaking ice.

All at once, the glass cracked and shattered, tiny shards tinkling to the ground.

Mari crunched over the broken glass and through the gaping window frame, never missing a step.

Aset and I exchanged a look, then hurried after Mari into the restaurant's interior dining room, Dom racing in from the far end of the room, having made his roundabout way in through the door.

We followed Mari through the commercial kitchen, which was partially open to the dining room, the stainless steel surfaces covered in a faint coating of dust. We found Heru in the back of an oversized pantry area, filled with rows of empty shelving that must have once held non-perishables but had likely been picked over by locals in the two months since the Netjers unleashed hell on Earth.

Heru shoved against the end of an enormous chest freezer set against the back wall. In the dim light leaking in through the open doorway from the kitchen and dining room beyond, I could just make out the outline of a metal floor hatch peeking out from beneath the freezer. Dom rushed forward to help Heru, and after a half minute of manly grunts and screeching metal, the rectangular floor hatch was uncovered.

Heru crouched to grip the handle, then stood, pulling the hatch open on creaky hinges. A modern staircase constructed of diamond tread aluminum steps descended into absolute darkness. Heru hovered at the top of the descending stairs and Dom stood on the adjacent edge of the opening, both peering into the cellar.

"Here," I said, holding my hand out in front of me as Aset, Mari, and I moved closer. Raw *At* pooled in my open palm like liquid quicksilver, and with a focused thought, I shaped the otherworldly material into a baseball-sized orb. As it hardened, it took on the usual, opalescent quality of solidified *At*, and with a little coaxing on my part, it started to glow. I handed it to Heru.

He accepted my offering, then raised his foot to take the first step into the cellar.

"Wait," I warned him, my eyes locked with his. "You're not going down there alone."

Heru's jaw tensed, but he set his foot back down on the floor.

I quickly created three more glowing *At* orbs, which I passed out to the others, then made one final orb for myself. "All right," I said, raising my eyebrows and nodding toward the dark abyss.

Heru started down the stairs, and with each step, his glowing orb pushed the heavy darkness further back. Mari followed behind Heru, me trailing her, with Aset close on my heel. Dom hung back, guarding the hatch against any who might attempt to ambush us and trap us underground.

Normally being trapped wouldn't be a concern, what with Heru's ability to teleport into or out of nearly any place, but based on Heru's inability to sense Tarset in her prison, there was a good chance this underground area was teleportation-proof. We couldn't risk being imprisoned alongside Tarset in a botched attempt to free her.

When I reached the bottom of the metal stairway, I was surprised to find a relatively mundane-looking cellar. Wine racks lined the chiseled stone walls, and boxes of foodstuffs had been stacked into piles. I wondered if we had found the missing food from the shelves in the pantry above.

Was this the work of Atum—or whoever had taken Tarset? Had her captors moved the supplies down here, then covered the hatch with the freezer to keep their stash—and their captive—hidden?

The lead light from Heru's *At* orb moved into a narrow passage at the far end of the cellar. I pushed past Mari to keep up with him. The ceiling in the main room was plenty high, but it dropped in the narrower back passage, forcing Heru to bow his head and hunch his shoulders as he moved deeper into the cellar.

Squat, narrow doorways had been cut into the walls on either side of the passage, leading into narrow rooms, maybe six wide and ten feet deep. Looked like we had found the ancient dungeon. The ceiling was a little higher in the cells. The walls had been covered in plaster and painted with vibrant scenes a millennium or two ago, but the plaster was crumbling too badly now to make out the images. Large patches were missing, revealing portions of the original, rough-hewn stone walls beneath.

I peeked into each cell, but only found more boxes of food. More cases of wine. One cell was filled entirely with rolls of toilet paper.

The passage ended in a solid, unbroken wall of stone after the fourth set of cell doors. Heru stood in the final doorway on the right, peering into the small room, looking utterly defeated. I knew before I reached him that Tarset wasn't in there. She wasn't down here at all.

"I don't understand," Heru said, his voice a choked whisper. "She's supposed to be down here."

I moved closer to the cell opposite his. The doorway was blocked by a padlocked wrought-iron gate, the interior empty. Because of the locked gate, obviously. There was something odd about the exposed stone portions of the walls, like the rough chisel marks had been disrupted by some sort of carvings or engravings too faint to make out clearly from this distance.

I held my hand over the padlock and closed my eyes, pushing raw *At* into the opening to shape the perfect key. Once I had the form of the lock, I solidified the *At* and turned the key. The padlock popped open, and I quickly pulled it free from the latch on the gate and dropped it on the floor.

Heru turned to watch as I pushed the gate open and stepped into the cell.

"What is it?" he asked, his hushed voice resonating off the stone walls in the creepiest way.

He had already peered in here through the bars, having turned away when he didn't find his daughter imprisoned within. He hung back in the doorway as I moved closer to the left-hand wall, my luminous *At* orb brandished in front of me.

I raised my free hand to trace my fingertips over the writing scratched into the walls. It was the faintest etching, a mere ghost of words. "Tarset was here," I breathed.

"What do you mean?" Heru followed me into the cell, scanning the walls, ceiling, and floor like he might find Tarset hiding in some small crevice. "How do you know?"

I reached behind me for Heru's hand and pulled him closer to the exposed patch of stone wall I was examining.

"Look." I held my *At* orb closer to the wall, the light deepening the shadows of the engravings. My whisper hadn't been an interpretation of the writing that had been carved into the concealed stone wall. It had been a recitation.

TARSET WAS HERE

Those three words—in English—had been scratched into the stone wall over and over again.

Heru moved closer to me, squinting as he leaned in toward the wall.

I peeled back a chunk of ancient plaster, revealing more iterations of the repeated phrase underneath.

Heru picked at the plaster, crumbling a small chunk between his fingertips, then sniffing it. "This is lime plaster, likely Roman," he commented, dry washing his hands.

I nodded. That had been my conclusion as well. And it *covered* Tarset's words.

"She *was* here," I said softly, resting my hand on Heru's biceps and glancing at his baffled face.

I smiled to myself in wonder, shaking my head, and returned to gazing at Tarset's words. I supposed that *I*, of all people, should have considered this possibility sooner.

"We've been thinking about this all wrong," I told Heru. "We've been so focused on figuring out *where* Tarsi is, but not once have we considered *when* she might be."

But here, right in front of us, was the answer to a question we hadn't even known to ask. We couldn't find Tarset, here and now because she was stuck in the past—the *ancient* past, based on this evidence.

Now, we just needed to figure out *when* exactly she was. Then we would find a way to bring her home.

ANCIENT TIMES

TARSET

I ROLLED MY SHOULDERS, attempting to increase the blood flow to my upper extremities. My arms tingled, and my hands were half-asleep. It was more difficult to grip the length of rope extending up from my bindings now than it had been when the guards first tied me up, maybe three hours ago. At least, that was what my internal clock estimated.

It was impossible to gauge the passage of time based on the muted sliver of sunlight leaking in through the crack under the solid slab of wood that functioned as the door to my cell. Not that much sunlight made it down into this oh-so-delightful dungeon beneath the storeroom, but a little flooded in through the open doorway that led down here.

Thick, rough rope had been knotted around my wrists—each wrist individually first, then tied together—before being threaded through a copper ring anchored in the wall a couple of feet over my head, still an inch or two out of reach when I stood on the very tips of my toes. After the rope passed through the ring, it stretched across the corner of the cell to the adjacent wall, where it had been knotted to a wall anchor beside the door.

In my initial panic, I had tried pulling the ring loose using my bodyweight, but the thing was solidly lodged into the wall, and all I had accomplished was wasting energy while making my shoulders ache and my wrists bleed.

Around the one-hour mark, I had stopped panicking and accepted that I wouldn't be able to brute-force my way out of this mess. I wasn't the brute-force type anyway. I was more of the overseer type, who found other, stronger people and delegated the brute-force work out to their more capable muscles. Only problem was, there was nobody around to convince to help me.

But eventually, someone would come. And when they did, I needed to be calm and clearheaded.

I shifted my weight to my right foot, shaking out my left foot hokey-pokey style, then rolled my ankle, first one way, then the other. There was enough slack in the rope that I could bend my elbows at *almost* a ninety-degree angle but not enough for me to kneel, and my feet were hurting from standing in place on the rough stone ground for so long.

I set my foot down and leaned back against the wall, once again curling my fingers around the rope to ease the pressure on my wrists, and settled in for more waiting. Someone would come eventually—Inyotef, Temu, Kiya, *someone*—and when they did, I was determined to bargain my way out of this.

A muffled ruckus drew my attention to the door. I straightened, angling my ear toward the door as I listened. There was a grunt followed by a clatter of metal on stone.

"I'm here on the overlord's orders." That razor-edged voice was the most beautiful sound my ears had ever heard. Temu was here. "If you disagree," he added, "take it up with Inyotef."

My lip curled at the mention of Inyotef's name, but not even the revulsion and hatred I felt toward my captor could squash the hope soaring within me. Temu was *here*. This was the moment I had been waiting for.

I took a small step toward the door.

There was a muted scraping sound as the wooden bolt slid free, unlocking the door. I recognized the sound from when I had been locked in. The door swung outward on creaking hinges, and I squinted against the flood of filtered sunlight.

"Give us some privacy," Temu ordered, moving into view through the doorway. He carried a torch in one hand, his large frame hunched in the low-ceilinged passage outside my cell. "*Now.*"

I inhaled sharply, my heart suddenly pounding. He was pissed—like, scary mad. Maybe enlisting his help would be even easier than I had thought.

Temu ducked his head further to pass through the doorway, then straightened to his full, towering height once he was inside the loftier cell. He turned his back to me, not yet looking directly at me, and reached out through the doorway to pull the cell door shut. He placed the torch in a wall sconce between the door and rope anchor. Then, finally, he turned to face me.

His guarded expression belied the simmering rage I had heard in his voice. I hadn't imagined it, had I? He scanned me from my bare feet up to my bound wrists, his outward lack of emotion disconcerting.

Temu took a step toward me, his eyes shadowed to dark pools in the flickering torchlight.

I backed into the chiseled stone wall, pressing my shoulder blades against the cool surface.

Temu took another step toward me. Another, and he loomed over me, so close I could have pressed my body flush against his if I ever grew a spine and stopped cowering against the wall. With each step, his emotionless mask cracked and fell away, his features tensing and his eyes glinting with dark ferocity. He planted his palms on the wall on either side of my head and leaned in.

Suddenly, I wasn't so sure I wanted him in here with me.

"I told you to be careful," he whispered, his breath brushing the shell of my ear.

My eyelids drifted shut, and I shivered, mildly ashamed by the swell of desire blossoming low in my belly. This was not the time, and *really* not the place for my lady bits to be getting excited.

Temu made a low, rough noise and pulled back enough that he could see my face. His nostrils flared, no doubt scenting my flush of arousal. Gods, this was embarrassing. When his eyes met mine, they held a dark promise, and I had to consciously hold myself back from pushing forward and rubbing against him like a cat in heat.

My body's infuriating response to his nearness sparked an idea. A potential way out of this mess. Once again, I wondered if our hyper-reactivity to one another was caused by our souls' perfect compatibility. By our potential to form a soul bond.

While I did *not* want to bind myself to Temu and seal my fate with his—trapping myself in the past—I wanted to *not die* even more. On the off chance that we were potential bond-mates, then sex would seal our soul bond, linking our lives together permanently. Temu would *have* to keep me close—and alive—or the withdrawals from my bonding pheromone, that he would experience in my absence, would eventually kill him. It was a big what-if. But, at the moment, it was all I had to work with.

A plan quickly formed in my mind.

Temu wanted me. That much had been apparent since I first spotted him watching me in the market. All I had to do was play on that desire until he gave in and took me right here, against this wall. The dank cell was hardly the most romantic setting, but some people fantasized about this sort of thing. Hell, I had experienced the thrill of being naked and tied up a time or two. Of course, then it had been consensual. And I hadn't been in an actual dungeon.

I shoved the distracting thoughts from my mind. Eyes on the prize. On Temu. On getting him to lose control and claim me—to bind our souls together—right here, right now.

"You reek of him," Temu murmured.

My eyelids snapped open, and I shied away from Temu's accusing stare. I narrowed my eyes to a glare. "I didn't have a chance to bathe before he *locked me up in his dungeon*," I hissed, anger emboldening me. "You're such a hypocrite." I sniffed and looked away.

To Temu's credit, I couldn't smell Nitocris on him. There was only his enticing scent, sweet and spicy, like honey and mulled wine. He must have soaked in the baths half the night to erase the residue of their coupling.

Temu moved one hand from the wall to the crook of my neck, the pad of his thumb settling into the hollow at the base of my throat. I watched him out of the corner of my eye. His gaze skimmed over my face, almost like he was etching the lines and angles into his memory.

"I didn't anticipate this turn of events," he said after a time, his voice hushed. His focus shifted to the wall behind me, and his stare grew distant. "But then, I suppose, neither did you." He glanced at me, one eyebrow hitched slightly higher than the other. "A pity your backup plan didn't work out."

I narrowed my eyes. What an odd thing to say.

But then realization struck, and my eyelids opened as wide as they would go. "It was you. *You* gave me away." I glared at him. "What did you do—tattle to Inyotef?"

"No," Temu said with a low laugh. He refocused on me, his gaze drifting down to my mouth. His tongue slipped out, wetting his lips. "I convinced Nitocris to leave you behind."

I clenched my jaw so hard my teeth ground together. "Is that why you fucked her?" I asked, my voice harsher than I had intended.

It didn't make any logical sense, but Temu's physical betrayal cut deeper than anything else about this nightmarish situation. And *that* wasn't even a true betrayal because *he wasn't mine.*

"It was her price," Temu admitted. "And I would have paid it a hundred times over to keep you away from her." Not to keep me *here*, but to keep me away from *her.*

His words were a knife blade buried deep in my heart. Unexpected tears burned in my eyes, and I searched Temu's face for some explanation. "Why?"

He closed his eyes as though it hurt him to see my pain. "It was too dangerous."

"For me to go with her?" I asked, shaking my head. I didn't understand. There was no logic to his words, not when staying here had led to my imprisonment.

"It doesn't matter," Temu said, inhaling and exhaling deeply. He opened his eyes, his stare spearing through me, skewering my soul. "What's done is done."

I wanted to scream to him that it did matter. His reason for betraying me mattered more than anything else ever had. But I choked on the words. On the hurt.

"Why don't you just do what Inyotef asks?" Temu's thumb stroked up and down the column of my throat. "He would release you and honor you above all others. You would be his true queen, regardless of his betrothal to Nitocris."

I jutted out my jaw and turned my face away, watching the shadows flicker over the stone wall as disgust at the thought roiled in my belly. "I can't," I whispered. "I won't."

"But you were willing to view the Echoes for Nitocris," Temu reminded me.

"It was a *bluff*," I snapped, spearing Temu with a sharp glare.

For a moment—a single, brief *thud thump* of my heart—horror flitted across Temu's face, there and gone in a blink.

My lips parted, my breath catching in my throat, and I searched his shadowed eyes. "That's why you did it." I coughed a single, bitter, disbelieving laugh. "You convinced Nitocris to leave me behind because you didn't want me to view the Echoes for her."

"You really wouldn't have done it?" he asked, his stare boring into me.

I should have spat in his face for what he did to me. But even now, I fought the urge to press my body against his. Locking my limbs in place to prevent myself from giving in, I shook my head.

"Why not?" he asked.

"For about a million reasons," I admitted, refusing to look away.

"Name one."

"Because it's too dangerous," I spat, throwing his own words back in his face.

Temu narrowed his eyes. "For you?"

"For everyone."

Temu tilted his head to the side as though considering my responses very carefully. What if he didn't like my answers? Would he walk away? Would he leave me locked up in this cell to rot? I was running out of time to make my move.

Before I could lose my nerve, I inched forward, pressing my body against Temu's from knees to chest. I angled my face up toward him and licked my lips. My breaths came faster, and not only for show, though I supposed a heaving bosom never hurt during a seduction. This was simply how my body reacted to his.

Temu's stare dropped to my lips and stayed there.

"Release me," I whispered, my mouth hovering a hairsbreadth from his. "Help me escape, and I will do anything for you."

Temu dragged his gaze back up to my eyes, his stare searching.

"*Anything*," I repeated.

And then I closed the distance between our lips and let my eyelids flutter shut. The first, gentle contact sent an electric zing shooting straight to my core.

I kissed Temu, slowly, sweetly, coaxing his lips apart until our breaths mingled. His hand curled around the back of my neck, holding me in place as he deepened the kiss. His tongue swept into my mouth, and I moaned brazenly. His other hand glided down my side, skimming the swell of my breast and dip of my waist, then slid behind me. He pressed his palm flat against my lower back, pulling my body closer to his. The hard length of his shaft jutted against my belly, and I was desperate to have my hands free so I could wrap my fingers around him.

Temu clutched me to him, claiming my mouth the way I had so recently seen him claim another woman's body. *That* was what I wanted. What I needed. To be well and thoroughly taken by this man. I was so lost to the lust that I couldn't even remember why I needed him to take me—to claim me—right here, right now. I simply wanted him. *Needed* him.

"Please," I groaned into his mouth. "Temu, please . . ."

Temu broke the kiss, pressing his forehead against mine. Both of us were breathing hard.

Slowly, so incredibly slowly, Temu's hands fell away from my body. He closed his eyes and, after a long, shuddering breath, took a single step backward.

"Temu?" My voice trembled, icy dread taking root inside me where a moment ago there had only been heat and desire. "Temu, look at me." Tears welled and spilled over the brims of my eyelids.

I was losing him. I could practically see the invisible wall he was building between us, brick by brick.

"Please," I whimpered. "Please, don't leave me."

Temu opened his eyes with such painful reluctance that I knew—I *knew*-—he was making himself look at me because he wasn't sure he would ever see me again.

"Temu?" His name came out as a sob.

He turned his back to me, yanked the torch out of the sconce, shoved the door open, and left the cell, slamming the door shut behind him. And just like that, I was alone again.

Temu left me. He really left me.

And I didn't think he was ever coming back.

THE HOURS DRAGGED BY. I sang softly to myself to pass the time, eventually falling into something of a waking trance. I periodically switched which foot bore the brunt of my weight, bent and straightened my arms, flapped my elbows like butterfly wings, and clenched my fists and stretched my fingers.

Through the crack at the bottom of the door, the flickering light from a torch eventually replaced the steady, if dim, daylight. My stomach groaned with hunger, but it was the thirst that was really getting to me. And here I had hoped I would never experience severe thirst again as I had during that first day trekking through the desert.

I let saliva pool in my mouth, then swallowed, hoping to trick my body into thinking it was getting something to drink. My bladder grew unbearably full, which didn't make any sense because I wasn't taking in any fluids. Regardless, I eventually had no choice but to let it go. I cried softly as the urine ran down my legs.

My eyelids grew heavier with each passing hour. Around the time daylight once again leaked under the door, I could no longer fight the exhaustion. I slumped back against the wall as sleep dragged me under.

I was startled awake by the sound of groaning wood. Fire seared in my shoulders, radiating a throbbing pain up my aching arms and down my back. My hands felt dead from me essentially hanging by my wrists.

I scrambled to get my legs under me and almost passed out from the cresting wave of agony that spread out from my shoulders to my arms and into my waking hands. Spots of imaginary light sparkled across my vision as I swayed on my feet, the pain nearly too much.

Slowly, the spots receded as the agony waned to a manageable level, and my grasp on consciousness grew steadier. I licked cracked lips with my sandpaper tongue and drew in ragged breaths. My mouth felt like I had been gurgling glue, and my stomach was a yawning void of hunger.

How long had I been in this cell?

"What are you waiting for?" someone said from outside my door. It was a woman. My sluggish mind dredged up a name. Kiya. "Open it," she ordered. "*Now.*"

The door to my cell swung outward, and Kiya moved into view, her petite form silhouetted by the comparably bright light pouring in from the dungeon beyond. A bucket dangled from one of her hands, and she gripped a torch in the other, a rolled bundle of fabric tucked under her torch arm, between her elbow and her side. She stood in the doorway for a long moment, her features masked in shadows.

Finally, she stepped into the cell, nodding once to a guard who remained out of sight. The door slammed shut, sealing her in with me.

Kiya set the bucket down by the door, then placed the torch in the wall sconce. She wore only a schenti. Her top half was completely bare, exposing her breasts—as well as the red, angry welts crisscrossing over her entire back. Such nudity wasn't uncommon for women in this time period, but it *was* unusual for Kiya.

She hugged the bundle to her bare chest and faced me, affording me my first good look at her face. She was barely recognizable, with two black eyes—the left swollen completely shut—and a misshapen nose that had to have been broken and left out of alignment.

"Inyotef did that to you?" I asked, my voice a hoarse rasp. Just when I thought I couldn't hate him more, he had to go and prove me wrong.

Kiya nodded, then crouched and reached into the bucket. She pulled out a ceramic cup, dripping water. My hatred for Inyotef fled as all of my focus shifted to that glorious cup of water.

She moved closer and lifted the cup to my lips. I choked on the first mouthful of water like I had forgotten how to drink, and most of it dribbled down my chin.

"Sorry," Kiya murmured, again tilting the cup and pouring a little more water into my mouth. By the time the cup was empty, I was taking full-mouth gulps.

"Thank you," I said, breathing hard as I watched Kiya scoop more water from the bucket.

She returned to me to let me drink some more, then refilled the cup three more times. After I drained the fifth cupful of water, she set the cup on the floor beside the bucket and picked up the cloth bundle. At first, that was all I thought it was—a roll of fabric—but after unwinding at least a dozen linen scraps, Kiya reached the prize hidden at the center. A trio of honey breads.

Kiya glanced at me, raising one finger to her lips to tell me to keep quiet. Did that mean feeding me was a no-no?

I nodded vehemently. I would have agreed to almost anything if it would get her to shove those honey breads into my mouth. I could already smell the tantalizing pastries, their sweet promise making my stomach groan with renewed need.

Kiya carried the honey breads over to me, setting two down on a scrap of linen on the floor beside my feet, but held onto the third to break off chunks and feed to me. "Hurry," she breathed, shooting frequent, fearful glances at the door. "I don't know how much longer we have."

I hardly needed her urging. I devoured the pastries in quick succession, and when I was finished, Kiya fetched me one more cupful of water. I drank greedily, giddy at feeling some energy return to my body and clearheadedness to my mind.

"Why did he beat you?" I asked Kiya when she lowered the empty cup.

"Because he could," Kiya murmured, shrugging one shoulder.

She turned away from me to retrieve the bucket and the small pile of cloth scraps she had discarded when unwrapping the contraband food. She returned, setting both on the floor at my feet, then drew the knife from the sheath on her weapons belt. I eyed that gleaming knife blade as she moved closer, pressing myself back against the rough stone wall.

"I will not hurt you," Kiya reassured me. "I just need to cut away your dress so I can wash you."

I relaxed a little, only flinching when the blade skimmed over my skin as she cut the shoulder straps. She tugged the soiled linen shift down over my hips, and I lifted my feet so she could take it away. Kiya dropped a handful of the cloth scraps into the bucket of water, pulling out one and squeezing her hand to wring it out.

"You haven't emptied your bowels yet," Kiya commented as she reached up to scrub my arms. "When I finish, I can hold the bucket for you, if you'd like."

My cheeks flamed and tears welled. I turned my face away, hiding my humiliation from her, and choked on a sob as I nodded. "I would appreciate that," I said, my voice barely a squeak. "Thank you."

Once I was as clean and refreshed as was possible while still being tied up in a dank cell in an ancient dungeon, Kiya set the now soiled bucket and linen scraps by the door.

She returned to me and touched the side of my face with gentle fingertips. "I'm sorry," she whispered, a single tear gliding down her bruised cheek.

The door swung outward on creaking hinges, and Kiya snatched her hand away from me and hastily backed up. She bowed her head and hustled to the door, bending to retrieve the bucket before slipping out of the cell around my next visitor.

"Good morning, divine one," Inyotef drawled, his lips twisting into a secretive smile.

A guard outside closed the door, shutting me away with my captor. Inyotef clasped his hands behind his back and scanned my exposed body, his smile turning faintly lascivious. That single look made me feel filthier than I had been before my sponge bath.

I clenched my jaw and pressed my lips together into a thin, hard line. If Inyotef came near me—if he tried to *touch* me—I was going to knee him in the balls so hard he wouldn't be able to get it up for weeks. His gaze lingered on my unbound legs, and his smile faded. I wondered if his thoughts had gone to the same place as mine and if he now recognized the danger he would be in if he moved too close to me. Maybe, because he kept his distance.

"Have you reconsidered my request?" Inyotef asked, his eyebrows raised expectantly as his focus returned to my face. "Are you feeling any more cooperative?"

I considered spitting on him, but I feared doing so would give away the fact that Kiya had smuggled in food. She had already suffered enough for me; I didn't want to make more trouble for her, especially when she was, quite possibly, the only person I could rely on right now. The only person I could trust.

My eyes stung as stray thoughts of Temu and his betrayal and abandonment shouldered their way into my mind. I set my jaw and shoved them away, transforming my hurt into rage and channeling it out through a silent glare at Inyotef.

Inyotef chuckled. "You're a bit of a masochist, aren't you, divine one?" He turned to the side, slowly walking past me and deeper into the cell. "No trouble at all. I will be glad to accommodate you."

Wait—was he talking about *torture*? Wasn't he afraid of repercussions from the other Nejerets? From *my dad*? Unless he had somehow puzzled out that I was estranged from my people. That my dad and the rest of the

Nejerets—at least in this time—weren't concerned about what happened to me.

Dread twisted in my gut, and a cold sweat broke out all over my body. I could handle a little imprisonment, but torture—I held no misconceptions about my ability to withstand an abundance of purposely inflicted pain.

When Inyotef reached the wall, he turned, pausing to glance my way. "If you change your mind, all you have to do is say the word." He ambled back toward the cell door. "Agree to be my seer, to view the Echoes at my behest, and this can all be over. It's really very simple." He stopped in front of the door and turned to face me once more. "Then we can go back to being friends."

My lip curled into a silent snarl.

Inyotef took a step toward me, then another, his gaze skimming over my body. "Of course, I already have many friends. What I really need is a pet." His eyes met mine, his stare level. "A supple, willing, obedient pet."

Outrage burned in my veins, and I stepped out from the wall, moving as close to Inyotef as my bindings would allow.

His expression sobered, and he backed away, moving closer to the door, propelled by whatever he saw on my face.

"If you ever touch me again," I hissed, "I will cut off your dick the first chance I get. I will slice it up and feed it to you, piece by piece." I lowered my chin toward my chest, my lips pulling back to bare my teeth at him. "So, think very hard about what you want to do with me, *Inyotef*." I narrowed my eyes to slits. "Even if you think you've broken me, in the back of your mind, you'll always wonder—is she really mine, or is she just biding her time?"

Inyotef studied me for a long moment, and I thought he may have truly been seeing me as a person for the first time and not merely the tool he believed he could forge me into.

Soon enough, though, his bravado returned, and he grinned coolly. "You look lonely," he said, turning away and placing one hand on the door. He glanced back at me over his shoulder. "I'll send someone in to keep you company." The apples of his cheek tensed in the hollow approximation of a smile, and then he pushed the door open and left the cell, shutting the door behind him.

I gritted my teeth as I listened to the bolt sliding back into place, and I was left to simmer in my rage alone. But I wasn't alone for long.

The door opened again a few minutes later, admitting a guard carrying a narrow rectangular table followed by a cherubic middle-aged man hugging a rolled leather case against his exposed paunch. The cherubic man directed the guard to place the table against the wall opposite me, then waited patiently while the guard wrangled my legs, binding my ankles together, then left.

"Divine one," my visitor said, bowing deeply. His voice was high and soft in a way that made me wonder if he was a eunuch. And it fit his cherubic appearance so perfectly, that I couldn't help but nickname him "Cherub" in my mind.

"I thank you for this incredible honor to work together," Cherub said.

At a loss for words, I didn't respond.

Cherub turned away from me once more and set his leather case on the table, unrolling it with an unsettling *clink* of metal. Copper instruments gleamed in the flickering torchlight, looking like oversized dental tools. Or, considering when and where I was, *embalmer's* tools.

I couldn't look away from the assortment of instruments as I imagined all the painful things they could do to my body. By the time Cherub faced me once more, gripping what appeared to be an elegant, elongated copper butter knife, I was trembling from head to toe.

"Please," I whimpered, huddling back against the wall. "Please don't hurt me."

Cherub's brow furrowed, but then he brightened and turned back to the table. He unwrapped what appeared to be a golf-ball-sized chunk of beeswax and tore off two smaller pieces, stuffing them into his ears.

"The screams," he said as he approached, offering me a bashful smile. "They can be so distracting." And then he raised the copper knife and showed me exactly what he meant.

"What would Kat do? What would Kat do? What would Kat do?" I murmured, over and over and over, the words transforming from a mantra to a chant to a prayer. Kat was basically a god, so why the hell couldn't she spare a moment to pop in here and smite this asshole already?

Cherub hummed to himself as he worked on my body, possibly to drown out whatever residual noise from my cries and screams made it past his earplugs. He was cautious and meticulous, cutting and re-cutting my thigh, then waiting for the wound to heal. Each successive slice of his copper blade cut a little deeper. Every so often, he paused to make notes on a roll of papyrus that had been stashed in his leather tool case.

Eventually, I stopped healing quickly enough for it to be noticeable. But Cherub didn't stop cutting.

I thought the torture might go on forever, or at least until I bled out. I would have welcomed the end to the pain. Inyotef, however, wasn't done with me yet.

After a few hours of slow, intentional cutting, Cherub repacked his papyrus and tools, rolled up his leather case, and hugged it to his chest. I felt woozy but still nowhere near passing out from blood loss. My torturer bowed deeply to me before approaching the cell door and knocking three times. A moment later, the door swung outward, and Cherub left.

Before the door shut again, Kiya slipped in with a fresh bucket of water. This time she also carried a woven basket slung over one shoulder. She set both burdens down by the door and crouched to rummage through the basket, eventually pulling out a waterskin. As she drew closer, a rich, meaty scent reached my nose.

The waterskin contained thick, fatty broth, instead of water, and I drank every last drop. Kiya returned to the basket to exchange the empty waterskin for another, this one filled with cream. She was stuffing me full of high-calorie foods to give me the energy I would need to heal. Dear gods, I loved this woman.

My eyelids weighed about a thousand pounds by the time I drained the second waterskin, and my head lolled forward, no matter how hard I tried to keep it upright. Was this regenerative sleep calling to me? I had never been injured severely enough to experience a Nejeret healing coma firsthand, but that had to be what this was. Now that my cells had the energy they needed to repair themselves, my body's instinctive regenerative process was taking over.

Kiya crossed the cell to the anchor holding the tail end of my binding rope and let out a few feet of slack. I swayed on my feet, and Kiya returned to me just in time to ease me down to the floor and lean me back against the rough stone wall.

"Rest now," Kiya murmured once I was sitting, my legs stretched out in front of me and my hands clasped together like I was praying.

Her touch was gentle as she cleaned the open wounds on my legs, and the pain faded as regenerative sleep dragged me away.

34

"**S**USIE. SYRIS. BOBBY. DAD. Lex. Reni." I finished the litany of names for the umpteenth time, then inhaled to start again. The syllables all blended together, turning the list of individuals into a unified whole. Into something new. A purpose. A reason to hold out. The only thing keeping me sane while, layer by layer, the flesh was being peeled away from my thighs.

During his second visit, I learned Cherub was a man of many occupations—priest, embalmer, scribe, physician. Every time he visited—this was session number six—he treated me with the utmost respect. Other than the torture part. He explained that he didn't enjoy hurting me, but that he couldn't pass up this opportunity to study the internal anatomy of a living subject. Apparently, I was going to help him make grand discoveries in medicine. For him, the ends easily justified the means.

For me, there were only the means. The torture. The agony. The promise of more. And it was breaking me down to my component parts.

After each session, I was more fractured. It was harder and harder to hold on to cohesive thoughts. To remember why I was letting this continue. Why I wasn't giving in. Why I shouldn't agree to give Inyotef any fucking thing he wanted from me.

My body. He had already had it.

My dignity. It lay shredded at my feet.

My life. I wished he would just take it already.

The future. My family. That was where I drew the line.

I had to protect them. That was why I continued to repeat the list of names. It was a reminder of why I could never give in. Inyotef could shatter me completely, but so long as I held those names in my heart, where he couldn't reach them, I would never—*never*—view the Echoes for him.

"... Kat. Nik. Nef*feeeeeee*." I screamed the ending of my half sister's name as Cherub did something near my knee that sent agonizing spasms shooting down to my toes.

I risked a glance down my body—I couldn't help it—but my mind wasn't able to make sense of what I was seeing. The musculature of my right thigh was completely exposed around the entire circumference of my leg.

As I stared at the horrific sight, I felt myself detaching, my awareness of self pulling away from the physical sensations until it was impossible to link the visual input with what I was feeling. That was someone else's leg. A picture in an anatomy textbook. Part of a cadaver in a bodies exhibit. Not me. Not *my* leg. Not my muscles seeping blood. Not my tendon about to be severed by a thin copper blade.

This time, the agony of that blade slicing into my flesh whited out my vision. For a heartbeat, a synesthetic moment, pain was my entire existence. It was sight and sound, taste and smell. It was all I had ever been, and all I would ever be.

And then it was gone, and I was nothing.

When I came to, I was alone in my cell. Some of the slack had been let out on my bindings, allowing me the freedom to sit, though not to lower my arms. I didn't want to feel gratitude toward Cherub, but I did. He could have left me hanging there, unconscious, waiting for Kiya to come and tend to me. It was a small, unnecessary kindness.

My right thigh itched and burned simultaneously, telling me the healing had only just begun. A quick glance down revealed the exposed muscles were now covered in a thick, leathery scab the unsettling blackish-brown of necrotic flesh and surrounded by an oozing, yellowish border. I figured I must have awakened before fully entering a regenerative coma because my body didn't have enough energy to heal.

As terrible as my leg looked at the moment, I had done this enough times by now that I knew I would be good as new after a couple of regenerative cycles. *But,* my body wouldn't enter that rapid healing state until I had received enough nourishment to fuel the exhaustive process.

Kiya would come bearing food soon. There was nothing for me to do now but wait.

I curled my left leg underneath me, careful to leave my grotesque right leg extended straight out in front of me for fear of tearing the leathery scabs. I wasn't feeling sturdy enough to stand, but I did rise up onto my left knee, which allowed me to lower my swollen, blood-deprived hands to my chest. My shoulder joints groaned as I tucked my elbows down against my sides, and a deep, throbbing ache radiated from my shoulders all the way down my back to my hips.

Sensation gradually returned to my hands as the disturbing dark red hue faded to a more natural copper brown. I wiggled my fingers, one by one. It was such a treat to be able to use my hands, I didn't even mind the pain.

I couldn't go on like this. Eventually, I would break down. Give in.

I shut my eyes and bowed my head. "What would Kat do?" I murmured to myself.

But I already knew what she would do in my position. A vivid mental image formed in my mind's eye. Kat's lifeless body cradled in a bed of snow. She would do anything—sacrifice anything—to save those she loved. She had proved that, repeatedly.

When I heard the now familiar scrape of wood telling me the wooden bolt on my cell door was being unlocked, I opened my eyes and raised my head to watch the door swing outward. I knew what I had to do.

Kiya entered the cell carrying her usual bucket and basket, but I had no interest in either. I only had eyes for the knife sheathed at her hip. She placed a torch in the sconce, set down the bucket and basket, pulled a waterskin out of the basket—no doubt filled with thick broth or cream—and approached me.

When I finally tore my stare away from the hilt of her knife and looked up at her face, she stopped, hovering just out of reach. One more small step and I would be able to grab her knife hilt. Only faint green and yellow bruises remained on her face from her black eyes and broken nose, though she still went topless to let the wounds on her back heal undisturbed.

Kiya eyed me for a long moment, her mouth pressed into a thin, bloodless line. She knew what I was planning.

She backed away, drew her knife, and set it on the floor by the door. She set two smaller daggers down beside the longer knife, then faced me once more.

"Open your mouth," she said as she approached.

My chin trembled, and my shoulders shook. "Please," I begged on a sob.

I had been holding it together in the hope that this would all be over with the merciful stab of her knife blade. But now my chance at a swift death—at an end to the pain—was gone.

"Please, kill me," I wailed. I gazed up at Kiya, beseeching her to end it. To end me. "*Please*, kill me."

Kiya sighed and dropped to her knees in front of me, utterly defeated. "I can't," she said, her arms drooping until the waterskin rested on the floor. "If I kill you—if I even let you die by not taking good enough care of you, Inyotef will kill me, and then he will kill my mother, and my sister, and my nieces and nephew." As Kiya spoke, tears streamed down her cheeks.

My shoulders caved in, my entire body shaking with the force of my sobs.

Kiya released the waterskin and reached for me, wrapping her hands around mine like a protective shell. "I'm so sorry, but I can't do that. Not even for you."

I bowed my head, my heart heavy. I couldn't blame Kiya for choosing herself—her family—over me. Not when my entire purpose for resisting was based on the same commitment to protect my own family.

"It's all right," I whispered to our joined hands. "I understand."

ONCE THE HOPE OF a quick death at Kiya's blade was gone, I started to go dead inside. With each passing torture session, my hold on that precious list of names grew more and more slippery. Cherub's copper blades didn't only cut away pieces of my body; they shaved off chunks of my determination to resist.

I stared at the wall, my back a raw slab of meat after Cherub's latest anatomical exploration. Kiya would come soon, but I couldn't work up the desire to turn around. I would need to, for her to feed me, but I just didn't care. I didn't want her to feed me. I didn't want to heal.

I wanted it to end.

I rested my forehead against the rough stone wall, wishing she would just let me die. She didn't even need to kill me. She could just let me die.

The only upside to this whole fucked-up situation was that the combination of back-to-back regenerative cycles and minimal recovery time between torture sessions was causing me to waste away. My body didn't have enough time to rebuild itself, and my overall state of health was deteriorating rapidly. At the current rate, I thought I had two or three torture sessions left in me. Inyotef would have to keep Cherub away for a while and feed me *a lot* if he wanted to keep me around.

I didn't know Inyotef well enough to gauge whether or not he had the patience required to drag this out. There was always the chance he would get frustrated with me and cut his losses.

"Tarset..."

That name. I knew that name, though it felt like an eternity since I had last heard it. It was *my* name, spoken in the faintest whisper. Only one person in this time and place knew my name, my true name, and he hadn't visited me for weeks—or however long I had been a prisoner here. I had long since lost track of the days.

Was I hallucinating? Was my mind already that far gone?

I lifted my head, wincing as the motion tugged on my ravaged back. I had to know if I had really heard him. If Temu was truly here. Gritting my teeth, I inched my head around just enough to peek over my shoulder.

And there he was, like a being formed of pure shadow.

Temu stood close behind me. So close that I had to tilt my head sideways to see what I could of his face in the darkness. He hadn't brought a torch. It was just the two of us alone in the dark cell.

I glanced at the door without moving my head. When had he come in?

"You came back." The words emerged out as a muted squeak, and I hated my stupid chin for trembling. I hated my stupid eyes more for stinging with a sudden welling of tears. But most of all, I hated my stupid heart for caring that Temu had come back. I honestly hadn't thought I would ever see him again, and his excision of himself from my life had hurt as much as any session with Cherub.

Temu bowed his head. "I am sorry for the part I played in your suffering," he murmured. My eyes had grown so used to the darkness that when he raised his head again, I could make out the concern furrowing his brow and the emotion intensifying his shadowed gaze.

My shoulders shook, and the tears spilled over, streaming down my cheeks.

Temu pressed his forehead to my temple and stroked my greasy, knotted hair. "Calm yourself," he murmured. "This will all be over soon."

Temu straightened and stepped backward. Fear gripped my heart as he unsheathed a long dagger.

He had said this would all be over soon. Did that mean he was going to kill me? Was that why he had come? Had his guilty conscience driven him back to me to offer me the mercy of a swift death?

I relaxed, embracing the promise of peace, and fear loosened its death grip on my heart. If Temu was here to end my life, I wouldn't fight him. I was just glad I wouldn't be alone in the end.

But instead of plunging the dagger into my chest or sliding it across my throat, Temu turned the blade on himself, cutting a long, deep slice along the inside of his forearm. Blood welled in the wound, and he raised his wrist and clenched and unclenched his fist, causing blood to run down his elbow and pool into his waiting palm. Then he reached for me with that bloody hand.

I took a jerky, involuntary step to the side and away from Temu. But I was held captive by my restraints, and I couldn't get far.

A blinding starburst of pain shot out from my back as Temu's palm made contact with my ruined flesh. My entire body went rigid, and a harsh, guttural sob erupted up my throat.

Temu's clean hand curled around the front of my face, his hold gentle but firm over my mouth, muffling my cries. "Hold still and keep quiet," he commanded, the order no less potent for having been spoken in the faintest whisper. "This will only take a moment."

His bloody palm touched my ravaged back once more, and my spine arched, agony temporarily whiting out my vision. The pain gradually receded as his hand moved over my back, giving way to the most intense itching sensation I had ever felt as my flesh healed. It was then that I understood.

Temu wasn't here to kill me. He was here to *heal* me.

At first, I didn't understand how he was doing it. When his hand slipped away from my mouth, I craned my neck, watching him reopen the cut on his forearm. And then I knew.

His blood. He was healing me with his blood.

In the future, transfusions using the blood of Nejeret elders were often used when a younger Nejeret was injured. The older the Nejeret, the more potent their regenerative abilities, and the blood of an elder could greatly amplify healing in a younger Nejeret.

I held still as Temu reached for my back with another handful of blood and smeared it over the raw, exposed flesh. Again, the pain was sudden and intense, but it quickly gave way to the severe itching sensation of rapid healing.

In minutes, my entire back was coated in Temu's blood and healing impossibly quickly, even for a Nejeret. I writhed under the intensity of the itch. It was almost worse than the pain.

I watched Temu over my shoulder as he cleaned his blade on the underside of his schenti. Once he had re-sheathed the blade, he wiped his hands clean as well.

"How old are you?" I asked, needing a distraction from the extreme itching sensation.

For his blood to be so potent, Temu had to be ancient. I had known he was a child of Nuin, but with his subdued otherness, I hadn't considered the possibility that he was one of the ancients, like my grandfather, Osiris.

"Who *are* you?" I added.

Temu finished wiping his hands and adjusted his schenti to drape undisturbed around his knees. His gaze skimmed over my back like he was checking his work. "I must go," he said. "Kiya will be here soon, and none can know I have been here."

A vice tightened around my heart, and my gut twisted into knots. "But—"

"Rest," Temu whispered, reaching out to brush a few snarled strands of hair away from my face. "Eat." His thumb traced the edge of my face, from temple to jawline. "Regain your strength. You need at least one regenerative cycle. When you are stronger, I will return."

"What do you mean?" I breathed, searching his shadowed eyes. "I need one regenerative cycle for *what*? You're going to return to do *what*?"

"Tell no one I was here," Temu said, his voice hushed but still steamrolling my questions.

He brushed the pad of his thumb over my lips, and then he backed away and strode for the cell door. He paused in front of the door, his hand pressed flat against the slab of wood like he was waiting for something.

After a long moment, he pushed the door open and slipped out of the cell. He eased the door shut without a backward glance, leaving me alone to wade through an ocean of confusion.

But I wasn't alone for long.

Kiya came soon enough to wash and feed me, and if she noticed the extra blood on my back, she didn't mention it. I took Temu's words to heart—rest, eat, regain your strength—devouring everything Kiya offered me. And as I drifted off into a regenerative coma, hope wrapped around me like a security blanket.

Because Temu had said he would return.

I WOKE SCREAMING AS something sliced into my sternum, the tip of the blade grinding against my breastbone. My eyes snapped open, and when I saw who stood before me, the scream died in my throat.

"Good morning, divine one," Inyotef purred, a devilish grin curving his lips. Torchlight flickered across his face, revealing his true, hellish nature. He pulled the dagger away from my chest and rested the tip of the blade against his fingertip, lazily twisting the knife back and forth.

Inyotef was here in my cell? Why? He hadn't come since the beginning, and it seemed like too much of a coincidence that he was visiting so soon after Temu was here.

Was it possible—had Temu lied? Had his visit been a subterfuge? Had he come into my cell on Inyotef's orders? He had given me hope, and I couldn't help but wonder if that had been the point. Had his visit been just another form of torture, psychological instead of physical?

"I see you've redecorated since I was last here," Inyotef said, scanning the wall behind me where I had, during the few waking hours I had alone, claimed this space as my own.

TARSET WAS HERE

The words covered as much of the wall as I had been able to reach. I *had* been here, damn it, and everyone who entered this cell after I was gone would know it.

"I miss you," Inyotef said, pointing the dagger at me again. He pressed the tip between my breasts, about an inch below the cut he already made. This time, he didn't break the skin.

I held very, *very* still, my breaths short and shallow.

Ever so slowly, Inyotef dragged the dagger lower. Another inch and the point would be below my breastbone. I doubted he was planning on stabbing me through the heart, but with enough force, I thought I could maybe do it for him.

Inyotef stopped the dagger's downward progress just shy of where I needed it to be, instead tracing the underside of my right breast with the flat of the blade. He tilted his head to the side and raised his eyes to meet mine. "Do you miss me?"

I sucked in a shaky breath and turned my face away from him, staring into the darkest corner of the cell, opposite the torch. Tears leaked from my eyes and silent sobs racked my chest.

The shadows in the corner moved. At first, I thought they were simply shifting in the flickering light from the flames. But then the shadows intensified, gaining density and form.

My breath caught in my lungs as I stared at a towering figure composed of pure darkness. The shadows shifted and slithered like snakes, slowly unfolding to reveal something so impossible that I truly believed I was hallucinating.

It was Temu, but not the Temu I knew. This man was *more*.

His skin was as dark as ever but had gained a faintly iridescent quality, and his scars shimmered gold in the torchlight. His eyes were pools of midnight, darker even than the shadows, and the angles of his face had sharpened, lending his appearance an almost alien quality. Otherworldly energy crackled around him, radiating off him in waves.

He had been stunning before when he had been masquerading as human. Now, he stole my breath. Captured my heart. Branded my soul.

He couldn't possibly be real.

"Look at me," Inyotef hissed, increasing the pressure on his dagger until the tip of the blade bit into the tender flesh beneath my breast.

I clenched my jaw and refused to give Inyotef what he wanted, redoubling my focus on the apparition of Temu. Maybe this was just the kind of rejection that would push Inyotef over the edge.

With a jerk of his arm, Inyotef shifted the dagger lower, pressing the flat of the blade against my inner thigh. "Look at me!" he demanded.

Apparently, this was exactly the kind of rejection that would push him over the edge. Just not in the direction I had hoped.

The edge of the blade sliced into my inner thigh, and I looked at him. I couldn't help it, not with that knife poised so precariously between my legs.

"*Enough!*" the apparition of Temu thundered, his booming voice loud enough to make the stone walls tremble.

Inyotef went rigid. But before he could turn around and face the glorious being in the corner of the cell, he flew backward, slamming into the opposite wall. His dagger clattered to the floor, and he slid down the wall, settling in a boneless heap.

I stared at Inyotef long and hard, trying to tell if he was still alive, but it was impossible to determine whether he was dead or merely unconscious. It took me a few seconds to notice the thick, iridescent vine coiled around his middle. A vine of *At*.

My stare snapped to Temu as this larger-than-life version of the man I had thought I knew stalked out of the corner of the cell. My lips parted, and I backed against the rough stone wall behind me.

I wasn't hallucinating. Temu was really here.

And he could control *At*.

Temu stopped in front of me, and I shuddered as all of that otherworldly power washed over me. It was like swimming through a thundercloud.

He scanned me, his stare lingering on the cut between my breasts, then moving lower to the crux of my thighs, where Inyotef's blade had been only a moment ago. Temu clenched his jaw, turning the angles of his face razor sharp, and his nostrils flared on his next inhale. Finally, his eyes met mine, and I drowned in those midnight pools.

Without a word, he reached up and sliced through my bindings though I hadn't noticed him draw a knife. Maybe he hadn't. He could control *At*, after all. He could will one into existence with a simple, focused thought.

Temu lowered my arms with the utmost care, and the pain was exquisite, but I couldn't stop staring at him. At this man, this Nejeret.

Here was the son of Nuin, the prince of gods. He was a revelation. The fulfillment of a promise I hadn't even realized had been made to me.

Temu sliced a short but deep cut along his forearm, apparently his favorite paint palette, and swept his thumb through the welling blood. He brushed the blood-soaked pad of this thumb down the valley between my breasts, over the bone-deep wound opened by Inyotef's dagger.

My flesh immediately started to itch as the cut healed. Temu gathered more blood, then traced the pad of his thumb along the underside of my breast to help the knick there heal, as well.

My eyelids fluttered closed at his gentle touch, and my breath hitched.

Behind him, Inyotef coughed, shattering this sudden bubble of peace.

I leaned to the side, craning my neck to peer around Temu's insanely broad shoulders so I could glare at Inyotef. Seeing the world through a red haze, I sidestepped around Temu on shaky legs, swiping the knife from the sheath on his weapons belt, and started toward Inyotef.

He was dead. So very dead.

Temu grabbed my arm, keeping me from my well-deserved revenge. When I looked back at Temu, he shook his head, his expression grim. "You can't kill him."

I stared at Temu, too stunned to respond.

I *had* to kill Inyotef. He knew about my mom, and he was exactly the kind of person who would take out his retribution on the family of one he believed had wronged him. And that was exactly how he would feel about me when he woke to find me gone.

But Temu's hold was unrelenting.

Acting on instinct, I lashed out at Temu with his own knife. I didn't actually want to hurt him. I just needed to distract him long enough to reach Inyotef and stab that fucker in the heart.

But I was weak and slow after my extended stay in the dungeon. Temu caught my knife hand easily and twisted my wrist until the sudden pain made me release the hilt of the weapon.

Before I could process what was happening, Temu released my wrist, pulled back his arm, and backhanded me across the face.

And yet again, darkness swallowed the world.

37

I CAME TO SLUNG over someone's shoulder. Temu's shoulder, I realized before I even opened my eyes. His intoxicating scent surrounded me.

With each step, the dry ground crunched under his sandals, and his shoulder joint jutted uncomfortably into my queasy belly. My brain and the entire right side of my face throbbed in time with my heartbeat, and the world felt topsy-turvy, even with my eyes closed.

Groaning, I lifted my eyelids but immediately slammed them shut again, blocking out the blinding sunlight and the dizzying sight of the narrow road six feet below.

Despite the headache and nausea, joy surged within me followed by the single greatest high I had ever experienced. I was *outside*. As in, not in my cell. As in, *free*.

Apparently, the sudden rush of giddiness was too much for my shocked body. My stomach lurched, and I vomited over Temu's shoulder.

Temu went still beneath me. A moment later, he slung me forward and set me on my feet.

Too dizzy to stand, I dropped to my hands and knees, only Temu's hold on my elbow slowing my descent to the ground. Temu backed away as I emptied my stomach of what little was left of the last meal Kiya had fed me, then gagged a few more times, spitting bile onto the hard-packed dirt road.

Once my stomach was empty, the nausea abated, and I sat back on my heels, squinting against the bright afternoon sunshine to look up at the man silhouetted before me. He appeared human again, and I wondered if I had been so out of it in the cell that I had imagined his altered appearance.

I pushed my greasy hair away from my face and wiped my mouth with the back of my hand, glaring accusingly at Temu. "You hit me," I ground out.

He stood a few steps away, arms crossed over his broad chest and expression bland. "I did," he agreed.

I jutted out my jaw, huffing angrily, and covered my bare breasts with crossed arms. My focus shifted past Temu to the road stretching out beyond him, where I could see the top of the palace walls peeking over the crest of the road. It blurred in and out of focus, but my desire to return and end Inyotef's life was unwavering. I considered making a run for it but dismissed the possibility almost as soon as it popped into my head. I was too weak. I wouldn't make it more than a dozen paces before Temu caught me.

"I have to go back," I said, refocusing on Temu. I had seen far too many movies to know leaving the bad guy alive will always come back to bite you in the ass. "He knows who my mom is. He'll go after her to get to me."

"I can't let you kill Inyotef," Temu said. "He's too important."

I scoffed. "I don't care if he's the emperor of the whole damn universe," I said, my voice rising as I climbed unsteadily to my feet. I took a stumbling step to the side, away from my pile of vomit, and Temu rushed forward, steadying me with a hand under my elbow.

"Thanks," I grumbled.

"Put this on," Temu said, pulling out a small white bundle of fabric that must have been tucked into the back of his schenti. He unfurled it, revealing a simple linen shift.

I snatched the dress out of his hands and pulled it on over my head. It felt wrong to be donning the clean garment when I was filthy, but the simple act of covering my nudity restored a surprisingly large amount of my dignity.

"Can you walk?" Temu asked.

The worst of the dizziness had passed, and I felt much steadier. Weak as hell, but steady enough to put one foot in front of the other. I nodded.

Temu tugged on my elbow, pulling me into motion as he glanced back up the road toward the palace. "We must be on our way. I am too drained to jump us away, so we must travel by foot. Inyotef will send his men after us, and I had not planned on killing anyone today."

I watched Temu out of the corner of my eye as I automatically fell in step beside him, thinking his words were terribly odd. He wanted to get moving because he hadn't planned on killing anyone today. Not because he feared for his own life. And not because he feared we would be captured. He didn't want to kill anyone. It was as if the prospect of Inyotef's guards injuring or capturing *him* was absurd, but Temu killing *all of them* was a foregone conclusion.

I waded back through my slippery memory of those last moments in the cell. After emerging from the shadows, Temu had attacked and restrained

Inyotef with *At*. Which meant Temu was one of those rare, powerful Nejerets with a *sheut*. And, like Nik, his *sheut* enabled him to wield the otherworldly material of *At* with barely a thought. When I took that into account, his proclamation made a lot more sense.

But that left pretty much everything else about him knotted into one big question mark.

Why had Temu saved me? And why not at the beginning of my imprisonment? Why had he waited until I had been tortured to the point of welcoming death? Had he been unsure about rescuing me, or had he been waiting for something? What had been the deciding factor for him? What had pushed him over the edge?

My brain still felt too foggy to process the situation properly, so I trudged along in silence beside Temu. I would voice the questions later, when I was more clearheaded.

Temu led me toward the east bank of the Nile, where he had a small canoe waiting for us. I was just about out of gas when we reached the boat. He helped me into the narrow vessel, settling me on the hull near the bow, then joined me in the canoe and used an oar to push off from the riverbank.

"There's food and water in the basket behind you," Temu said as he sat with his back to me, situating the oars in the water and adjusting his grip just so. "Help yourself."

I twisted on my narrow bench and found the aforementioned basket. I was starving—literally—and not feeling remotely picky. I grabbed the waterskin on top, hoping it contained something more substantial than water. It didn't, but the water was clean and cool, and I hadn't realized how thirsty I was. I drained the waterskin so quickly that I gave myself a bellyache.

Once the waterskin was empty, I traded it for a linen-wrapped bundle of jerky. My mouth watered as I raised the first piece of dried meat to my lips. It had been so long since I had eaten anything that required actual chewing, and my jaw ached with the desire to tear into the meat. But I stopped my hand with the jerky just shy of my mouth.

I was in bad shape. As soon as my body had stored up enough fuel to begin repairing itself, I would pass out. The need for regenerative sleep would take over, and there would be nothing I could do to stay awake. For a time, essentially, I would be dead to the world. Temu could take me anywhere, do anything with me. While grateful to him for the part he had played in freeing me, I wasn't feeling all that trusting at the moment.

I forced my hand to lower, my stomach groaning in protest, and re-wrapped the bundle of jerky to return it to the basket. I knotted my fingers together to keep myself from reaching for more food.

Temu had settled into a steady pace rowing across the river, periodically glancing over his shoulder to ensure we were still on course. The next time he looked over his shoulder, he focused on me. "You're not eating."

I gripped my fingers more tightly. "I don't want to fall asleep yet."

"I won't hurt you," Temu said, facing forward once more. "You have my word."

I let out an unladylike snort. "Says the guy who knocked me out."

Temu was quiet for a long moment. "I had my reasons," he finally said.

"Yeah, well, I have my reasons for wanting to stay awake," I snapped, crossing my arms over my chest and clenching my jaw.

"Suit yourself," he said, his tone suggesting he couldn't care less. His silence during the remainder of the crossing, however, was heavy with disapproval.

I couldn't tear my eyes away from Temu as he rowed across the Nile and not only because I was completely enthralled by the rhythmic flexing of the defined muscles covering his arms and back, though that was part of it. He didn't make any sense to me, and I didn't trust my concussed brain enough to puzzle out fantasy from reality in my memory of whatever had happened in the cell.

If Temu noticed my scrutiny, he didn't comment.

When we reached the west bank of the Nile, Temu guided the boat through a field of lily pads and purple lotus flowers and into the wide mouth of an irrigation canal. He drove the bow of the boat straight into the silty riverbank, causing buried rocks to scrape against the wooden hull.

Temu stood and tossed a small leather pack onto the canal bank, then hopped out of the boat himself. He waded through the shallow water toward the bow and held his hand out for me to take.

I hadn't even attempted to stand on my own, and my legs trembled like I was a newborn calf when I stood with his help. He curled an arm around my back and lifted me out of the boat, setting my feet down in a few inches of water and releasing my back but keeping a firm grip on my elbow.

I gazed longingly at the clear water funneling into the canal, the surface as smooth as glass. I didn't know where Temu was taking me, but I hadn't had anything more substantial than a soapless sponge bath for quite some time. My hair was a greasy rat's nest, and I reeked, even to myself. If the smell was bad to my nose, it had to be awful to Temu. I had lost just about every shred of dignity when I was locked in that dungeon, and I was desperate to reclaim what remnants I could.

"I'd like to bathe," I said, glancing up at Temu's face but quickly averting my gaze to our feet. "If we have time before we go . . ." I trailed off, no clue where we were headed from here.

"Of course," Temu said, letting go of my elbow.

He crouched to fish through his bag, eventually pulling out a linen-wrapped bundle small enough to fit in the palm of my hand. He handed it to me, and when I unwrapped the linen and unveiled the little square bar of soap, tears welled in my eyes.

I sniffled, wiped under my lashes, and offered Temu a shaky smile. At that moment, the little bar of soap was worth more to me than gold.

I gripped it tight in one hand as I pulled my shift off over my head and handed the garment to Temu. His gaze was heavy on my skeletal back as I waded out into the deeper water, the little bar of soap clutched to my chest. I wondered what he saw when he looked at me now—the woman I had been, or the weak, stick-thin creature I had wasted away to under Inyotef's unique brand of hospitality.

It was easier to keep my balance with the pressure of the water supporting me. I sank into the river up to my chin and rubbed that precious bar of soap all over my body until barely a sliver of soap remained. My body felt foreign to me, like it belonged to someone else. There were too many sharp angles and jutting bones.

I combed my fingers through my hair, wincing as I worked out the worst of the snarls. At least my hair wasn't as long as it had been when I first arrived in this time. That would have been a nightmare to untangle.

When I reemerged from the water, I felt like a bit of the old me had resurfaced. I wrung out my hair as I waded back to the riverbank, swiping away as much of the water from my skin as I could.

Temu stood in the river up to his knees, waiting for me with my dry shift draped over his shoulder. As the water became shallower, my steps grew unsteadier, and by the time I reached him, I could barely shamble forward on my own. He hovered at my side as I struggled to raise my shaking arms high enough to pull the dress on over my head.

Chin trembling, I sucked in a shaky breath. "I think I might need you to carry me," I said, staring down at the surface of the water. "If you don't mind."

Temu's knuckles grazed down my cheek to my chin, and he gently tilted my face upward until I dragged my eyes up to meet his. While the rest of his appearance had reverted to human, his eyes were different from before, reminding me of the dark midnight sky shot through by silver starbursts around his pupils. These were the eyes of the god-prince I had met in the prison cell.

"I don't mind," Temu said, the low rumble of his voice resonating in every cell of my being.

He moved closer, and the space between us crackled as though we were competing forces and our very nearness charged the air. He curled one arm around my shoulders, then crouched to slip the other behind my knees, scooping me up like I weighed nothing at all.

Despite all the uncertainties surrounding this man, I felt strangely at peace cradled in his arms. I wrapped my arms around his neck and rested my head on his shoulder, relaxing in his hold.

When we reached the edge of the water, Temu set me down to retrieve his leather pack and the basket of food. Once both were situated on his shoulders, he scooped me up again and set off toward the barley field bordering the riverbank.

Temu carried me for an hour or two, gradually making his way toward the limestone cliffs dividing the fertile river valley from the arid desert. He climbed up a path that appeared to end nowhere but a steep drop-off and a sheer cliff face. When we reached the apparent end of the trail, he turned toward the cliff face.

Without putting me down, Temu extended one hand out in front of him and pressed his palm flat against the rock wall. In a blink, the color drained out of a rectangular patch of limestone, revealing that this part of the cliff face wasn't rock at all, but a barrier of solid, iridescent *At*. The barrier shimmered, then evaporated into a glittering mist, leaving behind a seven-foot-tall opening in the cliff face.

Temu stepped through the opening and into the darkness beyond, then paused, turning back toward the bright, golden sunlight. I watched over his shoulder as he rebuilt the barrier, plunging us into absolute darkness.

My whole body tensed, and for a moment, I was back in that cell. Had I never left? Had my escape been little more than a twisted dream?

The subtlest, silver light gradually thinned the darkness, pushing away my cresting panic. At first, I couldn't tell where the light was coming from. It seemed to be ambient and sourceless.

It was the walls, I realized. The walls and ceiling. Temu must have coated them in *At*, and imbued them with the ability to glow.

The light remained dim, like moonlight, but bright enough to afford me a good view of the cavern. It was large and disk shaped, with smooth, curved walls and an even ten-foot ceiling. There was a sunken fire pit in the center of the cavern, though the logs stacked within appeared to be made of *At* rather than wood. A colorful patchwork of rugs surrounded the firepit, and a low square table—also constructed of *At*—sat off to one side, a pair of bedrolls on the other. Baskets stuffed full of I-didn't-know-what had been stacked up near the wall in the back, as though Temu had been stashing things here for a while in preparation for an extended stay.

Temu waved his hand at the firepit, and the *At* logs glowed orange, emitting a gentle heat that warmed the cool cavern.

A sizzle of energy drew my attention back to the man cradling me in his arms. I watched as Temu's appearance shimmered, his dull human facade falling away, letting his dazzling otherness shine through.

My lips parted, and all I could do was stare into his inhumanly beautiful face. Familiar but different. Other.

Temu gazed down at me with those midnight eyes, his expression distant, cautious. Almost afraid. He set me down carefully, placing my feet on the floor but keeping a hand on my waist to steady me.

"Who *are* you?" I breathed.

He held my stare for a long moment, his jaw clenching and unclenching.

I had the impression that, even now, after bringing me to this secret place and revealing his true nature to me, he was uncertain about divulging who he really was. Like his identity was the deepest, darkest secret of all. I couldn't imagine how such a thing was possible. How could his name be any more of a shock than everything else he had already revealed to me?

Temu—or whoever he was—turned his face away from mine and peered into the flameless fire pit. He inhaled deeply, then held his breath.

"My true name is Atum," he finally said, releasing the words through gritted teeth like some external force was dragging the confession out of him.

My mouth fell open, and a shiver cascaded down my spine. Now I understood his hesitation. That name—his name—was terrifying.

Atum was a myth, a legend. A nightmare. I gulped and instinctively backed away. Just one step, but I might as well have run screaming for the impact it had on Atum.

His expression hardened, and he glanced at me sidelong, a dangerous glint to his eyes. "I see you've heard of me."

38

"**B**UT—BUT YOU *SAVED* ME."

My mouth watered and my stomach groaned as I stared down at the feast Atum was laying out on the low table—the jerky I had shirked in the boat, as well as dried fruit, nuts, a stack of flatbread and a pile of honey breads, and a trio of waterskins that most likely contained something so much more nourishing than water.

When Atum poured the contents of one waterskin into a deep *At* bowl he created out of thin air and the scent of savory beef broth as thick as gravy reached my nose, I took an involuntary step toward the table. He pushed the bowl closer to the edge of the table. Closer to me.

I took another involuntary step forward, then stubbornly rooted my feet to the ground. "Atum doesn't save people," I said, tearing my stare away from the broth and focusing on Atum, who was now pouring thick cream into another bowl. "He—he kills them."

That was the terrifying truth staring me in the face. Atum was believed to be a myth because no living Nejeret had ever met him. Or, more accurately, no Nejeret had ever met him and lived to tell the tale.

Atum glanced at me without moving his head and pushed the second bowl closer to me.

I could smell the honey sweetening the cream, and I licked my lips. My salivary glands were like a faucet inside my mouth, and I swallowed repeatedly.

"Are you going to kill me?" I asked, my voice high and thready. Was this some demented version of a last meal?

Atum stared at me for a long moment. Each second that passed without him denying any deadly intent amped up the fear and adrenaline thrumming through my blood. I felt suddenly energized, my wasted limbs ready to run. But I was sealed inside this cavern with Atum, and there was nowhere for me to run *to*.

"A few days ago, you begged Kiya to kill you," Atum finally said.

I blinked, stunned by the statement. "How—" I shook my head, my mouth working but no more words coming out. Finally, I grappled my nerves—and my voice—into submission. "Did Kiya tell you that?" How else could he have known?

Atum inhaled deeply through his nose, releasing the breath slowly, evenly. "Whether you die by my hand is entirely up to you," he said. "You have a choice to make." With a sweep of his arm, he gestured to the food spread out before him on the low table. "Come. Sit and eat, and I will explain."

I pulled my bottom lip between my teeth, chewing on the chapped skin as I eyed the feast. And then, unable to resist any longer, I stumbled forward and fell to my knees. I lifted the bowl of beef broth and gulped it down in the least dignified way possible, leaving thin brown streams dripping down my chin on either side of my mouth. Once that bowl was empty, I swapped it out for the bowl of sweetened cream. While I chugged that, Atum refilled the broth bowl.

I would have sworn I could feel the food breaking down to its essential parts in my stomach and soaking into my body. I felt stronger—and sleepier—already. Which meant the clock was ticking on how much time we had to discuss this supposed life-and-death choice of mine before I conked out for some untold number of hours.

I set the second bowl down and picked up the linen napkin Atum had surreptitiously placed in front of me on the table to wipe my chin. "I'm eating," I said, reaching for the stack of flatbread. I snatched two off the top and raised my eyebrows. I was fulfilling my end of the bargain. It was time for him to do the same.

The corners of Atum's mouth tensed. "You have a choice to make," he started. "Your life is one of great potential. You can either hand that potential over to me and assist me in my work or not."

I chewed the mouthful of bread the bare minimum of times and swallowed, reaching for the *At* cup of water Atum had set on the table. "And if I don't choose to *assist you in your work*, you'll kill me." I stared at him point-blank over the rim of the cup as I drank.

Atum nodded once. That confirmation stung.

"Why?" I asked, spontaneously tearing up. I tried not to let the welling sorrow and fear show, but my voice came out tremulous, regardless. "What did I do?" After all I had survived, this seemed like a cruel joke. Fate was punking me.

Atum's expression softened. "You dared to exist when you should not," he said, his voice a gentle rumble.

So he knew my biggest secret then. He knew I didn't belong here—that I didn't belong *now*. My chin trembled as I attempted to hold the unraveling pieces of myself together.

"You are what I call an *anomaly*," Atum explained. "Your presence in this time and place is unnatural. I have detected other anomalies before, but they never stayed put long enough for me to observe them properly." He nodded his head to the side. "Well, there was Alexandra, but she is a special case, her temporal displacement was orchestrated by my father and was woven into the time tapestry."

As I listened, understanding about half of what Atum told me, I forced myself to continue eating, tearing off pieces of flatbread and chewing them robotically. When regenerative sleep claimed me, I wanted the healing coma to be as effective as possible so I would be in a better mental and physical position to deal with this impossible scenario when I eventually woke.

Atum was quiet for a moment, watching me eat. "I am well aware of the rumors surrounding me," he said, his stare shifting past me, growing distant. "That I kill without thought or mercy. Without reason or remorse." As he spoke, he pressed his hand to his chest over his heart, his fingertips tracing a few of the small, gold scars. "That I choose my victims at random." He refocused on me. "But I do not. I have a purpose. A singular reason for being, and every person who dies at my hand, does so to fulfill that purpose."

I reached for the bowl of nuts and pulled it closer to me, scooping up a small handful and shoveling them into my mouth.

"When Nuin brought me into this world," Atum continued, "he groomed me to protect the one true timeline—the singular path this universe must travel to achieve what *must be*. All other paths lead to the destruction of all that is."

Atum's words transported me back to the Netjer war that had claimed my life in the distant future, and I couldn't help but wonder if it was the culmination of Atum's *singular path*. If the same events that had led to my inopportune trip back in time were part of his *one true timeline*, and if my death at the hands of a Netjer was included in the *what must be* he spoke of.

"I missed you when you first arrived," Atum admitted. "Like all anomalies, your lifethread doesn't appear on the time tapestry, and as you moved through the desert, your impact on the weave was almost imperceptible." A small smile played across his face, a mere whisper of amusement, there and gone in a blink.

"I didn't actually notice you until the attack on the caravan. You exploded into a vortex of pure chaos, warping and snapping the lifethreads of all around you. I retraced your path, following you backward through the desert. Your path crossed with a few Nejerets, and it was as though your mere presence near them made their lifethreads tremble. I have never seen anything like it—anything like you."

Atum laughed under his breath, but there was no humor or joy in the sound. "I knew then that you were too dangerous to let live."

The bite of jerky I was chewing turned to sawdust in my mouth, and I had to consciously force my jaw to open and close.

Again, Atum's focus drifted past me, like he was seeing another time, another place. "But then, I watched you in that warehouse. You took pains to spare the lives of that girl's attackers, even when their deaths would have served you—and the people of Waset—better. You had killed before, and I could see no reason for you *not* to kill again, other than some internal awareness of your impact on the timeline." He paused. "Only then did I consider another option—one where you were allowed to live."

I gulped, finally swallowing the bite of jerky-turned-sawdust, and fought a gag as the food moved down my throat. I switched back to liquids, lifting the broth bowl and sipping as Atum continued his tale.

"You see," he said, "when a human strays from the weave and creates a dissonance in the pattern—even someone with a significant lifethread like Inyotef or Nitocris—I am often able to course-correct the trajectory of their life by inserting myself into their world. I can usually correct the dissonance and repair the damage to the time tapestry without bloodshed, without death."

"Is that why you were there—staying at the palace and following Inyotef's orders?" I asked. "Were you attempting to course-correct their alliance?"

"To prevent it, yes," Atum said with a nod. He drew in a deep breath, then sighed. "Though clearly, I was unsuccessful. Our kind can prove even more stubborn. An immortal's lifethread is longer, thicker, and far more stubborn than that of a human, more like a wire than an actual thread. I have tried time and again to take the gentler route to repair the dissonance caused by a straying immortal lifethread, and not once has it worked. In the end, the lifethread must always be severed and the surrounding ones rewoven around the sudden absence."

Atum fell quiet for a moment, and I swapped out my now empty broth bowl for the plate of honey breads and dove in.

"But with you," Atum continued after a considering pause, "one whose mere presence acts like a chaos bomb, destabilizing even those stubborn immortal lifethreads, I have been given an alternative. I can drop you into the life of the straying Netjer-At, let your intrinsic chaos weaken their lifethread, making them more open to redirection, then pluck you back out and clean up the mess you have left behind."

I frowned and furrowed my brow, not quite understanding his logic. "Wouldn't the weave, or whatever, be *more* disrupted then?" I mean, he had used the words *bomb* and *mess* in relation to my impact on this *tapestry* thing, and neither felt all that flattering.

"Perhaps," Atum said, tilting his head to the side, the corners of his mouth tensing. "But I am very good at cleaning up messes. It is the stubborn Netjer-At lifethreads I struggle to shift. *That* is what I need you for. Through you, Tarset, immortal lives may be spared. Lives that would otherwise be lost and damned prematurely to an eternity in Aaru."

I sucked in a breath to respond but found I needed more time to process Atum's words. I bit into another honey bread instead. Very little of what he had shared made sense to me. I was too exhausted, my eyelids growing increasingly heavy and regenerative sleep already tugging on the edges of my consciousness.

I swallowed the bite, then inhaled again. "So—and please correct me if I'm wrong—you're saying you think I can help you kill fewer people?" I paused, rearranging my thoughts into something semi-logical. "And, if I don't agree to work with you to help you kill fewer people, then you're going to kill *me*, instead?" I raised my eyebrows, silently asking if I understood the basic elements of the situation correctly.

"That is correct," Atum said, closing his eyes in a prolonged blink and bowing his head.

I frowned, narrowing my eyes. "Maybe I'm not seeing the complete picture here, which is likely, because I didn't understand most of what you just told me, but I feel like the answer is obvious—why *wouldn't* I agree to help you? Is there some downside that I'm missing?"

Atum nodded, a lone, bitter laugh shaking his chest. "You must step away from this world," he said. "You can never be known as you truly are. You must become nameless and unknown to those you will devote your life to saving."

The way he said *this world* made me wonder if there was some other place I would belong—if I agreed to work with him—but my focus was slipping, and there was something far more urgent I needed to ask before I committed to anything. Yes, my life was hanging in the balance, but I wasn't about to make a deal with the devil just to keep on breathing.

I stared at Atum for a few heartbeats while I chewed and swallowed the last bite of jerky. "You said you had some idea of how you could use me when you watched me fighting those guys in the warehouse," I said, wording the premise of my question carefully and keeping my eyes locked with his. "So why did you leave me to rot in that cell for so long? Why did you let Inyotef imprison me at all?"

I wasn't even sure how many days had passed. Enough to matter. Too many for Atum's answer to be anything but stellar.

"I had to be sure about you," Atum said with no hesitation. "The more I watched you, the more I came to suspect that the source of your anomalous existence was that you had suffered a temporal displacement. Heru had a daughter once who bore your name, but she now rests in the Netjer-At Oasis, frozen in time. You are not her—"

I sucked in a breath to correct him, but he beat me to it.

"Or rather, she is not you . . ." Atum tilted his head to the side to emphasize his next word. "Yet."

I closed my mouth, impressed by his ability to deduce the truth correctly.

"You are who that child will become in some era beyond the reach of the time tapestry, in the distant future," Atum said. "I had to be sure that protecting that future was your absolute priority, especially after your bargain with Nitocris. Even though you claimed you had not intended to fulfill your end of the bargain and view the Echoes for her, I had to know you spoke the truth. I had to know you would die to protect that future you so cherish if need be."

Atum's stare bore through my flesh and bone, flaying me open to expose my soul. "And so, I waited twenty-six days until I was sure."

I closed my eyes, and a pair of tears sprang free, gliding down my cheeks. Twenty-six days. Not even a month. Shame burned in my heart at how quickly I had shattered.

I started when I felt Atum brush away my tears with the pads of his thumbs. My eyelids snapped open, and I found him crouched before me, balancing on the balls of his feet.

Atum gazed into my eyes, no hint of pity on his face. "You were ready to make the ultimate sacrifice," he said, his voice a gentle rumble. "You would have done it—given your life to protect those you hold in your heart. I can see that you view this as a weakness, but in time, I believe you will come to see it as I do."

I sniffled and wiped my runny nose with the back of my hand. "Which is what?" I asked, voice wobbly.

Atum offered me a small smile. "Your greatest strength."

I WOKE FROM DREAMLESS regenerative sleep to find myself alone in the cavern. The entrance was sealed shut, and the only light came from the orange glow of the *At* logs in the firepit. A fresh feast of packable foodstuffs had been laid out on the table, and my stomach groaned with hunger at the sight of all that food up for grabs. I rolled from my back onto my side, then pushed myself up to a sitting position.

Rubbing my bleary eyes, I scanned the cavern once more, but there was no sign of Atum. I glanced down at my bedroll and the blankets piled around me like a nest. I couldn't remember lying down to sleep, and I wondered if I had passed out in the middle of eating. My cheeks heated as I pictured myself face planting in a plate of honey breads. Or worse, in a bowl of broth.

I started to stretch my arms over my head, but the movement caused a sudden, panic-inducing flashback to all the time I had spent in that dank cell with my arms tied over my head. I hugged my middle and stared at the glowing *At* logs, reminding myself that I had escaped. That I was free.

I glanced at the *At* barrier barring the cavern's exit. Free-ish.

I was incredibly grateful to Atum for saving me from that awful fate. I would have died in that dungeon. I had likely been days away from that eventuality. I still didn't forgive him for leaving Inyotef alive, but I wasn't too proud or stubborn to give credit where credit was due. Atum's reasons for helping may have been far from altruistic, but I wasn't about to look a gift horse in the mouth. Because of him, I was alive, and my family—in the future, at least—was safe.

It was my family living in present-day Men-nefer I now worried about. My mom and siblings. Their children. How long until Inyotef came after them, seeking retribution like it was the only balm that would soothe his wounded ego?

My stomach growled, renewing its claim on all that food just sitting there across the firepit, waiting for me to devour it. I shifted onto my hands and knees and crawled around the firepit toward the low table, my concerns for my mom and siblings shifting to the back of my mind. Not that I couldn't do anything to help them right now, trapped as I was in this cavern with another cycle of regenerative sleep breathing down the back of my neck.

I wolfed down pretty much everything on the table, which shouldn't have been physically possible, because nobody's stomach was that large—unless they had a Nejeret metabolism running on overdrive, breaking down and burning up the food with incredible efficiency.

I was barely able to drag myself back to my bedroll by the time the impending regenerative cycle pulled me into a deep, dreamless sleep.

When I next roused, I wasn't alone.

I heard Atum's heartbeat before I even opened my eyes. The gentle *whoosh* of his breath as he inhaled and exhaled was music to my ears, and I lay curled up on my side on the bedroll for some untold amount of time, listening to Atum. I probably should have been nervous or afraid of him, rather than soothed by his presence, but the cavewoman part of me was comforted by having the biggest, baddest Nejeret *ever* looking out for her.

At least, he would look out for me so long as I was on his side. So long as I helped him. I had yet to give him my answer because I had yet to decide.

Yes, I wanted to live. I was especially eager to keep on breathing now that I wasn't suffering from physical torture nearly every waking minute. But at what cost? What would I have to do for Atum, beyond being my apparently naturally chaotic self? Would I have to hurt people at his direction? Would I have to kill people? And what had he meant when he said I would have to *step away from this world*? Did that mean I could never go home?

The desire for answers wedged my eyelids open. I groaned and rolled onto my back, indulging in a delicious full body stretch.

I felt stronger. Not strong, but stronger, which was progress. I ran my hands down the sides of my emaciated body, noticing the defined ribs, hollow middle, and jutting hip bones. I still had a long way to go in my path to being healed, but my body—and my heart and mind—were on the mend.

When I sat up and peered around the cavern, I found Atum standing with his back to me near the wall beyond the table on the far side of the sunken fire pit. At first, I thought he was watching a movie or show on a large flat-screen TV mounted on the cavern wall. But that made little sense for about a million reasons, and when my mind finally caught up with reality, I noticed that the "screen" of the not-a-TV was embedded in the *At* wall, displaying a scene of a woman in her late twenties or early thirties, kneeling beside a bassinet on the floor, tucking a blanket around the drowsy infant swaddled within. Was this some kind of window to another time and place? Was Atum watching an *Echo*?

I had never heard of a Nejeret being able to view Echoes here on the physical plane of existence. Even the most powerful Nejerets, like my dad, had to leave their bodies and enter a higher dimension to view them. Or, at least, they *used to* do it back before we had been locked out of the Echoes completely.

I climbed to my feet and bent down to pick up a thin blanket, wrapping it around myself as a makeshift robe.

Atum glanced over his shoulder as I shuffled around the table—once again laden with food—and made my way over to him.

"What is it?" I asked when I reached Atum, clutching the blanket more tightly around me.

Atum eyed me sidelong, then stepped closer to the wall and raised one hand. He pinched his fingers together in front of the window or screen or whatever it was, and the scene shrank away, the woman and child melting into a rose-tinged iridescent stream that stretched horizontally across the altered patch of wall. That rosy stream shrank further, thinning and elongating, and I had the impression that we were zooming out on whatever we were looking at.

Soon, another stream—this one gleaming gold, but with that same rosy tint—intertwined with the original iridescent stream. They thinned further, and more iridescent streams appeared around them, lazily weaving through and around the original stream. Those that crossed the original stream gained a faint hint of rose to their gleaming iridescence.

"This is a patch, displaying a portion of the time tapestry," Atum explained.

My eyes opened wider, my thoughts whirling. My recollection of everything Atum had told me when we first arrived here was a little hazy, especially the things he had shared while I fought the pull of regenerative sleep. But I *did* remember him mentioning the time tapestry multiple times.

He had made it sound pretty damn important, like it basically directed his every action.

Atum raised one hand and traced the original rose-tinged stream even as it thinned further and more joined the visible area. "This is a lifethread," he said. "These are all lifethreads." He pressed his palm against the patch of the time tapestry, and it stopped zooming out.

Most of the left half of the patch was composed of iridescent lifethreads, along with that single gold thread. Around the middle of the patch, the original thread started turning pink. As it progressed toward the right side of the patch, the thread reddened further and seemed to swell, the lifethreads winding around it taking on an increasingly rosy tint. The transformation made me think of a spreading infection.

"Is this a *dissonance*?" I asked, pointing to the reddening half of the patch.

Atum nodded. "Indeed, it is," he said, glancing at me sidelong, his eyebrows raising like he was mildly impressed.

With another pinching gesture, the area visible on the patch zoomed out farther and hundreds—thousands—more lifethreads appeared. I could make out a few other faintly pink areas, but nothing so obvious as the original dissonance Atum had been observing, which remained near the center of the visible area. From this more distant view, the dissonance appeared even redder and seemed to pulse with wrongness, like a diseased heart.

"This displays all the lifethreads in and around Men-nefer over a three-year period," Atum explained. He touched his fingertip to a point slightly to the left of the original dissonance, and a shimmering vertical line appeared, bisecting the patch and crossing directly under his fingertip. "This is now."

"As you can see," Atum said, "the choices that will lead to a significant disturbance in the pattern are fast approaching. Free will is such that there is still a chance the corrupt lifethread may correct itself, but the chance of such a self-correction decreases with each passing day."

I chewed on the inside of my cheek, my brow furrowing. I had been taught that free will was an artificial construct, at least within the bookends of Lex's time travel adventures. All choices between her stint in ancient times and about two decades before the start of the Netjer war were supposed to be set in stone. And now, my trip into the past locked in those two decades following Lex's return to the future, because for me to be in the past, the future *had* to have happened in the exact way to lead me here. I was no expert on the time-space continuum, but that was the way I understood time travel.

I opened my mouth, inhaled to speak, then pressed my lips together once more, unsure how to voice my emerging question.

After three more breaths, I tried again. "I thought everything already happened," I said, shaking my head immediately after I spoke the words aloud. "I mean, I didn't think there was still room for free will." I frowned, exhaling through my nose. That hadn't sounded right either.

"You're thinking about time linearly, like someone trapped within the weave of the time tapestry," Atum said. "Like you are the same as any other lifethread." He nodded to the side. "Which is understandable, considering that until your temporal displacement, you were."

My eyebrows inched upward. "But I'm not anymore?"

Atum shook his head. "Your lifethread no longer appears on the time tapestry. You are a ghost, an invisible force altering the lifethreads around you as you move through the tapestry unseen. If not for your chaotic effect on the pattern of the weave, you would be virtually undetectable."

"Really?" I said, eyebrows climbing higher and higher as he spoke.

Atum nodded. "The time tapestry is always changing, always evolving," he explained. "It's why I am needed. When I'm not in the tapestry as I am now, I remain outside of it, monitoring the entirety of the pattern, waiting for new dissonances to appear."

Again, I chewed on the inside of my cheek. "But, each time you fix a dissonance, doesn't it make other changes . . . lead to more dissonances?"

"You would think," Atum said with a slight tilt of his head. "But the pattern of the tapestry is stubborn, the threads woven together so tightly that if a few are redirected or cut, the pattern will—usually—self-correct."

"Huh," I said, raising one hand to pinch my bottom lip. I frowned as a new thought occurred. "So, if free will always exists, and there's always a chance for new dissonances to form, when does your job end?"

"You are thinking linearly again," Atum commented, making no indication of saying more.

Did that mean his role as guardian of the timeline would *never* end? Was he doomed to watch over the time tapestry and to step in—and to kill, when necessary—for *all eternity*? I could only imagine all the terrible things he'd had to do to correct the pattern. All the awful things he had yet to do, and would do, however reluctantly.

Even considering the possibility of being stuck in such a purgatory horrified me.

But if I accepted his bargain to spare my life in exchange for assisting him in his never-ending work, my fate would join his. I would be trapped in Atum's purgatory alongside him, damned to do anything and everything to eradicate dissonances and protect the pattern of the time tapestry. I finally comprehended the monumental nature of the decision I had to make.

"So, um, . . ." I cleared my throat, searching for something—anything—to ask that would change the subject.

If I thought too much about the grisly nature of my potential role at Atum's side, I would chicken out. And then I would die.

"What you were watching before—was that an Echo?" I asked.

Atum eyed me askance, and I heard his silent criticism loud and clear. *Stupid question.* Got it.

A moment later, his lips parted, his eyes widening with dawning understanding. "You don't know how to walk the Echoes."

Embarrassment heated my cheeks, closely followed by a wave of defensiveness. "It's not my fault," I told him, my tone mildly snippy. "In the future, where I was before this, nobody has been able to *walk the Echoes* for a couple of decades. The Echoes—and time travel—were shut down."

Or, at least, time travel was *supposed* to be locked down. No clue how I ended up here, other than it having been a weird byproduct of dying.

I felt Atum's steady gaze on the side of my face, but I refused to look at him, instead staring at the patch of the time tapestry like it contained all the answers I was searching for. To be fair, there was a chance that it did.

"You were awakened after the nothingness set in," Atum said quietly.

I glanced at him for the briefest moment and nodded. The nothingness took over the Echoes around when Lex was sucked backward in time—the first time. I had been unfrozen soon after, a dying four-year-old plunged into a terrifying new world, where her mother had been dead for thousands of years.

"That era is beyond the reach of the time tapestry's pattern," Atum shared. "This explains much."

In my peripheral vision, I watched him extend a hand toward me, but he stopped short of touching me. Instead, he redirected the motion and clasped his hands behind his back, returning his attention to the patch on the wall.

"I will teach you to walk the Echoes," he said.

I looked at him, surprised by the statement. "I would like that," I admitted.

"*If* you agree to work with me," he added, tainting the offer with the reminder that if I *didn't* agree to work with him, he would kill me.

But, if I accepted his bargain, the Echoes would at least give me a way to see my mom again. All my life, that had been my only wish. If I agreed to work with Atum, I could watch Echoes of her whenever I wanted.

I blinked, my mouth falling open. Echoes weren't the only potential window into my mom's life. Another was right in front of me, staring me in the face.

"My mom should be in Men-nefer," I said, my voice tight with anticipation as I stared at the time tapestry patch displaying all the lifethreads currently in that region. My mom was likely one of them. "Could I check on her now?" I asked, glancing at Atum.

Atum stared at me for so long that I thought he was going to deny my request. "I will teach you to navigate the time tapestry, so you may view your mother whenever you like," Atum said.

I looked at him, warm hope swelling in my chest, thawing some of the damage caused by the events of the past month.

Atum shifted his focus to the patch. "*If* you agree to work with me."

O BVIOUSLY, I SAID YES.
As soon as I agreed, Atum reached into a small pouch attached to his weapons belt and pulled out a gold necklace—a simple quarter-sized *At* pendant hanging from a medium-weight gold chain. He moved closer to my side and guided the necklace over my head. The gold chain felt cool on my shoulders, but the pendant was notably warm as it settled between my breasts, and it emitted a barely perceptible vibration.

"This will allow you to interact with the time tapestry," Atum said. He lingered at my side, like he was struggling with distancing himself from me as much as I was with him, but finally stepped away, returning to his original position.

Peering down at the pendant, I traced a fingertip over the winged scarab etched into the solidified *At*.

"Since you have a personal link to your mother, refocusing the patch to display the surrounding pattern should be easy enough." Atum gestured toward the faintly glowing portion of the time tapestry on the wall. "Step forward and touch your hand to the patch, holding your mother in your thoughts, and it will recenter on your mother's lifethread."

"Really?" I asked, stunned by the simplicity of the task. My greatest wish. My deepest desire. Something that had been utterly impossible for two decades was now within reach.

I had been desperate to see my mom again since I first realized *when* I was and that seeing her again was a real possibility. But now that she was a literal arm's reach away, I felt like a tangled ball of nerves. What if she was already dead? What if I stepped closer to the wall, touched my hand to the patch, and her life thread *wasn't there*? I wasn't sure I could survive such a crushing disappointment. Not after everything else I had already been through.

Nietzsche was wrong. What doesn't kill you *doesn't* always make you stronger. Sometimes it leaves you brittle and fragile.

"She still lives," Atum said softly. "If that is your reason for hesitating."

I glanced at him through welling tears. I already had myself half convinced she was dead in an attempt to guard my heart against the grief of losing her again.

"You're sure?"

Atum nodded once.

Clearing my throat, I flashed him a grateful, if slightly wobbly, smile. And then I stepped closer to the wall, reaching for the patch. My hand trembled as if I were reaching for my mom herself.

The instant my fingertips touched the smooth surface, the view on the patch shifted, the pattern becoming an iridescent blur. When the motion stopped, the patch displayed roughly a dozen interwoven lifethreads. Slowly, the display zoomed in on one thread weaving through the heart of the cluster. As the focal lifethread thickened, images appeared, like the still frames on a film reel.

As a single one of those frames overtook the screen, I could see there was nothing *still* about it. When my mom came into focus, I sucked in a breath and brought a hand up to my mouth.

She sat alone on a cushion in a lush courtyard, grinding grain on a long, curved hand mill. She looked noticeably older than I remembered her, with fuller curves, fine lines on her face, and gray streaking her wavy black hair, but there was no mistaking her. My mom. She was right there.

My hazy mental image of her sharpened, becoming crystal clear. I would never forget her again. I sniffled and swiped a tear from under my eye. This was worth the eternity I had promised Atum. *She* was worth it.

"When I was younger, I used to imagine what I would have been like had I been given the chance to grow up here with her," I murmured, unable to take my eyes off my mom. The faintest smile curved her lips, making me think she was humming, though I couldn't actually hear her. "Who would I have become if I didn't have this gaping black hole in my heart?" I said, covering my heart with my hand.

"Had you remained, you would have died," Atum said.

I laughed a soundless, joyless laugh. He was right, of course. Even with the help of modern medicine, I had nearly died.

After another sniffle and swipe of tears, I glanced at Atum over my shoulder. "She's in danger," I reminded him. "Inyotef knows about her. He'll target her to get to me."

Atum crossed his arms over his chest. "Not so," he said.

My eyebrows shot up my forehead.

"While you were unconscious, I touched Inyotef's mind," Atum explained. "He no longer has any recollection of your link to Seshseshet."

Mouth hanging open, I turned to face Atum. "You *touched* Inyotef's mind?" Did that mean his *sheut* gave him power over people's memories, as well?

Atum nodded once. "I had to alter his memory to make him believe he intercepted me as I was helping you escape anyway. Couldn't have him retaining any latent recollection of my true nature. It wasn't any trouble to cauterize the knowledge of your parentage, as well."

I stared at Atum, only now realizing how little I knew about what this man—this relative *god*—could do.

"Pity you didn't erase his memories of me completely," I grumbled. It would have been the next best thing to killing him.

"Ah," Atum said. "But then his memory of the past two months would have been out of sync with the memories of those around him. Eventually, his true memories would have resurfaced." Atum flashed me a hollow half-smile. "There are limitations to such mental manipulations. Subtlety is often the most effective and reliable option."

I frowned. I hadn't considered all of the other people who had seen me at the palace. I was beginning to understand why Atum might have to rely on killing more often than he liked.

"You should eat," Atum said, sweeping an arm out toward the low table. "After another few regeneration cycles, we can be on our way."

As though the mere mention of eating roused my hunger, my stomach groaned audibly.

The corner of Atum's mouth twitched.

I peered back at the time tapestry patch, watching my mom grind grain, that perfectly peaceful expression on her face.

"You can check in on her any time you like," Atum said, his fingers gripping my elbow. His hold gentle but firm, he guided me to the table. "Eat. Rest. Your mother will still be there when you wake."

My stomach and heart were in a tug of war, pulling me in opposite directions. My stomach won out, and I made my way over to the table without further coaxing. I sat, my legs curled beneath me, and reached for a flatbread.

"Where are we going from here?" I asked before taking a bite. I turned my attention up to Atum, who remained standing beside the table.

He gazed down at me with those fathomless midnight eyes, his expression unreadable. "To my home," he said, sounding tired all of a sudden. "To Rostau."

41

I SAT AT THE table, quietly munching on my fifth fig, honey, and cheese flatbread sandwich of the morning while I watched Atum through the cavern doorway. He had already been fully immersed in his morning ritual when I woke from my fourth regeneration cycle since escaping from Inyotef's dungeon, and this was my first chance to watch the ritual up close.

Atum worked his way over his arms, torso, and shoulders methodically, reopening each and every scar with that black-bladed dagger. With each cut, he muttered something under his breath, the syllables sounding different each time, but too quiet for me to make out clearly.

I studied the black-bladed dagger from afar. Now that I knew Atum could manipulate *At*, I was beginning to suspect that the blade wasn't onyx or obsidian, but anti-*At*, the dark, chaotic counterpart to *At*.

After all, *sheuts* could grow and evolve, enabling a Nejeret to expand their otherworldly abilities with enough practice and patience—and time. According to legend, Atum was Nuin's first-born child, which meant he was extremely old. Like, even compared to my dad, who was considered one of the ancients. I tried not to think too hard about the fact that I was insanely attracted to a man who made my father seem like a young buck in comparison.

Every dozen cuts, Atum stopped and dipped his fingers into a drawstring leather pouch that sat open in front of him. So far as I could tell, it was filled with gold dust, which he rubbed over the open wounds while they still bled. That made sense, as his scars had lightened to glimmering gold when he dropped his disguise.

Finally, Atum wiped the black blade of his dagger clean and re-sheathed it on his weapons belt. He unfolded his large body and stood, groaning as he stretched out. His dark skin was streaked with blood and gold from the renewing of his scars. I admired the long, muscular lines of his powerful body.

He turned toward the doorway, freezing momentarily when he noticed me watching him. Eyes locked on me, he returned to the cavern, turning away just for a moment to reseal the exit.

He crossed to the wall displaying the time tapestry patch and stood with his arms folded over his chest and his feet shoulder width apart, studying the threads wrapping around the dissonance he had been monitoring for the past few days. Apparently, he found no significant changes to the disrupted weave because he lowered his arms and turned away from the wall. He joined me at the table, sitting with one knee upraised and an arm draped over his knee.

"Why do you do it?" I asked him.

"Why do I do what?" Atum said, eyeing my fig sandwich concoction, but reaching for the bowl of roasted nuts instead.

Suppressing a smile, I plucked an extra ripe fig from the small mound and placed it on a fresh piece of flatbread. I folded the flatbread in half, smashing the fig and smearing it around a bit between the two halves, then cut a few slices of cheese and slid those into the middle. I finished it with a drizzle of honey before holding the flatbread sandwich out across the table, licking a droplet of milky fig sap from the pad of my thumb.

Atum was oblivious to my offering, his stare locked instead on my thumb, my lips, my tongue. There was no mistaking the heat in his eyes.

A dormant ember of desire flared to life deep in my belly—the first hint of lust I had felt in well over a month—and I blushed at the overtly carnal attention. "Here," I said, clearing my throat and giving the flatbread sandwich a little shake.

Finally noticing my offering, Atum reached out to accept the fig sandwich I had made for him. "Thank you."

I nodded a silent *you're welcome* and watched him take his first bite of my creation. It was nothing fancy, but it was damn good. Based on the way his eyes lit with appreciation, he agreed. I smiled to myself and grabbed a piece of flatbread to make another.

We ate in silence for a time, mounting sexual tension clouding the air between us. My gaze skimmed over his muscular arms and chest, watching the blood and gold smeared over his skin shimmer every time he moved. He truly was magnificent.

I really tried to squash my curiosity about his ritual, but my need to know him better won out. "Why do you cut yourself every morning?" I asked, returning to my earlier question. "Why do you rub gold dust into the wounds and force the scars to remain?"

Atum lifted his elbow and glanced down at the scars flowing over the defined biceps on his right arm, his brows rising just a hair and the faintest frown curving the corners of his mouth downward. He studied the raised, golden bumps on his skin for so long I wondered when had been the last time he really looked at them. How long had it been since he noticed the scars beyond the motions of his ritual?

For a while, I thought he might not respond. He had turned ignoring my questions into an art form after all.

"Each cut represents a life ended," he finally said, tucking his elbow in against his side once more and staring down at the half-eaten feast.

My heart drooped at the confirmation of my suspicions. "People you killed?" I clarified softly.

Atum nodded, still not looking at me. "Not because I wanted to," he explained. "But because I had to."

"To protect the timeline," I murmured, letting him know I understood.

Again, he nodded, and my heart wept for him.

What would that do to a person, having to kill over and over and over, not because of any wrongdoing by the victims, but because their actions strayed from a preset pattern? What scars would that leave on a person's heart? On their soul?

"Each cut is a life *I* ended," Atum said, emphasizing in the "I" as though he needed to express his ownership of those deaths. "I cut myself and recite their names every morning because they were innocent." Finally, he dragged his eyes up to meet mine, and the turmoil shining in his midnight gaze nearly brought me to tears. "Because nobody deserves to be forgotten."

His pain became my pain, and the need to comfort him grew until it was all-consuming. I set down my half-eaten flatbread sandwich and stood. I padded around the table and eased down to kneel beside Atum, sitting back on my heels.

He became a statue as I reached for him with one steady hand, barely breathing as I traced the pattern of raised, golden bumps on his forearm with gentle fingertips. I trailed my hand higher, over the swells of muscle on his upper arm and his tensed shoulder, then rose to my knees as I traced his collarbone, feeling my way over the macabre history written on his skin.

I raised my eyes, my gaze lingering on his sensual lips before making its way up to his heated stare. His pupils expanded, dark desire swallowing the starlight in his midnight eyes.

Atum made a rough, growly sound low in his throat and slid his foot out, lowering his raised knee as he turned his body away from the table. Toward me. One of his hands settled on my hip, then glided higher, curling around my back. He flexed his arm, pulling me closer to him.

I raised my knee and straddled his lap. The hand he pressed against my back slid higher, tracing the length of my spine until it settled on the back of my neck. His other arm snaked around my waist to pull my hips flush against his body. The hard evidence of his arousal nudged my core, only separated by a few thin layers of linen.

Atum's nose skimmed along my jawline, leaving a trail of electrified nerve endings in its wake. Our heartbeats merged into a herd of thundering horses. The air between and around us felt charged. Electric. His mouth moved higher, hovering over mine, and our breaths mingled.

I closed the distance between our mouths, brushing my lips against his in the lightest kiss at the same moment as I tilted my pelvis, grinding my core along his hard length.

Atum groaned, his hold on me tightening. His eyes remained locked on mine as I rocked my hips back and forth in a slow, tormenting grind.

I ached with need for this man. This god. All cautionary thoughts about us being potential bond-mates and the dangers of indulging in our extraordinary attraction fled from my mind as my body took over. In this moment, I wanted nothing more than to drive his pain away, to banish the scars from his heart and the ghosts from his mind, at least for a little while.

I pressed my palm against Atum's chest, directly over his heart. "I'm sorry," I breathed, the words caressing his lips. An exquisite inferno raged in my core, burning ever hotter with each rock of my hips.

"For what?" Atum asked, his voice a gruff whisper. Against my palm, his chest rose and fell with each quick, shallow breath. His body coiled tighter, his careful restraint slipping. I would find myself on my back soon if I wasn't careful.

I didn't want to be careful. I wanted him on top of me. Inside me. Filling me completely.

"For what you have to do," I gasped between breaths. "For what you have to live with."

Atum's entire body went rigid and not from pleasure. His arms loosened, and I fell still atop him, pulling back slightly to study his suddenly stony expression. The heat that had burned in his gaze only a moment ago had been replaced by an icy wall. Though I sat on his lap, my chest flush against his, it felt like he was a million miles away.

His stare slid past me, focusing on some point on the wall, and his hands settled on my hips. "Save your compassion for someone who deserves it," he said and tightened his grip on my hips. He lifted me off his lap, shifting me to the floor mat beside him.

In one fluid motion, he stood and strode away from me, heading for the time tapestry patch. He glanced back at me over his shoulder. "I do not."

42

AFTER TWO MORE REGENERATIVE cycles, my hunger returned to a normal level, and I no longer felt the need to pass out immediately after eating. Suddenly, I had all this free time and nothing to do with myself except to sneak glances at Atum and to feel insanely awkward as I tried not to choke on the tension—sexual and something darker and more sinister—filling the cavern.

His rejection the other day still stung, even though I knew it had nothing to do with me. He wanted me just as badly as I wanted him. A lack of attraction wasn't what was holding him back. I didn't think it was fear of a potential soul bond, either.

Our problem had to do with Atum's issues regarding his role as guardian of the timeline or protector of the pattern, or whatever he considered himself. Which was totally understandable. I mean, the guy had to kill innocent people to protect the greater good regularly. It bothered him—the killing. I suspected he believed himself to be a monster for being able to end all those lives, for being willing to do so. But that it bothered him so much convinced me otherwise.

Atum wasn't a monster. He was just a son whose father had put him in the most onerous position possible. Nuin forced Atum to become a killer. What a shitty dad.

After hours of sitting by the faux fire pretending I wasn't staring at Atum's back and psychoanalyzing him while he watched the real-time view of that same troublesome lifethread on the time tapestry patch, the tension finally grew too thick. I stood and wandered to the doorway in search of fresh air.

I stood in the opening, gazing out at the Nile valley. In the cloudless sky overhead, the late afternoon sun sank toward the top of our cliff. Far below, canals reached all the way to the outer edges of the fields bordering the river. I followed the steep trail down the cliffside with my eyes and spotted a clear path to one of the closest canals.

Suddenly, bathing was all I could think about. I estimated six or seven days had passed since Atum sprung me from Inyotef's dungeon, and I hadn't had more than a sponge bath since that day I scrubbed myself raw in the Nile. I was due for a thorough soak.

I turned sideways in the opening to look at Atum. His focus remained locked on the time tapestry.

"I want to bathe," I told him. "And wash some clothes." An entire basket filled with white linen sheath dresses had been stashed here for me, but a few were dirty enough to require laundering at this point.

Atum finally tore his stare from the scene displayed on the patch, glancing first at me, then at the vat filled with fresh, clean water in the back of the cavern, near the stacks of storage baskets.

"*Not* another sponge bath," I clarified before he could suggest it. "There's a canal right down there at the edge of the farmlands," I said, nodding toward the valley below. "The entire trail is visible from here." I raised my right hand like I was about to swear an oath. "And if I see or hear anyone coming, I'll be out of the water and on my way back up here before they notice I'm there." My lips curved into a hope-filled grin.

"Very well," Atum said, his focus returning to the time tapestry. "There are more bars of soap somewhere." He glanced toward the storage baskets. "You're welcome to them."

I suppressed a squee as I hurried to the back of the cavern to search for the promised soap. Not five minutes later, I moseyed down the trail with a small, tote-style basket over my shoulder and a pep to my step. Atum may have saved my life, but if I wasn't careful, his brooding dominance would suffocate me. The cavern wasn't big enough for the both of us, and the fresh air revived me in a way that no amount of regeneration cycles ever could.

Once I had finished bathing and washing the dirty clothes, I climbed back up the trail to the cavern feeling like a new woman. Or rather, a little more like my old self—the woman I had been before a Netjer stabbed me through the heart.

The sun slipped behind the cliff as I hiked up the trail, and twilight was settling over the valley. As I rounded the final switchback, I found Atum stalking back and forth along the ledge in front of the cavern entrance.

Instantly alarmed, I picked up the pace, striding quickly up the last quarter mile of the trail. I was gasping for breath and grasping my side by the time I reached the ledge. My body may have healed, but I was still grossly out of shape. Apparently, Nejeret regeneration had little to do with physical fitness, because I currently had the strength and stamina of a record-holding couch potato.

I stopped at the end of the ledge and bent over, hands on my knees, working on catching my breath. "What is it?" I asked between gasps. "What happened?"

Atum turned toward the opening in the cliff wall and strode into the cavern. "The dissonance requires correcting," his voice was razor sharp, telling me he was not at all pleased by this turn of events. "We leave immediately."

I hurried into the cavern after him. Four baskets sat in a line along the wall under the time tapestry patch, two huge, and two merely large. All four were stuffed to the brim with food and other supplies.

"Do you need me to do anything?" I asked, wondering if this was going to be the first test of my usefulness as his brand new chaos bomb.

"Just hold these," he said, handing me one of the smaller—but not *small*—baskets, this one stuffed with blankets and clothing.

I hooked my arm through the pair of handles and grunted as the full brunt of the basket's weight dragged on my elbow. What was in the bottom of this thing—bars of gold? The second of the smaller baskets was a little lighter, but still not light. Both were heavy enough that I had to strain to hold them.

"Um, Atum," I said, hitching the heavier basket higher into the crook of my arm. "I won't be able to carry these for long."

"You don't need to carry them," Atum said, hoisting one of the larger baskets onto his shoulder. His arm muscles bulged, the tendons in his neck straining. "Just hold them."

He added the second enormous basket to the same shoulder, then reached out and grasped my upper arm. His hands were so large and my muscles were so wimpy that his fingers could encircle my arm completely, and then some. He pulled me out to the ledge but stopped immediately outside of the cavern opening instead of starting down the trail.

"You may wish to close your eyes," he suggested, facing me. "I'm told this can be quite disorienting to those unused to traveling."

"What are you—"

My words died off as an iridescent mist, shot through by vibrant strings of every color imaginable, rose from the ground and swallowed the world.

For a brief eternity, I floated in a dark abyss, with no sense of up or down but at one with all things. Atum's hand on my arm was all that anchored me to my sense of self.

All of a sudden, my feet were planted on the ground again, and all the air whooshed from my lungs. My knees wobbled and my stomach lurched as a wave of dizzying vertigo crashed over me. I had only a moment to take in Atum's tensed features and the endless desert landscape surrounding us before the world fell away once more.

Between the second and third jumps, I realized Atum could teleport. That realization and the conscious effort to keep my knees locked so I didn't collapse were the only two thoughts going through my head.

Over and over we teleported north toward the dissonance in Men-nefer. Each time we stopped, Atum appeared wearier.

After the seventh jump, Atum's hand fell away from my arm. Without his support, I collapsed to my hands and knees, dropping the baskets on the ground. I squeezed my eyes shut and rested the side of my cheek against the cool earth, sucking in lungfuls of air. A warm breeze rustled my hair, tickling my temples and neck.

Slowly, the world stopped spinning, and eventually, I was able to open my eyes and raise my head. I was surprised to discover that I was alone. Well, unless you counted the enormous man-headed limestone cat guarding my back.

Sheltered between the Great Sphinx's massive forepaws, I tilted my head back, arching my neck to peer up at the monument. The Sphinx's face was pristine, so different from the age-worn, noseless visage it bore in the future. Haloing the headdress, the stars winked faintly in the darkening sky above.

There was a tall rectangular opening cut out of the monument's feline chest that definitely wasn't supposed to be there. Was the Great Sphinx another of Atum's secret hideouts?

Frowning to myself, I approached the opening and cautiously poked my head into the body of the Sphinx. The walls of the space hollowed out inside the Sphinx weren't glowing, but enough dim light poured in from outside for me to look around. The hollow within the Sphinx was long and narrow but otherwise much the same as the cavern in the cliffs west of Waset, with a sunken faux firepit in the center, a low table situated nearby, and bulging baskets stashed against the back wall.

Atum stood near the longer wall on the left side of the space, arms crossed over his chest. The enormous baskets he had carried were abandoned nearby as, once again, he monitored the troublesome dissonance on a new time tapestry patch. He didn't even glance my way as I dragged my baskets into the hollow.

I settled my burdens by the firepit and innocuously studied Atum's back. He cut as large and imposing of a figure as ever, but the slight hunch to his shoulders and barely perceptible sway to his stance suggested an unexpected vulnerability.

Teleporting all this way had sapped nearly all of his strength. It was both a shock and a relief to discover he had limitations. That he was not, in fact, all-powerful.

I unloaded my baskets, starting with the bedding. Once the blankets were unpacked, I discovered the cause of the one basket's heavy weight—waterskins. I set them on the table, then dove into my second basket. This one was filled with food.

I laid out a bountiful spread on the table, then approached Atum. He had taken care of me when I had needed it. Now, it was time for me to return the favor.

"Atum," I said, my voice hushed so as not to startle him. I placed my hand on his upper arm and repeated his name, giving his biceps a gentle squeeze.

Atum blinked, like he had only just realized I was standing beside him, and gazed down at me. His bold, angular features appeared weary. He was clearly exhausted, and I hated asking him to do more than he already had, but I had no choice. I had a feeling he was going to crash hard after he ate, and he needed to seal us into the hollow before that happened because I sure as hell couldn't do it.

"You need to seal the entrance," I said, sending a pointed look at the open doorway exposing our hideout to the world. "The food and bedrolls are ready," I added.

Atum glanced at the low table, then at the bedrolls arranged around the dormant firepit, then at the doorway. He took one step toward the opening, but it was unsteady enough to make me unsure of his ability to make it all the way there on his own. I scurried to his side to lend him support, tucking in close and pulling his arm over my shoulders with a firm grip on his wrist.

He leaned heavily on me while he raised his hand and formed the *At* barrier sealing us in, plunging us into darkness. Only the dim glow from the time tapestry patch lit the space, casting eerie, shifting shadows.

I guided Atum to the low table by the firepit and eased him down to sit on a cushion. He gazed up at me, crouched before him, and raised one hand to cup the side of my face. "Thank you, Tarset," he murmured, his eyes bottomless pools of darkness in the faint, shifting light.

Unable to resist, I leaned my head into his touch, and tension thickened the air around us. I swallowed roughly, nodding a silent *you're welcome.*

Atum's hand slipped off my face, and he reached out to press his fingertips against one of the faux logs in the fire pit. It took ages, but finally, they started to glow, emitting a gentle warmth and easing the haunting effect of the shadows cast by the time tapestry patch.

I sat on the opposite side of the table, curling my feet underneath me, and dug into the meal. For long minutes, we ate in silence, but finally, my curiosity got the better of me. "The woman causing the dissonance—did she do something bad?"

Atum chewed his current bite of flatbread a few more times, then swallowed. "There is no such thing as good and bad in my world," he said, his gaze steady as his eyes met mine. "There is only what *must be* and what *never can be*. The woman whose lifethread disturbs the pattern now walks a path that only leads to the latter. If left uncorrected, the dissonance she is causing could irreparably damage the timeline."

"Does that mean you have to kill her?" I asked despite already suspecting the answer.

I knew killing was a tool Atum used to protect the timeline—and to keep my family safe, however inadvertently—but hearing that he was preparing to take a life, especially the life of a young mother with a baby, made the horrors of his existence all too real.

Atum held my stare for a moment longer, then averted his gaze down to the table. "If I must."

I swallowed an apology, knowing firsthand how much he wouldn't appreciate it. More like salt in the wound.

So, I suppressed my curiosity and held my tongue throughout the remainder of the meal. Only when Atum was sound asleep on his bedroll did I approach the time tapestry patch displayed on the wall.

The woman at the heart of the dissonance lay on her side, her hand gripping the edge of the bassinet holding her baby, as though even in sleep she protected the child. If only she knew she was the one who needed protecting.

L OCKED AWAY WITHIN THE Sphinx, I stood in front of the time tapestry patch and watched for Atum within the scenes running along the length of the condemned lifethread.

In the scene that represented the present moment, the woman at the heart of the dissonance huddled on the ground in the shade of a tree while she fed her baby with the ancient approximation of a bottle, like a miniature waterskin with a leather mouthpiece in place of a nipple. It struck me as odd that she wasn't nursing the baby herself—the child couldn't have been more than a few months old—but I was no expert in breastfeeding or ancient Egyptian infant care.

Like watching a car crash, I couldn't look away. Atum hadn't flat-out admitted he was going to kill this woman, but my gut told me that was the case. I had to know for sure.

Suddenly, the view on the patch shifted, zooming out to display the complicated weave of all the lifethreads in Men-nefer, a pattern of iridescent threads shot through by streaks of gold. A new dissonance formed right before my eyes, bright red and pulsing like a beacon. It was located further to the right from the shimmering vertical line denoting the present moment, suggesting it would happen sometime soon.

Already fearing Atum would be forced to carry out yet another correction, I raised my hand and touched a fingertip to the new dissonance. The view shifted again, zooming in on the tangle of life threads forming the disturbance.

A flaming villa filled the visible area of the time tapestry patch. A burning figure stumbled out through the villa's front doorway—toward me—and collapsed to its knees, then fell forward onto a face that was barely recognizable as human.

I gasped, covering my mouth with one hand while I hastily navigated back to the current dissonance with the other. Adrenaline surged in my blood, and my fingers shook as I zoomed in on the woman and child once more. I squeezed my eyes shut, but the image of that burning visage was seared into the backs of my eyelids. Unable to find the escape I sought, I opened my eyes and focused on the scene displayed on the patch now instead.

Atum stalked into view, a towering, dark-cloaked figure who I thought must have birthed the myths about the grim reaper. My hand remained over my mouth as I watched with eyes opened wide.

He loomed over the cowering woman, the infant clutched to her chest. Tears welled in my eyes as vines of At snaked around the woman's arms, legs, and neck, restraining her. Strangling her. The infant wailed, the sound thankfully muted to my ears, a flailing bundle of limbs and blankets on the woman's lap.

As the first vine crept toward the baby, I squeezed my eyes shut and turned my back to the horrifying scene. I hadn't considered the possibility that the woman wasn't the sole root of the dissonance. That it just might stem from the baby, too.

By the time I had worked up the nerve to look once more, the woman, the baby, and Atum were gone. Only the tree remained.

My stomach twisted into a tangled knot of disgust. I zoomed out on the time tapestry patch, searching all of Men-nefer for their lifethreads. But they were gone. Snipped. Dead.

What had I agreed to? I couldn't do this. I couldn't help Atum. I wasn't like him. I couldn't live with myself after doing what he had just done, and it repulsed me to think that he could. No wonder he was so twisted up inside. He had told me he didn't deserve my pity, and he was right. Sure, I had heard the rumors. But I hadn't been willing to accept the truth of his existence until I saw it with my own eyes.

Only a monster could do such things and live with themselves after.

Trapped within the hollow in the Sphinx's body, I paced around the fire pit, hugging my middle with one arm while I chewed on my thumbnail. My anxiety ramped up higher and higher with each lap.

I couldn't—wouldn't—let Atum turn me into a stone-cold killer like him. I would rather die than suffer that fate.

At the first tingle of otherworldly energy, I stopped pacing and turned to face the entrance to the hollow. The At barrier melted away, revealing Atum silhouetted by bright midday sunlight as he stood in the valley between the Sphinx's forelegs.

I gritted my teeth, my lip curling, and hugged my middle like I was trying to hold myself together. "How *could* you?" I asked—demanded—shaking my head in disgust. "The *baby*? There must have been some other way."

Atum stood immobile, like my contempt had frozen him in place. Finally, he stepped through the doorway and into the hollow.

I backed up as though his very presence repulsed me.

Atum turned his side to me, reforming the *At* barrier over the doorway. It no longer felt like something shielding me from the outside world. It felt like a trap. This was just another prison.

"Have you changed your mind then?" Atum asked, angling his face toward me, a very real, very palpable threat in his voice.

If I changed my mind about working with him, then there was only one other option for me. Death. He *would* kill me. The only remaining question was—how? Would he strangle me as he had the mother and child? Or would he slice me down with an *At* blade?

I blinked, setting a string of tears free, and choked on a semi-hysterical laugh at the thought of being stabbed through the heart by *At* for a second time.

What if there was another option—one Atum didn't know about? I could leave. Just walk away. Disappear.

Atum had admitted that my lifethread didn't appear on the time tapestry. Once I was out of his sight, he could only track me by the way I warped the lifethreads around me. But if I stayed away from everyone, if there were no other lifethreads around me, he would have no way to track me. I could lie low and bide my time until Aramei came into her power at the Hathor temple, and then I could hitch a ride back to my family in the future and out of Atum's murderous grasp.

"No," I said as I unfolded my arms from around my middle. I straightened my spine, pushing my shoulders back and down. I inhaled, filling my lungs, then slowly released the breath through my nose. "No, I haven't changed my mind," I lied.

Atum studied me for a long moment, then nodded. "We will speak about this correction later. First, I must ensure it has worked." He strode over to the time tapestry patch and took up a wide-legged stance in front of it, crossing his arms over his chest. "You should get some rest," he tossed over his shoulder without looking at me. "We'll leave for Rostau in the morning."

That was my window. My ticking clock. I had until morning to plot my escape, and then I would slip away.

"All right," I said and retreated to my bedroll. I laid down, curling up on my side, my back to Atum, and closed my eyes, pretending to sleep while I planned my escape.

No matter how I looked at it, I could only see one way out of this mess. I had to leave while Atum was engaged in his morning ritual. He entered an almost trancelike state while he reopened his scars, and he never sealed me in when he did it. If I was quick and quiet, I thought it shouldn't be too difficult to sneak away while he was distracted. By the time he finished and noticed I was gone, I would be too far away for him to track.

Muffled footsteps alerted me to Atum's approach as he made his way around the firepit. I kept my breaths slow and even in mimicry of sleep, but there was nothing I could do about my racing heartbeat. I only hoped he attributed it to a troubling dream. I heard a rustle of fabric in front of me and pictured him kneeling before me.

"Tarset?" Atum whispered. "Are you awake?"

I feigned sleep for all I was worth, and after a brief eternity, he left me alone. I lay like that throughout the night, waiting for the sun to rise. Waiting for my opening. I would only get one shot at escape.

The night seemed to stretch on forever, but eventually, Atum rose from his bedroll and gathered our things together in preparation for our departure after his morning ritual. There were the telltale *clinks* and *rustles* of food items being laid out on the table, followed by Atum's steady footsteps as he strode toward the blocked doorway. Finally, with a tingle of otherworldly energy, he removed the barrier blocking the only exit.

I waited a few more minutes, until I was sure he would have begun his ritual outside the hollow, then sat up as quietly as possible and glanced over my shoulder at the doorway.

"*Shit!*" I mouthed when I realized the glaring error in my plan.

Atum knelt on the ground between the Sphinx's forepaws, just a few steps beyond the doorway. The Sphinx faced due east, which meant that even from where I sat, I could see the sun peeking over the eastern horizon. Atum hadn't needed to take more than a few steps out of the hollow to be showered in light from the rising sun.

I studied the narrow alley between the walls of limestone forming the Sphinx's forelegs. There was enough room for me to squeeze past Atum on either side of him but not without him noticing me.

I momentarily considered attempting to climb over one of the forelegs, but I doubted any attempt at scrambling up and over a stone wall taller than myself would be any less noticeable than me trying to squeeze past Atum.

How the hell was I supposed to get myself out of this mess?

I stood and stalked toward the wall displaying the time tapestry patch, stopping by the table to snatch a flatbread from the short stack on my way.

The patch was zoomed out to display the pattern of all the interwoven lifethreads in Men-nefer.

The dissonance that had appeared yesterday still pulsed red slightly to the right of the shimmering vertical line marking the present moment. It looked like the events that would initially disrupt the weave would happen sometime tomorrow.

I wondered if Atum's brutal correction had caused this new dissonance. That would serve him right. My lip curled into what was undoubtedly an ugly sneer, but it felt good and nobody was around to see it, so I didn't care.

I glanced over my shoulder at Atum to make sure he was fully immersed in his ritual, then returned my attention to the time tapestry patch. I tore off a bite of flatbread with my teeth and reached out with my other hand to touch the illuminated display on the wall. Closing my eyes, I thought of my mom.

If, by some miracle, I managed to sneak away from Atum, I doubted I would ever see my mom again. I may not have agreed with the methods Atum employed to protect the timeline, but I recognized the danger I would put my future family in if I walked my chaos-causing self into my mom's home. Not an option. Besides, Atum was sure to look for me there.

I opened my eyes and was pleased to find my mom now displayed on the patch. She carried a basket through an orchard, the half-risen sun lighting her from the side. A pair of giggling children skipped along behind her. Were they her grandchildren? My own niece and nephew?

Smiling to myself, I pinched my fingers together, zooming out to the film-reel view to monitor my mom's immediate future. Her life thread gained a disconcerting pinkish hue around sunset today. By full dark, her thread was bright red and pulsing, an unmistakable dissonance.

"No," I breathed, shaking my head in denial.

So far as I could tell, the dissonance originated with my mom, then fanned out from there, looking like a wildfire consuming the time tapestry. The impact on the pattern was utterly devastating—so much worse than the dissonance Atum had corrected yesterday.

I zoomed in on my mom's lifethread, focusing on the point where it shifted from rosy pink to burning crimson.

The fire. It was *her* home. On the patch, I watched her being dragged out by her hair, kicking and screaming. Inyotef stood off to the side, his expression smug.

I stumbled backward, clutching my middle, too stunned to fully comprehend what I was seeing.

If Inyotef was at my mom's home, then Atum had lied to me. He hadn't erased Inyotef's memory of any knowledge of my parentage. Of my mom.

Atum wasn't just a cold-hearted killer, he was a bald-faced liar. Panic coiled around my chest, squeezing until I couldn't breathe.

In desperate need of fresh air, I bolted for the doorway, pushing past Atum and running for the open space beyond the Sphinx's paws. My toe caught on the edge of a dip in the paved platform surrounding the Sphinx, and I tripped, stumbling forward and landing on my hands and knees.

I stared down in mute shock at my hands. They glowed with a hazy golden light, the radiance pulsing brighter with each beat of my heart.

"Tarset!" Atum yelled my name, and the sound of his traitorous voice set my nerves on edge.

"You lied to me!" I shrieked, spinning on my knees to face him.

He was on his feet but hung back between the Sphinx's forepaws.

"You lied about Inyotef!" I shouted, hurling accusations at him like spears. "You never erased his memory of my mom!"

"Tarset, no," Atum said, taking a step toward me and raising one hand. I knew that gesture. *At* vines would rise out of the ground soon enough. He was trying to restrain me. To capture me. To trap me. "You need to calm down."

Calm down? *I* needed to calm down?

His words were lighter fluid on the flames of my anger.

I reared back on my knees and arched my spine, screaming as the rage overwhelmed me. Golden light exploded out of me, tearing paving stones out of the ground and sending them flying outward.

For a single heartbeat, I was a supernova of fury, and time slowed, almost seeming to stand still. Chunks of limestone paving stones hovered in the glowing ring surrounding me.

On my next heartbeat, the explosive golden light sucked back into me with an audible *whoosh*. All around me, chunks of rock and bits of debris shot outward.

I scrambled to my feet and spun around, watching the chunks of stone rain down from above. I stood in the middle of a crater at least ten feet across.

Atum held steady in his position between the Sphinx's forepaws, a curved wall of iridescent *At* shielding himself and the Sphinx from whatever the hell I had just done.

Wide-eyed, I stared at him, momentarily more terrified of myself than I was of him. What *was* that?

I balled my hands into fists and shook my head. It didn't matter. Inyotef was going after my mom, and I couldn't trust Atum to help me save her. I couldn't trust a damn thing that came out of his lying mouth.

For all I knew, everything he had ever told me was a lie.

My skin still glowed golden as I stumbled to a walk, and then to a run, heading for the low wall bordering the Sphinx complex and the barley field beyond. I tore the necklace bearing Atum's pendant off over my head and threw it on the ground, fearing he could use it to track me. Every few steps, I sent frantic glances over my shoulders.

But Atum didn't follow. He must have been afraid of setting me off again. I wasn't just a walking chaos bomb. I was an *actual* bomb.

I could see docks and boats lining the riverbank beyond the field ahead. If nobody wanted to ferry me across the Nile, I resolved to steal a boat and make the crossing myself. I *would* reach my mom before Inyotef. That bastard had already taken too much from me. I wasn't letting him take anything else.

Not today.

Not ever.

44

I HAD STOPPED GLOWING by the time I reached the harbor, which was about the only thing that went right.

It took me all day to figure out where my mom lived. I avoided asking around Men-nefer proper, not willing to risk running into my dad or detonating in the middle of the city. Even in my frantic state, I was coherent enough to be aware of just how detrimental either occurrence would be to the timeline.

Dark had fallen by the time I turned off the main road and jogged up the path to my family's estate. It was about a mile outside of town, surrounded by sprawling fields and a zigzagging network of canals.

I thought it was a trick of the eye at first. The fire wasn't supposed to happen until tomorrow. But the hint of light ahead quickly grew to the all-too-recognizable eerie orange glow of fire, and my heart sank into my stomach.

The villa was already burning. I was too late.

I picked up the pace until I was flat-out sprinting.

Three people stood out in front of the burning villa, dazed and clinging together, watching the inferno that had once been my family's home. None appeared to be Inyotef or any of his men.

I headed straight for the small group and skidded to a stop in front of them. I stood before them, examining each of their faces, but none bore my mom's visage or even remotely resembled the siblings I had left behind two decades ago. These people were strangers, likely servants or field hands.

I turned away from the terrified trio and jogged closer to the burning villa, only stopping when the fire grew too hot. There were more trees in this part of Egypt, near the Delta, which meant more wood was used in construction in place of fire-resistant mudbrick. Even so, the blaze seemed excessive, as though an accelerant had been used to get it going fast.

Skin stinging from the heat resonating off the fire, I stumbled back a few steps, raising a hand to shield my face. Nobody could have survived that blaze. If anyone was still in there, they were long gone.

I turned away from the burning villa and hurried back to the huddled trio of onlookers.

"What happened?" I asked, searching each of their distraught faces for whichever of them was the most coherent.

Of the three—a middle-aged man and woman, and a teen girl—it was the girl who seemed the least panicked. Tears cut trails down her ash-stained cheeks, but her eyes were clearer and more alert than those of the older pair.

I sidestepped to stand in front of her and grabbed the girl's upper arm, bending my knees to bring my eyes in line with hers.

"What happened?" I repeated.

The girl blinked, and her eyes slowly focused on me as though only just realizing I was there. She sucked in a stuttering breath, and then the words tumbled out of her in a jumble. "There—there was a—a man. He walked in when the whole family was inside. I—I was tending the goats." She glanced over her shoulder to a lean-to inside a pen, where a handful of goats trotted around and bleated in panic. "And then the fire started. It happened so fast," she said, wringing her hands. "The fire—it started so quickly. There was nothing we could do."

"Did they get out?" I asked, gripping the girl's arm tighter. "Did anyone get out?"

"I don't—I don't know." Her shoulders bobbed with suppressed sobs as she shook her head. "I—I don't think so."

"This man who entered the villa," I said in a rush. "What did he look like? Were there others with him?"

The girl shook her head, her focus shifting past me. "I—I don't know. I think he was alone."

Inyotef hadn't been alone in the scene I had witnessed on the time tapestry, but then, according to what I had seen, the attack shouldn't have happened until tomorrow. Was this Atum's accursed *free will* at work, altering what the pattern had predicted?

"He was tall," the girl volunteered. "Th-the man who did this. He was really big, and he wore a long, black robe."

I released her arm as ice replaced the blood in my veins, and a chill cascaded down my spine.

"The robe—it was open at the front," she added, touching a hand to one of her shoulders and drawing it across her chest. "He had all these scars."

Her words were a physical blow, and I staggered backward, clutching my middle. All other sensory input faded away as the world tunneled down to the girl's description of the lone man who had destroyed my family. All I could see or hear was Atum.

Atum had done this, not Inyotef.

"Y-y-you're glowing," the girl said, her words piercing the ice forming a shell around my awareness.

I glanced down at my hands, and my eyes opened wider when I saw my skin was emitting a faint golden light. The last time this happened—the only time this happened—the glow preceded an explosion.

I stumbled away from the trio and fled down the path leading away from the burning villa, running as fast as I could. The glow dimmed, then faded as the numb of shock set in.

But even then, I didn't stop. The need for home drove me onward, and I ran.

MY EMOTIONS WERE A tsunami, pushing me onward. My feet moved, one step in front of the other, with no conscious awareness of where I was heading. It was like moving through a dream. I was running. I was on a boat. I was running again.

The sky was just beginning to lighten in the early morning when I finally stopped, the emotional numbness of shock setting in.

I blinked, awareness dawning as I realized where I was. My mom's tomb. The closest thing to home that existed in this ancient era.

The tomb stood before me, a small pyramid encased in gleaming, polished limestone, the entrance wide open for the workers who were still finishing the designs carved into the walls of the antechamber and burial chamber within. Designs I had memorized long ago, far in the future, when my mom's mummified body had been entombed within.

There would be no mummy in there now. I wasn't sure there would even be a body to seal into the sarcophagus. What kind of remains would that inferno leave behind?

In the back of my mind, I wondered if the tomb had actually been empty all along. All those times I had visited my mom's grave, so far in the future, had I been talking to an empty sarcophagus?

But that didn't make sense. My dad would have known her body wasn't really in there. Unless he had lied to protect me.

I hugged my middle. I felt hollow. Empty. Exhausted.

I trudged toward the pyramid's beckoning entrance. My eyelids drifted shut as I passed through the doorway and into the darkness, and I wrapped myself in the intangible embrace of this place. Of my mom's legacy. For a brief eternity, I stood there in the tomb's entrance, neither here nor there. Neither now nor then. I hovered in that liminal place and time—in that *between*—where there was no such thing as life and death. Where there was only existence.

Where my mom wasn't dead.

Eventually, I peeled my eyelids open and peered around the small pyramid's shadowy antechamber. Tears streamed down my cheeks as I walked around the familiar space, skirting the baskets of tools piled in the corners, the fingertips of one hand tracing over the images and hieroglyphs etched into the walls. It was my mom's life, her memorial, carved in stone.

I wandered deeper into the tomb, through the doorway to the burial chamber. The granite sarcophagus stood empty in the center of the smaller room, a shadowy outline in the darkness. I retreated to the back corner and sank down to the floor, huddling in the joint between the two walls. How many times had I sat here, in this very spot, confessing my fears, my sins, my deepest desires? This was the only place I had ever felt comfortable baring my soul—alone in a tomb that may very well have been empty, even of the dead.

I reached for the wall on my right, my fingertips searching for the carved words I had traced hundreds of times. But the familiar grooves in the stone wall weren't there. That made sense. They hadn't been original to the tomb's interior design. They were in English and carved by an unskilled hand, likely gouged into the stone by some sneaky tourist.

Even so, the words had made an impression on me when I was younger, even forming the backbone of one of my songs.

Out of time, and without a place,
I linger here, no heart, no face.
My ribs are cracked, my soul laid bare.
I search for you, but you're not there.
You're never there.
Were you ever there?

I should have listened.
I shouldn't have run.
My ignorance killed you.
I'm the smoking gun.

I sat up a little straighter, spinning thoughts pushing back some of the numb fog.

The words had always felt personal, like they were a message written specifically for me, the daughter mourning her long-dead mother. But now, the words were too perfect. Their connection to my current situation was impossible not to make. What if the message *had* been written specifically for me—*by* me?

I recalled navigating around the baskets of tools in the antechamber. All those chisels and hammers ripe for the taking.

In a daze, I climbed to my feet, using the wall to pull myself up, and trudged back to the antechamber. I crouched by one of the tool baskets and plucked out a pointy copper chisel, then returned to my favorite corner of the burial chamber. I eased down to my knees, raised the chisel to the wall, and carved those remembered words with manic intensity.

Only when I sat back on my heels to admire the finished product in the filtered moonlight did I begin to understand the ramification of what I had just done. I hadn't simply carved the same words into roughly the same place on the wall. I had carved the same words in the *exact* same way as they had appeared—would appear—in four millennia.

Here was irrefutable proof. *I* carved the message on my mom's tomb wall. It had always been me. A message that had been there *before* the killing blow that had sent me tumbling backward in time. *Before* Inyotef captured me and learned about my mom. *Before* I struck my bargain with Atum, and *before* I fled from him.

What did that mean?

Was this all supposed to happen? Had it *already* happened? Even though my lifethread didn't appear on the pattern of the time tapestry, was my presence in the past an essential part of the timeline that had led to the future that I had left behind? Was this all part of some sort of fixed time loop?

Brow furrowing, I shook my head. I didn't have the mental bandwidth to comprehend this right now. There was only enough space in my head for one thing: I needed to know why.

Why had Atum killed my mom?

I stood and walked a slow circle around the sarcophagus, using the motion to reel in and focus my spiraling thoughts. When I reached my starting point, I continued onward, making another loop, then another.

Was Atum punishing me? Did he kill my mom—her whole family—because I ran away? Because I broke our bargain?

I shook my head, dismissing the questions as soon as they entered my mind, and raised my hand to my mouth to chew on my thumbnail. Retaliation wasn't Atum's way. He didn't kill for such petty reasons, not like Inyotef would have done. Atum valued life. His scars were proof of that. I had never even seen the man eat a bite of meat.

Besides, Atum's actions were guided by his rigid moral compass. He only killed to protect the timeline. He would do anything to preserve his precious pattern on the time tapestry. Like killing a mother and her baby. With him, everything was about the greater good. There was no room in his heart for personal vendettas.

Which meant, it had to be about the time tapestry. The pattern. The timeline.

A horrific sense of dread sprouted in my gut.

The dissonance surrounding my mom's life thread on the time tapestry hadn't formed until I touched the patch when Atum was out on the correction. It was as though me witnessing Inyotef's impending attack on my mom's villa caused the initial disturbance, not Inyotef's attack itself.

Except, my mom wasn't supposed to die in a fire. She was supposed to have drowned during an unfortunate boating accident alongside my brother, while the rest of my siblings and their own children were to have survived. That was the story my dad had always told me.

I frowned, considering that story. I had never thought to ask where the boat was taking them or whose boat it had been. I hadn't wanted to know the details of how they died.

If my presence had always been part of the timeline—as suggested by the carved-in-stone evidence in the back corner of this very burial chamber—was my mom *supposed to die* on Inyotef's boat? Had it always been her fate to be captured by Inyotef in retribution for my disobedience?

But then I interfered, striking the first discordant note that started the dissonance. Or, at least, I had tried to interfere. I had wanted to save my mom. To stop Inyotef. To change her fate.

But if I had succeeded, I would have changed the timeline itself. Possibly irrevocably so. The dissonance I viewed on the time tapestry was catastrophic. Had Atum only been stepping in to fix my mess? Was this—the murder of my family—merely another correction?

Had *I* forced Atum's hand?

Was this all my fault?

I paced around and around my mom's empty sarcophagus, and with each circuit, it became harder to ignore the glaring truth.

Atum killed my mom—my entire ancient family—because of me. Not because he was hurt or angry, and not because he wanted to punish me. He killed them because of what I had been intending to do. Because *I* had endangered the pattern. *I* had threatened the timeline.

My family was supposed to be captured by Inyotef, and his boat was supposed to wreck, and my mom and brother were supposed to die. But I would have prevented all of that from happening.

To protect the timeline, Atum ensured my mom *did* die, just a few days before she had been scheduled to according to the time tapestry. And the rest of her kids and grandkids perished in that burning villa alongside her, ending their lives prematurely, all because of my attempted interference. I inadvertently robbed my siblings and their children of their remaining years. Apparently, their untimely deaths weren't as damaging to the timeline as my mom's continued existence would have been.

I hugged my middle, my fingernails gouging into my sides until I felt the warm trickle of blood running down my hips.

What had I been thinking? What if I *had* saved them, and in doing so, changed the future? What if the changes killed my dad—oh gods—or Reni? Or Lex or Nik or Kat or any of the other people absolutely essential to all the impossible, crazy shit that had gone down—would go down—to ensure the continued existence of the entire fucking universe? What if I had saved my mom, only to doom every other person who had ever existed and ever would exist—*ever*?

"You idiot," I hissed, smacking the side of my head hard enough to make my ears ring. "You stupid idiot!"

I *hadn't* been thinking. I saw something I didn't like and reacted rashly. I was a loose cannon, a fucking vortex of chaos, just like Atum had said. I was too dangerous. My very existence was a threat to the future I was trying to protect.

It was impossible not to see that the universe would be better off without me around to screw things up worse than I already had. I vowed to walk into the Nile and to never walk out. To end the continued threat of my existence.

Cutting my last lap around the sarcophagus short, I headed for the tomb's exit. I stood in the doorway, staring out at the shadowed shapes silhouetted by the starry night sky. The trio of enormous pyramids Giza was famous for stood tall and proud along the horizon. Countless other, smaller pyramids sprouted up from the desert all around them.

And there, half-hidden by the gentle slope of a dune, the Great Sphinx held its head high, a stoic guardian of the night, just as the man sheltered in the hollow carved out of its body guarded the timeline. Atum was in there, searching the time tapestry for any sign of me. I knew it absolutely.

I needed to see him—to confirm this horrible suspicion. I needed to know for sure that *I* was the reason my mom was dead. The reason he had been forced to kill her.

I needed to know if the person I should exact my revenge on *was me*.

PRESENT DAY

46

"**I** CAN'T BELIEVE I didn't make the connection sooner," Heru said as he led me by one hand through the necropolis toward Sesha's tomb. The trio of Giza's iconic pyramids stood tall against the blue sky, untouched by the Netjers' assault on our world.

"I thought it was just graffiti," Heru went on. "I considered having it removed, but anytime I mentioned it to Tarsi, she told me to leave it, like her subconscious knew the words had always been hers."

I squeezed his hand. "You couldn't have known."

Apparently, this necropolis of small mastabas and pyramids was mainly populated by the remains of humans with Nejeret affiliation. Heru touched the exteriors of many of the tombs like he was offering a silent greeting to the deceased interred within. I wondered how many of these tombs belonged to former wives of his. How many held the remains of his children?

It was easy to settle into the idea of living forever without thinking about the potential downsides, but then someplace like this would slap that reality in my face. Humans died. They burned bright for a handful of decades, a century if they were lucky, and then they were gone, their bodies decaying and their souls reintegrating into the great river of soul-energy in Duat. Whenever around a place like this necropolis, I could easily understand why so many Nejerets avoided humans like the plague. Because they *were* a plague—on our immortal hearts.

"Here we are," Heru said, stopping in front of a pyramid about the height of a modern two-story house.

The gleaming white limestone casing on the pyramid's exterior was far better preserved than any of the larger, more well-known pyramids in the Cairo area. But then, this entire necropolis was like that. It was a well-kept secret carefully maintained by Nejerets over the millennia, turning it into something of a time capsule. None of these tombs had been violated during the difficult times in Egypt's history. None of their polished casings had been stripped and tossed into limekilns. They were perfectly preserved and truly marvelous.

The entrance to Sesha's pyramid was blocked by a heavy-duty wrought-iron gate rather than sealed with a stone slab, and a keyless smart lock hung on the gate in place of a traditional padlock.

Heru released my hand and pulled his phone out of his trouser pocket. Several taps of his thumbs later, the smart lock popped open. While Heru stowed his phone, I removed the lock from the gate and stashed it in my messenger bag. Heru pulled the gate open, then held out one arm, gesturing for me to enter Sesha's tomb ahead of him.

I created a ball of iridescent *At* in the palm of my hand and willed it to glow, then offered the illuminated orb to Heru. After he took it, I made one for myself.

Glowing *At* orb held out on my upraised palm in front of me, I held my breath and gingerly stepped across the threshold. A shiver cascaded over me from head to toe.

I was an archaeologist by trade. Entering the abodes of the deceased was no big deal. But walking into the tomb of a woman I had known fairly well during my brief but memorable trip to the ancient past was another thing entirely.

The walls in the antechamber of Sesha's tomb were covered with a collage of images from her life. She was displayed dozens of times in the carved reliefs alongside Heru and their children, tending the land, sailing the river, dancing, cooking, celebrating, and eating. I smiled to myself, remembering the kind woman who had welcomed me into her home, knowing full well who and what I was to her husband. But those were different times, and Sesha had been an exceptional woman.

"It's back here," Heru said, crossing the antechamber, heading for the doorway to the burial chamber in the back half of the pyramid.

I turned away from the depictions of Sesha's life to find Heru standing in front of her red granite sarcophagus, his hands pressed against the carved surface and his head bowed, mourning her death. A twinge of jealousy stabbed through my heart. He had loved Sesha very much. Clearly, part of him still did.

But then, Heru had loved many women over the millennia. None of them shared the Nejeret soul bond with him as I did, I reminded myself. They had held his heart for a little while. Now, it was mine for the rest of time.

"I remember the moment I received word of her death so clearly," Heru murmured.

I joined him, curving one arm around his waist and resting my cheek against his shoulder. "How did she die?"

"A fire," he said, his voice thicker than before. He cleared his throat. "It claimed our whole family, save for Aksel and Shila, who were with me for training at the time." I recognized the names as two of the children I had met while staying in Sesha's home and assumed they must have manifested Nejeret traits when they were grown.

Tears pricked in my eyes, my heart breaking for Heru's loss. I knew the thousands of years he had lived had been rife with loss, but this—nearly an entire family wiped out in a fire—was devastating.

Heru cleared his throat again, more forcefully this time. He straightened, removing his hands from the sarcophagus, and turned away. "It's over here," he said, his voice huskier than usual.

Heru made his way around the sarcophagus, heading for the back, left corner of the burial chamber.

I scanned the walls as I followed, recognizing familiar scenes and spells from the coffin texts engraved into the limestone. On the left-hand wall, the spells surrounded a stunning rendering of Rostau, where Osiris's body lay waiting in the underworld surrounded by a wall of flames and serpents.

Heru crouched in the corner of the burial chamber, tracing his fingertips over the words carved inexpertly into the stone.

> *Out of time, and without a place,*
> *I linger here, no heart, no face.*
> *My ribs are cracked, my soul laid bare.*
> *I search for you, but you're not there.*
> *You're never there.*
> *Were you ever there?*

> *I should have listened.*
> *I shouldn't have run.*
> *My ignorance killed you.*
> *I'm the smoking gun.*

Tarset's despair and desperation were palpable, even across the vast chasm of time. She must have been there when her mom died. And worse, she clearly blamed herself for Sesha's death.

"*He* did this," Heru said, the words coming out in a low growl. "Atum. This is his fault."

I looked at Heru and sucked in a breath. "Heru . . ."

His skin glowed golden, subtle but slowly increasing in intensity. The air around him crackled like it was charged with static electricity.

"He dragged Tarset into the past," Heru raged. "He trapped her there. He must be the one who started the fire."

My heart was suddenly galloping, my instincts telling me to run. I licked my lips and swallowed roughly. "Heru, your skin," I said, gradually standing. "It's—it's *glowing*."

But Heru wasn't hearing me anymore. He was lost to his rage, the golden glow pulsing steadily brighter with every beat of his heart like it was building toward something.

I backed away, bumping into the sarcophagus with my hip. I glanced over my shoulder, searching for the doorway to the antechamber, and shifted my trajectory. I had just reached the doorway and was turning to bolt when Heru threw his head back and roared.

Before I could even think about creating a shield of *At*, a concussive wave of golden light exploded out of Heru, lifting me off my feet and flinging me backward into the antechamber. I slammed against an unyielding stone wall, and all the air whooshed out of my lungs as searing agony erupted from my ribcage and spine. My vision momentarily whited out as I slumped down onto my side on the tomb floor.

I blinked, my ears ringing, and tried to push myself up onto my elbow, but the starburst of pain in my back forced me back down to the stone floor. I sucked in shallow breaths, each one sending dozens of daggers stabbing into my lungs as small pieces of limestone showered down on me from the ceiling.

"Lex!" Heru appeared in front of me in a burst of iridescent mist. His skin was the usual golden-brown, no hint of a glow, but his eyes were alight with panic. "I'm sorry!" He leaned in, his hands reaching for me, hovering but not touching. "I don't know what happened. I didn't mean to—"

The mass of limestone overhead groaned, and we both looked up, the sound turning my bones to ice. My eyes rounded as cracks appeared in the stone ceiling. The crack running across the center of the chamber widened, the whole ceiling bulging.

Heru lunged for me, gripping my shoulders and sheltering me with his body. I cried out, the renewed burst of pain pushing me momentarily into unconsciousness.

Groaning when awareness returned, I dragged my eyelids open. I was lying on my back on the sand-swept stone path outside of the tomb. Heru knelt over me, his eyes wild.

Based on his distraught expression, I assumed I looked pretty bad. I felt awful, like all of my ribs had been snapped in half and were stabbing through my lungs, and I couldn't feel my feet. Or my legs.

I squeezed my eyes shut, fighting back the surging panic at the thought of being paralyzed. I was Nejeret. So long as I wasn't dead, my body could heal from nearly any injury, even a broken back.

Heru brushed his knuckles down my cheek, and my eyelids fluttered open. He gazed down at me through a brave mask, but there was no way for him to hide the fear shining in his burnished gold eyes.

"We have to make another jump," he told me, his voice rough, like he was holding back tears. "This is going to hurt, Little Ivanov. But I will get you home, and you *will* heal."

My chin trembled involuntarily as I anticipated the pain. I gritted my teeth. "Do it," I said, not wanting to prolong the moment.

Heru bent his body over mine, leaning in to kiss me softly, tenderly. While his lips were still pressed against mine, the world fell away.

KAT

"**A** BRAND NEW ISLAND just *ppears* in the middle of the Mediterranean Sea?" Nik said, his back to me as he scrambled eggs at the stove, sweatpants slung low on his hips and not a stitch marring the upper half of his glorious body.

From my countertop perch, I tilted my head to the side, admiring the play of muscles shifting under all that inked skin on his shoulders and back. Sausage links sizzled in another pan and hash browns warmed in the oven, the small feast giving off an aroma that made my mouth water, but I wasn't sure which I wanted to eat first—breakfast, or him.

"I think it's at least worth checking out," Nik added.

"Mmhmm," I mumbled as I raised my mug to sip my coffee.

Nik peeked over his shoulder at me, a playful smirk twisting that sinful mouth. "You didn't hear a thing I said, did you?" He lifted the egg pan off the burner and set it on a hot pad waiting beside the stove on the counter.

I took another sip of coffee. "How am I supposed to concentrate on something like *listening*, when you're dressed like such a floozy?"

Nik coughed a laugh and turned away from the stove, first glancing down at himself, then looking at me, his eyebrows raised and pale eyes dancing. "You have issues, Kitty Kat."

"I have one issue," I corrected. "You, standing over there." I parted my knees, the hem of the shirt I had borrowed from his dresser hiking up to my hips to reveal the absolutely nothing I was wearing on the bottom. "When you should be right here."

Nik narrowed his eyes. "The food'll get cold."

I pouted my lower lip and reached out for him with one arm. "Then you better hurry up," I said as I set down my coffee mug and scooted closer to the edge of the counter. "I'd hate for all your hard work to go to waste."

Nik emitted a low, growly noise that made my belly do a delicious flip-flop.

The tiny hairs all over my body stood on end and not because I was suddenly insanely aroused. I snapped my legs shut and sat up straighter.

Nik must have felt the otherworldly tingle too because his eyes darted around the kitchen and living room.

"Someone's coming," I said, staring into the living room where the influx of otherworldly energy was concentrating.

"No shit," Nik murmured.

A billowing iridescent cloud exploded into existence out of nowhere, shot through by swirling streaks of every imaginable color. The vibrant mist dissipated to reveal Heru. He was filthy, every inch of him smudged or caked with dirt. But underneath the grime, his skin glowed with the unmistakable golden aura of an immortal Nejeret soul.

Heru scanned the cabin, searching for something. Me, apparently, because when his thunderous stare locked onto me, he stalked toward the kitchen.

A shimmering barrier of *At* sprang into existence in front of him, quickly expanding until Heru was completely enclosed in an impenetrable bubble of the otherworldly material. Even he wouldn't have been able to teleport out of the trap.

Heru moved to the very edge of the transparent barrier, his hands balled into fists and his chest rising and falling with each heaving breath. That golden, soul glow pulsed in time with his heartbeat.

Heru closed his eyes and took deep, even breaths. Gradually, his golden aura dimmed until it extinguished completely.

Nik approached the *At* prison he had created, and I trailed close behind him. "Uncle," Nik said in greeting.

Heru opened his eyes, his stare locking onto me. "I need your help," he ground out. "Something's wrong with me." He clenched his jaw. "I think I came back wrong."

Nik stopped near the iridescent barrier and gave Heru a once over. A moment later, the barrier melted into a shimmering mist that quickly evaporated into nothing.

I hung back a few steps, resting my hip against the edge of the kitchen island and crossing my arms over my chest. I tilted my head to the side, studying Heru. "I take it this isn't the first time your soul got all shiny?"

Heru shook his head, his shoulders drooping. "It just happened ten or fifteen minutes ago. Maybe longer. I—" He raised one hand to rub the back of his neck, smearing blood over his golden-brown skin. "I don't know. It's all a blur."

"You're bleeding," Nik told him.

"What?" Heru looked at his hand like he'd never seen the appendage before. "Oh, no. It's not mine." He cleared his throat. "Not my blood."

It was unheard of for him to be so flustered. I could only think of one thing that could rattle him to this degree. A chill crept down my spine and I straightened from the counter. "Where's Lex?"

"The oasis," Heru said, his voice breaking. "I—we were following up on a lead, and I—I don't know what happened. I was so angry, and this—this energy just burst out of me." He jutted his jaw forward, his nostrils flaring. "The energy—it hit Lex. Threw her against a wall."

"What?" Nik exploded, rushing Heru. Nik gripped his uncle's shoulders and shook him like he could force the story out of him faster. Nik had every right to be concerned. He had devoted thousands of years of his own life to ensuring Lex returned to the present safely.

"Is she all right?" Nik urged.

"The lower half of her spine shattered on impact," Heru said, looking like he was about to be sick. He swallowed roughly, tears welling in his eyes and overflowing in a matter of seconds. He sucked in a shaky breath, then collapsed against Nik, making a noise that wrenched my heart into jagged pieces.

I covered my mouth with my hands while Nik wrapped his arms around Heru. Tears streamed down my cheeks as silent sobs racked my chest.

"Is she still alive?" Nik grated out, his voice gruff.

Heru nodded against his shoulder. "She's with Aset," he managed to say between shuddering breaths.

"Good," Nik said. "That's good. Mom'll fix her up. She'll be okay." Nik turned his neck, peering over the back of Heru's head to look at me. "Do you have any idea what could be happening?"

I lowered my hands, doing everything I could to hold my shit together. Lex was alive. She would heal. Aset would make sure of that.

But what ailed Heru had nothing to do with his physical body; something was off with his soul. No amount of Nejeret regeneration could heal something like that.

"I—" I licked my lips. "I don't know. Maybe. I need to check something," I said, hurrying toward the hallway on the other side of the living room. "Hold on."

I rushed into our bedroom and retrieved my tarot deck and a sketchbook from the nightstand then returned and sat at the dining table, curling one leg underneath me on the chair. I bounced my other foot as I hastily shuffled the deck.

"Just grab whatever to wear," Nik said as he pulled out the chair on my right and sat.

Based on the sound of Heru's retreating footsteps, he was heading down the hallway to our room to change and wash up.

Nik glanced to the side, watching Heru go, then leaned forward, resting his forearms on the table and clasping his hands together. "You have an idea, don't you?" he asked me, his voice pitched low and quiet.

I, too, turned my head to glance toward the hallway, then nodded. "I'm not positive," I whispered, pausing my shuffling to lean in toward Nik. "But I think the aura we saw when he first showed up—that golden glow—was his soul. It was almost like his body wasn't strong enough to keep it contained." Again, I glanced toward the hallway. "I think something went wrong during the resurrection."

Nik frowned, his eyes narrowing as he considered my words. "What if his soul doesn't like being contained after getting to experience being free of its physical shell? We were a *lot* more powerful in energy-being form . . . before Isfet resurrected our bodies."

I snorted a humorless laugh. "Like his soul is too big for its britches?"

"Pretty much, yeah," Nik said, nodding his head to the side.

I shrugged one shoulder and refocused on the cards, tapping the edge of the stack on the table to straighten out the deck. "Only one way to find out."

Nik raised his eyebrows in a silent question.

"I need to talk to Isfet," I said and tapped the tip of my index finger against the charged deck of tarot cards. They practically hummed with otherworldly energy. "I just need to figure out *how* to do that."

Blowing out a breath, I drew the top card from the deck, flipping it over and laying it down on the table.

The Hermit. Traditionally, it represented withdrawal, healing, and solitude. Unsurprisingly, the lone figure depicted on the card was me, standing atop a vast, snowy mountain range, clad in my standard jeans, black leather coat, and combat boots. The inked version of me held out my sword, Mercy, in front of her, more like a torch than a weapon, the crystalline At blade glowing brightly.

Five of Cups, reversed. There are only two cards in the deck where the reversed meaning offers a more positive outlook than that of the upright card, and this was one of them. Upside down, the Five of Cups hints at recovery after hitting rock bottom. It represents the strength that can only come from extreme adversity. It can also suggest that a reunion is close, that a relationship that has fizzled will be revived.

Again, a likeness of me appeared on the card. In the upside-down image, I sat at this very table, my back to the viewer, three empty whiskey glasses resting on their sides on the floor, two more upright on the table, half-filled with amber liquid. Swirling tendrils of rainbow smoke crept in from the corners of the card.

I narrowed my eyes, leaning closer to the table as I studied the card. Was that supposed to be soul-energy? Corners of my mouth tensing, I sat up straighter and flipped the next card.

The Empress represents wisdom, secret knowledge, and the spiritual realm. I didn't appear on this card. Rather, the lone figure standing in an ethereal white gown in front of a backdrop of swirling, multicolored soul-energy was pretty, waiflike Isfet, the personification of the soul of this universe. I knew her well. I had merged souls with her to defeat the Netjers, but I hadn't seen her since she helped me restore the physical bodies of all Nejerets after my people's mass execution at the hands of the Netjers.

I blew out a breath. Looked like the Five of Cups represented a reunion after all.

I touched the deck of tarot cards, but the otherworldly zing was gone. The cards had shared all they would right now. I returned my attention to studying the three-card spread, tapping the tip of my index finger on the corner of the middle card, where the swirls of soul-energy reached for the upside-down likeness of myself.

The cards confirmed it. The only way for me to reach Isfet was to enter Duat and to speak with her among the streaming soul-energy.

I had entered Duat a half-dozen times before, but all save for the first and last times had required me to pay a steep price—my life. I wasn't looking to die today, not even one of the temporary deaths I had managed before, especially not now that Aaru had been destroyed. By me. We had no clue about what happened to the immortal souls of Nejerets who died now, post-Aaru, and I wasn't about to find out.

The last time I entered Duat, I had been in full control of my powers and hopped up on otherworldly energy. Maybe my scarred soul had healed some over the last few months, but I wasn't delusional. I knew I couldn't manage an interdimensional trip in my current state.

But the *first* time I entered Duat, I had been pushed into the higher dimension by Anapa, the friendly Netjer who inspired the ancient Egyptian myths of Anubis. Anapa was the one who had first warned me this universe was in danger, and later, he had helped me defeat his people when they invaded. I hadn't seen or heard from him since shortly after the battle. I wasn't even sure if he was still in this universe, let alone on this planet, but if he was around, I sure as shit could have used his help right now.

I huffed out a breath through my nose, shoved the tarot cards away, and dragged the sketchbook closer. I pulled the pen free from the coil binding and flipped the cover open, rummaging through the middle pages until I found one that was unmarked. I set the sketchbook down, rested the head of the pen on the clean sheet of paper, and started to draw.

Anapa, I thought as my pen scratched over the page. *Where are you?*

48

KAT

HUGGING MY DOWN PARKA shut—stupid, broken zipper—I stepped through the brand new gateway and into the least inviting environment I could have imagined. Snow crunched under my boots as I set foot on the mountain peak I had drawn on the kitchen wall, and an icy wind sliced the skin around my eyes—about all that was exposed of my face between the wool beanie and the scarf I had wound around my neck and face.

A field of glaciers and snow-capped mountains spread out toward the horizon in every direction. The view was breathtaking. Well, that, and extremely oxygen-deficient up here on the top of Mount-fucking-Everest. It wasn't lost on me that this setting was essentially the scene that had been depicted on the Hermit card brought to fruition.

Okay, other than one factor: I wasn't alone.

Already shivering, I trudged away from the gateway to give Nik and Heru room to follow me through.

The air several paces in front of me shimmered, and Anapa appeared, donning the human-esque form he preferred when he entered the physical realm. He was still a little too tall, his eyes were a little too big, and his features were a little too pointy to pass as anything of this world, but it was a good effort.

"Katarina," Anapa said, beaming. His outfit was absurd for the alpine setting, consisting of a long, loose tunic over equally loose pants that reminded me of something a yogi would wear. He strode toward me, bare hands outstretched in front of him.

"It's cold as balls, Anapa," I grumbled, unwilling to release my death grip on my coat to hug him. Instead, I snuggled in close to his body, soaking up some of his abundant warmth as he wrapped his long arms around me. "Aren't you freezing?"

"Of course not," Anapa said, laughing like my question was utterly ridiculous. He released me to greet Nik and Heru in a more subdued fashion, then clasped his hands behind his back and turned to face me. "To what do I owe this honor?"

"I need your help," I said, wincing a smile as I pulled down the layers of scarf covering the lower half of my face, and only partially because the frigid air *literally* hurt. I really hated to be *that* kind of friend. The taker. The one who only reaches out when they need something. But here I was, doing that very thing.

Anapa bowed his head, apparently unbothered by my neediness. "Anything for you, dear Katarina."

I rubbed my gloves up and down my arms and hopped in place on the balls of my feet. "I need to get into Duat," I said, teeth chattering. "Preferably without dying."

Anapa's brows drew together. "I would not advise it," he said with a slight shake of his head. "Your *ba* is still healing. Exposing it to raw soul-energy could be very dangerous."

Pressing my lips together into a thin, flat line, I glanced at Nik. The soul bond we shared meant me risking my life risked his, too. But what other choice did we have?

While I had been drawing the gateway, Heru had received word from the oasis that he wasn't the only resurrected Nejeret experiencing these soul explosions. How long until Nejerets were detonating all over the place? What if this was also happening to Tarset while she was trapped in the ancient past? How long until it started happening to Nik, too?

Nik gave an almost imperceptible nod, telling me I had his support.

I returned my focus to Anapa. "I have to try," I told him. "I need to talk to Isfet, and this is the only way."

Anapa studied me for a long moment. "Very well," he said finally and extended a hand toward me. "Come."

I took two steps closer and placed my gloved hand in his.

Moving faster than my eyes could track, Anapa slammed his other hand into my solar plexus. I coughed, but the reflex didn't just expel air. It expelled my soul.

I stumbled backward, extremely disoriented by the scene in front of me. Nik and Heru stood frozen in a moment between moments, staring at me. Or rather, at my body. Which I was no longer in.

On the plus side, I was also no longer freezing, so that was cool.

I stepped around my time-frozen body, to where Anapa stood, waving his hand in a circular motion, like he was washing a car. About three yards away, a circular vortex formed, warping reality as it grew larger with each rotation of Anapa's hand. Soul-energy streamed past the hole Anapa was boring between dimensions in a whirlwind of color.

"Come now, Katarina," Anapa said, once again holding his hand out for me to take. "Let us be quick."

I placed my hand in his, and together, we approached the portal to Duat. The closer we drew, the stronger the pull of the other dimension. I couldn't recall feeling this pull before, which was more than a little disconcerting.

But, again, what choice did I have? I needed to speak with Isfet, and this was the only way.

I stepped through the portal into Duat, and I was momentarily swept away by the current of the soul-energy. Only Anapa's tight grip on my hand kept me anchored in place. It took a shit-ton of concentration, but finally, I managed to get my feet on the ground—or under me, or whatever, because there was no *ground*, so to speak, in Duat.

I glanced back at the portal. I could still see Nik and Heru standing with my body in that same freeze-frame moment. I turned back to Anapa, who looked the same as he had back on Mount Everest. But something about the way he was looking at me told me *I* looked different.

Curious, I peered down at myself. All the other times I had entered Duat, my soul had appeared a brilliant gold with inky black and shimmering iridescent marbling caused by the *At* and anti-*At* fused to my soul, thanks to some poor life choices I had made in my youth. I had grown accustomed to my soul's unusual appearance—it was what gave me my unique and sometimes powerful connection to the universe.

My soul didn't look the same anymore. The black and white striations were still there, but the gold appeared faded and murky, almost like it was tarnished. People joked about having a tarnished soul; lucky me, I actually had one.

"Peachy," I commented.

As I stared down at the dulled golden sheen of my hand, tendrils of lime green, fuchsia, and tangerine soul-energy coiled around my wrist and between my fingers. They tightened around me, tingly but not uncomfortable. The way the strands flattened against my soul reminded me of bandages over open wounds.

"Anapa?" I asked, unable to look away from the strands of soul-energy wrapping themselves around me. "What's happening?"

"I do not know," he said, his voice ringing with alarm.

I gulped, despite not actually having a physical throat to gulp with, thinking his response fell into worst-case-scenario territory. Anapa knew *pretty much* everything. Anything that alarmed him scared the shit out of me.

"Make haste, Katarina," Anapa urged. "Send your message now, so we may leave this place."

I nodded, panic rising. Closing my incorporeal eyelids, I pictured the angelic being that embodied the soul of the universe, with her silver blond hair, porcelain skin, and sky-blue eyes. I recalled the musical sound of her voice and the unique vibration of her soul.

"Isfet," I whispered. "I need you."

I felt the call leave my soul, more than words. More than sounds. A signal. It hurtled through Duat toward Iusaaset, the magnificent tree of pure energy at the very heart of the universe.

Suddenly, the tingling stopped. I opened my eyes to discover that the streaming, clinging soul-energy was gone. I was no longer in Duat but had returned to the physical realm to once again stand on top of Mount Everest. My time-frozen body was right where I had left it, standing in a triangle with Nik and Heru.

I glanced down at my hand, seeking reassurance that whatever had happened between the soul-energy and my tarnished soul back in Duat was over.

Once again, my soul resembled my physical body which, in my limited experience, seemed to be the norm for when it was lurking around body-free in the physical realm. My soul was bundled up, a perfect reflection of my body, standing a few yards away.

I tugged at my left glove, wanting to get a look at my skin. Or, my soul's skin, or whatever. But my glove refused to budge.

"You cannot remove it," Anapa explained. "This is a mere projection of your physical self."

"Well . . ." I strode closer to him—maybe a little too close for comfort—and angled my face up toward him. "How do I look? Am I still covered in strips of soul-energy?"

Anapa's eyes scanned my face, and his brow furrowed. He took too long to respond for the answer to be anything reassuring.

"How bad is it?" I asked, swallowing the resurgence of panic. I raised my eyebrows, urging him to say something.

Anapa sighed. "There is, ah . . . a shadow."

My eyebrows climbed higher. "A *shadow*?" I shook my head. "What the fuck does that mean?"

"If I knew, I would tell you," Anapa said, frowning. "I'm sorry, dear Katarina. Be cautious. We are in uncharted waters here."

I took a step back, moving out of Anapa's immediate personal space, but continued to hold his stare. "This is some serious bullshit," I told him, fully aware that it wasn't even remotely his fault. But he was the messenger and, damn it, it *was* bullshit.

Anapa placed a heavy hand on my shoulder. "I know." That was it. All the words he had for me. No comforting platitudes or pretty lies. Just an acknowledgment that he understood.

I inhaled deeply, then blew out the breath, my shoulders drooping. "Thanks for your help," I said, flashing Anapa a weak smile.

Anapa gave my shoulder a squeeze, then removed his hand.

I turned away from him and trudged back to my waiting body. The instant I touched my own shoulder, my soul was sucked back into my physical form, and time resumed.

ANCIENT TIMES

TARSET

49

I CROUCHED BEHIND THE low stone wall surrounding the Great Sphinx complex, peeking over the top of the wall periodically to check if the doorway on the Sphinx's chest was still sealed or if Atum had emerged. The brightening dawn light had long since banished the stars, and any minute now, the first sliver of the sun would peek over the eastern horizon.

Atum should've been outside by now, preparing for his morning ritual. I was growing increasingly concerned that I had assumed wrong—that Atum wasn't still at the Sphinx after all and had already moved on to some other place where I would never find him.

Then I would never know the truth.

I felt the tingle of a surge in otherworldly energy first. It charged the surrounding air, giving rise to a wave of goose bumps over my skin.

I peeked over the short wall, my stare locked on the Sphinx's chest. The limestone facade disguising the *At* barrier shimmered, then dissipated, revealing Atum's tall, broad-shouldered form.

My heart turned leaden at the sight of him standing in the doorway, gazing out at the eastern horizon. My mother's killer. The future's savior. All my thoughts and feelings about him tangled into a snarled mess until I could no longer recognize good from bad or right from wrong.

There is no such thing as good and bad in my world. There is only what must be and what never can be.

I was one of those things that could never be. I accepted the sad truth.

Rolled mat tucked under his arm, Atum scanned the area surrounding the Sphinx.

I ducked down as he reached my portion of the low wall. I silently counted to thirty, then slowly poked my head over the top of the wall to see if he was finally settling in for his ritual. I planned to sneak closer while he was distracted, figuring he would be more likely to answer truthfully if I caught him off guard.

But he wasn't kneeling between the Sphinx's forepaws, as I had expected. He was stepping over the low wall on the opposite side of the complex. For a solid thirty seconds, I watched him stride into the desert beyond the wall, and then I scrambled to my feet and jogged around the outer perimeter of the wall to follow.

Atum climbed to the top of a squat dune, then continued walking down the other side, disappearing from sight.

I picked up my pace from a jog to a run. By the time I crested the dune, Atum was already atop the next, unfurling his mat. Beyond him, compact mastabas and tombs spread out, an entire city of the dead.

I backpedaled a few steps, then crouched to watch Atum. He laid the mat on the ground, then knelt, drew his black-bladed dagger, and rested the blade on his lap while he watched the eastern horizon. As the initial bright golden rays of sunlight burst over the horizon, Atum made his first cut.

I stood and started down the dune, the leather soles of my sandals slipping and sliding over the loose, dry sand. I moved slowly and quietly, not wanting to alert him of my approach.

At twenty paces away, I closed in from directly behind him. I worked to keep my breaths shallow and measured as I crept forward.

Just ten paces to go.

Five.

"Thank you for returning," Atum said, wiping the black blade of his dagger on the underside of his schenti and re-sheathing the blade on his weapons belt.

I froze, a scant four paces away, one foot in front of the other. My heart lodged in my throat, blocking my voice.

"There is much for us to discuss," Atum said as he reached into the leather pouch sitting open on the mat in front of him and scooped out a small handful of gold dust to rub over his open cuts.

Upon hearing his voice, tears welled with a sudden surge of emotions. The numb shock that had comforted me throughout the night shattered, exposing all the suppressed rage and sorrow. The heartbreak. The betrayal.

"Tell me *why*," I demanded through gritted teeth.

Atum stood, his body unfolding to its full, impressive height.

"I need to know." My voice broke as a sob convulsed in my chest. Fresh tears streamed down my cheeks.

Atum turned to face me, his expression guarded.

"Was it me? Did I cause this?" I asked between sobbing breaths. "Did *I* kill them?"

Atum's eyes widened, and I thought I detected a glint of fear in their dark depths. Probably because I was glowing again. Good. If he was afraid of me, I was more likely to get the answers I needed.

"You didn't kill them, Tarset," Atum said, raising one hand slowly like he was reaching out to calm a frantic wild creature. He took a cautious step toward me. "Just calm down, and I'll explain everything."

"*Don't tell me to calm down!*" I shrieked. "Just tell me why! *Why* did you have to kill them?"

I could feel it this time, like the funnel of a tornado gaining speed and strength as it reached down from the sky. It was as though the wild emotions raging within me agitated my soul, making it expand until it was too big for the shell of my body to contain.

"*WHY?*" The word tore out of me in a roar, riding a wave of explosive golden light that silenced the world.

For a dozen heartbeats, I was the sun. A star. A supernova. The only sound was my straining heartbeat.

Tendrils of golden energy snapped out around me like solar flares. With each heartbeat, another concussive wave pulsed from my soul, sending waves of sand and chunks of limestone flying. Beneath my feet, sand crackled as it melted, reforming into glass.

Atum created a shield of pure *At*, but those whipping, lashing eruptions of golden energy ate away at the barrier like acid on flesh. A massive tendril whipped out, demolishing Atum's shield on contact and exposing him to the full brunt of the concussive golden waves pulsing out of me.

The force of the strike threw him backward, and Atum crashed into the side of a mastaba, the impact cracking the limestone. He slid down the stone wall, leaving behind a huge dent in the surface, and slumped on the ground. Blood leaked from his ears, nose, and mouth.

Shock cut through my flailing emotions, and the wild outpouring of energy from my flaring soul sucked back into me. In a blink, sound returned to the world, and I found myself standing in the center of a ten-foot glass crater. My mouth hung open as I took in the utter devastation I had caused.

I could hear people behind me, voices raised to shouts, but I only cared about one thing—one man. The one person whose sole objective was to ensure the continued existence of the future *I* needed.

"No," I breathed, rushing forward. The leather soles of my sandals sizzled on the molten glass underfoot, but in two strides, I was out of the super-heated crater and hurtling toward Atum.

At first, I thought he was dead. He was so still, his body so broken. Small gashes covered every exposed inch of him. He coughed, and blood sprayed from his mouth. His eyelids cracked open, and his pain-glazed eyes locked on me.

"Atum!" I skidded to my knees beside his slumped form, my heart leaden. My hands hovered over his bleeding broken body, fluttering over him, afraid to touch him and inflict even more damage.

Atum was in such rough shape that I couldn't believe he was still conscious, but his stare didn't waver.

What had I done? This wasn't what I wanted. I had come to him for answers. That was all. I had come here to hear him confirm my suspicions—that *I* was responsible for my mom's death—not to exact revenge on *him* personally.

He caught my wrist with one hand, and I froze. "I never . . . lied to you," he ground out, his jaw clenched. "Nitocris knew . . . about your lineage." He took a shallow, convulsive breath. "Reminded Inyotef . . ."

My eyes widened, and my mouth fell open. I had forgotten about Nitocris—that she knew about my parents. That she was, in fact, the one who had originally made the connection and mentioned it to Inyotef.

Atum's focus shifted past me, and I spun on my knees, reaching for the hilt of his ritual dagger and drawing the blade from his weapons belt in one smooth motion. I would fight off all of Men-nefer if necessary to keep him safe. Atum wasn't dying today. Not on my watch.

When I saw who approached, my fingers loosened on the dagger, and the weapon slipped out of my grasp, landing on the sand with a dull thunk. I was struck dumb and momentarily paralyzed by the sight of the two women skirting around my sizzling glass crater.

One was an unfamiliar Nejeret.

The other was *my mom.*

50

"**W**HAT HAPPENED?" THE NEJERET asked as she rushed forward, ahead of my mom.

My *mom.*

She was *alive.*

The Nejeret was tall and lean, with the same dark skin and eyes as Atum. The same angular features. The resemblance was too striking not to assume that she was his daughter. But I couldn't give her more than a passing glance, not when my mom trailed behind her.

My mom was *alive.* Which meant Atum hadn't killed her.

Thoughts looped in my mind, skipping like a broken record.

She was supposed to be dead. But she was here. She was alive. Atum didn't kill her. He *didn't* kill her. She was alive. She was here. Right here. Right in front of me.

Alive.

"What have I done?" I breathed, tearing my stare from my mom to gaze down at Atum.

He sat propped against the exterior wall of the mastaba, his head slumped to one side, his eyes shut. He had held onto consciousness as long as he could. Long enough to say what he needed to say. Long enough to show me how wrong I had been.

"What happened?" the Nejeret repeated, enunciating the words very clearly. She dropped to her knees on Atum's other side.

My mom stood at his feet, wringing her hands as she scanned the tombs in the necropolis beyond like she might find whoever was responsible for the attack on Atum. Like she had no idea that the culprit knelt a few feet away from her.

I looked from one woman to the other repeatedly, the motion slowly transforming into a head shake. "I–I don't know," I said, and it wasn't a lie. *I* had done this, but I didn't know how.

The Nejeret pulled a compact mirror from a pouch tied to her belt and held it near Atum's nostrils. The glass fogged faintly with his next, shallow exhale.

"He still lives," she said, glancing first at me, then at my mom. "But I don't think we should move him. The damage to his body is extreme. I'm not sure he can heal this on his own, and my healing gifts lie elsewhere."

"My husband's sister is a skilled healer," my mom volunteered. "She is in town," she added, nodding toward the ancient city on the far side of the river.

"Aset?" I asked, and my mom's attention turned to me, her eyes narrowed. "Is she at the Hathor temple?"

My mom nodded, her stare scrutinizing, like she recognized me but couldn't quite place my face. I could hardly blame her. The last time she had seen me, I was four years old and being frozen into a statue of *At*.

"I'll fetch her," I said as I stood, wiping my suddenly clammy hands on my skirt. I kicked off my damaged sandals, hoping nobody noticed the clumps of glass stuck to the soles, and started down the sandy hill. "Just keep him alive," I tossed over my shoulder, and then I picked up the pace, settling on a fast run.

I leapt over the low wall on this side of the Sphinx complex and ran toward the opposite wall. Movement at the doorway between the Sphinx's forelegs caught my attention, and I slowed to a jog. A young woman emerged, maybe twenty years old, her resemblance to my mom uncanny. My mom had been pregnant the last time I saw her, some twenty years ago, and I wondered if this was my baby sister, all grown up.

The young woman held an infant cradled in her arms. At first, I thought it must be her child. But then I recognized the lotus pattern on the blanket—the same as the pattern on the blanket that had been wrapped around the infant in the original dissonance. Was this *that* child—the baby I had accused Atum of killing?

The moment between one stride and the next stretched out into an eternity.

Had Atum saved them—my family *and* this baby? None of this made any sense. I had seen the time tapestry. I had watched him suffocating the mother, and after, the baby's lifethread was gone, vanished from the pattern. Unless Atum had teleported the child away from Men-nefer, meaning it wouldn't have appeared in the portion of the time tapestry that had been visible on the patch.

My thoughts couldn't keep up with my shifting understanding of the events of the past day and a half.

My foot hit the ground, and my focus snapped back to the urgent task at hand. Atum was dying. And if he died, the timeline—and the future I would have given my life to protect—didn't stand a chance.

I kicked it into high gear as I approached the low wall on the far side of the Sphinx. I hurdled over the wall, then sprinted down the paved causeway leading to the river and the boats docked at the harbor. The journey across the river and to the Hathor temple passed in a blur.

Men-nefer had long been the seat of Nejeret power in Egypt, and the people of this region held my kind in great reverence compared to the reception I had received at the harbor in Waset. The first boatman I approached was eager to ferry me across the river. When we reached the eastern bank and I asked him for directions to the Hathor temple, he jumped at the chance to lead me there himself.

I marched through the open gateway into the Hathor temple, blinders on as I scanned the pillared courtyard for Aset. When I didn't see her, I approached the nearest priestess, a middle-aged woman sprinkling something into the long, rectangular pond that spanned the center of the courtyard.

"Where is Aset?" I asked as I strode toward the priestess. "I must see her immediately."

The priestess stared at me with wide eyes. "Of course, divine one," she said, bowing deeply before turning on her heel and scurrying deeper into the temple.

I paced along the length of the pond, wishing the priestess would hurry so I could return to Atum. It was ironic that I had been so focused on reaching this temple since I first realized where and when I was, but now, all I could think about was getting *away* from this place. Getting *back* to him.

The priestess returned less than a minute later, Aset following close on her heels. The priestess stepped off to the side, allowing Aset to pass her as the two women approached me.

I turned away from the pond and hurried toward Aset. "I need your help," I said as our paths converged near the end of the pond.

Aset eyed me, scanning me from my bare feet up. Her gaze lingered on the lower half of my dress.

I glanced down to see what had snagged her attention. Blood was splattered and smeared over the white linen. "My—" I hesitated, uncertain what to call Atum. "My friend is gravely injured."

"I can see that," Aset drawled, one eyebrow hitching higher. Finally, she dragged her eyes up to my face, her stare meeting mine. She was uncertain about helping me, which was totally understandable. She didn't know me, after all. At least, not in this time period.

I licked my lips. "Sesha sent me," I said, needing to hurry Aset along.

At the mention of my mom's name, the resistance left Aset's eyes, and her expression relaxed. "Where is your injured friend?"

"Across the river," I told her in a rush. "At the edge of the necropolis near the southern side of the Sphinx. I can take you to him straight away."

Aset nodded once, her stare unfocusing as it shifted past me, almost like she could see the place I meant. "Human or Netjer-At?"

"Netjer-At," I told her. "We must hurry. He's not healing as he should."

She refocused on me, her stare hawkish. "What is the nature of his injuries?"

"Ah . . ." I blinked, unsure how to answer. "He was caught in a blast of energy, like an explosion. I think he has damage on the inside of his body—that his internal organs are bleeding."

Aset's eyes widened, and she scanned me again, studying me with renewed interest. "You have some knowledge of the body yourself."

"Not enough," I murmured. Everything I knew, I had learned from her, but she didn't need to know that.

Aset placed a gentle hand on my shoulder. "Let me gather my things, and then we can be on our way."

51

I HUFFED AND PUFFED behind Aset as we jogged along the western quay toward the road that led to the causeway up to the Sphinx and the Great Pyramid beyond. Clearly, Aset was in much better shape than me, not that such a thing was all that shocking.

I still had piddly stamina from my extended stay in Inyotef's dungeon and the resulting week of regenerative cycles. Plus, my muscles felt like jelly from the mad, adrenaline-fueled dash I had made *to* the Hathor temple to find Aset. It was all I could manage to not be left behind.

A cluster of armed and armored men stepped into our path, where the end of the quay met the road. Five burly warriors stood shoulder to shoulder, purposely blocking the way out of the harbor.

Aset slowed to a walk, then stopped a few paces out from the human barricade.

I caught up, gripping my side and breathing hard.

In the boats tied off on either side of the quay and all along the walkway, sailors and workers stopped what they were doing and turned to watch.

"Out of my way," Aset commanded, raising her chin imperiously.

A sixth man pushed through the living barrier, and I instinctively backed up a step. Inyotef's stare locked on me, his lips spreading into a fiendish grin.

Tremors shook my body as, in a single heartbeat, I relived the nightmarish string of days during which Inyotef held me prisoner. My stomach knotted, then lurched, and I feared I would be sick.

Inyotef switched his attention to Aset and bowed deeply. "Divine Ones," he said with such sincere deference I might have bought his act if I hadn't already known what a depraved piece of shit he was.

Aset took a step toward Inyotef as he straightened. "Move," she demanded, her voice quieter but somehow more commanding than before. Something in her tone told me she wasn't buying his act.

Inyotef glanced over his shoulder and nodded to one of the thugs in his entourage blocking the end of the quay. The man took a step backward, angling his body to the side to let Aset pass.

Aset started forward, slipping through the gap.

When I made to follow, Inyotef stepped in my path.

"Just her," Inyotef murmured, one corner of his mouth lifting into a cruel sneer. "Not you."

Aset peered back from the other side of the line of armed men. The guard who had let her through returned to his original position to fill the hole in the line.

She was going to argue, to demand they let me through. I could see it in the hard glint in her copper eyes, in the tensed set of her jaw. This stupid, pointless confrontation was going to delay us even further, and we didn't have time to spare. For all I knew, Atum was already dead. But on the off chance that he wasn't, she needed to get to him as quickly as possible.

"Go," I said, surprised by the iron in my voice. Inside, I was shivering tin foil. "I have business with this man," I told her, lying through my teeth. "I'll be right behind you."

Aset held my stare through the dip between two of the thugs' shoulders for a long moment. I feared she would press the matter, but finally, she nodded once and turned away, setting off at a fast jog. She didn't look back.

"Follow her," Inyotef ordered. "I want to know where she's going in such a hurry."

"Don't." I balled my hands into fists and clenched my jaw, my nostrils flaring. If Inyotef's men followed Aset, they would find Atum. They would find my mom. Hell, my whole family was out there for all I knew.

I couldn't let that happen.

I stepped forward and swallowed roughly. "Unless you want me to make a scene," I said, flashing Inyotef a wooden smile.

Inyotef studied me, his index finger tapping against the outside of his sword sheath. "If I let her go, you will come with me willingly?"

I sucked in a shaky breath, pursed my lips to prevent myself from lashing out with all the hateful words I had saved up for him, and nodded.

Inyotef narrowed his eyes like he was weighing the worth of my silent promise. "Where is our valiant hero, the prince?" Inyotef made a show of scanning the harbor for the man he knew as Temu, Atum's previous human identity.

"Not here," I said. "Gone." But not dead. At least, I hoped that was the case. The universe had yet to collapse in on itself, which seemed like a promising sign.

Inyotef sniffed dismissively. "No matter. I wanted to punish Temu. But you—" He smiled lazily and took a step closer to me, reaching out to skim his fingertips along my jawline.

I jerked my face away from his hand.

Inyotef's smile widened. "You, I plan to break, slowly and precisely." He withdrew his hand. "You will be a wedding gift for my bride. Her very own pet Netjer-At." He gestured toward the far end of the quay with one extended arm. "Come now, let us be on our way."

My chin trembled, but I refused to cry. I wouldn't give him that satisfaction. Instead, I gritted my teeth and held my chin high as I started toward the boat at the end of the quay. I just hoped Atum still lived to give meaning to my sacrifice.

At least, if he was already dead, none of this would matter. The timeline—and the universe—didn't stand a chance without him.

I smiled to myself as I led my captor down the quay. Either way, Inyotef would lose. And that knowledge was more than enough of a win for me.

52

I NYOTEF'S BOAT CARRIED US directly to the palace, which was practically a small walled city all on its own on the outskirts of Men-nefer. I walked at his side of my own volition, hardly seeing any of the wonders around me. My thoughts—and heart—were across the river with Aset.

With my mom.

With Atum.

Inyotef led me through a warren of brightly painted hallways. I didn't even bother attempting to keep track of the twists and turns we took. I wouldn't be leaving this place.

Nothing had changed about my situation in relation to the timeline. If anything, I was more resolved now than ever to remove the greatest danger to the future—me.

Eventually, we stopped in front of a locked door composed of thick boards bound by bronze bands. A small, square opening had been cut into the door at face height and a copper mesh screen was built into the hole.

I waited at Inyotef's side as a guard stepped up to the door and lifted the wooden beam barring it shut. The guard pulled the door open, then stepped backward in the hallway, giving us room to pass.

"I hope the accommodations are to your liking, divine one," Inyotef said, holding his hand out toward the doorway to my new prison cell beyond.

I pressed my lips together to prevent myself from rising to his bait and stepped past him and into the cell. A quick scan revealed no ropes or restraints, which was an upgrade from my last cell. Even better, there was a small window cutout in the far wall, a simple horizontal opening about four inches high and maybe two feet wide. It was too high in the wall, and the wall itself was too thick for me to see anything outside, but at least it afforded some natural light.

There was a grimy bucket in one corner—my toilet, I assumed—and an even grimier-looking bedroll laid out along the left-hand wall. I wrinkled my nose and shivered involuntarily. I wasn't going anywhere near that thing. I refused to die with lice.

I moved into the center of the cell and gazed up at the sorry excuse for a window. "Does she know?" I asked, my voice low and steady, reflecting the deep pool of resolve welling in my heart. Soon enough, this would all be over.

"Who?" Inyotef asked. "My beloved Nitocris?"

I suppressed a snort and turned my head just enough that I could see Inyotef over my shoulder in my peripheral vision. "Does she know I'm here?" I clarified. "Does she know what you did to me—what you're planning to do?"

"Why bore her with such petty interpersonal matters when she has a country to rule?" he said.

In other words, he had kept Nitocris in the dark about the less savory details regarding our *interpersonal matters*. I wondered if she had any idea of what had befallen me at the hands of her betrothed after she cast off from Waset.

"You will be such a welcome surprise," Inyotef said. "Just what we need to reunify the lands."

I sniffed a laugh and returned to staring up at the window cutout in the wall. He was a fool if he believed Nitocris welcomed any sort of surprise. She believed everyone was plotting to kill her. She had confessed as much to me herself. Oh no, a woman as paranoid as Nitocris preferred to know every single thing going on around her.

The sound of Inyotef's retreating footsteps told me he was leaving the cell. I supposed I wasn't as fun to toy with when I was ignoring him.

The cell door thudded shut behind me, and with the groan of wood, I was locked in. Panic fluttered in my chest, but I quickly trapped and caged it. All it would do was wear me out, and I would need all my wits and strength to see this through to the end.

I kicked the filthy bedroll toward the door, then huddled in the empty back corner opposite the toilet bucket. I curled up my legs and hugged them to my chest, resting my cheek on one knee.

Atum had better still be alive. I wondered what he thought of me now. Did he hate me for endangering the pattern? Had he concluded, as I had, that the timeline was a lot safer without me around to muddle things up?

I was like Midas, transforming everything I touched, except instead of turning to gold, the things I touched turned to shit. And that wasn't even including whatever the hell was going on inside me with these insane energy explosions.

For hours, I sat in the corner of the cell, alone with my wandering thoughts. My well of resolve deepened, becoming bottomless, and I found peace there.

Atum would live. He had to. My family—both ancient and future—would be safe, thanks to him. Inyotef could torture my body as much as he liked, but he couldn't touch my heart.

In the early afternoon, or so I gathered from the light pouring in through the narrow cutout high up in the wall, muffled voices outside my cell drew my attention to the tiny mesh window in the door. One voice was deep and masculine—a guard, I assumed—the other decidedly feminine and familiar. Looked like the queen had come to pay me a visit.

"I was given orders to only open this door for Inyotef," the guard said.

"And tell me—who do you serve?" Nitocris asked, her voice razor sharp. "Inyotef, or your queen?"

A few seconds later, I heard the groan of the wooden beam being lifted. I raised my head as the door swung outward, and Nitocris darkened the doorway. She hovered there for a full ten seconds, surveying my cell—and me—then stepped inside, a pair of guards slipping in behind her.

I stood, my back still wedged into the corner, and pressed my palms flat against the stone walls on either side of me, letting Nitocris and her guards know I was no threat to her. Belatedly, I wondered if maybe I *should* attack her. I felt certain they would kill me, but I needed to draw this out. To buy Aset time to work, and Atum time to heal.

"I am sorry for this," Nitocris said, with no showy sighs or apologetic smiles. She offered the simple truth, which I appreciated.

She was going to despise being tied to a man like Inyotef, and I wondered how long it would take her to realize the mistake she had made with him. Would she come to her senses before he tried to kill her and steal her throne, or would she only realize his true, vile nature once it was too late?

"He told me you didn't know I was here," I volunteered, hoping to sow discord between Nitocris and Inyotef.

Even if I wasn't planning on being around to watch the fallout from their union, I was still going to plant my flag firmly on her side of the battlefield. This would end in bloodshed. I just hoped that blood wasn't all hers.

Nitocris barked a laugh. "I haven't stayed alive this long by being oblivious, divine one. Nothing happens inside these walls that I don't know about," she said. "I don't agree with his decision to hold you captive, but I won't release you, so don't ask. Our alliance is fragile and Inyotef has such a delicate ego." She raised her eyebrows, tilting her head to the side. "You have spent so much time with him. Surely you understand. Besides, I can't risk you returning to your people and drawing their wrath down upon us."

The corners of my mouth tensed. "What makes you think they don't already know—that they're not already on their way?"

Nitocris speared me with a level stare. "My dear, Inyotef held you prisoner and tortured you for weeks in Waset, and nobody came for you then. Why would it be any different now, here?"

I returned her stare, giving nothing away.

Nitocris narrowed her eyes as she studied me. "Inyotef believes you have been exiled by your people and are hiding from them," she mused. "He believes you would rather die than let them know where you are. It is the only reason he dares to act so boldly with you."

"And what do you believe?" I asked coolly.

Nitocris let out a low, hollow laugh. "I believe you are a woman in a very difficult position. Inyotef thinks he can break you down and reshape you into something he can control." She raised her eyebrows, her lips curving into a secretive smile. "I, however, think he underestimates you." She rolled her eyes. "He is a *man*. A clever man, and a devious man, but a man, nonetheless. He doesn't understand that true strength comes from within."

"You can't trust him," I warned her. "One day, when you're no longer of use to him, he *will* turn on you."

She smiled to herself. "Oh yes, I know," she said, her rising pitch telling me she had already accounted for that eventuality. She had a plan.

What a miserable pair Nitocris and Inyotef would make, both waiting for the other to bury a knife in their back.

"I appreciate the warning," Nitocris said, bowing her head. "And so, in return, I will offer you this—at sundown every evening, I will send one of my most trusted servants to check in with you. If your suffering grows too great, I will ensure that it ends."

She was offering to set me free—not free of this cell, but free of my body. A mercy killing.

"You need only say the word," she said.

It was my turn to bow my head. "Thank you." When I raised my head again, the queen's back was to me.

She strode through the doorway, pausing in the hallway to peer back at me. We stared at one another for a long moment, some deep, wordless understanding passing between us. I would never see her again, and we both knew it.

Then, Nitocris turned away and stepped out of view.

My cell door slammed shut, and once again, I was alone. But at least I wasn't hopeless, as I had been in Waset. I wrapped the queen's promise around me like armor, already planning my final performance.

D AYS PASSED IN A blur of alternating periods of agony and
unconsciousness. If I was awake, I was hurting. Inyotef made sure of
that personally.

No cherubic priests stepped in to slice my flesh with a steady, restrained
hand or to study my living anatomy. Inyotef's misguided sense of vengeance
and masculine entitlement drove him to be rougher and crueler with his
torture than Cherub had ever been, but it actually worked out in my
favor. Cherub's restraint enabled him to make a session last hours. But
Inyotef's eagerness to hurt me—to break me—pushed him to beat me into
unconsciousness within minutes of starting.

I learned quickly that Inyotef was a sadist, relishing my pain. My
whimpers brought him pleasure, my screams the greatest joy. But my
silence—that enraged him completely and was the reason so many of our
sessions ended so quickly.

Inyotef fed me the bare minimum to guarantee regeneration, but while
my wounds healed, the limited nourishment ensured my body wasted away
under the constant strain. I quickly lost track of the days and number of
regeneration cycles. I would already have called in Nitocris's promised favor,
except I was never conscious or coherent enough when her servant visited.

And then, one day, the torture stopped, because Inyotef never came. Food
arrived in his place, always a large bowl of sweetened gruel and a pair of
waterskins—one filled with broth, one with water.

I ate and slept the deep, dreamless sleep of a regeneration cycle three
times without a single visitor beyond the guard who brought me my food

and emptied my bucket. Time and again, I tried to hold out on eating until evening fell so I would be awake when Nitocris's servant visited, but I never could do it.

After the third such torture-less regenerative cycle, someone new entered my cell. The door swung inward, and an emaciated woman with a shaved head scurried in carrying a bucket of water and a white linen dress slung over her elbow. She kept her face angled downward, her eyes trained on the floor.

It took me a long, incredulous moment to recognize her as Kiya. *My* Kiya.

I gawked, my mind unable to process the once-proud warrior's drastically altered appearance. Her head had been shaved clean, and she wore nothing but the skimpy linen briefs of the lowest servants. She was far thinner than she had been, scrawny where she had once been leanly muscled. But it was her spirit that had changed the most. She had been broken.

The guard tossed in a waterskin before slamming the cell door shut.

I clambered to my feet, using the wall for support, then rushed toward Kiya. I waited for her to set down the bucket and dress, then threw my arms around her frail frame. She clung to me, her face buried in my neck and her whole body convulsing with sobs.

Gone was the bold, self-assured woman I had known. I could only imagine what Inyotef must have done to her to strip her bare of all her internal armor and reduce her to this frightened creature.

I stroked Kiya's shaved head and rubbed her scarred back, waiting until she had calmed somewhat. Once her sobs had quieted, I loosened my arms and pulled away, raising my hands to cup either side of her face. I searched her haunted brown eyes but found no inner spark. No fire. It was as though the Kiya I had known had been snuffed out.

"I am so sorry," I told her, meaning the apology with all of my heart. "Tell me what he did to you, Kiya, and I swear to you, I will do everything I can to ensure he suffers worse."

Maybe I was all bluster, but I knew firsthand how damaging it could be to suppress a traumatic experience. There was catharsis in turning the unspeakable into words. I could give her that, at least.

Kiya closed her eyes, setting a fresh string of tears trailing down her cheeks, and shook her head.

"Kiya," I breathed, my chin trembling. "Please, tell me."

Her lashes fluttered as she opened her eyes. She parted her lips, but instead of speaking, she opened her mouth wide, revealing the raw, swollen stub where her tongue had once been.

I clenched my jaw, refusing to display the horror I felt. Rage simmered in my veins, and I inhaled deeply, letting out the breath slow and measured. I couldn't afford to let my emotions get the better of me and trigger another of those soul explosions, not when Kiya was trapped in the cell with me.

I wondered if I could hold on to the rage, bottle it up to be released at a later time when Kiya was gone and Inyotef was the only one who would be caught in the blast zone.

Kiya stepped backward and averted her gaze to the floor once more. She gestured to the bucket of water, then to me. She was here to wash me.

Much as I relished the prospect of being clean—or, at least, clean*er*—I was far from eager to discover why Inyotef wanted me presentable. This was no kindness. No mercy. Such things no longer existed in my world.

Kiya was a message. One I heard loud and clear.

Once I was cleaned up, worse was to come.

54

I wasn't sure what to expect after Kiya left. It felt strange to be relatively clean and to wear anything more than my skin. Or to have time awake when I wasn't being brutalized or force-fed. For the first time since being imprisoned here, I had a chance to think.

The amber light streaming in through the narrow window cutout high in the wall transitioned to sunset orange, then faded to twilight gray. I paced circuits around the perimeter of my cell, chewing my nails to nubs as I considered Inyotef's reasons for this sudden change.

Why clean me up? Why dress me? For appearances, obviously—he wanted me presentable for some reason. Or for some person. But for who, exactly? Was he planning on showing me off—to prove how powerful he was? So, possibly some important official or dignitary? Maybe a foreign ruler?

Or maybe the Council of Seven had heard rumors of a Nejeret held captive in the royal palace, and Inyotef needed me to convince their representative I was here of my own free will. My blood ran cold at the thought.

With the groan of wood, someone unlocked my cell door. I retreated to my corner but didn't cower. I refused to give Inyotef the satisfaction of seeing my fear.

The door swung inward, revealing Inyotef standing in the doorway, backlit by the flickering torchlight in the hallway behind him. His gaze skimmed over my body from the toes up, a faint smirk twisting his lips. He made an appreciative sound in his throat that sent a swarm of invisible spiders scurrying down my spine. I shivered involuntarily.

"You do clean up nicely," he said and stepped backward, sweeping out one arm to invite me to join him in the hallway. He grinned, an eager glint in his eyes. "Come, our guests are waiting."

I gulped, then stepped away from the wall. Anything that excited Inyotef set me on edge. But whatever this was about, it couldn't be as bad as torture. At least, that was what I told myself.

I passed through the doorway, but leaving the cell only afforded me the illusion of freedom. Of that, I was certain.

Inyotef offered me his arm.

I suppressed a cringe and a shudder, turning my face away from him.

My rejection only seemed to amuse him further. He started down the hallway, and when I didn't immediately follow, he stopped and turned partway to settle a level stare on me. He didn't have to say anything. The threat was implied. Cooperate, or else.

I considered bolting back into my cell. The door was still open, and I thought I could probably dive inside before the guard slammed the door shut.

But that *or else* hung over me.

If I cooperated tonight, maybe Inyotef would extend my reprieve from the torture. I chewed on the inside of my cheek. I could at least go wherever he wanted to take me and assess the situation once I had more information. Relying on Nitocris to end my misery hadn't been working out all that well, but maybe this change in setting would give me a chance to take care of matters myself.

Squaring my shoulders and raising my chin, I approached Inyotef. When I reached him, he fell in step beside me. This time, he didn't offer me his arm.

I attempted to keep track of the turns we made as we moved through the palace, but the place was a warren, and I quickly lost all sense of direction.

"Here we are," Inyotef said, nodding toward a wider doorway than those we had previously passed through.

I could see a few columns painted with vibrant designs immediately beyond the doorway and some planters overflowing with greenery further in, suggesting we would be entering a courtyard. Flickering orange torchlight lit the space, and the lively sounds of a party set my nerves even more on edge.

Inyotef stopped a few steps from the doorway and gestured for me to continue on.

I hesitated only for the briefest moment, then passed him and entered the courtyard.

It was both more grandiose and more barren than anything at Inyotef's palace, with massive painted limestone columns reaching high overhead like they were guiding the eye toward the sky. There were no pools, and there was only a quadrant of planters filled with lush greenery in the center of the large, open space. A huge wooden gate blocked one end of the courtyard, making me think this was possibly the entryway to the palace.

Armed men milled around the courtyard, ceramic cups in hand, laughing raucously and shoving one another. More than a few appeared unsteady on their feet, suggesting the festivities had been going on for a while.

I paused between two columns, hanging back as I scanned the crowded space. What was this all about? Why had Inyotef brought me here?

One of the inebriated men stumbled toward my row of columns, stopping a few columns away. My eyebrows rose when he hiked up his schenti, gripped his flaccid penis, and started urinating, right there on the floor between two columns.

Only then did I see the ropes tied to one of those columns, the fingertips peeking around the curved, painted limestone, the toes being showered in the man's urine.

Dread pushed me farther into the courtyard, and I craned my neck to see who had been tied up between the two columns.

And then I saw her. Kiya.

Stripped nude and gagged, she had been strung up between two columns, a veritable Vitruvian woman. She stared up at the darkening sky, her eyes vacant. She was alive, but she had gone somewhere else in her mind. I could only imagine what further horrors Inyotef and these animals had inflicted on her to cause such a mental retreat.

Hands balling into fists, I rounded on Inyotef.

He lounged against one column bordering the doorway, that cruel smirk twisting his lips.

"Where is Nitocris?" I asked through gritted teeth.

She would never allow something like this to happen, regardless of her fragile alliance with him or whatever other queenly bullshit she had going on.

"Away," Inyotef said, pushing off the column.

I sucked in a breath to spit some serious vitriol in Inyotef's face.

Rough hands closed around my arms and wrists, cutting off my tirade before it even started. Two of Inyotef's ruffians dragged me down the line of columns toward Kiya. I twisted and jerked in their hold, but it was no use. They were too strong, and I was pathetically weak after my second bout of imprisonment and torture.

"The men are a little wild," Inyotef said, strolling along behind us. "You see, they've been on the water for weeks and only just arrived from Waset this afternoon."

I struggled as my captors dragged me past Kiya to the neighboring space between one of her columns and the next one over.

The drunken urinator staggered away, and Inyotef eyed his back for a moment before stopping in front of Kiya to admire her exposed position. He tutted as he shook his head as though she was his greatest disappointment.

My captors wound ropes around my wrist, knotting them painfully tight.

Inyotef moved past Kiya to stand directly in front of me, his arms crossed over his chest, hanging back to oversee his henchmen's work.

They stretched out my arms, wrapping the length of my binding ropes around the columns on either side of me.

"As soon as she left your cell," Inyotef said, "I set up Kiya out here to give my men a taste of what they're in for with you . . . with instructions to keep their hands off her until you arrived. Couldn't let you miss all the fun."

Now that my arms were secured to the columns, Inyotef's thugs crouched to work on binding my ankles. I managed to kick one in the face, receiving a satisfying crunch and a shouted curse for my efforts. But the man still tied the rope around my ankle, even with the blood dripping from his nose.

My legs were jerked apart, my ankles crushed against the bases of the columns. The skirt of my dress hiked high on my thighs, and the extremely vulnerable and exposed position sent panic flitting through my chest. My soul stirred, swelling, pushing at the boundaries of my physical form.

Inyotef stepped closer to me, hanging back just out of reach of my feet on the off chance I got one leg free again. "You're going to listen while they destroy her," Inyotef purred, a disturbing grin curving his lips. "You'll hear what they're going to do to you. And when she is little more than meat and bone, they'll move on to you." He raised his eyebrows, his grin vanishing. "Unless you give in. Unless you walk the Echoes for me right here and now."

I gritted my teeth, reminding myself that my death—even at the cost of Kiya's demise—would be for the greater good of the timeline. The outrage agitating my soul dwindled, slowly fading away.

Inyotef moved closer, emboldened by my inability to lash out with my legs. He thoroughly invaded my personal space, raising one hand to trace along my collarbones with his fingertips. "You have the power to stop this," he said, stroking the column of my neck with his knuckles. "To save her." His hand moved higher, the pad of his thumb gliding over my chin and brushing across my lips.

I struck without thinking, opening my mouth and snapping my teeth shut around his thumb. Inyotef's eyes widened, his sinister glee vanishing as my incisors sank into the joint, and I bit down as hard as I could. A spurt of blood gushed into my mouth, making me gag. My jaw opened reflexively, and I released Inyotef's thumb.

Inyotef stumbled backward, clutching his injured hand to his chest and staring at me with pure astonishment, like he really thought this would break me.

I almost laughed out loud. What a fucking moron.

I had one foot out the door. Senioritis for living. As soon as the opportunity presented itself, I was out of this useless physical shell, more than ready for an extended vacation in Aaru. I had earned the peace I would find in the land of the dead. And even better—I would never have to see Inyotef's disgusting face again, because he was human, fated to return to the streaming soul-energy in Duat when he died.

A blood-curdling scream cut through the raucous sounds of the gathering. A hush fell over the crowd as even the most inebriated of Inyotef's men looked around for the source of the scream.

In the sudden quiet, I heard a faint crackle, like ice spreading across the surface of water. It sounded like it was coming from the gate, and I stared hard at the pair of heavy-duty wooden doors, searching past the foliage blocking my view of the gate for the source of the noise.

The men closest to the gate slowly backed away, retreating deeper into the courtyard. At first, I didn't understand why. But then I saw it around the edge of one planter. The bottom half of the oversized doors no longer appeared to be made of wood but had been transformed into iridescent *At*, gleaming like moonstone in the torchlight. The otherworldly material was spreading, consuming the doors.

Looked like Atum had survived his injuries after all.

A low, sinister chuckle cut through the vacuous quiet, and it took me a moment to realize the laughter was coming from me.

Inyotef glanced my way, his eyes rounded, his pupils swallowing his irises.

I let the chuckle die out on a satisfied sigh.

Atum was alive. The proof was staring me in the face from across the courtyard. Whatever happened to me next didn't matter because Atum was *alive*, which meant the timeline was safe.

Surely Atum would see me as the threat I was after I had nearly killed him. Surely he wouldn't—couldn't—let me live. *Surely* this would all be over soon enough.

That shimmering opalescence consumed the last sliver of wood, and then cracks spread across the surface of the gate.

The men who had been binding my ankles to the columns abandoned their tasks before they had finished and stepped away. The rope looped around the columns slackened, giving me free movement of my legs. I brought my feet together and stood straighter, relieving the pressure on my bound wrists, and held my breath. The cracks continued to spread, branching out, breaking the gate into smaller and smaller pieces.

With a thundering boom, the gate exploded. Shards of *At* hurled into the courtyard, peppering the nearest of the gathered thugs with otherworldly shrapnel. Just as suddenly, the shards froze in midair, a deadly shell hovering around the wide-open gate.

Atum's large, shadowed form darkened the palace entrance. Long, billowing robes as black as night cloaked his imposing frame, and a cowl shadowed his face, the grim reaper coming to collect his promised souls. His head slowly turned as he scanned the courtyard, and I felt more than saw his eyes lock on me.

Atum was here for me, either to kill me or to save me. I honestly wasn't sure which. But his target was obvious—me.

He stepped into the courtyard, and the bubble of hushed anticipation burst. The shards of what had once been the gate flew outward, a deadly cloud of throwing daggers cutting down the men all around Atum before they could even think about running. Whole bodies were reduced to bone shards and meat chunks and sprays of blood right before my eyes.

As Atum crossed the center of the courtyard, moving down the aisle between the planters, the shards of *At* regathered into a cloud, gracefully flowing around the courtyard like a swarm of lethal heat-seeking locusts, hunting down and obliterating every last one of Inyotef's men.

A mist of blood hung in the air, the copper scent tinged with the acrid stench of bile and bowels. Bone crunched beneath Atum's feet as he drew nearer, accentuating the intermittent splat and plop of fleshy bits hitting the ground.

Inyotef scurried away from the carnage, still clutching the hand I had bitten to his chest. He fled around the column to my right but backpedaled into the courtyard a moment later, pushed backward by a wall formed of glittering *At* shards. The swarm spread out, sealing Inyotef in with Kiya and me. A gap in the barrier appeared straight ahead, letting Atum into our cage before quickly resealing.

"No, please," Inyotef begged, backing closer to me. "Wait. Please." He ducked under my outstretched arm and hid behind me.

I twisted and tugged on my bindings, trying and failing to get away from the coward.

Two shards of *At* shot out of the wall encircling us, heading straight for me. I squeezed my eyes shut and turned my face away. This was it. The last moment. The end of me.

The lengths of rope binding my wrists to the columns snapped. I dropped to my knees, stunned by the unexpected freedom and even more so by the simple fact that I was still alive.

Did that mean Atum wasn't here to kill me?

Splashing through inches of standing blood, I scrambled away from Inyotef and crawled closer to Kiya, who was still strung up between the columns. I snagged a knife from one of the blood-soaked weapons belts lying half-buried in the crimson pool that had become the courtyard floor. As I sawed through the rope binding Kiya's right ankle to the column, I watched Atum stalk closer to Inyotef's cowering form.

Inyotef huddled behind the next column over, his hands raised to shield himself from Atum's rage.

The rope binding Kiya's right ankle finally gave way, and I shuffled sideways to get to work on freeing her left leg.

Atum pushed back his cowl, giving Inyotef his first clear view of his attacker's face.

Inyotef lowered his hands, his lips parting and brow furrowing. He shook his head, squinting like he was peering through a fog. "Temu?" Inyotef visibly struggled to reconcile the nightmare looming over him with the biddable prince he believed had betrayed him.

A pair of crystalline khepesh swords coalesced out of thin air in Atum's hands, moonstone *At* marbled with obsidian swirls on the sickle-shaped blades. Atum stepped closer to Inyotef, the muscles in his broad shoulders and burly arms bunching as he prepared to raise his weapons.

An image from the distant future flashed through my mind's eye—my dad with Lex and sweet little Reni. Atum had said Inyotef was important to the timeline. Killing him would threaten that future. It would threaten my family. It could very well threaten the whole damn universe.

"Atum, don't!" I blurted.

I dropped my knife barely halfway through the tough rope, the metal blade landing with a *splat* in the pooled blood, and scrambled to my feet. I lunged at Atum and clasped both hands around his forearm to hold him back. Otherworldly energy rolled off him in waves, thrumming up my arms and through my soul.

"You can't kill him," I reminded Atum. "The pattern—you'll damage the timeline."

Atum dragged his stare away from Inyotef, and for a long moment, his midnight eyes searched my face. His focus shifted to Kiya, still strung up between the columns, then dropped to my hands on his forearm, lingering on the cut ropes knotted around my wrists. His jaw clenched, his nostrils flared.

Out of the corner of my eye, I watched Inyotef slowly regain his feet, emboldened by my pleas for Atum to spare his life.

Atum's arms relaxed, his swords gradually lowering until the tips of the blades skimmed the blood pooled on the floor. His focus returned to Inyotef. Tension hummed through Atum's body, the muscles of his forearm coiled and flexed under my hands as his grip on the sword hilt tightened.

"Atum," I said, my voice a soothing coo. "Don't do it. We have to protect the pattern, no matter what. It's more important than everything else. It's the most important thing in the entire universe."

Atum tore his stare from Inyotef and gazed down at me, his midnight eyes skimming over my face, lingering on my lips and the blood staining my chin, the tears streaking down my cheeks, the pleas in my eyes.

"Not anymore," Atum hissed.

And then he ripped his forearm free of my hold, raised both swords high overhead, crossing his wrists, and whipped the blades down, slicing an "X" across the front of Inyotef's torso.

Inyotef barely had a chance to clutch his middle in an ineffective attempt to hold his guts inside his body before Atum raised the swords again and scissored the blades through Inyotef's neck.

Inyotef's head dropped to the floor, landing with a sickening splat. His body swayed for several seconds, blood spurting from the severed trunk of his neck. Finally, his knees gave out, and his body twisted as it collapsed.

Nausea knotted my stomach, the horrors of all I had witnessed in the past few minutes finally sinking in. I hugged my middle, but it only reminded me of Inyotef doing the same thing just a moment ago while his intestines bulged from his gut wounds. I covered my mouth with one hand and closed my eyes, breathing through my mouth to avoid the pervasive stench of blood and guts and death.

Atum just saved me.

But it was more than that. He *avenged* me. He killed Inyotef, disregarding the potentially catastrophic damage the action could cause to the timeline.

And he had done it *for me*.

I WALKED THROUGH THE palace's demolished gate alongside Atum, choking on all the unsaid words that hung between us. As soon as we finished cutting Kiya's bindings, he had wrapped her in a shimmering blanket of *At*, and now he carried her cradled in his arms.

With each step along the road leading to the palace harbor, we left bloody footprints on the paving stones, looking more brown than red in the silver light from the crescent moon. That blood was the only clue we left behind as to what had befallen Inyotef and his men.

Atum had swept the courtyard clean with a staggering wash of otherworldly power, turning all organic material save for the three of us into *At* and sending it *away*. I imagined some other plane of existence littered with the discarded remains of all of his dead.

Inyotef had deserved to die—nobody would have argued that, me least of all—but even more than death, he had deserved to suffer. For all he had done to me, and for the unimaginable things he had done to Kiya to reduce the once strong, proud warrior to the meek creature shivering in Atum's arms. For everyone he had crushed in his mad quest for more power.

In minutes, we were striding onto the palace's private quay. Those few minutes hadn't been nearly enough time for me to work up the courage to speak.

A string of boats bobbed in the river, tied off to the intermittent stone cleats that bordered the walkway, but only the largest ship moored at the end of the quay showed any activity. One of these things was *really* not like the others, and not only because the other boats were currently unoccupied.

The craft, which looked much more like a pirate ship one might find in the waters of the Caribbean than an ancient riverboat, gleamed like moonstone in the starlight. The entire ship appeared to have been formed from *At*, from the broad, deep hull to the single, tall mast and many sails, to the spider web of lines and rigging.

Gaping, I paused mid step to stare down the quay at the ship that was very clearly Atum's.

"We must hurry," Atum tossed over his shoulder without actually looking back at me. His black robes billowed as he continued down the walkway.

I squeezed my eyes shut, then opened them again, making sure I wasn't hallucinating. The ship was still there, gleaming under the crescent moon, looking as out of place as ever.

I jogged to catch up to Atum. "Is that a *galleon*?"

Atum glanced at me sidelong. "No," he said, implying that he knew what a galleon was. He threw me further off balance by adding, "It's a sloop. Single sail, fast, can move through shallow waters, and it doesn't require a large crew."

I stared at the side of Atum's face as we walked.

"You should really look where you're going," he said.

I snorted derisively. "*You* should really—" I didn't have a chance to finish my brilliant retort, because I tripped over a basket and barely caught myself before tumbling over the edge of the quay and into the river.

Righting myself, I blew out a breath and pushed my hair out of my face before stomping after Atum. I caught up to him as he was crossing the ramp to the ship's deck. The river's low level made the deck line up almost perfectly with the quay. The ramp wasn't wide enough for both of us, so I trailed behind Atum onto the ship.

A few Nejerets moved around on the deck, nodding a silent greeting to me when our eyes met. I recognized the female Nejeret who had stayed behind to watch over Atum with my mom after *the incident* near the Sphinx. She trotted down the stairs from the upper deck, skipping the final two steps.

"Father," she said as she approached, her focus shifting from Kiya in Atum's arms to me, then back to Atum. "You said you would only be returning with one woman." She fell in step beside Atum as he headed for the door to the cabin tucked under the upper deck while I trailed behind. "We only have extra provisions for one more passenger."

Atum turned partway and shouldered the door open. He ducked to pass through the low doorway, then straightened, the cabin's ceiling just high enough for him to stand without stooping. The only light source was a lantern of glowing *At* hanging over the desk near the back of the cabin.

It heartened me to know I wasn't the only person Atum withheld responses from.

Atum strode over to the long, narrow berth tucked along one side of the cabin and gently laid Kiya on the bed. He pressed the pad of his thumb against her forehead, directly between her eyebrows, and her eyelids fluttered closed, her body going limp.

I crossed my arms over my chest and narrowed my eyes, wondering how many other tricks Atum was hiding up those voluminous sleeves. This man was the greatest enigma I had ever encountered, and I planned on uncovering every single one of his secrets.

Atum straightened and turned to the woman—his daughter—hovering at his side. "Only this one will make the journey to Rostau with you," he said, nodding to Kiya as he finally answered his daughter's question.

Atum's daughter glanced at me. "And her?" she asked, pursing her lips.

"She's coming with me," Atum said.

"To where exactly?" his daughter asked.

Atum looked at me, his stare distant and unreadable. "To Waset to help me clean up the mess we just made."

I raised my eyebrows at the word *we*—I wasn't the one who shredded all of those people—but I suppressed the urge to scoff on account of him having just saved my life. Again.

"Would you like me to join you once I get the refugees settled?" his daughter asked. "Or to send Shu?"

Atum inhaled and exhaled through his nose ponderously before inhaling again to respond. "You will join us," he said, then pointed to Kiya with his chin. "Learn as much as you can of this one. You'll be taking her place."

His daughter bowed her head.

Atum stepped around her, reaching for me. His fingers curled around my arm, and he pulled me toward the exit. I went with him, mostly because his grip was an iron vice and I had no choice, but I peered back at Kiya's sleeping form. Atum's daughter now perched on the edge of the bed, her eyes closed and the fingertips of one hand pressed against Kiya's temple.

"Kiya will be fine," Atum said. "Tefnut is gifted at healing the mind."

I looked at Atum. "Inyotef—he cut out her tongue."

Atum shook his head, but he didn't look surprised. I shuddered as a wave of revulsion cascaded over me. I couldn't believe I had ever let that psychopath touch me. That I had ever welcomed his touch.

Once I noticed the women waiting at the top of the ramp connecting the ship deck to the quay, all thoughts of Inyotef fled, and Atum no longer needed to pull me along. It was all I could manage not to rush my mom and throw my arms around her.

"I'll give you a minute to say your goodbyes," Atum said, releasing my arm and stepping away.

I watched him approach one of the Nejeret sailors on the far side of the deck, then returned my attention to my mom. My steps slowed as I neared her, and I flashed her a tentative, tremulous smile.

Starlight shimmered in her eyes, highlighting her unshed tears. She knew me now—knew who I truly was. Her chin trembled as I approached. "My sweet Tarsi," she said, opening her arms to welcome me in for a hug. Atum must have filled her in on my true identity while I was imprisoned.

A sob ripped its way out of my chest, and I fell into her arms. My mom rubbed my back and made soothing sounds pulled straight from the deepest recesses of my memory. For a moment, I was a little girl again, seeking comfort in my mother's embrace, and it was pure heaven.

Too soon, my mom pulled away enough to see my face. She wiped away my tears with gentle thumbs, completely disregarding her own. "You grew into such a strong, beautiful woman." She sniffled, her cheeks trembling as she smiled. "I want to hear all about your life in the future. You must tell me everything when you come to Rostau."

I swallowed roughly and nodded, too choked up to speak.

She leaned in, pressing her lips to my forehead, then wrapped her arms around me once more. "I love you, my sweet girl." She tightened her embrace. "You are always in my heart." Her arms loosened, and she stepped back.

Only then did I realize Atum had rejoined us.

My mom kissed her fingertips, then reached out to press them to my lips. "Be safe," she said, her eyes lingering on my face for a few seconds before she turned and headed for the open door to the captain's cabin.

"Thank you," I breathed, tearing my stare from my mom's retreating back to peer into Atum's midnight eyes.

We stood there for a dozen heartbeats, simply staring at one another. I licked my lips, and Atum cleared his throat.

"We should go," he said, the low rumble of his voice resonating with every cell in my body. With every fiber of my soul. His hand slid along my lower back, pressing me into motion.

I crossed the ramp ahead of Atum and stepped off to the side of the quay as I waited for him to join me. "Will I see her again?" I asked, peering back through the open cabin doorway. She believed I would join her in the mysterious land of Rostau at some point, but I wanted to be certain before I let my hopes begin to rise.

"That is my intention," Atum said, his footsteps echoing on the wooden ramp. He stepped onto the quay, and I turned away from the ridiculously out-of-place ship, falling in step beside him.

I had about a million questions for Atum, but none of them seemed all that urgent. My entire life, I had held one wish in my heart—to see my mom again. Every shooting star, every birthday cake, every coin thrown into a fountain had been tied to that same wish.

And against all the odds, it came true. I saw her again. I held her. We cried, and it was everything I always thought it would be. My heart's greatest desire had been fulfilled.

Now, trapped thousands of years in the past and heart unexpectedly unburdened, I discovered I desired something else. Something new. Something I wanted even more than I had ever yearned to see my mom again. I watched Atum out of the corner of my eye as we made our way down the walkway, the corners of my mouth tensing with the hint of a smile.

And that *something* had absolutely nothing to do with finding my way home.

PRESENT DAY

+ KAT

I SPLASHED COOL WATER on my face over the sink, then straightened and turned off the faucet. I dried off my face with a washcloth and leaned in closer to the mirror on the medicine cabinet over the sink, looking for any hint of the *shadow* Anapa had mentioned. But all I saw was my usual pale-verging-on-pasty skin.

"Ugh," I mumbled. I needed to get outside more. A little vitamin D would do me some good.

And then I smirked, snorting a laugh as twelve-year-old me silently countered that Nik gave me *plenty* of vitamin D.

I pulled the mirror door open and plucked my toothbrush and the tube of toothpaste out of the medicine cabinet, then shut the door. And shrieked, dropping both the toothbrush and toothpaste into the sink.

An angelic, silver-blonde woman stood behind me in the reflection.

I slapped my hands over my mouth to stifle the scream, but there was nothing I could do to quiet my pounding heart.

I forced my hands down from my face and gripped the thin strip of counter at the front edge of the sink. "Is—Isfet?" A hasty peek over my shoulder revealed that she wasn't really here in the bathroom with me but was only in the reflection.

Isfet nodded, and she raised one delicate hand, pressing the tips of her slim fingers against the other side of the mirror. I lifted a shaking hand, doing the same.

"It is good to see you, Kat," Isfet said as soon as my fingertips touched the mirror's surface, her words flowing straight into my mind rather than through my ears.

"You too," I said.

"I cannot stay for long." Isfet's brow furrowed. "Why did you call me here?"

I took a deep breath, then cleared my throat. "It's the resurrected Nejerets," I said, then I quickly explained what was happening to Heru and a handful of others.

Isfet listened closely, and when I finished, she remained quiet for a long moment. "I must consult with the others," she finally said, disquiet clouding her clear blue eyes. "Fear not, Kat. I shall return with answers."

I sucked in a breath to ask her *what others*, but before I could, Nik knocked on the bathroom door. "Kat? Are you okay?"

"Yeah," I said, glancing at the door. "It's Isfet. Give me a sec." I still needed to ask Isfet if she could help in retrieving Tarset from her prison in the past.

But when I looked back at the mirror, Isfet was gone.

"Fuck," I hissed and slapped my palm down on the counter.

I huffed out a breath, comforting myself with her promise to return with answers. She would be back, and we would get to the bottom of all this.

With any luck, she could find Tarset too and finally bring her home.

EPILOGUE

TARSET

"W E NEED TO TALK about what happened," I said, finally slicing through the choking tension clouding the air in the hollow of the Sphinx's body. I sat on a floor cushion at the low table by the firepit, staring at Atum's broad back as he studied the time tapestry patch, his arms crossed over his chest.

Atum turned his head just enough to peer at me over his shoulder.

I held my last inhale in my lungs. Neither of us had said a word since leaving the ship. Not the entire hour-long trek to the Sphinx, and not while I set out the meal that now sat untouched on the table. I was hesitant to eat until we had cleared the air because once my belly was full, regenerative sleep would sweep in to whisk me off into unconsciousness. And some things needed to be said before that happened.

Atum's arms relaxed, and he turned away from the time tapestry patch to stalk over to the table. He eased down onto a floor cushion opposite me, placed his elbows on the table near the edge, and clasped his upraised hands together. His midnight eyes locked with mine, and my heart stumbled over its next few beats.

I licked my lips and cleared my throat, then inhaled to speak.

"Did you know you could do that?" Atum asked first.

I blinked, surprised by his question. "Wait, what?"

Atum's stare was unwavering. "Release a blast of energy from your soul. Did you know you could do that?"

I shook my head. This was nowhere close to the subject I wanted to discuss. "No, I-I have no idea where that came from," I confessed. "I think it has something to do with how I got here." I lowered my gaze to the stack of flatbread on the table. "To this time, I mean."

"And how *did* you get here?" Atum asked.

Biting my lip, glancing up at him, just for a moment. "I, um . . . I died." My shoulders hiked up toward my ears. "I don't know much more than that. I died, I entered Aaru, and then it sort of exploded, and I woke up in the middle of the desert . . . four thousand years in the past." I raised my gaze to meet Atum's.

He studied me for a long moment, then let out a throaty grunt. The sound fanned the embers of desire to life within me.

I sucked in a deep breath and held it for long seconds, working up the courage to broach the subject *I* was most interested in discussing. "You know about my dad and Lex, right?"

Atum's eyes narrowed slightly. "I know of them, yes," he said.

I looked down at my hands, picking at a barely-there hangnail alongside my thumb. "And you know about their soul bond?" I peered at Atum, waiting for confirmation.

He nodded, his eyes never leaving mine.

I swallowed roughly. "I, um—" I cleared my throat, suddenly overheating. "I think we might be like them. I think we might be potential bond-mates."

There. I had said it. I had put it out there. The subject was broached. The elephant in the room acknowledged. There was no taking it back now.

For a dozen heartbeats, Atum and I stared at one another. Not moving. Not even blinking.

Again, I licked my lips and looked down at my hands, though my attention remained on Atum. "We should keep that in mind," I said. "Before we do anything that makes this thing between us permanent."

A low chuckle touched my ears, and my stare snapped up to Atum.

The hint of a sly grin turned up the corners of his luscious mouth, and his dark eyes burned into me. "I have no problem with making this permanent."

My heart lodged in my throat. He had no problem with the idea of bonding with me—of tying our lifethreads together, forever.

But regardless of how much I desired Atum, *I* did have a problem with making this permanent. Because if we consummated our relationship and bound our souls together, then I could never go home. I would never return to my future. I would never see my family again. And I wasn't sure I could commit to giving them up. Not now. Maybe not ever.

I stared at the man—the god—sitting across the table from me, branding my soul with his gaze. I wasn't willing to give up on the chance of being with him, either.

Atum leaned forward just a little. "It looks like you have another choice to make."

Thanks for reading! You've reached the end of *Song of Scarabs and Fallen Stars*, but Tarset's adventure is just beginning. The Fateless Trilogy continues with *Darkness Between the Stars*, available for pre-order now.

Sign up for Lindsey's newsletter to receive updates on the Fateless Trilogy as well as to gain access to her FREE subscriber library, including four full novels (ebook and audiobook), two exclusive novellas, and more!

https://www.authorlindseysparks.com/join-newsletter

ABOUT
LINDSEY SPARKS

Lindsey Sparks lives her life with one foot in a book—so long as that book transports her to a magical world or bends the rules of science. Her novels, from Post-apocalyptic (writing as Lindsey Fairleigh) to Time Travel Romance, always offer up a hearty dose of unreality, along with plenty of history, intrigue, adventure, and romance.

When she's not working on her next novel, Lindsey spends her time hanging out with her two little boys, working in her garden, or playing board games with her husband. She lives in the Pacific Northwest with her family and their small pack of cats and dogs.

www.authorlindseysparks.com

FB Reader Group: Lindsey's Lovely Readers
TikTok: @authorlindseysparks
YouTube: Author Lindsey Sparks
Discord: discord.gg/smTeDHQBhT
Facebook: @authorlindseysparks
Instagram: @authorlindseysparks
Pinterest: @authorlindseysparks

Made in the USA
Las Vegas, NV
02 June 2022

49694790R00203